WALKING

to

GATLINBURG

BOOKS BY HOWARD FRANK MOSHER

Disappearances
Where the Rivers Flow North
Marie Blythe
A Stranger in the Kingdom
Northern Borders
North Country
The Fall of the Year
The True Account
Waiting for Teddy Williams
On Kingdom Mountain
Walking to Gatlinburg

WALKING

to

GATLINBURG

A Novel

HOWARD FRANK MOSHER

SHAYE AREHEART BOOKS

New York

Copyright © 2010 by Howard Frank Mosher

Published in the United States by Shaye Areheart Books, an imprint of the Crown Publishing Group, a division of Random House, Inc., New York.
www.crownpublishing.com

Shaye Areheart Books with colophon is a registered trademark of Random House, Inc.

Library of Congress Cataloging-in-Publication Data

Mosher, Howard Frank.
Walking to Gatlinburg : a novel / Howard Frank Mosher.—1st ed.
p.   cm.
1. United States—History—1849-1877—Fiction.   I. Title.
PS3563.O8844W36 2010
813'.54—dc22   2009030441

ISBN 978-0-307-45067-8

Printed in the United States of America

DESIGN BY AMANDA DEWEY

1   3   5   7   9   10   8   6   4   2

First Edition

For my son, Jake

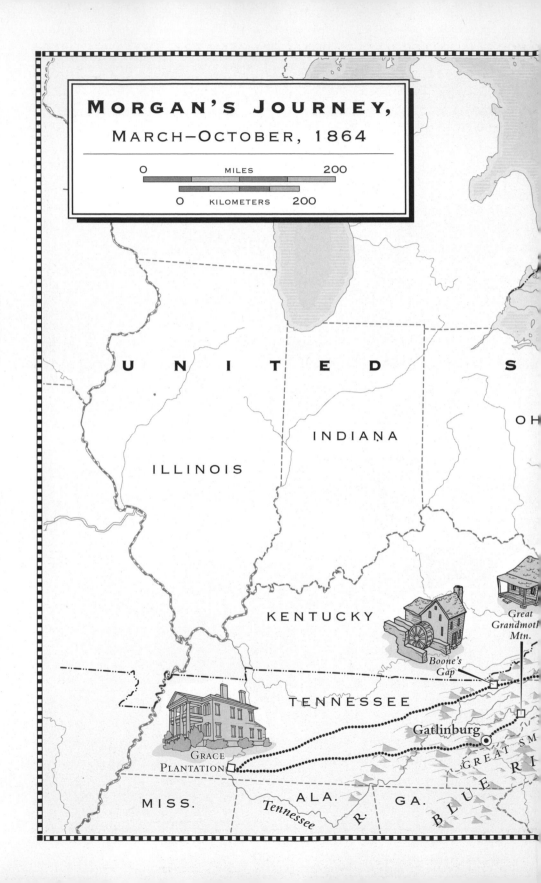

Morgan's Journey,
March–October, 1864

0   MILES   200

0   KILOMETERS   200

U   N   I   T   E   D   S

ILLINOIS

INDIANA

OH

KENTUCKY

Great
Grandmother
Mtn.

Boone's
Gap

TENNESSEE

Gatlinburg

GRACE
PLANTATION

GREAT SM

BLUE RI

MISS.

ALA.

GA.

Tennessee   R.

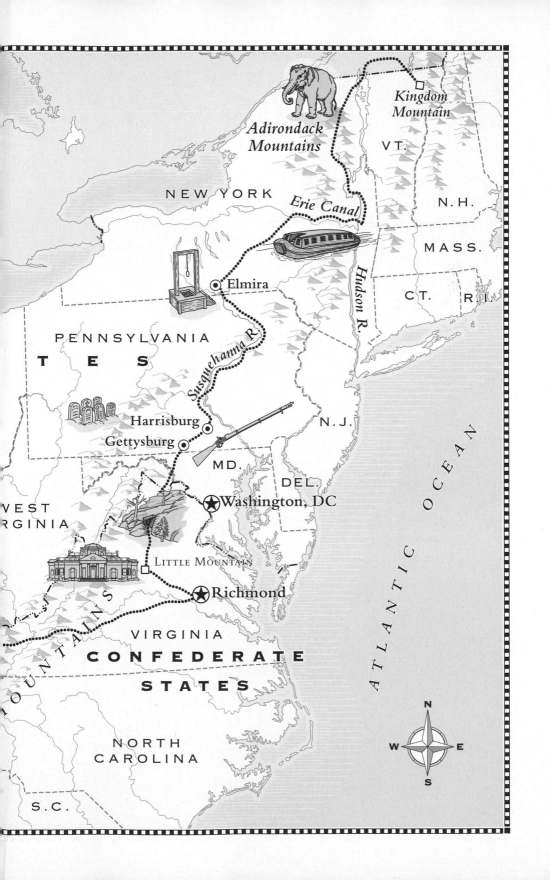

Kingdom
Mountain

Adirondack
Mountains

V T.

NEW YORK

N. H.

Erie Canal

MASS.

Hudson R.

Elmira

C T.

R. I.

PENNSYLVANIA

T E S

Susquehanna R.

Harrisburg
Gettysburg

N. J.

MD.

DEL.

Washington, DC

WEST
VIRGINIA

ATLANTIC OCEAN

LITTLE MOUNTAIN

Richmond

OUNTAINS

VIRGINIA

CONFEDERATE
STATES

NORTH
CAROLINA

N
W   E
S

S. C.

WALKING

to

GATLINBURG

THURISAZ

ᚦ

Years later Morgan Kinneson would conclude that it was probably reading that had gotten him and his brother, Pilgrim, into
trouble in the first place. The Kinnesons of Kingdom Mountain
had always been great readers. Shakespeare's plays. *Pilgrim's Progress.*
Paradise Lost. His mother had delighted in reading Miss Austen and
Mr. Dickens to Morgan and his brother. Their father, Quaker Meeting Kinneson, read aloud regularly from the papers and gazettes out
of Boston, Washington, and Philadelphia. After Pilgrim left Kingdom Mountain for Harvard, he sent Morgan books by his professor
and friend, the Swiss-born naturalist and glaciologist Louis Agassiz,
and by Emerson and Thoreau, the Concord freethinkers, and, most
recently, the book by that strange Englishman Darwin, which was
like no other book Morgan had ever read.

Of course the Vermont Kinnesons also read the Bible. The elderly female cousin several times removed who had quartered herself upon the family since his father was a boy had read to Morgan, with a satisfaction bordering on gleefulness, the vengeful old scriptures of cataclysmic floods and fire raining out of the sky to incinerate entire wicked cities, and wicked giants laid low by boys with slings, not to mention women turned into salt for the least imaginable infraction, and innumerable millions wailing and gnashing their teeth in everlasting fires for reciting their prayers one way instead of another. "Take from the Bible what you can use and ignore the rest," Pilgrim had advised him. "Just as you would from any other book. It's the book our ancestors were raised on. It can't be all bad."

"It's the book I was raised on," said the elderly cousin many times removed, whose name was Mahitabel, but whom Pilgrim and Morgan called Cousin Sabbath School. She gave Pilgrim a dark look. "It has served me well. It will serve him"—meaning Morgan—"well. When he is judged, at the end of what I prophesy will be a short and ill-spent life, he will know why he has been consigned. There will be no brook fishing or roving off night and day there, I assure you." Exactly where Morgan would be consigned, Cousin Sabbath School never specified.

"That sounds like the kind of threat a brimstone preacher would make to scare a fellow into going along with his way of thinking," Pilgrim said. "Around comes the long-handled collection basket, boys. Pay your dues or it will go hard with you by and by."

"We shall see what we shall see," Mahitabel said.

"On that much, at least, we can all agree," Morgan's father said, hoping thereby to end the discussion.

"Aye," said Cousin Sabbath School. "We can."

Of all the Kinnesons, Pilgrim, who was five years older than

Morgan, was the most voracious reader. He studied books about medicine and trees and animals and rocks. Until he went to war he had been studying at Harvard to become a doctor. He had even spent a year studying surgery with Joseph Lister at the renowned medical college in Glasgow, Scotland. Before leaving home for Harvard and beyond, he had taught Morgan a good deal about the animals and plants and birds of Kingdom Mountain. He had shown Morgan how to shoot with Hunter, Pilgrim's old cap-and-ball musket, converted from their grandfather's flintlock. And while Morgan quickly became a good shot, his brother remained the expert marksman in the family. Even after he had stopped hunting, stopped killing things altogether, Pilgrim was the best shot Morgan had ever known. For his part, Morgan had an uncanny natural woods sense, which he had honed ever since he had been allowed to go to the woods on his own. As his father sometimes said, you couldn't haul the boy out of the woods with a yoke of oxen, though he too read avidly himself, travel accounts mainly, by explorers like Marco Polo and Captain James Cook. As for Morgan's formal schooling, that had ended after the episode with Dogood.

In a way it had been the Kinneson mania for reading that had resulted in Pilgrim's trouble as well. In the third year of fighting, Pilgrim had enlisted in the Union army. Like his father, who operated the northernmost station on Vermont's Underground Railroad, Pilgrim was an abolitionist. But the rift with Professor Agassiz had led to his leaving college to enlist. It was Darwin's *Origin of Species* that had resulted in the break, though by then Pilgrim and his parents had already quarreled over the matter of Manon Thibeau. Not that Morgan believed there was any lesson to be learned from such reflections. You couldn't just stop reading, any more than you could help falling in love. Still, he had to acknowledge, at least to himself, that reading was the main problem, as true in his case as it was in Pilgrim's. If he'd never encountered those travel books, he might never have come up with the idea for his own great odyssey after Pilgrim had gone missing at the place in Pennsylvania called Gettysburg.

FOR A TIME after Pilgrim went off to college, Morgan dreaded going to places on Kingdom Mountain that he and his older brother had once frequented. Places where Pilgrim had taught him to wait for a buck to slip down to a stream to drink. Brooks where they'd caught the vividly colored little native trout that lived in every rill on the mountain. The big lake, Memphremagog, which stretched twenty-five miles north into French Canada, where they'd watched the snow geese alight, thousands of them, sailing out of the dense clouds in family gaggles of four and five and six on their way north to Baffin Bay or south to the Chesapeake. Once, while they were trolling on the lake in the birch canoe they had made, Morgan had hooked a huge deepwater fish, probably a lake trout but possibly a sturgeon. The fish had towed the canoe for almost a mile over the border, between the steep mountains rising abruptly three thousand feet out of the water, before breaking off with Morgan's homemade red-and-white lure in its mouth.

The two brothers loved to camp overnight on top of Kingdom Mountain, high above the treeline, where you could see four different states and deep into Canada. One night, tenting on the mountaintop with their cousin Dolton Kinneson, a great bear of a fellow who was Pilgrim's age but in his head much younger than Morgan, they'd watched the entire northern sky flare blue, green, red, silver, yellow, and pink from the northern lights. Pilgrim had told them about the Canadian voyageurs, fur traders in colorful tuques and sashes, who paddled thirty-foot-long *canots du nord* in grand flotillas from Montreal to Lake Athabasca and a place with the wonderful name of Flin Flon—twenty-five hundred miles and back again, racing to beat the onset of winter, singing their stirring paddling songs, penetrating wilderness never before seen by anyone save a few scattered bands of Cree. At twelve and thirteen and fourteen, Morgan had longed to go north with these bold adventurers.

He and Pilgrim and Dolton had brought Professor Agassiz to the mountaintop to examine the glacial erratics, boulders carried down from the Far North by the great ice sheet. They'd showed him the Balancing Boulder, a gigantic round rock as big as their farmhouse, perched on a smaller flat-topped boulder, with strange glyphs that the professor called runes carved into it beside pictographs of a whale, a walrus, and a reindeer. The professor believed that the pictographs and the runes might have been carved by Norse explorers hundreds of years before, but neither he nor anyone else could tell for certain. Only that the carvings were very ancient. Sometimes Morgan and Pilgrim played a variation of blindman's bluff at the Balancing Boulder, shutting their eyes and reaching for the boulder to see which rune they touched most often. Even when he tried not to, Morgan usually touched the symbol ᛏ; Pilgrim, ᛉ.

At all of these familiar places Morgan had felt terrible pangs of loneliness ever since Pilgrim had gone missing in Pennsylvania. The plan had been taking shape in his mind for some weeks. After Pilgrim went off to war he continued to write to Morgan, though not to their parents. He told Morgan that he felt they were still close in spirit because they both loved the same places on the mountain. Pilgrim had liked to josh, calling Morgan "soldier" or "Natty," after Natty Bumppo, the fabled scout in Fenimore Cooper's novels. Morgan's parents were too serious-minded to do much joshing. As for the aged cousin, she had never joshed in her life.

"Did Lord Jesus of Nazareth sit around the woodstove cracking wise with his cronies?" she said. "Did he, cousin?"

"I believe not," Morgan's father admitted.

"I believe not, too," Mahitabel said quite viciously. "Lord Jesus of Nazareth never laughed in his life. Not once. Nor did Paul."

"Laughing wasn't Jesus' department," Morgan's father conceded. "It wasn't Paul's department either, from what I can gather about Paul."

"They knew that laughter is a sin," Mahitabel said. "That laughter besmirches the creation. I detest laughter."

The old woman opened her daybook, in which she kept a careful running account of all that she detested, along with clippings of crimes and atrocities culled from the gazettes Morgan's father subscribed to. "Look you," she said, removing a cutting from the *Washington Intelligencer* of two weeks ago. "Do you call this funny? Do you laugh at this?" The heading read, FIVE HARDENED KILLERS ESCAPE FROM YORK STATE PRISON CAMP. Below, in smaller type, "Family of Four Found Hanged. Murderers Said to Be Bound for the South."

The article, which Cousin Sabbath School now proceeded to read aloud with relish for the third or fourth time, was especially painful to the Kinneson family because Quaker Meeting's brother, Colonel John Kinneson, was the commandant of the prison, and during the breakout John's wife had been shot by one of the killers. It described how, in an incredibly violent and audacious action, the killers had been broken out of the Union prison at Elmira on the morning they were supposed to be executed. The article reported that the five escaped war criminals were the worst dregs that the conflict between the states had produced. Their numbers included a slave killer, a child murderer, an unfrocked minister, and a disbarred army doctor who, so far from healing the wounded soldiers under his care, had practiced vivisection upon them. The family they were thought to have murdered the next day had been connected with the Underground Railroad, a point that delighted Mahitabel, who had long opposed the Railroad and was a staunch anti-abolitionist, on the grounds that the Children of Israel had owned slaves, and what right did abolitionists like Morgan's father and Pilgrim have to oppose a tradition sanctioned by the Lord God of Abraham and Isaac?

"Show me," Mahitabel demanded, "where the Lord God of Abraham and Isaac told Moses to free *his* slaves. Show me where Jesus ordered the Romans to free *their* slaves."

In fact the aged cousin had inherited, from yet another aged cousin, a half-interest in a ladies' cotton undergarment factory near Burlington, which had recently gone bankrupt because of the war, a misfortune for which she blamed abolitionists in general and Morgan's father in particular. She also blamed Morgan, who, after Pilgrim left Vermont for Harvard and then joined the army as a medical adjutant, had been conducting passengers over the border to Canada himself.

That's what Morgan was doing on this gray afternoon in late March of 1864. Not yet eighteen, tall and athletic, light-haired, with wide-set eyes the color of the big lake just before a summer storm, he was guiding a single passenger—there had been many fewer since the president's proclamation just over a year ago—up

7

the Kinnesonville Pike over the saddle on the east ridge of Kingdom Mountain. He was taking the man, known to him only as Jesse Moses, to the last station before Canada, a seasonal maple-sugar house that Pilgrim had named Beulahland, on the back side of the mountain. There they would rest and eat the cold supper Morgan's mother had packed for them. Then he would guide Jesse Moses the rest of the way through the Canadian forest to Magog and put him on the morning train for Montreal. Morgan's father had already wired Auguste Choteau, the Montreal Underground stationmaster, that a passenger from the South would be arriving so that Choteau could be at the terminal to meet Jesse.

Morgan and Pilgrim had made this trip so many times that as Morgan trudged through the deep snow high on the mountain, he could hear his brother's voice in his head, telling about Professor Agassiz's great ice sheet creeping down from the north, carving out the lake and creating the vast bog called the Great Northern Slang. Telling him the names of the boreal plants clinging to the mountain above the tree line, plants found in few other places south of Labrador, explaining how birds had originated from lizards and humans from something more like monkeys. That's what had caused the falling-out between Pilgrim and his teacher. The professor would have none of Mr. Darwin's monkeys. He and Pilgrim had quarreled bitterly over the matter while on a working holiday together in the Southlands, up in the remote mountains between Tennessee and North Carolina. The quarrel had marked the end of their friendship. Now Pilgrim had gone missing. No doubt buried, according to Morgan's uncle Colonel John Kinneson, in a mass grave for the unknown fallen at Gettysburg. And Morgan would have none of that. He knew for a fact that Pilgrim was alive, though how he knew he couldn't say. He simply did, just as he knew that eventually spring would follow winter on Kingdom Mountain, and summer, however brief, would follow spring.

When Jesse Moses had arrived at the Kinneson place, he had not been dressed for late winter in the North Country. He had no coat, just a ragged blanket with holes for his arms and head, and rags wrapped around his feet for boots. Morgan's mother had outfitted him with wool stockings and a shirt and some oversized trousers. There had been a fresh dusting of snow earlier in the day, with more on the way. Morgan could smell snow on the sharp north wind, see it coming in the slate sky over the mountain. He'd brought his musket, Hunter, in case he came across a bear early out of its den. Jesse followed him, carrying a tow sack around his neck and wearing a red wool jacket and felt boots Morgan had long ago outgrown. Morgan was glad Jesse was warm but aggrieved to have to give up his boyhood clothes. The red coat had been Pilgrim's before it was his. Even with it buttoned up around his throat, Jesse was shivering. More from fear, Morgan thought, than from the cold. The old black man continually looked back over his shoulder.

"They coming," Jesse said.

"Who?" Morgan said. "Who is coming?"

"They coming, I reckon," Jesse said again.

They crossed the saddle of the mountain and started down toward the maple orchard. The trees on the wild north side produced wonderful syrup and sugar. The sap here ran late, often not starting to flow until early April. The syrup was light amber, the sugar a lovely blond, a full shade lighter than Morgan's light hair. When the sap was running Morgan and his mother sometimes stayed at the sugar camp for several days. Returning to the camp through the inky maple trees at twilight behind the big red oxen, his shoulders on fire from lugging full sap buckets all day, seeing the red sparks climb high over the black woods where his mother was sugaring off, Morgan would pretend he was an Esquimau coming home from a seal hunt. He loved sugaring time, and this afternoon, guiding Jesse Moses down the mountainside, he looked for any sign that spring and sugaring were close at hand. A blue jay in some black spruces made its late-winter rusty-hinge cry. That was all.

It began to snow lightly, hard pellets sifting through the bare branches at a slant. Morgan came to a place where something had crashed out of the snowy woods and crossed the old tote road. It was a huge, cloven-footed animal like an ox—but what would an ox be doing on the far side of the mountain before sugaring time? And where an ox's belly would have dragged in the snow, this animal left no belly furrow. It was, Morgan realized, a moose deer. He was overcome by the hunter's urge to strike out and track it down. His grandfather Kinneson had married an Abenaki woman. Yet Morgan, with his light hair and complexion and ice-gray eyes, seemed to have inherited all of the Indian ways in the family. Pilgrim, who was dark-complected and looked more like an Indian, was the scholarly brother. He'd have been able to say the moose's scientific name. Morgan just wanted to hunt the animal.

There was a good supply of wood at Beulahland. Last fall Morgan had cut several cords against this spring's sugaring season. He passed under the rowanberry tree in the camp yard, marked with the rune ᚦ, *Thurisaz*. A black man, an Underground conductor himself, had carved the symbol deep into the tree many years ago, when Morgan's father was a boy. There was a similar rune on the Balancing Boulder atop the mountain. Pilgrim's professor had said it meant "gateway," which made sense because the Kinnesons' Underground station was the gateway to Canada.

Morgan lifted the latch of the plank door, went inside, and poured a little coal oil on some kindling in the stove to get a fire going.

Jesse Moses started to unbutton his borrowed jacket. "I gone give you back you warm red coat, mister tall boy," he said. "Put me in mind of that Joseph coat."

Morgan smiled at Jesse's "mister tall boy." He was ashamed of his selfish unwillingness to part with something no longer of any use to him. "You keep that coat, sir," he said. "It's just a mite small for me."

Snap. Outside, a snow-laden branch broke off a maple tree, as loud as a pistol shot. Jesse started. "It's all right," Morgan said. "Just an old tree limb."

Morgan could not seem to stop thinking of his brother. Pilgrim had no great love for hard physical labor around the farm—making hay, threshing oats, cutting firewood—but he loved sugaring season, loved to come to the camp to help celebrate the first exhilarating task of the approaching spring.

As Morgan unpacked ham, bread, baked beans, and pie from his haversack and laid them out on the unplaned table, he ran his eyes over the titles of the books on the window shelf. Most had belonged to Pilgrim. Gray's *Anatomy.* The *Complete Plays of William Shakespeare.* Chaucer's *Canterbury Tales.* The professor's great book on glaciation.

"We waits here till somebody come for me?" Jesse Moses asked Morgan. "Somebody will come?"

Morgan thought how frightening all this must be to Jesse. The gathering snowstorm, the deep north woods, the rough mountain-side cabin miles from anywhere. He wanted to tell him that the president's proclamation freeing all slaves had gone into effect more than a year ago, that they were four or five hundred miles from the nearest slave state, that he was as safe, as Quaker Meeting liked to say, as a toad in the palm of God's hand. But Jesse's eyes were terrified.

Morgan smiled at him. "By this o'clock tomorrow, Mr. Jesse, you'll be in Montreal."

"Where that?" Jesse asked.

"Canada."

"Promise·land," Jesse Moses said.

"Yes. The promised land."

"A young gal 'bout you age been through here lately? Runaway gal, pretty as a pitcher, maybe gots a little boy with she?"

Morgan shook his head

"You staying with Jesse, I reckon," Jesse said. "You daddy say you staying with Jess. Put him on the cars. I gots something to tell you. Something important."

Thinking about the moose, Morgan said, "I'll be back. By nightfall or shortly afterward."

"I gots to tell you—"

"I won't be gone long. No one will find you here."

Morgan knew he should remain with the frightened man. What if, while tracking the moose deer, he was overtaken by the oncoming blizzard and couldn't return to the camp? But he had to get on the animal's trail while there was still tracking light. When he'd first seen the track, it was all he could do not to send Jesse on alone to Beulahland while he lit out after the animal then and there. He'd never shot a moose deer. *L'original,* the French Canadian trappers who sometimes brought furs down the pike to sell in Kingdom Common called the moose. On this one animal his family could live for an entire year, preserving the meat in the icehouse. He would feel better about putting his plan into action knowing that they had that moose. So he told himself.

"I'll be back by one hour after dark," he told Jesse Moses. "I promise."

The old man gave Morgan an uncertain smile and reached out and patted his arm. Morgan smiled back. Then he was out the door into the small driving grains of snow betokening more snow to come. He peered up the mountain through the dark maple boles and judged that he still had half an hour of good light. He started back up the trail at a trot.

MORGAN WISHED that he'd thought to bring along his snow-shoes. If Monsieur *L'original* got into the slang, where the March snow still lay four feet deep, he'd need them. Climbing up the mountain from Beulahland, now running on the snowy trace, he thought he saw where a bear had come out of its den in the tumbled boulders at the foot of a cliff, then had returned to sleep out the balance of the long northern winter. High in a yellow birch tree beside the trail a partridge was nipping off buds, its small head bobbing herky-jerky like a yard hen's. Once he and Pilgrim and their cousin Dolton had found one hundred and sixty-two alder leaves neatly folded one atop the other inside the crop of a cock partridge that Morgan had shot off its drumming log. Morgan knew the exact number of alder leaves inside the bird because Dolton had counted them out in his loud, deliberate voice, the way a child might who had just learned to count to one hundred and beyond. "You're a good counter, Dolt," Pilgrim had said, and Dolton nodded, happy to be complimented by his cousin. After Pilgrim enlisted, Dolt too had attempted to go to war. Twice he had been rejected as unfit for service, once in Vermont, once in Albany. Dolt had decided to stay on in York State because there he would be closer to the war, and who knew, he might yet find a way to join the army.

Morgan came to the place where the moose had crossed the tote road, its strides a full yard-measure apart. Just up the slope he saw where it had been browsing. Several striped-maple trees about twenty feet tall were barked from the snowline up to eight or nine feet above the ground. When the feeding animal heard him and Jesse coming, it must have rushed across the trail, breasting through drifts a deer would have to leap or go around. Its track was three times the size of a big buck's.

Think like a moose, Morgan told himself in the dwindling daylight. How did a moose think? Did a moose think? What else besides striped-maple bark did it eat? Where would it go to find its next meal?

The animal seemed to be headed down the mountain toward Pond Number Three, which the professor had called a glacial tarn. Morgan was running again, angling away from the tracks. He planned to cut the moose off at the base of the mountain before it got out onto the frozen slang beyond the tarn, where it would easily outstrip him. With luck it would stop to feed on the cedar branches and alders along the edge of the slang. If he was fortunate enough to kill it, he'd have to borrow his father's yoke of Red Durhams to skid the dead animal around the foot of the mountain to the home place. Either that or butcher the moose where he shot it and pack out the meat in several trips. He was getting ahead of himself. First he had to shoot it. He ran faster, his felt boots throwing off scoops of snow like a winter hare bounding through high drifts. If the slang beyond the tarn was open, the moose would circle out around it and he could still intercept it before full dark. It was snowing harder. Morgan's hunter's blood was up. He ran faster. The hunt had become a chase.

Morgan was five feet eleven and one half inches tall and still growing, with long legs like a racehorse. He was as farsighted as a hawk. Three years running, at the Harvest Saturday turkey shoot in Kingdom Common, he'd placed five of five balls in the bull's-eye at one hundred paces with Hunter. He was confident that if he could get that close to the moose with any shooting light at all left in the sky, he could kill the animal. That was all that mattered to him as he leaped over a blowdown, cleared a crease in the snow where a rill cut diagonally down the slope, glimpsed dark water ahead at the base of the mountain where the flume dropped into the pond. Water. Not ice. He believed, hoped, that the moose would avoid the frigid open water at this time of year. The swirling snow fell thicker, blotting out the slang beyond the tarn. The air smelled like spent gunpowder, like wet hay smoldering, like more snow coming.

Morgan thought he heard church chimes. Here on the back side of the mountain, that could not possibly be, though once from the mountaintop, when the wind was out of the southwest, he'd heard church bells floating out from the Common, faint and mysterious. Yet he was almost certain he heard music. He even recognized the number, *"Sucre d'érable"*—"Maple Sugar"—maybe played on a zither like his mother's. Running to intercept the animal, he thought of church music, thought of a herd of lean moose devouring a herd of fat moose to the bright wild strains of *"Sucre d'érable,"* like the cattle in Joseph's dream. A year ago at the Sabbath school pageant at church, Morgan had recited the story of Joseph to the entire congregation. Then he had told them straight out in his sharp, carrying voice that if he'd had a raft of good-for-nothing jealous brothers

15

like Joseph's and they'd shoved him into a pit to be devoured by wild beasts, he'd have found a way out and hunted them down one by one, little brother Benjamin excepted, and done unto them as they had done unto him. The congregation had been horrified, especially the somber old churchmen and the ancient churchwomen who shared Mahitabel's opinion of the place where Morgan and his like would spend eternity. In fact, he had deliberately outraged the churchgoers in retaliation for their urging his parents—not that they had needed much encouragement—to forbid Pilgrim to marry Manon Thibeau, a French Canadian Catholic, on the grounds that such a union would condemn the young couple to eternal hellfire. Manon's parents, who attended Our Lady of the Green Mountains in Kingdom Common, felt the same way, threatening to send their daughter to a convent in Quebec City if she continued to keep company with Pilgrim. Shortly afterward Pilgrim had enlisted. Heartbroken, Manon had wandered off into the slang and vanished forever.

After the pageant Morgan's parents had stopped making him attend Sabbath school and church, so when he finished his barn chores on Sundays he had all day to hunt and fish. That had been the second part of his design in telling the sanctimonious old churchfolk that in Joseph's place he would have hunted down his treacherous brothers from one end of the Holy Land to the other. At the same time he'd spoken in deadly earnest. Maybe it wasn't in Joseph's nature to see justice served, but it was in his.

He came out on the edge of the cedar bog at the north end of the tarn. Along the slang draining the bog were the moose's tracks, and out on the frozen surface, as black as a bear in the falling snow, the huge animal was making fast toward an island of cedars, where the ice ended and the open water of the slang began. It was moving in ponderous, loping strides entirely different from the bounding of a deer, and it was well beyond the killing range of Hunter. The moose disappeared in the patch of cedars. If Morgan had been five minutes earlier he'd have had a perfect shot broadside at close range.

Through the thickening snow he marked a beaver lodge jutting up through the bog just this side of the cedar island. The lodge squatted round and dome-roofed like the Esquimau icehouse in his old school geography. Across from it, on the opposite side of the open lead of water through the ice, stood a dead pine tree. Many years before, the pine had been struck by a bolt of lightning, which had corkscrewed its way down the trunk from top to bottom and riven the tree wide open in a spiraling crease, exposing the heartwood. In the top of the pine sat a fish hawk's nest abandoned for the winter. The stick nest was nearly as big as a hayrick. Morgan studied the beaver house and the osprey nest. He tried to think what the moose might do next. A true deer would bed down in the cedars and wait out the storm. Toward dawn if the snow stopped, it would come out to feed. He supposed that a moose deer might do the same. He decided that at first light the next morning he'd be back here waiting for the animal. He'd spend the night in the sugar camp with Jesse and be here ready at dawn. Then he would take Jesse along to Magog and the railway.

Again he swore he could hear chimes floating over the bog. The music was eerie. "Rock of Ages," he thought. It faded in and out of earshot. *I gots something to tell you. Something important.* What was it Jesse wanted to tell him? Morgan couldn't imagine. Just as he turned to start back up the mountainside he heard the first gunshot, muffled by the falling snow but followed seconds later by another.

. . .

H E SPRINTED BACK UP the mountain, his feet finding the trail, which he could discern only by looking ahead at the narrow opening between the tops of the snowclad fir and spruce trees delineating the path below. There were tracks in the road where two men had come through after him and Jesse, headed in the same direction. Ahead the tote road forked. The left branch went west to the big lake, then hooked north. The right branch led directly to the sugar camp. It was hard to tell which way the men he was following had gone. The falling snow had sifted deep into their tracks and drifted over them, but from a slantwise indentation, little more than a shadow on the snow, it appeared to Morgan—who could trail a deer or bear over hardpan ledge by the faintest imprint in the lichen, or by a snapped-off saxifrage blossom or a hair caught on a Labrador tea plant—that the men had taken the route to the sugar camp. When he and Pilgrim played the tracking game they called Chase, Pilgrim had taught him to watch for a single bent-back blade of grass, a wool thread snagged by a bull thistle, half a heel print in the swale. Spring or fall, summer or winter, Morgan read the woods the way Pilgrim read books. From the inside out.

He moved quickly over the snow. He was quite certain he would overtake the men soon and was hoping against hope to come up on them before the sugar camp. The snow was letting up. Behind the thinning clouds he could see moonglow.

On the mountaintop the Balancing Boulder shone like a huge crystal ball in the emerging moonlight. Ahead, Morgan smelled wood smoke. In the pale moonlight he saw smoke standing straight up from the chimney of the sugar camp. Searching for the pole star to tell the time, he looked up through the black and leafless branches of the rowanberry tree outside the camp door. A corpse dangled with its feet just above Morgan's head. Jesse Moses. Hanging dead on the rowanberry tree.

The cabin door opened, and Morgan slid behind a tree. In the pale starlight a black bear stood upright in the doorway and pissed in the snow. No, not a bear. A huge man in a bearskin coat with the head of the bear still attached and pulled up over his head. The animal's front legs were tied loosely over the massive chest of the man in the shaggy coat, each bear paw as big around as the bottom of a milk pail. The bear-man saluted Jesse Moses hanging in the rowanberry tree, and as he did so, snapping off the salute neat and brisk as you please, Morgan raised Hunter and fired. The man gave a surprised howl and reeled backward into the cabin, gripping his left shoulder. In his haste Morgan had aimed high.

"What is it?" a voice inside the camp cried out. "Did you spot the nigger wench? For God's sake don't kill her."

The cabin door slammed shut. Morgan started running back down the mountainside toward the cedar bog.

A T DAWN Ludi Too eased downslope in Morgan's tracks. The entire eastern sky was suffused with alternating bands of gold and crimson and turquoise. Ludi, wrapped in his reeking bearskin, elided into "Marching to Georgia" on his hammered dulcimer. He'd created the instrument from a washboard nailed over a rectangular ammunition box. The strings had belonged to a piano in a darky church that he'd fired. Chestnut-wood pegs, a black cherry soundboard. Inside the cut-down ammo box was a loose rattlesnake rattle to give the instrument vibrato and resonance. The dulcimer hung around his neck on a thick strap made from mule reins stained dark with sweat. He beat the strings with two mallets of yellow poplar, for of all the trees in the forest the tulip tree made the most melodious music in a windstorm. And oh, the dulcimer sounded like a whole marching band going off to war. Out of it Ludi could coax the wail of a fiddle, the ringing notes of a banjo, the feeling sentiment of a Spanish guitar, the percussive beat of a kettledrum, even the brassy blare of a bugle, cornet, or trombone. How he conjured such concerts from his homemade mountain instrument no one knew, least of all the musician himself. Even with an injured left shoulder where Morgan's musket ball had torn through flesh and grazed bone, Ludi was a wonder musician. It was said in the coves and hollows of Ludi's mountains that he could lure a wild rabbit out of a laurel thicket, the heart out of a pretty maid. The troubador could charm fish from a brook right into his fry pan, quail to his horsehair quail trap, could still a storm like the Lord on Gennesaret. Ludi Too could play the venom out of a moccasin, money from a miser, silence from a preacher, the fight from the fightingest enemy. If A.D.'s wench was laying low nearby, he had no doubt he could conjure her out of her hidey-hole with the magical dulcimer.

Ludi was as uncanny a shot with his breech-loading Yellow Boy carbine as he was a musician. With the Yellow Boy, both south and north of Mason and Dixon's Line, he had dispatched more than three hundred Union and Secesh soldiers. This morning, all-merciful Jesus willing, he'd dispatch the bushwhacker who had winged him the night before at the cabin on the mountain. And, if not before then afterward, he'd run down the gal into the bargain. He might have her himself before turning her over to A.D., aye, he might. But he would have to keep the mad doctor off her. It had been all Ludi could do to prevent the vivisectionist from ripping out the old nigger's live beating heart with his dreadful gleaming instruments before they hung him up in the tree to bait the gal in. Ludi made up his mind to put a bullet in Doctor Surgeon's brain the moment they captured the wench.

Ludi carried a second weapon, which resembled a long horse pistol such as cavalrymen sometimes wore. But instead of one barrel, it had two snugged up side by side, with two hammers and two triggers. One barrel threw buckshot, the other a four-ounce ball capable of penetrating an oaken door. Ludi wore this weapon around his neck on a lanyard of human gut. Its cracked walnut stock was held together with a spare string from the dulcimer. Etched on the barrels were several demonic faces.

The Yellow Boy was mounted with a slim telescopic tube, through which Ludi now scanned the frozen swamp below. The swamp stretched out for miles in the clear morning sunlight. Good light to shoot by, Ludi thought, though whenever possible he preferred to work with the sun at his back. Also he preferred to work alone. That's why he'd made the clubfoot remain behind in the cabin. Doctor Surgeon had wanted to come along, but Ludi had important work to do this morning, and he did not want the lame little medical man getting in his way. Why King George had brought the clubfoot with them during the escape, or the actor and the Prophet either, was a mystery to Ludi. He and George could easily have taken care of the business at hand themselves.

Except for a black thread of open water winding through it, the swamp was snow-covered. Here and there islands of evergreen trees stood up. The largest one lay only about an eighth of a mile away and occupied no more space than a mule could plow from sunup to sundown. Just across the dark water from the island stood a dead pine tree, with a very large bird's nest at the top. Between the island and the lightning-snag pine, a beaver lodge of peeled sticks jutted out of the frozen swamp. Ludi couldn't tell for certain, but he believed that the tracks he'd been following approached the beaver lodge and stopped there. So much the better, he thought, as he jacked a shell into the chamber of the Yellow Boy.

M ORGAN SPENT THE night in the woods at the foot of the mountain. Toward dawn his battle plan had come to him all of a piece. The haunting music from up the mountain was still quite faint, and as he walked across the frozen bog and along the edge of the open slang he knew that he had time. He approached the beaver lodge and ripped some dead sticks away from the side. Then he walked backward in his tracks to a stump beside the slang. He removed his felt boots and woolen stockings and rolled his wool pantaloons up above his knees. Without hesitation he stepped into the water. It was well over his knees and shockingly cold. He gasped, caught his breath, felt his way over the silty bottom to the lightning snag.

He put his boots and stockings back on and began to climb up the dead stobs jutting out from the pine trunk. Up he went, hand over hand, marveling at the whorling wound gashed deep into the trunk of the great tree. He scooped the snow out of the osprey's nest and pulled himself into it. Carefully, he upended his gun, poured powder from his horn down the barrel, ramrodded it home, dropped in the wadded ball, ramrodded again, placed a brass cap under the gooseneck hammer. He drew back the hammer, then pawed more snow out of the nest to make a hollow for himself. To his astonishment he found a fish skeleton four feet long in the bottom of the nest. In the fish's skeletal jaw was the faded red-and-white homemade lure he'd lost years ago when he and Pilgrim were trolling in the big lake and he had hooked the great fish that had towed them and their canoe into Canada. The three hooks hanging from the bottom of the lure were rusted to points. What this curious reminder of the outing with Pilgrim might signify, Morgan had no idea. Nor could he imagine how the osprey had carried the fish, which must have weighed thirty pounds or more, to its nest. But now a man was coming out of the woods at the foot of the mountain. He was wearing a bearskin coat and playing a zitherlike instrument depending from his neck. Morgan wedged deeper into the nest.

He waited until the musician drew near to the beaver lodge. Waited until he raised his rifle and cut loose with a thunderous volley. Waited until he had discharged both barrels of the scattershot into the lodge as well. Then Morgan fired, and the rifleman sat down in the snow, holding his side.

"YOU'VE KILT OLD LUDI DEAD, Yankee boy," Ludi Too said, pressing his blood-soaked hand against his side. "Deader'n pork. And smashed my instrument to boot, damn your cold gray eyes."

"You killed Jesse Moses," Morgan said. He didn't like it that Ludi had noticed the color of his eyes. He reached out and lifted the strange pistol with two barrels over Ludi's big head.

"I'm paunch-shot," Ludi said. "Hand me back over that double horse cock of mine so's I can finish it."

Morgan kicked the big pistol over to Ludi. The killer picked it up, cocked both hammers, called Morgan a misbegotten bushwacking bastard, pointed the gun at him, and pulled the triggers.

The hammers clicked on empty chambers, as Morgan had known they would. He'd seen and heard Ludi fire at the beaver lodge with both barrels. Even so, it was terrifying to have a man cut down on him with a mortal weapon from six feet away.

"They goddamn!" Ludi shouted, and hurled the gun feebly at Morgan. It fell at his feet, and the boy picked it up and hung it around his neck by its lanyard.

"Well, then," Ludi said. "I've played out my hand. End it, old son. Put a ball in my head. For I don't care to bleed out here in this arctic fastness. Hark. I'll sing me a hymn to pass over on."

Ludi reached into his bear coat pocket and brought out his poplar mallet, and on the shattered dulcimer he played a bar of "Rock of Ages."

"Let me hide myself in thee," warbled the minstrel. "Come, boy, join in. We'll make a duet of it.

"For the sake of Jesus seated at the right hand of Jehovah, put a ball in my breast, lad. I'm begging you. Put a ball in my breast and take my instrument and sing in a ballad that I died game. Finish me, man. Only tell me first. Where be the nigger's stone? Does the gal have it?"

Morgan stared at him.

"Never mind," Ludi said. "Anno Domini will get it. One way or another, old A.D. will come at it when he finds the wench."

It was clouding over again in the west beyond the mountaintop. Big flakes of snow were dropping out of the sky.

Morgan said, "Toss me your ammunition belt."

"Eh?"

"Your ammunition."

Slowly, Ludi unbuckled the two bandoliers crossed over his chest under his bear coat and heaved them in Morgan's direction. He was bleeding harder now.

Morgan fetched the Yellow Boy, half buried in the snow nearby, and reloaded it with one bullet from Ludi's belt. He set the rifle upright against a cedar tree, training his musket on Ludi lest he snatch up the loaded rifle and turn it Morgan's way. "I'm leaving you your gun with one shell in the chamber to do with as you see fit," he said.

"How do you propose that I pull the trigger?"

Morgan knelt at the musician's feet and pulled off Ludi's right boot and stocking.

"Wigwag your toe."

"What?"

"Wigwag your great toe. Do you have life in it?"

Ludi moved his toe, as black as his boot.

"That's how," Morgan said and began backing away toward the cedar island, the musket in his hands pointed at Ludi.

"A curse on your yallow head, boy. Unto the seventh generation."

Morgan faded into the cedar trees on the island, trotted to the other side, and began to run toward the foot of the mountain. The snowflakes were as big as the palm of his hand and coming faster. A minute later he heard a muffled shot from behind him.

Quartering with the northwest wind on his left cheek, he reached the shelter of the woods at the foot of the mountain. He wanted to return to the cabin and deal with the second man, whose tracks he'd seen going over the mountain with Ludi's the night before, but his wet feet and legs were freezing. He had no choice but to stop and pull some loose bark from a yellow birch and break off dead limbs close to the trunk of a skunk spruce, make a brush pile, and build a fire. Otherwise he'd freeze his feet, and that he could not risk. If there was one part of him that Morgan Kinneson knew he would need over the coming weeks, it was his feet.

TWO

RAIDO

R

The second snowstorm was a full-fledged blizzard. It lasted almost twenty-four hours, pinning down all living things on the mountain. All Morgan could do was wait it out for a day and a night while maintaining an economical fire from the dead limbs of the softwoods along the edge of the bog at the foot of the mountain.

During this interlude Morgan thought about Dogood, the schoolmaster. A year ago, at a Saturday-night spelldown at the schoolhouse, Morgan and Dogood were the last spellers standing. The word was "vengeance."

Dogood, tall, rawboned, a brawler and a bully, had been hired not for his knowledge but because he could keep order with his fists. It was rumored that he had paid a cousin from New Hampshire

two hundred and forty dollars to go to war in his place, prefer-
ring to lord it over a schoolroom of children than fight to preserve
the Union. Dogood went first. "Vengeance. V-E-N-J-A-N-C-E.
Vengeance."

"Nay," said Quaker Meeting Kinneson, who was serving as spell-
master. He looked at Morgan. "Vengeance. As in 'Vengeance is
mine,' saith the Lord."

"Vengeance," said Morgan, who, though he detested every minute of his life spent in school and away from his beloved woods, had
a memory like glue. "V-E-N-G-E-A-N-C-E."

"Correct," Quaker Meeting said. "And vengeance belongs to?"

"The Lord," Morgan said, but Dogood, publicly humiliated by
one of his own scholars, evidently thought differently. The schoolmaster bided his time, and soon enough that time arrived. One evening when Quaker Meeting was off doing chores for a sick neighbor,
Morgan did his father's barn work as well as his own and thus failed
to complete his lessons for the next day. When he arrived at school
unprepared, Dogood drew a small circle on the slate behind his
desk and ordered the boy to stand bent over with his nose in the
circle while he beat him with his ironwood pointer. After the beating, a dozen hard licks, Morgan turned around and challenged the
teacher to bare-knuckles fisticuffs that Friday night at the schoolhouse. Then he walked out the door.

Word spread like brushfire that Master Dogood and the young
firebrand Morgan Kinneson were to square off at the schoolhouse.
Every ne'er-do-well in Kingdom County was on hand to see Dogood, stripped to the waist, his suspenders hanging from his worn
serge trousers, lift his fists against his pupil. Morgan had asked his
cousin Dolton to second for him. The schoolmaster had no cor-
nerman but he assumed a formidable attitude with his fists turned

up, his elbows down, his long, cruel horse face tucked between his rugged shoulders.

"No head-butting, no gouging, no biting, go in and fight to win," roared old man Kittredge, and Morgan rushed the teacher with a haymaker that would have felled a stallion.

Dogood slipped the blow and flicked out a looping jab that stung Morgan's left eye like a bumblebee. He knocked the boy on the forehead with his right hand, then delivered a crunching blow to the breastbone that lifted Morgan off his feet and dropped him like the kick of a workhorse.

"Put your boots to the little bastard, Teach," someone yelled.

Spittle white as table salt glazed Dogood's lips as he drew back his boot. Before he could cave in the boy's ribs, Dolt Kinneson had him in a bear hug. "I reckon that's enough for tonight, Mr. Schoolmaster," Dolt said, lifting the thrashing pedagogue right off the schoolroom floor.

Dolt set the teacher down, went to the vestibule, and returned with the wooden drinking bucket. He dashed the full contents over the face of Morgan Kinneson, who came sputtering to his knees. Dolt grinned. "That's good for tonight, cousin. Sometimes a fella has to take a whopping to give a whopping. You're halfway there."

Now Morgan was alone in a blowdown, with the wind howling through the forest on all sides, Jesse Moses hanging from the rowanberry tree outside the cabin high on the mountain, the mad musician no doubt sitting dead as a stump in the bog, and another man, likely a killer himself, at large on the land nearby. For the first time in his life, he was the hunted rather than the hunter, a terrifying thought. Yet he knew that his life depended on his keeping a clear mind.

Rummaging in his jacket pocket, he felt something smooth and hard. He drew out an oval, grayish stone, about as large as his palm. It was attached, through a small hole drilled through the top, to a leather necklace. Etched into the surface on one side were the words *Jesse's stone.* Below the writing a jagged line of what appeared to be mountain peaks ran from north to south, interrupted at intervals by a dozen or so curious miniature drawings. A ruined fortress. A little ship perched high in a tree. What might be the entrance to a cave. Also a pillared manse on a hilltop, a windmill and waterwheel, and a field of flowers. Each drawing was accompanied by a symbol similar to the runes on the Balancing Boulder. The other side of the stone seemed, at first, to be smooth. But when he examined it closely, Morgan could discern, very faintly, many of those same symbols, rubbed nearly indecipherable like the words on an ancient coin.

Morgan continued to look at the carved images until they all started to run together. He could not imagine how the strange stone had gotten into his jacket pocket unless Jesse had tucked it there back at the cabin. The killer in the bear coat had referred to a stone—the "nigger's stone." Might this be it? What did it signify? And what about the girl the killer had mentioned? The voice inside the cabin had alluded to a wench, and Jesse had inquired about a runaway girl, Morgan's age and pretty as a picture. Who might she be? If only he had stayed at the camp with Jesse, listened to what the old man had wanted to tell him.

He slipped the rawhide loop attached to the mystery stone over his head and around his neck, then built up the fire again. All night Morgan fed the fire and considered his options. By dawn the blizzard had stopped. He counted the money in his wallet. Six dollars, the proceeds from his winter trapline. The time for his odyssey, months in the planning, was at hand. First, though, he must return to the cabin to finish the task he'd begun two nights ago when he'd wounded Ludi.

As he started to stand, Morgan glimpsed, proceeding at a halting pace down the snowy mountainside, a figure in a black cape wearing a great black hat with a sweeping brim like a wizard's of old. The man dragged his left foot, which was enclosed in a large black box, and carried a carbine with a yellow breech like Ludi's Yellow Boy. He was angling away from the brush pile where Morgan was hidden, already out of musket range. A terrifying thought crossed Morgan's mind. What if the limping creature with the rifle circled back to the home place?

Realizing that he must lure the gunman deeper into the woods, away from his family, Morgan shouted out for the man to stop and drop his rifle. Instantly the black-garbed figure dodged behind a spruce tree and fired a shot toward the brush pile. Though he had no chance of hitting him with his ancient musket, Morgan fired back. Then he began running in a northerly direction. Bullets whined through the air around him, clipping off evergreen branches. Morgan screamed as if hit, whipped out his buckhorn knife, shoved up the sleeve of his fringed jacket, and made two long, swift, shallow slices across his bare forearm, which immediately began to drip blood onto the snow. He screamed again. Behind him his pursuer had stopped to reload. When the shots began again Morgan sprinted up the mountainside.

P RESSING NORTH INTO Canada leaving a blood trail, in time Morgan emerged onto a tote road that had been packed down by a snowroller. There he met a country priest in a handsome cutter pulled by two bay horses.

"Where do you go, my son?" the man of God asked Morgan.

Morgan looked up at the priest, an elderly man with a kind face and inquisitive, friendly eyes. A patch of his clerical collar showed snowy white against his heavy black cassock.

"You're hurt," the priest said. "What did you do to your arm?"

"A scratch," Morgan said. "A small accident in the woods, nothing."

"Come up, come up, that must be looked at," the priest said, nodding at the seat beside him. Morgan climbed aboard, and they glided on north in silence behind the two big bays. From time to time Morgan looked back the way they had come. Not a soul was in sight in the wintery landscape.

"Who do you look for?" the priest said. "The devil?"

"Quite possibly," Morgan said.

"Well, he's as apt to be ahead of us. But if so, we'll say, 'Satan—'"

"'Get behind us,'" Morgan said.

"Ah," said the priest. "You know your scripture. But tell me, in all seriousness, where do you go with all your weapons? To the American war? You're headed in the wrong direction, I must tell you."

Morgan looked at the cleric. "I expect I'm going straight to hell," he said.

The priest smiled. "That's a crooked path, not a straight one," he said. "Tell me. What causes you to say such a thing as that?"

Morgan stared bleakly out across the snowy fields, then glanced back over his shoulder. The road was as empty as the moon.

"My friend?" the priest said.

"Have you seen a Negro girl?" Morgan said. "Possibly with a little boy?"

The priest shook his head. He glanced at Morgan, and for a moment the old and the young man looked into each other's eyes.

"Mon dieu," the priest said softly, and after that they did not speak again. At dusk the priest dropped him off at the tiny railway depot in Magog, then headed off toward a dark stone church with a soaring steeple sheathed in tin, on the north edge of town.

At the depot Morgan borrowed pen, ink, and paper from the stationmaster and wrote the following letter:

> *Dearest Parents,*
>
> *I am pained to write that on Tuesday last, a crazed and heartless killer murdered the passenger on the Underground named Jesse Moses, entrusted to my care, whom I had heedlessly abandoned. I came upon the scene of the murder too late to be of any assistance. I was able however to track down the killer and lure him into an ambush. I assure you that he will kill no more, though this is but meager consolation for the loss of Jesse.*
>
> *As for the second part of my message, for some time I have been determined to go south to find my dear brother, Pilgrim. I have the utmost faith he is still alive, though where he may be and why we have not yet heard from him I cannot say. Know that I am now and always will remain,*
>
> *Your loving son,*
> *Morgan Kinneson*

Morgan handed the letter to the stationmaster along with a shilling to frank and post it. "A man attired all in outlandish black with a hideous black box for a left boot will be along shortly," he said. "He is not a good man. Kindly tell him that I boarded the evening train for Halifax."

The stationmaster looked at Morgan for a moment, then nodded.

TWO DAYS LATER—TWO DAYS of hard walking through the rough backcountry farms and isolated hamlets of the borderlands, snatching an hour or two of uneasy sleep in a hayrick here, an empty schoolhouse there—Morgan continued to drive himself brutally, punishing his body to relieve his mind of the guilt he felt for abandoning Jesse. He had seen no evidence of a runaway slave girl with a little boy or of the limping specter in black, but he knew that the cloaked man with the flop-brimmed hat and the dragging foot might be lurking with his Yellow Boy behind any corncrib or outhouse. And who was the man Ludi had referred to as Anno Domini? Morgan believed he might be connected with the killers who had lately escaped from the Union prison at Elmira.

On the third evening of his trek a freezing rain set in. What had Pilgrim told him years ago? "Remember, brother, no matter how cold and wet you are, with flint, steel, and tinder you're always warm and dry." Near a hollowed-out maple tree on the bank of a large, north-running river that he had no means of crossing, Morgan gathered some wet boards from a collapsed horse hovel and built a fire to warm by. He had neither food nor the appetite to eat, nor was he sure that he had the strength or courage to continue for one more day. Huddled inside the rotted old tree trunk, desperately homesick, he feared that his resolve was flagging, that he might be undone not by the likes of Ludi Too and the clubfoot in wizard's garb but by his own terrible loneliness. Yet how could he return home without Pilgrim? He had given his word, not just to his parents but to himself, that he would find his brother. And what choice did he have? Where else could he go? As the warmth from the fire seeped into his bones, a thousand wild notions, each more fantastical than the last, ran through his head. He would run away to sea. He would lie about his age and enlist. Strike north to the great unbroken forests of the Hudson's Bay territory and run a trapline. He thought about the pretty fugitive girl and wondered if the little boy might be her own. Hunkered down in the hollow tree, he fell asleep to the crackle of his fire and the rush of the river.

En roulant ma boule, ma boule.
En roulant ma boule.

Out of the dawn mist on the river, putting in toward a gravelly bar just below the shattered old maple where Morgan had spent the night, came a long freighter canoe manned by half a dozen colorfully dressed men singing in French. The bowman, who wore a blue wool shirt, a yellow tuque, bright red leggings, beaded moccasins, and a bold green sash, splashed out of the canoe and drew it up onto the bar.

"Bonjour!" he called up to Morgan on the bank above.

When Morgan called back hello, Green Sash immediately switched to English. He said he had come up the Richelieu River recruiting men for the annual spring rendezvous of voyageurs at Montreal, and he invited Morgan to join them for breakfast. Sooner than Morgan would have thought possible, the paddlers had a kettle boiling for tea, and Green Sash was handing him a slice of warmed-over *tourtière,* which he wolfed down steaming hot.

"How long has it been, my friend, since you last ate?" Green Sash said as Morgan devoured a second helping of hot pork pie.

Morgan shrugged. Then, looking at the crumbs in his hands, "Five seconds. I last ate five seconds ago."

Green Sash laughed, but Morgan was appalled that he could make a joke, even a very lame one, after all that had recently happened. Also he felt shamed to take food from a stranger.

Green Sash, who was slender, with dark hair curling out from under his tuque and dark eyes that noticed everything, unchained from his belt a wooden cup, which he dipped into the cold river and offered to Morgan. It was a curious vessel, made, Morgan judged, from white cedar. Around its rim ran carvings of a moose, a leaping trout, a floating loon, and a voyageur paddling a canoe toward an Indian girl. On the bow of the canoe on the cup was the sign ᚦ, which Morgan recognized from the Balancing Boulder.

"You carved this?" Morgan said.

Green Sash shrugged. "I carve a little. *Mon pere* is the last true carver in our family." He put out his hand. "My name is Auguste Choteau."

As they clasped hands, Morgan told the young Frenchman his name. He pointed at the symbol on the drinking cup. "I believe you know my father. Quaker Meeting Kinneson? At the sign of *Thurisaz?*"

"Ah," Green Sash said. "It is actually my father, the carver, who knows your father. His name is Auguste as well. But look, Monsieur Kinneson. You really must come north with us. With your weapons you will be our hunter, eh? Some say this will be the last time the company sends out *coureurs des bois.* Join us. It will make a man of you. The Cree girls will make a man of you."

Auguste Choteau cut his black eyes at his paddling crew, already packing away their cooking pot and kettle in the long canoe. In French he repeated what he'd said about the Cree girls, and the voyageurs laughed and beckoned for Morgan to join them. He was tempted, oh, sorely tempted, to do so, thereby putting every consideration and promise and responsibility behind him for a carefree life of hunting and making love to beautiful Indian maids and feasting with good companions on beaver tails and moose steaks beside nameless northern lakes teeming with trout.

"Maybe another year," Morgan told Auguste. "For now, if you could just cross me over the river, I'd be grateful to you."

Choteau shrugged. "Another year may well be too late, *mon ami.* The Cree girls will be *très triste.* But yes, we'll carry you to the far bank. And keep the little drinking cup. I can make another in a night or two. Look. See the figures of the *coureur* and the young woman? This cup will perhaps bring you love. Give it to your sweetheart. A token from you and"—here his eyes flashed again— "Auguste Choteau of Montreal, Canada."

Approaching the northern end of Lake Champlain later that morning, Morgan felt more desperate than ever. To take his mind off the hideous scene at the sugar house, he got out Jesse's stone and tried again to make sense of it. At the top, along with the pictographs of the crumbling fortress and the ship in a tree, he recognized the rune from the cedar cup Auguste Choteau had given him, ᛏ, beside a drawing of a beaver. At the bottom was the symbol that Pilgrim had touched most frequently on the Balancing Boulder, ᛉ, accompanied by a most curious carving of a one-legged stick figure. There was no drawing of a girl with a child, nor did Morgan's rune, ᛏ, appear on the map, if a map it was, though he thought he recognized it, more by touch than sight, on the reverse side of the stone. Pilgrim had agreed with the professor that the wild seafaring Norsemen had probably ventured to America before Columbus and had left their magic signifiers on the Balancing Boulder on Kingdom Mountain. Morgan was quite certain that Jesse had slipped the heart-shaped stone into his pocket to prevent the killers from acquiring it. Pilgrim would have known its geological composition. All Morgan knew was that it was neither granite nor slate and was not native to Vermont.

ON THE WEST SIDE of the bay where the Richelieu River debouches from Lake Champlain sat a half-finished fort, its gaping cannon portals overlooking the narrows. Morgan thought it might be the razed old fortress depicted on Jesse's stone. A tall, elderly man in a cocked blue hat stood in a flat-bottomed wooden scow in a small inlet, stabbing at something in the water. He was dressed in a uniform of some sort, and as he punted the boat along the cattails and bulrushes near the shore, he stopped frequently to exchange his long pole for a barbed trident made from a pitchfork. He was spearing chain pickerel, heaving them green and flopping into the boat. Milk-white milt and bright yellow eggs like gold beads spewed out of their vents. A horned bullpout with spiky whiskers and fins squeaked like a frog as he threw it onto the pile of fish in the boat. With the next lunge of his trident he impaled a great northern pike, snaky-looking and as long as Morgan's arm.

With each furious thrust at the hapless fish, the lanky old gondolier shrieked out an imprecation. "Death to you, John Reb! Death to the Rebellion! And to *you* and *you* and to *you* too, general." When he forked up the long pike, squirming wildly on the pitchfork tines, he roared out, "Taken at last, Jeff Davis. You'll hang for treason."

The madman's blue claw hammer coat was bespattered with fish offal and covered with a tatterdemalion array of shiny tin scraps, shards of colored glass, shredded ribbons of every gay hue, and dozens of buttons studded all over the shoulders and back and seams and even the coat's forked tails. There were mother-of-pearl buttons, pewter buttons, buttons of amber, big brass buttons, and buttons fashioned from bits of white bone as well as from glossy black bitumin, not to mention drilled copper coins, silver dollars, and even a few golden double eagles. Around the man's neck on a string hung a child's tin horn. Wisps of snowy hair stuck out from under his blue tricorn. A scraggly white beard stretched to his waist. His eyes were pale blue. Mounted on a swivel affixed to the front end of the boat was a blunderbuss as long as a small cannon. At the rear a tattered American flag fluttered from an upright besom-broom with a few straws still attached.

The fish killer threw down his trident, picked up the punt pole, and drove the boat through the scratchy reeds onto the pebbly shore a few feet from where Morgan stood watching.

"Come aboard, ensign," the boatman commanded in a brisk military voice. "On the double now. We've not a moment to lose if we're to take back the fort. Avast there, step lively. Are you waiting to be piped on like Lord Nelson? Fine, then."

The white-beard lifted the tin horn to his lips and gave a great lusty blast.

Morgan stepped into the prow and sat on the forward thwart near the blunderbuss.

"Nay, not so fast," the old man said. "When the Admiral of the North speaks to you, lad, you'll salute him. You'll salute, by Jehovah, or I'll have you keelhauled and whipped the length of the fleet and back."

Trying not to smile, Morgan saluted. The Admiral in the meantime had seized his trident and speared another finny Rebel, which he added to the heap of insurrectionists in the bottom of the boat.

"This is how I'd do them Johnnies if they'd but let me enlist," the Admiral cried, and he fell upon the poor gasping fish with his punting pole, belaboring them left and right. In his frenzy he narrowly missed Morgan's head.

Suddenly the boatman began to weep. "Oh, lad, they kilt my two boys," he wailed. "Don't you see? They kilt my boys, and we must retake Sumter and set the world right again. We'll wind time back before the war and my boys won't never have gone for soldiers nor died in battle and all will be as it once was."

He pointed down the lake at the stone fort overlooking the narrows. "There she stands," he said. "Sumter. I retake her every morning. In the interest of bringing back my boys, you understand. Watch now, ensign. This Chesapeake Bay punt gun will play pure hell with the Rebs in that redoubt. We shall take her again, you and I together."

As they approached the empty fortress, the Admiral of the North told Morgan that it was locally known as Fort Blunder, because after the War of '12 it had been mistakenly built by Americans on Canadian soil. Just ahead a raft of wild ducks bobbed on the water, riding the chop on the lake like painted wooden decoys. "Quack, quack," the Admiral cried out. "Do ye see them, lad? Skirmishers dispatched from Sumter to lay water mines. Quack, quack, quack!" The ancient warrior gave a powerful push with his iron-shod punting pole. He leaped over the heaving pile of fish past Morgan and into the bow of the boat, all the time clucking to himself. Out of a squat keg, using a wooden flour scoop, the Admiral dipped a good pound measure of horseshoe nails, screws, bolts, nuts, and metal fragments, which he dumped rattling into the maw of the great Chesapeake gun on swivels. With the exactitude of an alchemist of yore, he poured in powder, placed a cap as broad as his bent yellow thumb under the hammer, then flung himself down on the shivering mat of fish in the bottom of the boat and trained the gun ahead. He smelled of some awful compound of unwashed flesh, wet wool stockings, fish scales, gunpowder, and despair.

"Ensign," he said. "Pole us forward. Toward the skirmishers."

Morgan moved to the stern, picked up the pole, and drove the boat closer to the ducks, which rose into the air in a great clamorous cloud. The blunderbuss went off with an astonishingly loud roar. An orange tongue of fire shot out of the mouth of the punt gun, and the sky rained bright feathers, gray and white duck down, and squawking ducks. The Admiral gave a tinny blast, signaling a charge, on the child's horn dangling from his neck. He seized the punt pole from Morgan and shoved his scow into the midst of the dead and wounded birds. In a desperate parody of hand-to-hand fighting, the elder began to club the ducks, shouting *take no prisoners, give no quarter, show no mercy,* ordering Morgan to gather up the dead and throw them into the bottom of the boat with the fish.

Morgan's ears rang from the detonation of the punt gun. The Admiral's exhortations sounded faraway and faint. "We'll follow

Nelson's advice, boy, and go straight at 'em. Damn the fancy maneuvers." The sun emerged, and the Admiral's buttons and bits of glass and metal sparkled like the waves on the bay as he poled directly at Fort Blunder in the manner of Lord Nelson. Although Morgan understood that the fort was unmanned, he could not rid his mind of the thought that at any moment the big guns might be run out, and he would be blown to Kingdom Come and never find Pilgrim. The punt boat had the north wind behind her and was fairly skimming toward the fortress. What if Morgan's pursuer was lying in ambush behind its walls?

"Now, lad, again, the switcheroo. Change stations!" cried the Admiral. Nimble as Jack Candlestick, he sprang into the bow. Morgan scrambled back to the stern and took up the pole as once more the madman poured a motley of clanking metal scrap into the blunderbuss. He fired at the fort. Chips of stone flew off the upper parapet above the top row of cannon portals. The Admiral leaped to his feet and shaded his eyes with his hand. Whipping off his blue tricorn, his snowy hair streaming in the wind, he waved the hat over his head and shouted out a great huzzah.

"They've struck their colors," he exulted. "Sumter is ours once more, ensign. Do you see? None of it happened. Time's all wound back on her spindle and my lads are alive. They're home turning mother's garden. They'll be there when I arrive. I'm a-going to set you ashore now. I want you to hold the fort. If the Rebels rise up, leave not one stone upon another. Put 'em all to the sword. Time's spooled back up and my lads are home spading in the garden and tomorrow we'll all go a-blackberrying together."

The man was weeping. Through his tears he cried to Morgan, "Step out on that grass tussock, boy. Go up boldly and occupy the fort and let all be as it was before."

"I need to go another short way down the lake," Morgan said.

"You need to obey your superior's orders," the lunatic roared. "Do you dare answer back to an officer? Do so again and I'll have you shot. Now will you hold that fort and hold back time or not?"

The old man's eyes were riven through with red veins. "Don't you see, lad?" he wailed. "The whole war's as much a blunder as this fort, and all you and I can do is keep retaking her, because come tonight she'll fall and the years will fly off God's great bobbin again. Oh, dear boy. They come for me last week from the village. They tried to take me up in a net, but I ran away like the gingerbread boy. They dogged me like a fish with a close-mesh net for that I lost my boys."

He was pouring another rattling miscellany of metal into his punt gun. Morgan picked up a dead mallard and stepped onto the tussock of marshy grass, felt it quiver and give under his foot, leaped to another and out onto the scree in front of the abandoned fort. He walked backward with his musket at the ready. He would not put it past the Admiral of the North to throw down on him with the great Chesapeake Bay gun and cut him clean in twain. Could the Admiral possibly be one of the killers himself? But no, the grief-stricken father was punting hard back into the lake, the flat bottom of the boat whishing over the dead rushes. The sun had disappeared. A chilling mist was falling as, out of the low clouds, winging their way north into the wind, came a flock of snow geese. The white undersides of their wings were fringed in black and they were honking encouragement to each other as they breasted the wind.

"Gunboats!" the Admiral roared. "They seek to flank us on our right."

Frantically he swiveled the punt gun up at the squadron of geese and touched off a barrage of whizzing nails and screws. The air was full of falling white geese as the Admiral punted over the waves in a world bereft of all reason.

Morgan gathered up some driftwood. Using a bit of birch bark in his pocket for kindle, he struck his flint and steel and started a fire in the lee of the fort to cook the duck he'd carried off the boat. As he plucked and cleaned the bird, he thought about the deranged Admiral. How could the local people allow the madman to work such rapine on innocent creatures, exterminating whatever swam in the lake or flew over it?

The spitted duck took a long time to cook, but Morgan did not want to eat wild fowl red. He dozed with his back against the fort. He dreamed of being called upon in school to recite and not knowing his lesson, woke with a start, sweating and light-headed. Something was burning. It was the mallard, charred and in flames. The waterbird was so old and tough that he could scarcely swallow a morsel. He'd hoped that the wing meat, what little there was, might give him strength, but finally he gave up on the bird and threw the blackened carcass into the fire. He got out Jesse's stone. Beside the drawing of the pile of stones that was Fort Blunder was the rune ᚱ. There was a code of some kind here if Morgan could but unravel it. Sitting with his back against the fortress, he fell asleep again.

SOMETHING COLD AND WET was pressing against the back of Morgan's neck. He jumped up and spun around, groping for Ludi's scattershot pistol, and found himself looking up into the solemn gray face of an elephant. Morgan had seen a live elephant once before, an underfed, ill-used animal with the Sykes Brothers Traveling Menagerie, which had come to Kingdom Common when he was a shaver. This elephant was half again as big as the Sykes Brothers', bigger than Morgan had known any animal could be. He wondered if it too might belong to a circus. It wore a spangled harness studded with bits of colored glass. On its back was a purple tapestry worked with rainbow-hued figures, dancing women in half-veils, warriors riding camels and fighting with curved swords, giraffes, hippopotamuses, even a crocodile with a small bird standing in its open mouth. The elephant had little black eyes and short bristly lashes, and to Morgan's amazement it was crying. It was shedding real tears, and on its long elephant face was the saddest expression Morgan had ever seen on the visage of man or beast.

"What's the matter?" he said to the weeping elephant. "You look like you just lost your best friend."

Morgan wondered if the animal might be hungry. He wondered what elephants ate. Maybe this one would eat hay if he could find some for it.

Gently, the weeping animal wrapped the end of its trunk around Morgan's wrist and gave him a tug like a biting fish. Still grasping Morgan's wrist, the elephant started walking toward the open gate of the fort. For a moment he wondered if the elephant was an apparition brought on by his exhaustion. But he could smell the animal's musky, comforting scent and feel the moist end of its trunk on his wrist and see the great tears sliding slowly down its face. This animal was as real as he was.

The elephant released Morgan's wrist and walked on ahead, looking back once like a smart dog that wanted to show him something. "What is it?" Morgan said. "What do you want me to see, my friend?"

Inside the fort stood a blue-and-green cart with a red canvas cover, its wheel spokes and tongue picked out in canary yellow, in the middle of an otherwise empty parade ground. On the side of the cart's high canvas cover, in faded black letters, were the words "Sabbati Zebi. Seer and Prophet. Fortunes Told 5¢. Prognostications 10¢. Prophecies 25¢." Below that was the rune ᚱ and the word *Raido*.

From the wagon came a groan. "Who is it, Caliph?" a voice said. "Who comes? Cossacks to finish me off, no doubt."

"It's Morgan Kinneson of Kingdom Mountain, Vermont," Morgan called out. "The elephant brought me."

The voice inside the cart did not reply. Morgan lifted the back flap and peered inside. An elderly gypsy man lay on a pile of straw, holding his stomach and rocking. He had long gray hair and a silver hoop in one ear. Over his legs and stomach was drawn a ragged quilt. Beside him sat an old trunk with a faded painting on the lid of a genie rising out of a bottle.

"I die now in a minute," the gypsy said to Morgan. "Because of your cursed war and all it unleashes."

Morgan looked at Sabbati Zebi. "It isn't my war," he said.

"Look," Sabbati said. "I am traveling the countryside north of here with the Caliph and minding my own business when suddenly I am overtaken by a clubfoot driving a fine sleigh and dressed all in black, with a sable hat. He sees the sign on my cart, *raido,* and asks what it means, and I make up some gypsy foolishness. He watches me with his snaky black eyes, and I know he does not believe the tale. Then he asks if I have seen a tall boy with fringe jacket and long, light hair."

A chill ran up Morgan's back. "Was this man armed?"

The gypsy shrugged. "Not knowing. Perhaps. His eyes are dead eyes, and I am afraid. So I tell him I am ill and must get to a doctor. That I have a bad tumor inside my stomach, is killing me. And he says is my lucky day, he is doctor. He gets from the carriage a carpetbag. He says he has the right medicine, will cure Sabbati. He presses my stomach and I pretend to shriek in pain. Then he asks me again. Have I seen a boy from Vermont with a musket and another gun around his neck. Or a long-legged black wench. I shake my head and groan as if in pain, and the clubfoot says he will examine my stomach, and out of the bag he whips his doctor's cutting knife and does this to me."

The gypsy pulled back the quilt. With his other hand he was cradling his own intestines, spilling out of a long rent in his stomach. "Look," he cried. "The so-called doctor sliced me open and pulled out my guts and trod on them with his great black iron shoe."

Morgan started and drew back, but the gypsy reached out and seized his hand. "The Caliph is bring me here. To the fort I also call *raido*. Is wounded?"

Morgan realized that Sabbati was referring to the elephant. "I didn't see that he was. But he's crying."

"Is cry for me, his brother. Elephants have souls, too, like gypsies. They cry tears. They smile with their eyes. They are beloved friends. And like a gypsy, mark me well, they are dreaded enemies who never forget a wrong. Thirty years the Caliph of Baghdad and I are together, peddling our wares and transporting our dark friends. Now this. Killed by a clubfoot who pulls out my guts and stomps them into the ground with a boot like a blacksmith's anvil. He will kill you too if he finds you."

"Not if I find him first, he won't. I'm going to fetch you a doctor."

"No doctor," Sabbati Zebi screeched. "Is doctor who turns me inside out. With his fine sleigh and well-fed horses."

"These horses," Morgan said. "What kind of horses?"

"Horses with four feet and a mane. What other kind is there? Bay-colored."

"Good Jehovah!" Morgan cried out. He was horrified to realize that he had not only led the second gunman from the frozen slang to Sabbati Zebi, but the clubfooted creature with the Yellow Boy had no doubt murdered the kindly priest who'd picked him up as well.

"Bring me a little water," the gypsy said. "A terrible thing it is to die thirsty."

The dying man nodded at a wooden bucket hanging from the tail of the cart. Morgan grabbed the bucket, sprinted to the lake, returned with the water. With his cedar drinking cup he scooped out water for the gypsy, who gulped it down.

Sabbati gave him a cunning look. Then he demanded more water but this time he could not swallow it. The crafty expression never left his face as he said, "How is it, Sabbati, you may say to me, that if you can prophesy future events, you couldn't predict being attacked by the crazy clubfoot?"

No such question had occurred to Morgan, who was certain that no one could predict the future. To Morgan fortunetelling was almost as great a fraud as Sunday school.

The gypsy shook his head. "Predict the future I don't. Only reveal character. Yours I find lacking."

Despite everything—the dying gypsy, the crying elephant, Jesse's death, his seemingly hopeless mission, and with the second killer and perhaps others as well closing in on him—Morgan smiled. "You're right," he said. "Now I'm going for the doctor."

"No. Only watch with me. When I pass, take what you want from the trunk, then set fire to my cart with me inside. Now swear that you will do this and that you will give Caliph to the best-hearted person you know. Swear."

"I'll see that your beast is well cared for," Morgan said. "In the meantime, what do you know about this?"

He got out Jesse's stone and handed it to the gypsy. Sabbati's black eyes snapped. "Where?" he said. "Where do you find this?"

"A black man named Jesse Moses gave it to me."

"Listen. You must throw this stone as far out into the lake as you can throw it. Is dangerous. Now watch with me a little. You owe it to me because I do not reveal your whereabouts to the clubfoot. Yes, I see you coming three days ago. I predict the present as well as the past. Don't fall asleep. I travel soon. Then you and the Caliph must leave here before the crazy returns with his long doctor's knife. And throw the stone in the lake. Do you promise?"

"I'll wait with you," Morgan said, then instantly wished he hadn't. How at this rate would he ever find Pilgrim? But having failed to keep his word to deliver Jesse Moses safely to the railway station, he was determined to watch with the gypsy.

"If he comes for you—I mean the doctor," Sabbati said, "go to Big Eva. She will protect you, at the sign of *Laguz,* on Henry Hudson's River, in the Mountains of the Bark Eaters. See? Here on the stone, not far south of my sign, *Raido.*"

"What does it mean? *Raido?*"

"Sojourner. As all gypsies are. I am now about to make yet another journey, one we each make only once. Tell the Caliph farewell from Sabbati Zebi."

"Sabbati," Morgan said, tracing his rune, ⸸, on the back of the dying man's hand with his finger. "What is this called?"

"Nauthiz," the gypsy said.

"What does it mean?"

"Ask Big Eva in the Mountains of the Bark Eaters," the gypsy told him, and then he closed his eyes and did not speak again.

ALL NIGHT Morgan waited with Sabbati Zebi until, toward dawn, he fell asleep. When he woke, the hand he held was cold. The sky was growing lighter. Soon day would arrive and with it, perhaps, the deranged doctor. He must leave the fort as soon as possible.

Morgan began to sort through the gypsy's belongings. A coal-oil lamp half full of oil, which he lighted. Some pots and pans and a brazier. Some glass jewelry. A bag of counterfeit brass coins. A few colored hair ribbons and combs. The trunk inscribed with the genie contained a small framed picture of Jesus delivering his sermon on the mountain, another of Moses gazing on the Promised Land, yet another of Jacob wrestling with his angel. Several miniature bottles containing a yellowish liquid labeled Sea of Galilee Water. A packet of St. Peter's writing styluses, a fragment of St. Paul's singed robe, and a splinter from the cross of the thief crucified beside Christ. Finally, a box of blue-tipped sulfur matches and a wicked-looking foot-and-a-half-long dagger with a round cork handle, a silver band around the top. The dagger was all Morgan wanted.

He looked out at the elephant, who was weeping again. "I know," he said, placing his hand on the rough, dusty folds of the animal's leg. "I know, Mr. Caliph."

Morgan sprinkled the oil from the coal lamp over the gypsy and the contents of the cart. He struck one of the sulfur matches on the barrel of Hunter and tossed the flaming match inside the cart, which ignited in a heartbreaking whoosh. Then, with the Caliph walking beside him, he headed south from Fort Blunder on the pike along the lake.

The sun rose behind the mountains across the water. Ahead a gigantic glittering bird, as huge as Sinbad's roc, was perched in the lower limbs of a lakeside willow tree budded out red for the spring. The fiery rays of the rising sun sparkled off the bird's multicolored feathers so that it hurt Morgan's eyes to look at it. The elephant let out a trumpeting bellow and began to shy away from the mythical bird in the willow tree, which was no bird at all but the Admiral of the North, his hundreds of bright buttons shining in the crimson sunrise, pinned to the willow by the throat with his own trident. His unmoored wooden boat drifted on the lake nearby. The Chesapeake Bay punt gun with which the Admiral had taken Fort Sumter afresh each day was gone.

SINCE LEAVING FORT BLUNDER THREE days ago Morgan had eaten nothing but a porcupine he'd clubbed in the road and a red squirrel clipping end twigs off a maple tree to suck on the rising sap. He'd killed the squirrel with Ludi's scattershot, but there hadn't been enough meat to get onto the tine of a fork. Twice he'd fed the elephant, once at a rundown farm where a man sold him a hundredweight of damp, smutty hay and again at a lumber camp, where the hay turned out to be mostly straw with all the nutritional value of sawdust. In the mountain hamlets he passed through, consisting mainly of a sawmill, a dozen or so battened dwellings, and maybe a log schoolhouse, he asked directions to the headwaters of Henry Hudson's River. People would point vaguely toward a jumble of snowy peaks off to the south. No one seemed to have heard of Big Eva or to have glimpsed any sign of the horrible box-footed creature in black, but Morgan could not shake the sense that he was not far away, perhaps toying with him, cat-and-mousing him for some fell purpose of his own. Surely, back at the fort, it would have been as simple for the vivisectionist to kill him as to kill the Admiral.

In one wretched assortment of hovels, children and loafers had pelted him and the Caliph with mud and snow, pinecones, stinking potatoes, frozen horse and ox dung. The grieving elephant walked on with its head down, oblivious to these missiles. The steep mountainsides were covered with felled trunks of hemlock trees, stripped of their bark and strewn about all higgledy-piggledy like the colossal white bones of some extinct race of giants annihilated in long-ago warfare amongst themselves. Yet these Adirondacks, or Mountains of the Bark Eaters as the gypsy had called them, were the mountains of Morgan's great hero John Brown, who from this fastness had helped many an Underground passenger move on to Canada and safety. Thinking of Brown gave the boy courage as he moved deeper into the forbidding peaks, hoping to elude the killer who had eviscerated the gypsy and, Morgan had no doubt, impaled the poor Admiral of the North with his own trident. Morgan's father had told him that by taking the law into his own hands in Kansas, removing fathers and husbands from their homes and hacking them to pieces, Brown had violated the most sacred commandment of the God he claimed to serve. Morgan could scarcely disagree. Yet he thought that later, at Harpers Ferry, Brown's error had been in his strategy, not in his principles. Tarnished though he was, John Brown was still the public figure

Morgan most admired. Given a chance, he'd have gone to Harpers Ferry with him. For a certainty Brown would have known how to deal with the clubfooted demon who was pursuing him and the Caliph.

IT WAS SNOWING AGAIN, with sleet and freezing drizzle mixed in. Ice formed on the elephant's head and sides and on Morgan's slouch hat. The day before he had taken a chill, which had turned into a hard ague. First fever, then shivering. Coughing steadily, he walked on into the Mountains of the Bark Eaters beside the elephant. From time to time the animal paused and looked back the way they had come with red and weepy eyes. Morgan thought that the gypsy must have had considerable goodness in him. Why else would the Caliph mourn him so?

That night Morgan heard wolves howling and a scream that could have been a cat o' the mountains, a great yellow painter. The elephant paid little attention to the wolves, but the painter's scream angered him, and he trumpeted back as if to keep this tiger of the north woods at bay. Toward morning Morgan dreamed that he heard his name being called out over the dark forest. "Morrr-gaaan. Give up the stone, Morrr-gaaan. Give up the nigger gal."

He sat bolt upright. Was it in fact a dream? From far off in the woods came a high, eerie threnody:

Young Morgan's body is a-moldering in the dust,
Young Morgan's musket's red with bloodspots turned to rust,
Doctor Surgeon's scalpel has made its last inquiring thrust,
A.D. goes marching on.

There could be no doubt. The apparition called Doctor Surgeon was sporting with him. Terrified though he was, Morgan resolved to sell his life as dearly as possible. The doctor might kill him, but not without mortal cost to himself.

Dawn, and racked by bloody coughing. The Caliph knelt in the snow trail, speckled with brown evergreen needles, and beckoned with his trunk. Morgan stepped carefully onto the animal's bent brow and then onto its back. For the rest of that day he rode on the elephant. Like the migrating geese overhead, he knew north instinctively so, putting his back to Canada, he and Caliph proceeded south along the lumber track through the snowy woods. How could runaways from the South who had never seen snow make their way through this boreal fastness? With a conductor like John Brown, he supposed. Morgan had been a conductor himself. Now he was a soldier. He was his own private, captain, and general, his own sutler, though a poor one, because both he and the elephant were near starving. He was his own outrider and his own artillery, his own pickets, his own rolling army of one. He was guilt-ridden and sick and in full retreat from an evil he did not understand. Very possibly he was dying.

A T FIRST Morgan thought that an avalanche had let loose from the upper slopes of the mountain ahead. The low rumbling rose to a steady growl as the woods road he was following crested a rise. Ahead he saw thousands of logs rushing down the whitewater rapids of a brawling river. Grinding together and creating a tremendous thunder, they sluiced downstream between looming black boulders.

Morgan jolted along on the elephant until he came to a place where all hell seemed to have let out for a holiday. In a bend just downstream, logs scrubbed clean of every shred of bark were piled thirty feet high. More logs were augmenting the jam every second, piling up against a black cliff that plunged directly down to the water on the far side of the river. The jam rose higher and higher up the sheer stone wall, though some few logs were still being guided through a narrow corridor of rushing water by red-shirted black men with pick poles.

More lumberjacks, also black, were using a yoke of oxen hitched to a long cable to try to free a mammoth debarked log, the butt end of a monstrous white pine. Branded on the side of each ox Morgan noticed the rune ᛏ. The animals' eyes bulged as they strained to free the pine log from the jam. A gigantic coal-black jack in a red shirt, a slouch hat as big as a five-gallon bucket, and voluminous trousers was urging the oxen on. From time to time the mountainous jam gave a groan and shifted. But it refused to give. The pine butt had it locked fast in the narrows below the cliff.

The huge black drover exhorting the oxen glanced up at Morgan and said, "This exactly what we need. I was just saying, what we need now, complete this bedlam, is an elephant show come by."

Morgan realized that the jack in the slouch hat was not a man but a tall, broad-shouldered black woman. "We're mired right down to Chiny," she announced with satisfaction. "The drive be hung on Big Eva's Crotch. The boys can't budge it and ain't *no*-body pleased with the walking boss, which is me. Big Eva. Tell you the truth, I ain't overly pleased with her myself. What you doing with old Sabbati's hefferlump, boy? Where at's Sab?"

In a few words Morgan told her of Sabbati's fate. Eva put her hand to her head. "I ain't surprised," she said, though it was obvious that she was. "In such parlous times as these, they entire Republic at war with itself, I can't say that anything surprise Big Eva. Except good news. I sorry to hear about Sab. He a fine man for all he gypsy nonsensicalness. Help one big slew of passengers over the line to Canady."

Morgan was studying the jam. "Here's some good news," he said. "I believe I can help you free up your logs."

"Not unless you got a crate of dyne-a-mite, you can't. We already tried every other method known to mortal man or woman. Every stick of dyne-a-mite in the North Country been sent south so we can blow up the other fella's bridge and railway so he can blow up ours. Blow up a great multitude of each other in the bargain. Without dyne-a-mite there no breaking loose God's Toothpick."

"God's Toothpick?"

"What I call that kingpin pine log fasten in all the others. God's Toothpick. River ain't big enough up here to float out a log like that."

Still coughing, Morgan watched the men and oxen straining to free the key log. Now they were hooking the chain wound around the log to a heavy wire from a drum windlass on a sled chained to a tree. Big Eva's lumberjacks cranked the wire taut, and it stood quivering in the hazy spring sunlight, flinging off sparkling drops of river water. God's Toothpick didn't budge.

"That steady pressure won't answer," Morgan said. "You'll have to jerk the key log free. You've got to snap him out the way he went in."

"I very glad to know it. Glad to go to school to a yalla-hair boy. We had enough dyne-a-mite, we could jolt free the whole riverbed. Where you ever get such a croup, boy? You don't take care of that bloody flux, you be as dead as poor Mr. Brown. What you big idea, bust out the jam?"

Morgan led the Caliph down the bank to the windlass. The wire was juddering with tension. As he'd suspected, the winching pressure was only wedging the mammoth log tighter into the jam.

"You need to pull it at an angle upriver, the way it went in," Morgan told the gray-haired black man turning the capstan winch.

"I see we got a new walking boss," the man said to Big Eva. "That the good part. Bad part, they new boss all of about twelve years old. Boy Jesusa at the temple, I reckon. Young Master Jesusa, 'structing they moss-backed old Pharisees."

"A steady pull won't do here," Morgan said. "It needs to be more of a jerk and a heave. To overcome inertia. My brother explained it to me."

"Oh, I sees," the gray-head replied. "He a big engineer, you brother."

"Maybe more of a conductor," Morgan said. "His name was—*is*—Pilgrim Kinneson." Out of the tail of his eye he saw Big Eva cut a glance toward him and just as quickly look away.

"Be my guest, by all means," the drive foreman said as Morgan cranked the winch backward and loosened the wire.

"We need to get the physics right," Morgan said, citing Pilgrim, who had studied physics at Harvard. But Eva said, "I physic you, boy, with a double dose of salts, you grand idea don't work out."

Morgan grinned. He liked this big, good-looking woman with a loud and ready reply for everything. He would not be surprised if she could tell him something about Pilgrim or about the girl—the pretty girl—the killers were after. When there was slack enough in the cable, he walked the elephant knee-deep into the river. He unclipped the wire hooked to the end of the chain around the log, then he fastened the chain to the ring bolt of the elephant's pulling harness and guided the Caliph a few paces up the fast current. The chain tightened.

"Hi! Hi yi hi!" Morgan yelled. The elephant gave a sudden terrific pull, surging into his harness with enormous force and springing the colossal pine trunk free. The jam began to shift. Morgan continued to exhort the Caliph to pull. The elephant plowed through the current, angling toward the bank, yanking the monstrous log into the slack water and thumping it up onto dry land like a stick of stovewood. The towering log jam began to turn on its axis, then collapsed in upon itself and slowly broke apart. Once again the logs ran freely down Henry Hudson's River.

"Zachias, come outen that tree!" exclaimed the foreman. "Leviathan hath spoken."

Morgan unhitched the iron hook on the end of the logging chain from the ring bolt on the elephant's pulling traces.

"No dyne-a-mite," he said to Big Eva, showing his open hands. "Just a flop-eared old elephant. Now, what can you tell me about—" Morgan sat down on a stump. He was having trouble catching his breath. His last thought as he toppled toward the ground was that as long as you were called upon to do it only once, dying was probably manageable. He was only sorry that he had not found Pilgrim first.

"'Bout time you come to."

Morgan opened his eyes. Eva's gray-haired foreman was looking at him through wisps of smoke. No, not smoke. Steam. He was lying on a bed of fresh cedar boughs inside a hut made of green cedar. The foreman was pouring water over red-hot stones in a shallow pit to make still more steam, which rose up through a lacy canopy of cedar boughs. The powerful scent of evergreen filled the hut.

Through a flap in the side of the hut came Big Eva. She bent over and pressed her ear against Morgan's chest. Then she straightened up as much as she could without striking her head on the woven boughs overhead. "Sound clear," she said. "Just a bad ague was what you had, boy. Maybe a touch of they walking ague. How long you think you been laying here, being minister unto?"

Morgan sat up, then fell back. "My guns," he said.

"You guns safe, don't worry. How long you think you been here?"

"Two days?"

"Try five," Eva said.

But Morgan had already sunk back on the cedar boughs, where he slept for yet another day and night. When he woke again he was ravenously hungry.

MORGAN KINNESON, STILL WEAK but no longer coughing, scooped smoking pork and beans into his mouth as fast as he could knife-and-thumb them. Mopped up the gravy with a chunk of yellow cornbread the size of a house brick. Oh, it felt wonderful to be well again. As for Pilgrim, Eva told Morgan she had heard through Underground scuttlebutt that Quaker Meeting Kinneson's elder son had vanished during the fighting in Pennsylvania. Be that as it might, Eva told Morgan that Pilgrim had not come through her station, *Laguz*. Nor had she seen a runaway girl, with or without a little boy. Not that she could say so directly if she had. It was absolutely forbidden for a Railroad employee to mention the name of any passenger or conductor, even to another Railroad employee. But Eva admonished him not to deceive himself with wishful thinking about his brother. When Morgan showed her Jesse's stone, she too implored him to destroy it, saying it jeopardized the safety of every stationmaster from Tennessee to Canada. "Get it by heart and then bury it in they woods, boy," she said. "Be sure you bury it deep."

Morgan pointed to his rune, ᛏ, on the stone. "Sabbati called this *Nauthiz*. He told me to ask you what it meant."

"Means everything harder than you think. And everything connected."

"And this one?" Morgan pointed to Pilgrim's sign, ᛟ, at the bottom of the stone.

Eva frowned. "*Othila*. Means separation. And that all you gone tease outen Big Eva. Bury that stone twenty feet deep, boy. Then go home where you belong. That you advice from me."

Morgan held out his empty tin plate to the cook.

"Thank you, sir, you welcome, sir," the cook said. "Boy wants to eat offen us wouldn't hurt him none to show some manners. Say please and thank you."

"I reckon he's earned his meal, please or no," Eva said. "Say, child. You hungry or what?"

Morgan scooped with the back of the gypsy's dagger, careful not to touch the blade with his tongue. It clicked and scraped on the sides of the refilled tin plate.

"You ever do get down South, watch out for they killers," Eva said. "They as soon do for you and you ellyphant as look at you."

Morgan stood up. He beckoned to the Caliph of Baghdad and climbed aboard his back. "What killers?" he said.

"*They* killers," Eva said. "Hundreds of thousands of they. Some wears blue, some wears but'nut. But they all killers."

Morgan touched the brim of his hat with his finger. Then he and the Caliph headed off along the river, a determined boy and a sad elephant traveling south through the mountains together in the uncertain spring of 1864. Thus far he had eluded the clubfooted killer with his deadly surgical instruments and long-range carbine, but he knew that the time was coming, and sooner rather than later, when he must confront and kill the devil or be killed himself.

THREE

MANNAZ

ᛗ

"They say," declaimed Steptoe, "that we are evil incarnate."

Doctor Surgeon tipped his glass toward the little player. "They say right."

Prophet Floyd chuckled. "Aye," he said. "Spake old Jeremiah, 'Men's hearts are devious and there is no help for it.' Who among us, brethren, can deny the evil that men do and are? Yet are we not made in His image? So must not He too be evil?" Floyd smiled and nodded in agreement with himself. Then he was off and raving in that private tongue known only to him and perhaps to God, the sacred language in which the angels' voices had enjoined him to kill so many of his flock, both before and after he anointed himself Messiah of the Grand Army, not of the American Republic but of the Republic of Satan himself.

"Shut your hole," King George said, and Prophet instantly did.

George, also known as Swagbelly, sat with his back to the window. He was so massive that he blocked most of what faint light crept into Albany's Sign of the Tippling Dutchman, and so dark that he seemed to absorb the rest. How, he wondered for the twentieth time, had he allowed himself to fall in with these madmen? Anno Domini had said he needed them to retrieve the girl, but back at the prison George had been tempted to take them up one by one and snap their necks like trout.

At his court-martial the player, Steptoe, who styled himself a spymaster, though in fact neither side took him seriously enough to entrust him with any significant information, had boasted of killing more than a dozen young girls and keeping their bodies preserved in a Pennsylvania icehouse so he could violate them repeatedly. Prophet Floyd, the self-proclaimed Messiah, sputtered gibberish day and night, disported himself with deadly serpents, and supposed that he was the instrument of retribution of some supremely wrathful power to whom the stern old Jehovah of the Bible was as benign as George's white-haired grandmother. As for the vivisectionist who called himself Doctor Surgeon, a man who had been chief medical officer of Union field hospitals at six major battles, he'd announced at his trial that by such fell means as introducing infection into open wounds, conducting unnecessary amputations, and prescribing lethal dosages of arsenic drops he had killed more Union and Confederate soldiers than any ten roaring cannons.

Indeed, George had long suspected that the blind man himself was at least half mad. What sane person referred to himself as Anno Domini, as if wherever he went there too went end-fire and Armageddon? Verily, the day would come when George would have a sufficiency of A.D.'s gold, and when that happy advent arrived, he would make the blind man pay as dearly as mortal man could pay. Yes, by God, George would. And then he would do for the others as well, the pleasant work of a quick moment.

"You were instructed," King George told the triumvirate of fools, in a voice like mountain thunder, "to fetch me the stone map and the gal. Instead you let the boy kill Ludi."

"But I killed the gypsy conductor," Doctor Surgeon said in a wounded tone. "Somehow the boy escaped with the elephant into the mountains."

"Where you played at bo-peep with him for your own diversion," George said. "Now you had best find him and the gal as well and kill him and bring me the stone and the wench, unharmed, as the blind man, I mean Anno Domini, instructed you. You"—pointing a forefinger as large as a German sausage at Doctor Surgeon—"to the canal. Your contact there is Captain Suggs of the boat *City of Buffalo*. You, Preacher, to Elmira. For the lad may stop there to consult with his uncle. And you, who call yourself Steptoe, to Pennsylvania. For that's his destination. If he proceeds so much as a mile beyond Gettysburg, or if you harm a hair on the gal's head, I'll come for all three of you myself. Or, worse yet, A.D. will. Do you want the likes of him, with his horrible green goggles, scouring the land for you? I shouldn't think so. Now. Fan out and do your work."

"Kill the elephant too," George called after Doctor Surgeon as the clubfoot hitched across the tavern floor toward the door, dragging the black box that enclosed his freakish appendage.

"The elephant? Why kill—"

"Because I despise elephants," King George thundered. "Now range out!"

.   .   .

TODAY WAS TO BE a great day in the history of Glens Falls, an otherwise humdrum mill town on the upper Hudson some forty miles above the terminus of commercial navigation. At two o'clock this afternoon the town would welcome and fête the president of the United States. Glens Falls, at least, would do all it could to help Lincoln in his steep uphill bid for reelection. American flags were draped across every storefront. Besides a pig roast, there would be speeches by local dignitaries of the Republican Party. It was rumored that Harriet Tubman herself might introduce the president. Unfortunately, he was slated to be in town for but two short hours, arriving in his special campaign railway car, delivering a brief speech, having a bite with his supporters—a country boy born and bred, Lincoln was known to have a tooth for the salty cracklin' on the outside of the pig—before tearing back to Albany for an evening rally.

By early afternoon the Falls was teeming with people eager to hear the president. Just south of town, where the Albany, Glens Falls, and Plattsburgh tracks crossed the river on a soaring trestle, spectators lined the banks three and four deep to see Lincoln's campaign train chuff into town. Morgan himself had little interest in viewing the man his father, for all his abolitionist sentiments, referred to as King Abraham; Morgan suspected that Quaker Meeting Kinneson privately blamed Lincoln and his war for Pilgrim's disappearance. But as he and the elephant headed south out of town, he discerned a north-bound engine stopped beside a wooden tank to take on water. The entire train consisted of the locomotive, a single passenger car painted red, white, and blue, and a caboose. As Morgan, aboard the galumphing Caliph, passed nearby, a tall man in his late middle years wearing a rusty black suit stepped down from the railway carriage and began voiding a rather halting stream of urine onto the cinder bank. The man relieving himself, who was the most tired-looking man Morgan had ever seen, looked up and grinned to see a boy sitting on an elephant and watching him.

A bulky man in a bowler hat swung down from the open coach door and shouted at Morgan, "Who in the blazing hell are you?"

"It's all right, Pink," the president said in a surprisingly soft voice. "The boy means us no harm."

Shaking himself off, the president said to Morgan, "You are well armed, son, if I do say so."

"Well armed!" the man called Pink exclaimed. "Why sir, he's a traveling arsenal. Get down off that animal, boy. Keep your hands right where I can see them."

"It's all right, Pink," the president repeated. As he buttoned up, the Caliph made a gracious curtsy in his direction, and Lincoln smiled slightly. The lines around his mouth looked as deep as crevasses. Still fumbling with his trouser buttons, he peered up at Morgan and said, "Though I will allow that this is about as awkward a way to launch a reelection campaign as any I can imagine: The water closet in my carriage is out of order, lad."

"What isn't?" Morgan said.

Lincoln looked at him again, sharply this time. Then the commander in chief did something he had not done in many months. He laughed. It was a rueful laugh, but it was beyond doubt genuine, though his eyes and face seemed no less careworn and weary.

Morgan decided that the conversation had lasted long enough. While he believed that he had temporarily given his pursuer the slip, there was no way to be sure. It would not do to have the madman lying close by in the hills above the river, even now drawing a bead on the president of the United States.

"You, sir," Morgan said to Pink, who had stationed himself directly in his way. "Do you give me the road or no?"

"By God, now," Pink said, his hand darting inside his jacket.

"Step aside, Mr. P, step aside," the president said mildly. "This lad is no danger to us." And as Morgan rode past, "God bless you, son."

Morgan, who wanted no blessing from God or anyone else, touched the drooping brim of his slouch hat with his forefinger. It occurred to him that for such a great man the president had a very commonplace nozzle to do his business with. Under different circumstances, Morgan thought, he might actually like the old fellow.

"COME UP, you long-eared sons of a whore. Wake up, roll along, roust out, and walk on, you hammer-headed brace of slackers."

The hoggee of the showboat *His Whaleship* out of Utica, New York, cracked his whip over his two canal mules. Down the towpath a hundred yards, Morgan watched as the cursing mule driver charged his stubborn animals. But instead of beating them he patted their heads and scratched their long ears like two highly favored dogs. No matter. The brace of mules refused to budge. Already canal traffic was backing up behind *His Whaleship*.

"Here's a pretty pass," roared the hoggee, still gentling his animals. "We've got as capital a mess on our—why, as I live and die, it's Morgie Kinneson!"

To Morgan's astonishment the showboat hoggee turned out to be his cousin Dolton Kinneson. The two young men stared at each other with amazed delight.

"What under the sun are you doing here, Dolt?" Morgan said.

Dolt caught Morgan up in a crushing bear hug. Then he explained that the Great Western Canal was as far south as he'd gotten on his quest to enlist. Some months ago he'd taken a job with the showboat, whose principal attraction was the gigantic head and jaws of a sperm whale, in which twenty ladies and gentlemen could sit as proud as Jonah and have their daguerreotype made. On the deck several black crewmen were watching the reunion between the cousins with interest.

"Meet the Caliph, cousin," Morgan said. Dolton gravely extended his hand. Equally solemnly, the elephant took it in his trunk and gave it a formal tug.

Not to be outdone, Dolton gestured at his boat. "Meet *His Whaleship,* Morgie. But these two mules are on their last legs. Say. I'll pay you five dollars to hitch your big boy to *His Whaleship* and haul her up to Ute for me. Will you do it?"

"I will," Morgan said. "And I won't take a round copper penny. Hitch him up, cousin. I've a great deal to tell you."

"And I you," Dolt said as he unhooked the mules and hitched the Caliph to *His Whaleship.* Dolt glanced significantly at the side of the showboat. Inscribed in black below its gilded name was the figure Ħ. "You won't believe what I'm truly doing here, Morgie."

As if by way of reply, the Caliph reached out with his trunk and planted a big, wet kiss, full on Dolt's mouth. Then Morgan would have sworn that the elephant gave him a sidelong glance and winked.

I N THE EARLY AFTERNOON they came to a place where the berm was covered with blossoming dandelions. Butter-yellow cowslips bloomed along marshy backwaters, and each little puddle pond had its own pair of mallards. Wild black cherry trees were blossoming white as new snow in the hedgerows. Ahead was a lock through which canal boats were floated up to the next level of the waterway. It occurred to Morgan that, with his great love of exotic travel books, roaming the land with an elephant and seeing such wonders as the canal and the president's private train would, under normal circumstances, be a splendid adventure. But he doubted, after all he had witnessed and participated in, that he would ever want to read a travel book, or perhaps any book, again.

With a proprietary air Dolt told Morgan that there were eighty-three locks on the Great Western and that the canal was forty feet wide and four feet deep and stretched three hundred and sixty-three miles from the Hudson River to Buffalo over a rise in elevation of five hundred feet. Eighteen cut-stone aqueducts carried side streams across the canal. Numerous dams let water drain in during drought time. The other boats waiting at the lock, their names gilded on their bows in gold flake, were *Canal Master, J. J. Belden, Tug Ridge, Watertown,* and *City of Buffalo,* this last a floating gin mill captained, Dolt said, by the infamous anti-abolitionist dandiprat and raging sodomite Captain Higgenbotham Suggs. Suggs, strutting the deck of his ship, stood four and a half feet tall and fully as wide across, and wore a yellow-and-red-flowered waistcoat, a tall castor hat, a high stock collar, and whipcord breeches tucked into glossy morocco boots with scarlet tops. He guyed Dolt mercilessly, inquiring whether he was expecting a flood and gathering up beasts from afar two by two, or was he hauling gold specie that he needed such a monstrous tusker to pull his boat? Could the elephant count to five with its foot? Recite the Lord's Prayer? Why in the name of King Herod were its ears so small and its snout so short? Dolt stood by the Caliph with his boots planted two feet apart and his prunella neck cloth fluttering in the spring breeze, and when Suggs's fountain of wit ran dry, which did not take long, Dolt lifted to his lips the horn used to warn passengers of low bridges and blared out a great scornful raspberry by way of reply.

"And what of you, my pretty soldier?" Suggs called out to Morgan. "Come aboard the *City of Buffalo* and I'll give you the cook's tour, lad, abovedeck and below."

Morgan was staring at the two reddish brown horses Suggs was using instead of mules to pull his barge. The two big bays looked familiar. Giving Suggs a hard look, he checked his musket and scattershot to be sure they were primed and loaded.

While they waited their turn to lock up, Dolt confided to Morgan that *His Whaleship* was owned by the wealthy Utica abolitionist Gerrit Smith and was frequently used to carry a cargo of far more importance than the jaws of a dead whale. Currently he was en route to Buffalo with five Underground passengers disguised as crewmen. From there they would be conveyed by steamship across Lake Ontario to Canada. Again Morgan's cousin gave him a look full of meaning. The whale, he said, was merely for flash and dash. Dolton Kinneson an Underground conductor on the canal! Morgan never could have imagined it.

At dusk Morgan hayed the elephant at a town named, elegantly, Mule Fart, then walked on along the towpath under a million wheeling stars, talking to Dolton, while a deckhand manned the tiller. Suggs's *City of Buffalo,* now crowded with gin-swilling revelers bound for annual Spring Rout in Utica, kept pace two or three hundred yards behind them. The reflections of its red and green running lanterns glimmered in the black canal water as the gin boat crawled through the night under a pale quarter moon.

Dolt too had heard that Pilgrim had gone missing at Gettysburg but scoffed at the reports that he might be dead and buried in a Pennsylvania ditch. "Old Pilgrim's too crafty to be killed, and that's a natural fact," he said. "I know he's alive."

"So do I, cousin. But sometimes doubt creeps in."

"What was it the old reverend at home used to say, Morgie? Faith without a measure of doubt ain't worth a brass farthin'. Doubt be damned, don't you never stop looking for your brother. Never. See here, cousin. Say you was the one missing. Do you think Pilgrim would stop looking for you? *I* guess he wouldn't. Now here's a hard question that I need to ask a smart person. It's about this war."

"I don't care much about the war, Dolt."

"Well, don't care about it, then. Just answer the question for me. They say the fighting ain't about slavery. Ruther it's about states' rights."

"So I've heard."

"All right, then. You tell me, Morgie. States' rights to do what?"

"Secede, I reckon."

"Secede why? Over what?"

Morgan laughed. "Well, Mr. Grand Inquisitor, over slavery."

"Then why ain't the war about slavery?"

"I suppose it is."

"I suppose it is too," Dolt said. "So don't you never stop looking for Pilgrim!"

Morgan laughed again and shook his head. Philosophizing with Dolt Kinneson, now a canalman and Underground conductor, in the middle of the night in the company of a dead whale and a live elephant. And while Dolt's private algebra eluded Morgan—the x's and y's equating the cause of the war with the imperative to find

Pilgrim—the justness of his cousin's sentiments did not. He too believed that he must keep looking for Pilgrim, if only because the looking might sustain his faith that his brother was still alive. As to the war, well, he did not disagree that slavery, the greatest evil mankind had ever devised, was the ultimate issue, but it had long seemed to him that the conflict had acquired a malignant life of its own. Pilgrim had slipped away from it. Morgan wanted no part of it. His sole concern was to stay alive long enough to locate his missing brother.

Later Dolt told him that according to Gerrit Smith, the sign on the boat, ᛗ, stood for *Mannaz,* meaning beginnings. The canal, one of the main passages to Canada, was where the new lives of the *Whaleship*'s fugitive passengers truly began.

Morgan was pondering this idea when he noticed, down the waterway in the thin moonlight, that the *City of Buffalo* had shortened the distance between the two boats by half. The bay horses pulling the barge were coming on at a sweeping trot.

"SUGGS MEANS to pass us up yonder in the Yellow Jack Fens," Dolt said, looking back over his shoulder at the oncoming barge. "He means to cut our towropes with his boat scythes. Can your big boy run, Morgan? Shall we give the old sod a run for his money?"

"He can," Morgan said. "And we shall. Hi, Caliph. Run! Run, boy!"

The elephant broke into a lumbering trot. *His Whaleship* bounced along behind on the moon-shimmered surface of the canal. Suggs, at the tiller of his gin boat, blew his warning horn, and the hoggee leading the *Buffalo*'s bays leaped onto the back of one of the horses and whipped them up. The chase was on.

As the boats entered the vast swampy region known as the Yellow Jack Fens, the *Buffalo* continued to gain on them, the revelers on deck howling the bays on. Suggs blared out a ringing charge on his horn, and a blinding orange tongue of fire, accompanied by a terrific crashing report, shot out from the bow. A torrent of flying metal raked the stern and port side of *His Whaleship*. In the moonlight Morgan could make out the long shining barrel of the Admiral's Chesapeake Bay punt gun jutting off the bow of the *City of Buffalo*. Furiously reloading the deadly weapon, over which he hunched like a great cloaked bat, his outsized hat as black as a pirate sail, was the clubfooted creature from the wintery bog in Vermont. "Hands high overhead now, niggers and nigger stealers alike," shrieked Doctor Surgeon.

Flinging his musket to Dolt and calling out to the Caliph to run, run, run, Morgan broke into a sprint, heading directly back toward the *City of Buffalo* and straight into the maw of the Chesapeake punt gun now swiveling his way. As Doctor Surgeon thumbed back the gooseneck hammer, Morgan whipped the cord of Ludi's two-barreled scattershot over his head. He leaped over the mouth of the punt gun just as it exploded again, clearing the flying death-charge of shot by scant inches. He landed on the foredeck of the *Buffalo* and threw down on Doctor Surgeon with the scattershot. The terrified horses shied, causing the bow of the boat to crash into the side of the berm. A barrel of high-proof gin flew off the roof of the cabin, emptying its volatile contents over the deck. Morgan was flung across the deck by the collision. He fired one barrel of the scattershot wildly into the night, striking a running lantern, which shattered and fell onto the deck, torching the spreading pool of gin.

From around the corner of the low cabin came Suggs, his ten-foot-long fending pole raised above his head. Morgan dodged aside and Suggs slipped and fell onto the flaming deck and instantly took fire, as if the tons of gin he had consumed over his lifetime had ignited to consume him. As the blazing captain leaped into the canal, Morgan sprang off the boat. Casks of gin in the hold were now exploding like barrels of gunpowder. One of the bay horses was missing, as was the creature in black. The revelers had fled back down the berm.

Another barrel of gin burst and another and yet a third, as the *City of Buffalo* burned to the waterline. Soon all that could be heard was the jingling chorus of spring peeping frogs and one lone late-flying snipe, winnowing through the night sky high overhead.

Then, coming from nowhere and everywhere, a trilling ululation. "Morrr-gaaan. Morrr-gaaan. The girl, Morrr-gaaan. Where is the girrrl?" Followed by curdling laughter. Followed by silence.

DAWN WAS an enraged red streak in the northeastern sky. Black clouds scudded low overhead as Morgan and the elephant plodded west along the berm while Dolt manned the tiller of the showboat, its skeletal jaws pointing the way, its elegant blue-and-white gingerbread trim riddled to scrapwood. Two of the Underground passengers had been killed in the battle the night before by flying shrapnel from the punt gun. Two others, badly injured, had been taken on ahead to Utica for medical attention by the driver of a passing lumber wagon. Dolt, who had never before lost a fugitive passenger, was close to distraction. Morgan blamed himself. He was the one who had led the mad killer straight to *His Whaleship* and the runaways. It seemed that wheresoever he went he brought nothing but death and destruction to all who would help him.

Ahead on the towpath a goose girl was driving to market a score of gray Toulouse honkers and several dozen turkeys, and the path was beslimed with the birds' copious phlegm-green leavings. As Morgan passed the girl, who was long-legged and saucy and as sharp as the little end of nothing, she beckoned to him lewdly and broke into wild gales of laughter. She wore a shift of goose feathers and down glued to a potato sack, and her legs were as brown from the sun as the muddy canal water; her feet and ankles were the green of weathered copper from the droppings of the geese and turkeys, which kept up a din you could hear half a mile away, a constant lunatic honking and gabbling and gobbling. And as she harried them along, the little hoyden gabbled back at them in a strange and uncanny approximation of their own peculiar tongue.

UTICA. AT THE JUNCTION of the Great Western Canal and the River Tug, which ran out of the dank spruces and hemlocks of an area called the Limberlost, the sun came streaming forth on the wharves of the town. The streets were thronged with country folk and townspeople gathered for the Ute Spring Rout, a species of licensed saturnalia where a sober man, or woman either, was a rare spectacle. The docks were crowded with every manner of line boat, freight craft, and pleasure packet. Drunken wagoneers whipped their teams down the muddy main street between high warehouses, clerks' offices, and whore-cribs. From the wharf where he unhitched the Caliph from *His Whaleship,* Morgan counted three separate fisticuff brawls in progress. Fishwives screeched from makeshift stalls, farmers had set up impromptu pens crowded with bleating spring lambs and grunching pigs. Bare-breasted women were hanging out of the upper windows of a canal-side doggery with a swinging sign upon which someone had painted in staggering scarlet letters MOTHER HUBBARDS FRESH GIRLS AND FINE SPIRITS.

Dolton had already begun his showboat spiel. In a singsong voice, standing on the whale's lower jawbone, he called out through his polished brass speaking horn, "Ladies and gentlemen of the metropolis of Utica, flower of the Great Western Canal and upper York State, for two dollars you may have your likeness made seated in His Whaleship's great jaws. Come all you York State Jonahs! Whilst you sit for your daguerreotype, Professor Dolton Kinneson, that's yours truly, will instruct you in the nomenclature of whales, of which there be Right, Sperm, Finback, Blue, and many another curious variety. You are invited to examine His Whaleship as close as you wish. If you find he be not a true and honest whale, your money will be cheerfully returned and you will keep your photograph as well."

Someone was pulling at the fringed sleeve of Morgan's jacket. Expecting another surprise attack from his assailant of the night before, Morgan spun around, already reaching for the gypsy's dagger at his belt. It was the little goose girl. "If you'll bargain for me cheap this afternoon at the poorhouse vendue, mister elephant boy, I'll do you each night and again each morning. But come. First I'll show you something amusing."

The girl, whose name was Birdcall, led him and the elephant

77

toward a spanking white wooden bandstand on a broad greensward. Thirty or forty young men were crowded around the stand listening to a war recruiter in a blue silk hat harangue them about the sovereign delights of going south for a soldier. The recruiter had a speaking trumpet and an insinuating lisp, and he rampaged back and forth on the bandstand bellowing like a man possessed. "Who'll sign on, gentlemen, for the lark of a lifetime? Yes! The North Country Sharpshooters' Regiment consists of none but gentlemanly men. It is a beautiful chance for those wishing to see something of this life away from home, boys. Yes! Our summer uniform is green, the color of God's good grass, and miller's gray for winter. Our vittles none but the choicest, our officers princes among men." The recruiter pointed the small end of his horn at Morgan. "Will you sign on for the lark of a lifetime, boy?"

Morgan shook his head, though several other young men surged forward to sign up at a table beside the bandstand, where three ensigns in uniform sat enlisting recruits. One recruiter was missing his legs and conducted his affairs from a large wicker basket like a sitting hen. Another seemed in the course of his soldiering to have misplaced an eye and an ear. The third had but one arm, having evidently left the other behind on his holiday in the South.

Dolton, in the meantime, had hired a trap and driver to take him to Mr. Gerrit Smith, to report to the fabled philanthropist and Underground conductor the attack on his showboat the night before. Morgan agreed to meet Dolt that evening at a canal-side tavern called the Robber's Roost, then he and Birdcall, with the elephant lumbering along at their side, made their way to the poorhouse where the spring vendue was to be held. Fleetingly, Morgan wondered if Birdcall might be the girl the killers were pursuing. But no, they were looking for an older girl, a negro fugitive, and pretty besides. The previous day, when he'd inquired of Dolt about the pretty runaway, his cousin had teased him quite mercilessly, but in the end, he had to admit that he hadn't seen such a girl, with or without a little boy. To Morgan she remained a phantom. A pretty phantom.

NEAR LOCK NUMBER FIFTY-FOUR, a mile west of town, stood a sooty stone building overlooking a field as stark as a brickyard, which had long served as Utica's poor farm, a catchall for every kind of hapless indigent. Elderly paupers with no family to care for them, waifs like Birdcall, disabled soldiers, the feeble-minded hoi polloi, whole destitute clans with not one place else to go in the wide world. Each spring the less infirm on the poor-farm roster were lent out to farmers and petty tradesmen in the surrounding rural precincts to be boarded for the duration of the good weather in exchange for a few dollars and whatever light work the residents might be able to perform, which often consisted of no more than standing in fields and flapping their arms to keep away blackbirds. The annual vendue of paupers was conducted much like an auction, with one notable difference. The poor-farm clientele was considered so entirely feckless and, by virtue of their noxious existence, so bothersome, that instead of renting their services, the good-hearted authorities paid local squires and householders a small stipend to take them off the town for a few months, with the prized rentees going not to the highest bidder but to the lowest.

"Why don't you just run away?" Morgan asked Birdcall. "You

and your geese were ten miles down the canal this morning. Who'd have known or cared if you'd hopped a boat east and never looked back?"

"That's been tried afore. They have to account for us to the board of overseers in Ute. Otherwise, they'd starve us orphlingers off and say we went runagate. If we does run, they send the beadles after us and chain us up in our kennels and feed us naught but bread and water."

"How did you come to be an orphan?" Morgan asked the child. "Have you no family at all?"

"None in the world," said girl, trilling her "world" in an Irisher's brogue. "Me mother and father and infant brother Joshua Jonathan perished of the bloody flux that they calls the cholera on the way over the great salt sea from Dublin town. That was two years back, and I've been on me own since. 'Bout six months ago I was taken up by two bully boys and sold into service at Mother Hubbard's as a crib gal. Mr. Gerrit Smith rescued me out of bondage at Mother's and placed me in the poorhouse, but that's little improvement. You must buy me, honey man. You won't regret it. Otherwise I'll be sold back into service to Mother Hubbard, the vile old whore. Hoy! They're running up the red flag. The vendue's about to commence."

Morgan was all but weeping with frustration. First an elephant with a sense of humor to care for. Then an orphan child from over the ocean. Not to mention the clubfooted killer who might, even now, from the upper story of some leaning beehive of a tenement or the roof of a warehouse, be sighting in with his Yellow Boy midway between Morgan's shoulders. He was desperate to be on his way to Gettysburg, but there seemed to be some maddening delay at every turn in the way. Still, a plan had been forming in his mind. If locating Pilgrim was indeed a kind of military campaign, one that might well necessitate going behind enemy lines, then he must travel as light as possible, unencumbered by elephants and foundlings. And he must be ready to recalibrate his tactics at a moment's notice. With luck, he'd be able to help little Birdcall and at the same time fulfill his promise to the gypsy to find a good home for the Caliph. Then there would be only the killer to deal with. And dealing with killers was a line of work that the soldier Morgan Kinneson was becoming proficient in.

Above the Utica almshouse a crimson pennant snapped in the spring breeze. The auctioneer wore a bottle-green coat and a tall velvet hat and emerald boots rolled at the top. He stood on the tail of a wagon, his addlepated indigents and almshouse dregs crowded around him, cowering together or standing singly and staring away into nowhere. A knot of hard-looking farmers and their hard-looking wives, canal boat captains, tightfisted shop owners, and know-all tradesmen coolly assessed the pickings. Morgan stood near the back of the crowd.

"Hi ho and away we go," cried the auctioneer. "Who'll take three dollars to board this beauty for the summer?"

He gestured toward a blind crone lashed into a bent-hickory rocker with filthy strips of linen, rocking vigorously away in the back of the wagon and gazing up with her sightless eyes at the sun. "She's an easy keeper, good people, and the chair goes with her. Set her rocking on a Sunday eventide and wind her up again in a fortnight like a two-week clock. Her head follows the sun, you can tell the hour by its angle. She's more accurate than a garden dial. Milly the human timepiece, we call her. A little fried mush every three days and a kick to remind her she's still alive will do very nicely for her. Who'll take three dollars to provender her till fall, and if she don't summer over, why, you pocket what's left. She victuals easy, boys."

"What can the hag do?" demanded a broad woman in a sun hat broader yet. "Crippled up as she is and blind as a bat besides?"

"Why, Mother Hubbard," the auctioneer said, "she can knit two and purl one without a dropped stitch, mumble a winter's tale in a chimney corner to chill your blood, run a dasher, and live on less than a little. Set her out in your kitchen garden and she'd keep off the devil himself."

"Why don't you just stone us all and be done with it?" the old woman in the rocker suddenly croaked out.

"I'll take her for six dollars, not a penny less," the woman in the sun hat said, and "Done!" said the auctioneer.

Next a soft-headed old man with a purple goiter the size of a rutabaga dangling from his chin was fobbed off on a farmer for seven dollars. Then a family was sold, a mother, a spratling of ten or eleven, and a sucking infant. The mother and infant went to a farm wife, but the sprat was seized upon for two dollars by an ancient in a black wig who wanted a replacement for his recently deceased goat to run a treadmill churn. The child screamed at being separated from his mother, who shrieked and lamented most grievously, but the auctioneer told them to be grateful they weren't black Africans on the block in Charleston, where a far worse fate would certainly await them and the infant itself would no doubt have been torn from its mother's breast.

A feebleminded boy of twenty was indentured out to work in a fulling mill. Several homeless girls in their teens were assigned as washerwomen or cookees on the canal boats. Then the master of ceremonies motioned for Birdcall to join him on the wagon tail. The goose girl hopped lightly up, signaling Morgan by running her finger down the side of her nose. Her feet were green from the goose leavings, and her eyes were as hard as green glass. Her hair was the color of barn paint. "Here's a mere slip of a thing just coming into her womanly own. With a mite of correction, a mite of stripping and whipping, she'll make a fine below-stairs serving gal. She was on the canal last summer with the *Niagara Queen,* and she can hoggee mules, sniggle-snaggle eels, serve breakfast hot, and warm your bed. She only wants a little correcting. Off we go, hi ho, hi ho, who'll take her for five dollars?"

"There'll be no bidders," an elderly hoggee with a hook for a hand told Morgan in a confiding voice. "She has a ruputation, young as she is. No respectable householder will tech her."

"I'll take her for a dollar and she'll have all the correction she needs," Mother Hubbard said. She shouldered her way up to the wagon and reached out and ran her hand up Birdcall's bare leg as if appraising a cut of meat at the market. Fast as a bull mastiff, Birdcall grabbed the matron's wrist and sank her sharp little white incisors deep into her thumb.

Mother screamed and danced a jig and held up her bleeding thumb, roaring out that she'd take the bitch back for nothing.

"Mr. Auctioneer," Morgan called out. "I'll pay you two dollars for her."

"What? What are you, boy, a millionaire-man?" With a well-aimed kick, the auctioneer booted Birdcall off the wagon. "Take her then and be damned," he said cheerily, snatching Morgan's money out of his hand.

"You and the hellcat are both tripe, boy," Mother Hubbard snarled at Morgan. "You are both dead as tripe. See if you ain't."

Morgan motioned for the elephant to kneel and told Birdcall to climb up on the animal's back. Then he led the Caliph, with the girl atop it hurling scurrilous epithets at the harridan and the laughing throng, back toward the town.

As they headed along the berm Morgan once again considered his situation. He needed to swing south toward Elmira to see his uncle John, who had been in the great battle at Gettysburg, in order to learn more of Pilgrim's disappearance. His uncle might also be able to tell him more about the killers who had escaped from the Union prison, particularly the clubfooted doctor. His cousin Dolton needed, above all, not to go south. Then there was the wilding, young Birdcall, who had attached herself to him like a canal leech, and the matter of what to do with the Caliph. Barring an unforeseen encounter with the doctor, his plan was nearly ready.

A S DUSK SETTLED IN, the Spring Rout was in full swing between the wharf where *His Whaleship* was tethered and Mother Hubbard's whore-cribs and tavern at the far end of Canal Street. There were beer tents and open-air eateries serving ribs braised with maple syrup, Hudson River oysters on the half shell, and hot cross buns. There were ring-toss and coin-toss booths, guess-your-weight-and-age charlatans, tinkers, and pack peddlers hawking yard goods and scissors and genuine silver spoons with the brass showing through. There were dancers on stilts. And in the quagmire in front of Mother Hubbard's, near a swing-bridge over the canal, a party of maskers accoutered in feather boas, cloaks of many colors,

and sashes glowing vividly in the flaring gas street lamps. Some
of Mother's whores pranced in the mud attired in top hats, eye
masks like highwaymen, and not one stitch else. Their gentleman
escorts wore gossamer gowns in pastel hues. A gigantic butler in
snow-white livery made a stately promenade along the street pouring a viscous, bright emerald liqueur from a retort with a long pipe
neck into crystal goblets held high by the masked bacchanals. Some
of the celebrants wore crowns of gilded paper, and all were mim-
ing the most clownish extravagancies that men and women deep
in drink and debauchery are capable of. No one seemed to think
Morgan's elephant extraordinary in the least. In fine, the spectacle
reminded Morgan of nothing so much as a scene from a collection
of passing strange tales by a writer named E. A. Poe that Pilgrim
had sent him for his birthday two years ago.

Dolt was sitting on a bench outside a beer tent with a supremely
foolish grin on his face, toward which he was ever so carefully advancing, with both hands, a flagon of amber ale a good two feet
high. "Morgie," he shouted. "Have you seen the Spanish Mute?
The knife thrower? You won't believe what the fella can do. Why,
he can pick a bluebottle fly off a fat man's arse blindfolded from
thirty foot away."

Morgan couldn't help laughing as, with the painstaking deliberation of a very drunken man, the Dolter tilted his tankard—in the
process sloshing half of the beer over his jacket—toward a motley
knot of equally intoxicated fairgoers just up the street. They were
gathered around a man in a flowing black cape and a death's-head
mask standing a little beyond the last street lamp. He had provided
his own illumination with a flambeau made of lighted rags soaked in
coal oil and wrapped on an upright spear with a razor-sharp flanged
point, thrust handle-first into the mud. Leaning against the flaming

projectile was a wooden spear extender, an ancient device Morgan recognized from a travel book Pilgrim had sent him, known as an atlatl. The blazing rags were bound just below the spearpoint.

As Morgan and Birdcall approached with the elephant in tow, the Spaniard in the death's head tossed, high above his head, three shiny blades that gleamed in the torchlight, and as each spinning, glittering blade descended, he plucked it neatly out of the air and hurled it with deadly accuracy into the blood-red bull's-eye of a target painted on the door of Mother Hubbard's outhouse.

"Huzzah!" cried the masked onlookers. "Hurrah for Sir Skull and Crossbones."

"Do it again, dumb Fernando," called out a creature in red tights, a red doublet, and a goat's mask surmounted by two red horns. "Do it once more and there's a double eagle in it for you."

The mute shook his satanical head as if he disdained to repeat any part of his repertoire. But he pointed at the gypsy's cork-handled dagger in Morgan's belt sheath. Curious to see what the thrower might do next, Morgan passed him the blade handle first. With no more ado than a housewife throwing salt, the Spaniard hurled the dagger backward over his shoulder into the three tight-clustered silver throwing knives in the bull's-eye.

The crowd clapped and showered the performer with jingling coins. But as Morgan approached the target to retrieve his knife, the mute suddenly cried out, "Tarry, young sir. There's money in this for you. Just tell me *where be the nigger gal?*"

Whereupon Doctor Surgeon ripped off the death mask and reached into his carpetbag for his floppy-brimmed warlock's hat, which he clapped on his head even as Morgan grasped the butt of the scattershot hanging from his neck. As Morgan lifted the gun over his head, the killer snatched from his bag the long surgical knife with which he had sliced out many a poor soldier's heart and hurled it with a wicked sidelong motion, pinning Morgan's gun hand to the outhouse door by the fringed sleeve of his deer jacket.

Doctor Surgeon seized the blazing spear, inserted it in his atlatl, and flung it too at Morgan. The boy ducked, but as the deadly missile sped past him, it nicked his earlobe and fastened his head to the door by his long hair. "How now, my young Absalom?" screamed the doctor, as Morgan tried to pull away from the flaming spearhead. "Do you render up the nigger's stone?"

Morgan, pinioned to the wall by sleeve and hair, struggled to reach his scattershot with his left hand. Once more Doctor Surgeon dived into his bag, this time producing a battle-ax of his own devising, which he called his separation hatchet, because with it, prowling the battlefields in his bloody surgical gown, he had separated dozens of wounded Union and Confederate soldiers from their own heads. He threw the hatchet high into the air, caught it neatly by the handle in its spinning downward arc, drew back his throwing arm, and shrieked, "I'll see you in hell, Morgan Kinneson!"

"Caliph!" Morgan shouted. Before the doctor could loose the hatchet, the looming bulk of the elephant towered over him on its massive hind legs then dropped all of his tremendous weight and force to trample the murderer underfoot. Again the animal rose. Again he came crashing down, like the ramparts of old Jericho, on the writhing remains of the vivisectionist. Emitting an enraged scream unlike any earthly sound heard before or since in the wretched canal town, the elephant reared and plunged onto his victim yet a third time.

Later, when he had time to reflect on the death of Doctor Surgeon, Morgan recalled the gypsy's warning. "Elephants are dreaded enemies who never forget a wrong." He could only conjecture that the Caliph recognized the voice of the monster who had eviscerated his master. Even after grinding the doctor into a paste scarcely identifiable as the remains of a human being, if human he ever was, the elephant continued to trumpet. Morgan yanked his pinioned sleeve away from the outhouse door and ripped his head free from the flaming spear, leaving a singed hank of his dark gold hair fixed to the target.

As the maskers scattered, Birdcall clung shrieking to Morgan. Someone fired off a shot, and Dolton came running. In the pandemonium, Morgan grabbed his cousin by the shoulders. "The elephant's yours to take care of, Dolt. He'll pull your boat, and I know you'll treat him well."

"Morgie!" Dolt said, clasping Morgan's hand.

"I'll see you when I see you, cousin," Morgan said, and started across the swing-bridge with Birdcall scampering by his side. He was sorry to part with the Caliph but certain that he had left him, as he'd promised the gypsy, with the best-hearted person he knew.

Morgan looked back once. The awful iron box encasing the doctor's clubfoot sat in the street in front of Mother Hubbard's, as innocent as a boot in a cobbler's window. Otherwise nothing remained of the creature that could not be scraped into the canal the next morning on the blade of a coal shovel.

Tally two, Morgan thought as he walked into the night with Birdcall clinging to his arm. He wondered what would become of the outsized black shoe. He wondered what would become of himself, adrift in a world compared to which the most fantastical depictions in E. A. Poe's stories seemed ordinary. He began to count his steps, hoping thereby to tether himself to what he could remember of his life at home in Vermont, where counting tallied hen's eggs and pounds of butter, not killers eliminated. He could not seem to get past two. *First Ludi. Now the doctor. Tally two.*

It occurred to him that after Gettysburg Pilgrim might have fled north to Canada. Or returned to Glasgow to study with Lister. No matter. Morgan could not have turned back now if he'd wanted to. He kept walking.

PERTH

ᚾ

Dawn broke over the desolate countryside, a forlorn study in browns and grays, muted tones for muted times when color, like hope itself, seemed to have been drained out of the land. Elsewhere in upper York State it was springtime, with bold new shoots of grass and nodding daffodils and spun-gold buds on the trees heralding the new season. In the hinterlands between Utica and Elmira all seemed dreary and diminished. The hills were not high enough to be called mountains, the streams too slow and narrow for true rivers, the kine in the farmyards as lean as those in Pharaoh's dream. The Hardscrabble, as this region was called, was not a war-torn land but for all the world looked to be, with its played-out fields grown up to thorn apple and river birch and juniper and barberry, its dilapidated houses and sagging barns with crumbling sandstone foundations, its dispiriting four-corner country stores reeking of coal oil and moldy cheese, horse liniment and manure. Poverty Ridge. Fool Hill. Second Coming. The River Styx. The names scrawled on the crooked signposts Morgan passed told well the tale of the Hardscrabble. Hollow-eyed women, widowed by the war at twenty, gaunt and aged at thirty, watched him and Birdcall from their dooryards. The children looked worm-ridden and rickety. The wind whistled out of the north. Morgan's musket and the scattershot hanging from his neck grew heavier with each mile, and he could not stop thinking of the war.

Some of the recruits clamoring to enlist in Utica were scarcely older than he was. Soon enough they would see combat so bloody that his encounters with Ludi and Doctor Surgeon would seem like schoolyard scuffles. Yet from the moment they donned their blue uniforms, their thinking would all be done for them, often in faraway citadels by gray-bearded men who, when they came to die, would do so in their own beds surrounded by loving kin. No one could do a soldier's dying for him, or his killing, either. When it came to that, the killing, Morgan believed he was at a moral disadvantage, because he could never claim he was under anyone's orders but his own. Still, he had not been in a stand-up battle against an opposing army. He doubted his mettle in such a situation and wondered if other soldiers, however fervent in their cause, doubted theirs. All he knew for sure was that he had not yet been truly battle-tested and that when and if he was, he had no idea how he would conduct himself. In many of the books he had read, men's journeys led to self-knowledge. Thus far his sojourn had resulted only in more and greater uncertainties.

Birdcall was an adept thief, stealing hens, ducks, eggs, wash off clotheslines. The child had no more concept of ownership than a cat. One afternoon she slipped up on a sitting goose and wrung its long neck. Flinging the goose over her back, she took to her heels as fast as a bounding fox. By the time the pursuing gander raised the hue and cry with its anguished honks, she was over the next hilltop, and that night they feasted on roast goose for supper. She could hook a steaming pie-plant pie off a farm wife's windowsill, coax a sucking lamb away from a ewe. They had a capital lamb dinner one evening near a town where a very foolish writer, in Morgan's estimation, had spun all kinds of yarns about Indians, scouts, frontiersmen, and an imagined way of life and fighting that never had existed, though in truth Morgan had greedily devoured every book Fenimore Cooper ever wrote. When he tried to tell the story of *The Deerslayer* aloud, Birdcall cut him off and declared that she never in her life would believe a word in any book, and under no circumstances was he ever to speak to her of books again. Watching her ravage a greasy lamb chop in the firelight, Morgan suspected that the girl could not read a single black letter. Yet she had a ceaseless curiosity and asked a thousand questions each day, often repeating them if his answer was jocular or unsatisfactory. Did he, at all, have any wives? If so, how many? Seven, Morgan assured her. One for each day of the week. How many men had he slain, and had he ever slain a woman? How old was he? How old was he when he made the beast with two backs with his first sweetheart? Yet for all of her wild talk and antic waywardness, there was something in Birdcall that he believed in. Something that made him think she might yet land feet-first if he could but find the right landing place for her. Frequently he looked back over his shoulder or off down the pike ahead at bends and likely spots for an ambuscade. The possibility that he might be killed by the remaining prison escapees before he found his brother was insupportable. The thought that Birdcall too might be murdered was worse yet.

South of Cooperstown they cadged a ride with a rum-befuddled wagoneer carrying hops poles to Elmira. The driver claimed to be a great hand at reading character through phrenology. "For instance," he said, glancing at Morgan, "I can tell by observing sector twenty-three of your skull, which denotes mirth, that you love fun and wit and laughter. But sector eleven, just behint your ear, tells me that you also know how to make a dollar. How much then, soldier, for the pinkling?

"The pinkling?"

"The split-tail. What will you take for her? You're going to war anyhow, I expect. I'll give you two round silver dollars."

"You'd soon offer me three to take her back," Morgan said.

At this, Birdcall, who was riding between them, whooped like a crane bird. Then she whispered to him to sell her as dear as he could and that night she'd stifle the wagoneer in his sleep and they'd make off with his hops poles and be rich as dukes.

The phrenologist, who continued to have recourse to his rum bottle with each new pronouncement, began to extol the virtues of hops, whose properties in flavoring beer he claimed to be the most sublime discovery in the history of the world since man tamed fire. He said that hops had a beautiful flower, yet the vines were shy and retiring, growing mainly in the night, sometimes as much as six inches from dusk to dawn. Then he offered Morgan five dollars to rent Birdcall for an evening.

When Morgan replied sharply, the hops advocate growled, "What would you do, young boy, was I to rotch out and take them firelocks away from you and boot you out of the wagon and drive off with the bitch?"

Morgan had been staring at an alder tree on the far side of a little brook slipping through a meadow of ragged robin in full pink blossom. Hanging from a branch of the alder was a cone-shaped hornets' nest as big as a peach basket.

"What would you do?" the drunken wagoneer repeated.

"This," Morgan said, raising Hunter. "Forgive me, bees." With that he shot the paper hornets' nest clean off the branch.

"I Jeroboam!" shouted the driver, reining in the horses, which had started violently when the gun went off. "But ain't you forgot something, boy?"

"I doubt that I have," Morgan said.

"Oh, yes, you have, too," said the wagoneer. "Now your chamber's empty. Hand the gun here and step down, or I'll batter out your brains with a hops pole and leave your carcass in the crick."

Before the wagoneer had finished issuing this disagreeable ultimatum, Ludi's two-barreled pistol with the devilish engravings running wild over it was pressed against the side of his head. In the same motion Morgan pulled back the hammer of the shot barrel.

"Rein in," Morgan said.

"Let's take his wagon and sell his poles," Birdcall said. "Let's skag him and plant him and see if he grows in the night."

"We're going to step down now," Morgan said to the wagoneer. "If you try to double back afoot or lie in wait for us up yonder, I'll cut you down like those bees. Hi, git!"

He slapped the near horse on the rump, and the team trotted off down the track. The driver looked back with a baleful glare. Morgan drew an admonitory bead on him with the scattershot, and the rum-soak cursed and whipped up his team. Morgan did not think the wagoneer belonged to the gang of killers, but in such times as these there was no way to tell friend from foe. He redoubled his vigilance yet felt more vulnerable with each mile south.

They came upon a potter in a roadside shop selling stoneware that was light gray and brown with delicate blue forget-me-nots painted around the rim. The potter, a benevolent-appearing, grandfatherly guildsman, invited the two young wayfarers to look into his clay kiln. "Cobalt-blue glaze with an orange-peel finish can stand TWENTY-TWO HUNDRED DEGREES. CAN A SLAVEHOLDER?" he suddenly roared out. On he raved, assuring them that his kiln was hot, hell's fire hotter still. Morgan and Birdcall backed off through his racks of cider jugs and vinegar jugs, milk pitchers, jars for putting up maple butter, deep crocks for pickles. The war was still some hundreds of miles away. The madness it had fomented infested the entire land.

COLONEL JOHN KINNESON looked across the desk at his nephew and the girl. He wished he were back in his classroom at the Elmira academy, where he'd taught before the war, inhaling the comforting schoolroom scents of floor wax and chalk dust and the musty pages of his familiar old Caesar and Cicero. And the faintly pungent aroma of ink, a scent he loved as much as the first sharp redolence of fallen leaves in Elmira's long and lovely autumns, with these two sitting at their desks waiting their turn to recite. *Gallia est omnis divisa in partes tres . . .*

The pair looked so innocent, for all of their strangeness. The green-eyed girl wearing some kind of feather-bedecked sack like Puck in the play. His young nephew—the commandant could not think of Morgan as other than a boy, though he was man-grown and then some, six feet high and broad through the shoulders and draped about with enough weaponry to make John Kinneson's old friend from the border wars, the southern general himself, gape in wonder—reciting as chilling a tale as any the colonel had ever heard. Morgan spoke quietly and in measured cadences, choosing his words deliberately so as not to exaggerate. And all the while he was recounting his Dantean narrative, the boy was watching and watching with those level gray eyes, his light hair—save for the burned hank he had left on the doctor's target—hanging to his shoulders, quite like the boys from Georgia and Tennessee at whom just last year the commandant had been shooting with intent to kill. Four short yet interminable years ago, the colonel would not have believed a word of his nephew's story. Now he had no difficulty giving it full credence.

The colonel, for his part, had no news of either Jesse—the old man had not, so far as he knew, passed through Elmira—or a runaway young woman with a little boy. After he recounted to Morgan what scant details he possessed concerning the surviving three condemned men—the necrophiliac child killer who styled himself an actor, the crazed Prophet, and the slave killer, King George—the boy asked him to describe the escape. The commandant paused for a moment, thinking back to the March dawn a month ago when he'd stepped out on the porch of his wood-frame farmhouse atop East Hill and looked down at the prison where, soon after sunrise, the war criminals were to be hanged. Then he told Morgan and the girl the following story.

THESE WERE TO BE the first executions at the Elmira prison camp and, Colonel John Kinneson fervently hoped, the last. With the possible exception of King George, the doomed men were as mad as hatters. By any measure the colonel was aware of, each of

the killers was entirely deranged, and he did not hold with execut-
ing bedlamites, however unspeakable their deeds. Standing in the
cold dawn on the porch, looking down at the prison in the valley
below and puffing the cigar his wife forbade him to smoke in the
house, sipping the bitter chicory coffee she'd made him by lantern
light when they rose, the colonel concluded that the condemned
men were living emblems of everything that was insane about all
wars.

Not that the Union officer and long-time Underground conductor, leaning against a wooden porch pillar inscribed with the sign
M and pulling on his boots one-handed, had any earthly idea what
should be done with such demons. Nor did he intend to lose a moment's sleep over their fate. It was simply one more question that he
did not know how to answer in a time of many unanswerable questions. Less than a year ago he'd been fighting in Pennsylvania, an
officer in charge of a feared unit of sharpshooters, a veteran of seven
battles. Then, in a fraction of a moment, he'd lost his left arm. It had
simply vanished from just below the shoulder, torn clear by a cannonball fired from exactly where he never knew. He'd been tossed
this sop, overseer of the hellhole prison camp known as Helmira,
because it was near his home. Running the prison without adequate
food and medicine for the captured soldiers in his charge was bad
enough. Then a week ago the killers had arrived under heavy escort
with express orders from the war secretary for their execution.

The colonel doused the stub of his cigar in his mostly undrunk
coffee and tossed the wretched stuff onto the frozen dooryard,
where a few March snowdrops blossomed through the icy crust.
This afternoon he'd pick them for his wife, a fine, strong woman
who, while he was away fighting, had not only worked their small

farm but continued to run their Underground station, *Ehwaz,* harboring all the passengers who came their way and sending them safely along to John's brother in Vermont and so to Canada.

The sky over East Hill, a deep indigo when he'd brought his coffee out onto the porch and lighted his cigar, was now the color of a dead-ripe orange. It was nearly time to go down the hill and preside over this latest charade. In the past several years John Kinneson had seen—and participated in—enough madness that he thought he should be used to it by now. But he was not.

From the prison, through the barred window of the stockade house, came the strains of "Just a Closer Walk with Thee," plaintive and funereal. The mad minstrel was at it again with his hammered dulcimer, the strangely mournful tune now acquiring volume, floating out the cell window over the parade ground, past the blockhouse and up the hill to the assembled spectators—the mayor of the town was just arriving in his new phaeton with his two young grandchildren—the tune eliding into "Rock of Ages" as smoothly as dawn elides into day, and then, before you could quite say how, "The Green, Green Grass of Home."

The commandant glanced up the hill above the farmhouse. Four crows appeared over the ridgetop, silhouetted dark and spectral against the red sky. No, by Caesar, not crows—tall black plumes bobbing like sooty featherdusters on the heads of four coal black horses cresting the hill in the cut through the woods and pulling a long black hearse sleigh escorted by four riders in blue uniforms. The colonel could hear the metal runners hissing on the snow, blue in the shadow of the woods. Blue snow, black horses, salmon-colored sky. The driver was beginning to come clear in the strengthening daylight as the hearse started down the steepest pitch of the hill. He too wore a blue uniform. But what mainly accounted for his macabre appearance was a large pair of emerald goggles extending halfway up his forehead and well down over his cheeks.

Now the colonel could hear, floating up from the stockade house, the sweet treble notes of Ludi's dulcimer playing "The Battle Hymn of the Republic." The spiked ice shoes on the feet of the trotting horses pulling the hearse sleigh gripped the silvering crust on the road as surely as horse hooves shod for summer gripped the packed dirt surface on a bone-dry day in August. The green-goggled driver looked like Death at a ball. What tasteless spectacle was this that the war secretary had staged? Why so elaborate a send-off for five murderous lunatics? The appointments of the hearse were ornate enough for a governor. As the Black Maria on runners glided by his house, John Kinneson noted that the door pulls were polished brass, so too the side rails inside the partially curtained glass panels, where he supposed the pillowed biers lay waiting. How was it that the condemned men, the very dregs of the Union, merited such panoply? On the black-fringed roof of the runnered hearse, held fast with gold and red cords, was a vast ebony coffin. The commandant supposed that it must be intended for the slave killer, King George, who was close to seven feet tall and weighed nearly four hundred pounds, so gargantuan he'd had to ride a Percheron plow horse while chasing down the runaways he killed as examples. The unearthly dulcimer music, the horse-drawn hearse and black-clad goggled driver—it was a scene from a tale told by a crone to frighten children.

Suddenly the goggled man stood up. Gripping the reins in one hand and the left front ornamental post atop the hearse in the other, he roared, "Open the gate, goddamn you, in the name of the president."

It was evident that the sleigh hearse was not going to slacken its pace. The gatekeeper, known to some of the prisoners as Cerberus, swung wide the reinforced door. As the hearse approached the entry the commandant realized what was wrong. It was the escort. Why four hale cavalrymen when soldiers and horses were so desperately needed in the war? Even as the timbered door swung open to admit the black hearse and its black-plumed horses, the commandant knew that this was all wrong.

Suddenly a great deal was happening at once. The standing driver in the green goggles began to crack the reins over the backs of his horses, flinging his arm wildly from side to side. Guided by the two cavalrymen in the van, the horses pulling the sleigh rushed through the entryway onto the prison parade ground. The other two riders stood in their stirrups, then leaped onto the backs of their horses and swung up onto the parapet beside the blockhouse, which they stormed like an entire army of blue men, shooting down the guards with their sidearms, commandeering the two swivel guns and blasting the gallows and scaffolding to flinders, reloading and sweeping with grape canister the assembling soldiers and the barracks beyond.

Then, sitting up in the large coffin atop the hearse, another blue man flung away a black crepe covering to reveal a strange machine. It was not a cannon, exactly, nor was it a swivel gun like those in the blockhouse. The machine was silver in the sunrise and beautifully fitted out with gleaming brass, like the brass appurtenances of the runnered hearse. It was operated by means of a crank handle on the side, and it spit bullets out of a ventilated barrel fed by a large revolving chamber at a steady rapid rate, chattering like a trip hammer as it mowed down the phalanx of guards marching to the stockade house to bring forth the condemned men. The commandant, now running into his house, boots and all, returning with his

Henry Big Fifty, had read of such a weapon. What was it called? In the meantime the driver of the hearse was lashing the plumed black horses around and around the parade ground, trampling the wounded and dying under the basket-sized, befeathered hooves as his cape billowed backward. Inside the guardhouse Ludi Too was beating out "Turkey in the Straw" on his dulcimer, his sweet voice ringing out over the scene of the massacre. "Ha, ha, ha, hee, hee, hee. Turkey in the straw and you can't catch me." One of the blue riders was busily hurling glass jars of Greek fire at the barracks, officers' quarters, commissary, and dispensary. The jars shattered, plastering the roofs and wooden sides of the buildings with a volatile paste of phosphorus and sulfur, which took flame as soon as air hit it. The one-armed commandant loaded the Henry awkwardly, standing the rifle barrel-up against the porch rail, kneeling down, and wedging the stock between his knees while he inserted six .50-caliber bullets one at a time with his single hand. He cursed his missing arm as if it had abandoned him of its own malign will.

The careering hearse stopped in front of the stockade house. A blue escort leaped off his horse and produced from inside the sleigh a heavy chain, one end of which he wrapped around the wrought-iron upswept curve of the sleigh runners, the other through the bolted ring-handle on the stockade house door, which the black horses yanked free of its hinges as if it were made of kindle. The strains of the dulcimer were louder now, then were drowned by another raking burst from the big silver gun on the hearse. What the deuce was that gun called? The commandant had read about it in a War Department publication. The thing had been invented by a physician and was heralded as a superweapon that would win the war for the North in a month. That had been more than a year ago. Colonel John Kinneson was incredulous that at such a moment

as this his forgetfulness would fret him so. He balanced the loaded
Henry on the porch rail and sighted on one of the two blue men
in the blockhouse with the swivel guns, a good five hundred yards
away. Maddeningly awkward as it was to shoot with a single arm, it
all came back to him. He'd always been a natural marksman, able
to concentrate so completely that he scarcely heard the crack of his
rifle as he shot the blue man on the right swivel gun squarely between his shoulder blades. He lowered the gun stock to the porch
floor, knelt, wedged it between his knees, lever-jacked another shell
into the chamber, steadied the gun on the rail, and fired at the second man in the blockhouse. This time he missed. A foot-long splinter jumped off the railing beside the swivel gun and flew directly
through the hearse. Why would a physician sworn to heal the sick
and do no harm invent such a fiendish machine? What was it called?
Levered, steadied, aimed through the peephole over the open end
sight—no windage this calm morning, but a good hundred-foot
drop in elevation to take into account—and shot the man operating
the silver weapon. The five condemned men ran out of the stockade
house and swarmed up onto the hearse, pulling Yellow Boy repeating rifles out as they clambered aboard, firing at soldiers and fleeing
spectators alike while the prison burned. If the commandant could
only get a line on the driver, he might stop this yet. Some of the
other prisoners were loose, fleeing across a cut cornfield toward the
river. A few remaining guards were firing on them. Wounded guards
and townspersons were screaming. The remnants of the scaffolding
and gallows were afire, the stockade house blazing.

The black hearse horses, guided by the mounted blue men, raced
toward the gate, itself in flames. King George picked up the blue
gunner slumped across the silver weapon, lifted him high over his
head, and flung him at a guard on the stockade wall near the gate,

who was training a rifle on the hearse driver. The corpse flew a good fifteen feet through the air, blue arms and legs aspraddle, and knocked the rifleman off the wall backward. As the hearse passed through the gate, the Prophet stabbed the fallen guard with a splintered length of stockade paling, shouting "SOUEE, HERE PIG PIG PIG," like a man at a hog-calling contest. Ludi began to beat out that next-to-impossible-to-sing new "Star-Spangled" number. The hearse raced past the cornfield toward the river. Ludi Too was sighting a Yellow Boy back toward the hilltop. Before the former commandant could draw a bead on him, the Henry burst apart in his hand, the end of the barrel peeling in two, a groove in the stock materializing as suddenly as the commandant's left arm had vanished at Gettysburg, the lever-action handle flying past the colonel's head. He was left holding the skeleton of a rifle with a split barrel. At first he thought the gun had blown up in his hand. Then he could hear the dulcimer again. Ludi had set down his rifle and picked up his mallets and was playing "When Johnny Comes Marching Home," and the commandant realized that the musician had deliberately shot his gun out of his hand at seven hundred yards. Ludi was toying with him. "Hurrah, hurrah! When Johnny comes"—more rifle shots—"Well, the girls will cry, the boys will shout . . ." A small roadside church on the river road burst into flames as if of its own accord as the death sleigh rushed past. Then the sleigh was concealed in a copse of yellowing willows by the river.

"I suppose they need you down there," the commandant's wife said. She was standing beside him on the porch, her hand on his shoulder.

Gently, almost tenderly, he set down the remnants of the Henry, as if it were a fallen comrade. "I suppose they do," he said, and started down the porch steps to see what order he could bring forth from the mayhem below.

In the past three years Colonel John Kinneson had had many horrifying experiences. He had seen a tinder-dry forest catch fire from shelling and incinerate alive hundreds of fallen men lying helpless in the path of the flames. Once, after running out of ammunition, he had covered the retreat of his men by beating off the advancing enemy with the stock of his gun, which he'd swung by the barrel like a war club. When Pickett's men were swarming up the hill toward his company at Gettysburg, he had fought with a two-headed felling ax. On the second day of that battle he had seen his own nephew, the beloved elder son of his beloved elder brother, a noncombatant surgeon, descend into the Slaughter Pen, medical bag in hand, and disappear without a trace, no doubt blown off the face of the earth by mortar fire, though of friend or foe it was impossible to say. But in all that time he had never witnessed anything like the scene below him now.

Gatling. That was it. The secret new weapon was called a Gatling gun, named for its physician inventor. But the commandant knew that neither it nor any other weapon would win this war. It was a war that no one could ever truly win, no matter who surrendered first. As he headed down the hill toward the inferno, he would have given nearly anything for a cup of real coffee to fortify himself. It didn't seem like a lot to wish for. Just before the escapees abandoned the hearse for the horses hidden beside the river, a mile or more away, Liza called his name from the porch. Her voice sounded surprised. At the same time he heard the distant, sharp report of Ludi's Yellow Boy. He spun around to see his wife collapse over the porch railing and pitch headfirst into the frozen dooryard, spattering the carved sign on the pillar, the railing, and the snowdrops he had intended to pick for her that afternoon blood red, changing his world forever.

MORGAN STARED AT THE BED of the shot-up hearse sleigh, abandoned a month ago by the escaped prisoners beside the river just south of the prison, where they'd split up to ride their separate ways. As he studied the wrecked old Black Maria, a thought occurred to him. He turned to his uncle. "With a hammer and saw and a sack of two-penny nails, anyone could turn this into a neat enough little conveyance."

"What would you pull it with?" the colonel said.

"A pair of oars," Morgan said. "In half an afternoon, I could cobble this into as tight a little rowing boat as any on the river."

"No boats!" Birdcall cried out. "I'se a-scart of water."

"You'll be fine," Morgan assured her.

The idea of proceeding from Elmira to Gettysburg in a metamorphosed hearse intrigued him, and appealed to his sense of irony, though whether because it reminded him of his own mortality or the killing fields of the South, or because it betokened the deaths of the killers he was now pursuing even as they pursued him, he could not tell. In fact Morgan was a rude fist with a hammer and nail—a gun was the only tool that had ever felt comfortable in his hands—but with his uncle's help it required only a few short hours to dismantle the ghastly thing and convert it into a very serviceable craft. A bit boxy, to be sure, and rather awkward to maneuver, but fine for the little Chemung and the broad, brown, shallow Susquehanna, which cut down through three mountain ranges of Pennsylvania, swept past Harrisburg, and then bowled along to Maryland and the huge estuary.

The commandant provided them with oars and a long cane pole with some line and hooks, also a letter to the southern general, his old friend, requesting that Morgan be given safe conduct and whatever additional assistance in locating his brother that he could provide. What Morgan's uncle had been unable to do was shed any new illumination on Pilgrim's disappearance at Gettysburg. The past summer, on the second of July, Pilgrim had been ministering to the fallen of both sides under heavy fire in the place called the Slaughter Pen when he had simply vanished. Presumably, like so many others, he had been blown to shreds by a mortar. Uncle John had all but implored Morgan to return to Vermont, telling him that the unknown dead buried in mass graves at Gettysburg were being exhumed and transferred to the new cemetery on the hilltop this very spring, and Pilgrim's remains would surely soon be identified. "No, sir," Morgan had said. "I reckon they won't be."

Morgan asked his uncle to write to his father explaining that he intended to proceed to Gettysburg, where he would relay to his family whatever news concerning Pilgrim, be it good or ill, that he discovered. And he asked John Kinneson to inform Quaker Meeting that the second killer, like the first, was no more.

As for the mysterious symbols on the Balancing Boulder and on Jesse's stone, all the colonel could tell him was that he believed that a black man had assigned the runes to certain Underground conductors, including Morgan's grandfather Freethinker Kinneson, many years before. The colonel had selected the sign ᛗ for his station after moving to Elmira to teach before the war, simply because it was this rune on the Balancing Boulder that his eye seemed most drawn to.

Morgan and Birdcall left Elmira in the hearse-boat late that afternoon, letting the current carry them down the river, which smelled strongly of fish and mud and spring. At first Birdcall, who couldn't swim a stroke, was frightened. As they drifted past bankside farms, little mill towns, islands with newly leafed-out swamp maples and willows still partly under water from the spring freshet, she began to enjoy herself.

A warbler flashed, a small bright flame in the limbs of a bankside elm. Birdcall called to a redbreast worming a plowed field, mimicked the low gurgling of a mating bluebird. Morgan and Birdcall, floating down the river on a warm evening in the season his mother had called the soft of the year. The girl buzzed low to a yellowthroat in a hazel bush overhanging a backward-running eddy speckled with foam like his mother's meringue pie, the sugary meringue toasted brown on its rim. She answered the *peabody peabody peabody* of a white-throated sparrow in the spire of a hemlock where a feeder brook tumbled down a gorge into the river. A red-wing, its orangered shoulder patches flashing like the epaulets of the preening Zouave bravos in Ute, called from a cattail above a skunk cabbage as large as a real head of cabbage. *Konkeree. Konkeree.* Back whistled the girl, *konkeree,* as natural as the bird itself. Yet the river was no haven from the pitiless universal code of survivorship informing all life on earth. A white-tailed field mouse swimming across a small lagoon vanished in a furious thrashing spray. "Hi!" Birdcall cried out with a child's satisfaction. Ahead, a pair of shiny green mantises, six inches long, were mating on a willow branch overhanging the current. As the boaters passed the romantical insects, the female swung her horizontal mandibles around and, without so much as a by-your-leave, snipped off her partner's head. The headless male mantis stolidly continued to perform his part of the transaction.

"Good on you, old gal!" Birdcall cried out to the long green spouse killer and hooted with laughter. Morgan had been sorely tempted to leave the child with his uncle, but what the old widower could do for such a wilding he had no idea. He knew he could not keep her safe much longer. The remaining escaped killers might well be hunting him at that very moment.

At sunset they passed a gang of several young boys wearing soldier caps made of paper. They were conducting a scouting mission along the riverbank, taking prisoner bullfrogs, worms, salamanders, minnie fish, and turtles, all of which they threw into a copper washtub of boiling water, which they called Andersonville. Morgan supposed that he might have done the same a few short years ago. What was the war itself but a crueler tale yet, writ large across the land? Pilgrim had written to him that in some southern states slavery was referred to as the "peculiar institution." To Morgan, spinning on down the current in the green dusk with Birdcall, mankind was of all species the most peculiar, and the cruelest.

As darkness fell, they kept to the middle of the river. Cabins with yellow lamplight in parchment windows sat on hillsides, and they glided past a town where lumber arks were drawn up to the shore. On one raft men danced to a squeeze box. Birdcall slept like a dead girl as Morgan rowed on into the night, his blistered hands wrapped in holey wool stockings. Toward morning he put into the mouth of a creek, where they covered the hearse-boat with fragrant honeysuckle blossoms and slept side by side in the former bier, the girl's frail arm flung over Morgan's shoulder. The next night they made forty miles by Morgan's reckoning, though once he dozed off and they nearly plunged over a spillway. He woke just in time to row out of danger and lower the boat around the dam works in the darkness.

They passed a troop of men with headlamps coming out of a hole in a hillside. An hour or two later they came to a lighted city that turned out to be no city at all but a paper manufactory, and the stench of sulfur and smoke clamped down on their throats like poison gas. The river bends were sharp and frequent. Morgan pressed on. He detected no sign that he and Birdcall were being pursued. Soon it might be safe to travel by day.

IF THE RIVER AT NIGHT was an alien place of strange illusions and dangers, the daylight world as well had turned topsy-turvy. An itinerant preacher, hitherto unknown in the region, had been vouchsafed a vision with the agreeable tidings that he was the New American Messiah. Unto him had been accorded a revelation in which one hundred thousand of his followers were directly taken up to the celestial sphere, translated on the spot like old Elijah, without first having to undergo the unpleasant formality of dying. The disciples of the New Messiah, though they numbered merely in the hundreds, were confident that the time of their ascendancy was at hand. Were not the signs everywhere? Within the last year the war had come north to Pennsylvania with a singular fury. Across the land multitudes had clashed like the Israelites and the Philistines, an eye for an eye and a bullet for a bullet. From these infallible signifiers, the Messiah and his acolytes had adduced that the end-time had arrived. In Oswego a black-and-white milch cow had given birth to a Percheron colt with two heads. Hail the size of small cannonballs had fallen on an onion field in a town called Allegheny, killing a scoffing nonbeliever named Sweeny Bill McGuire. In Binghamton a precocious nanny goat had pranced into a dancing academy and bleated out, "Repent, for the judgment is nigh." A floating hearse with two young angels, an avenging Gabriel and a female sprite wearing feathers, had been sighted on the Susquehanna hovering in the dawn mist above the current. Handbills proclaimed that on May Day, adherents of Floydism should adorn themselves in white sheets and ascend to the greening hilltops, at which time the iniquitous world would give up the ghost and the faithful would be taken up to heaven streaming radiant trails like comets. Yea, before the gleeful eyes of the redeemed, the unanointed would then be cast into eternal roiling flames.

Every hamlet and mill town and riverside city from the Great Western Canal to the Mason and Dixon Line was abuzz with talk of the millennium. On May 1, as Morgan and Birdcall made their way down the river into full spring, they passed families and entire communities of Floydites, wrapped in bed sheets and muslin curtains and even yellowing old wedding dresses, proceeding solemnly to hilltops overlooking the river in accordance with the vision of the New Messiah. Others clambered onto their rooftops or scaled church steeples. Some held forth in tongues and some blasphemed other religions, claiming Floydism was the only true path. Birdcall was beside herself with laughter, but Morgan feared that this new frenzy sweeping the land was yet another manifestation of the violence done by the war to reason and good sense. When half a million men had died of cannonshot, grapeshot, minié bullets, infection, typhus, cholera, and other diseases, and much of the divided land itself laid waste like cursed Gomorrah, these shenanigans struck Morgan as simply another outbreak of the epidemic of madness gripping the universe.

The Prophet himself seemed ubiquitous. On the night before the Taking Up of the Chosen, he had been sighted preaching in a country church near Canandaigua, lining out a hymn sing in Allentown, and performing an exorcism in Gloversville upon a seven-year-old girl possessed of a demon with a guttural voice who had dared to call Floyd a fraud and his apostles jackasses. In designating May 1 the Day of the Ascension, the Prophet had urged his apostles to render up to him their silver and gold coinage and to slaughter their fowl and beasts and raze their houses and even their churches. For after the Uptaking there would no longer be any need for money or temporal abodes or any worldly enterprises whatsoever. As Morgan and Birdcall floated south, they passed houses ablaze, crops and rich timbered woods afire in every direction. One man was using a ram with two great whorled horns to plow salt into his goodly tillage. Another husbandman had split open his tiled silo and spread out the ensilage therein for the beasts of the field and the birds of the air. Yet another was shoveling fresh dung from a cart into his parlor through broken window sashes while his wife and grown daughters warbled out Hosannahs. One devotee poleaxed his prize herd of Jersey cows. Householders who had not come under the sway of the Prophet had armed themselves and their families and were guarding their homes and fields against the rampaging Floydites. Fire bells tolled. The hills were covered with worshippers in scraps and tatters of white, some holding infants in lace dresses on high in the mild spring sunshine, others having lashed themselves to treetops, windmills, and wooden coal-mine towers to gaze at the sun through shards of smoked glass and sing the praises of Floyd.

Who, well pleased with that which he had wrought, now lay waiting with his comrade the actor on a small stolen ferry-raft in the mouth of a tributary near the riverine settlement of New Canaan. Morgan and Birdcall had just come into sight upriver. Prophet and Steptoe, arrayed in white themselves, were expecting them. Dimly outlined in the twilight, the hearse-boat floated like a cork as Morgan rowed past the tributary and the girl trailed one small bare foot in their wake. Steptoe trained the sights of his Yellow Boy square on the rowing lad's temple and squeezed the trigger. The pin fell on the empty chamber with a small *click,* which carried over the river's flat surface in the noiseless dusk like a hammer blow.

"You fool!" Prophet hissed. "You forgot to load."

"That's her," Steptoe said. "Oh, dear Jesus. That's the gal."

"It is not," Prophet said, staying Steptoe's hand as he tried to load his rifle. "The bitch we're after is black as your boot."

"I want the child, black or white, quick or dead," Steptoe begged. "I must and will have her."

"And so you shall, brother," Prophet said. "Be patient, and so you shall."

Morgan glanced toward the tributary. The raft was well hidden in a copse of bankside willows. He saw nothing untoward, only the close-ranked willow trees. He rowed on.

Prophet and Steptoe poled the raft, laden down with the spoils of the Floydites, into the gentle current as the hearse-boat passed out of sight around a bend. Prophet began to sing, in honor of the minstrel Ludi Too, *Dec'd,* a dirgeful hymn of his own composition.

Satan wears a sinful shoe.
Mind now, Morgan, or he'll slip it on you.
Render up the gal, boy, render up the stone.
Render unto Prophet and he'll leave you alone.

Downriver, as the spring night settled in around them, Birdcall cocked her head. "What's that? Do you hear someone a-singing?"

Morgan shipped his oars and listened. Now he too heard the

singing, heard his own name wafting down the river through the dusk. *Render up the gal, boy, render up the stone.* Followed by hysterical laughter not of this world. *They coming. Who is coming, Jesse? They coming.* Propping Ludi's scattershot and his charged musket on the thwart of the hearse-boat, Morgan began to ply his oars in earnest.

"Our father who art in heaven," Birdcall started to recite.

"Hush," Morgan told her. "Crawl into the bier and lie flat. Quick as ever you moved. Get in."

She did. He rowed. *Render unto Prophet . . .* The singing faded into the night of a land benighted, upon which little light had fallen for many years or would for years to come.

A LONG WOODED ISLAND LOOMED ahead in the middle of the dark river. Seeing that the hard current ran west of the island, Morgan rowed the hearse-boat down the slack water on the east side and nosed into a small cove lined with swamp maples. There he and Birdcall waited in the darkness. Presently they heard the singing again. *Tomorrow at rising sun, Satan's going to stop young Morgan's tongue.* Morgan readied his musket and scattershot. Far off over the fields across the river the moon was rising. The singing faded out of earshot again, and Morgan knew that their pursuers had followed the main channel on the west side of the island. For the time being he and Birdcall were safe. He drew the hearse-boat onto a mud flat and, taking her hand, headed along a path toward a large tree outlined in the moonlight on a knoll overlooking the rest of the island.

As Morgan looked up into the tree he noticed a small house shaped like a boat about twenty feet off the ground, cunningly guyed to the branches with ropes and shrouds. On its deck stood a woman in a peaked bonnet.

"Well," she called down in a friendly voice. "Art afraid of a shunned creature who dwells in a tree like a spectacled owl?"

"What kind of tree?" Morgan asked.

"A chestnut," the woman said. "A great spreading umbrageous chestnut tree. There is none other like it for fifty miles around."

"It's a fine-looking tree," Morgan said. "We don't have chestnuts in Vermont."

"I don't imagine you do," the woman said. "From what I've heard of Vermont, it's the next place to the North Pole for cold and misery. Here." She unfurled a rope ladder down the chestnut's massive ridged trunk. "Come aboard, thee and thy sister. We'll have a palaver, a sea confabulation. Only leave thine artillery on the ground below. I don't allow weapons aboard the good ship *Perth*. She flies a neutral flag."

Morgan sent Birdcall up the rope ladder and through a hatchway into the ship house, then went up himself, leaving his musket and scattershot at the base of the tree. Inside all was snug and shipshape, with the tree woman's household appurtenances and clothing stored away in wooden lockers, a sleeping hammock strung from the limb rafters, and four round portholes to admit good light by day. The decking planks, which were roped to tree-limb floor joists, had been holystoned to a soft sheen. A compact sheet-metal galley stove sat on the deck, its bent pipe jutting out of the side of the house. A lighted whale-oil lamp swung over the table. On a perch in a hanging cage sat a saw-whet owl, and a mewing black ship's cat arched its back and purred when Birdcall began to make of it. On the inside and outside of the hatchway cover someone had carved the sign that appeared on the drawing of the treehouse on Jesse's stone: ᚼ.

"I loves this vessel," Birdcall said. "Was you ever a sailor woman, mother?"

"I have sailed the world over in the good ship *Perth* without ever leaving this tree," the woman replied. "Yet not a single nail was used to construct it, for it was nails, thou knowest, that pinned our blessed Savior to His cross." In the light of the binnacle lamp the tree woman appeared to be in late middle age. She was quite stout, with a plain, good-natured face and sad, kind brown eyes. She was dressed all in somber gray, and her head was covered with a gray bonnet.

"My former brother, the smith Joseph Findletter, built this ship for me after my man and our two boys were killed in the war at Nash's Ford. Hast heard of the battle there? Thousands murdered on both sides, neither able to claim victory. My brother shuns me because I refused to shun my men after they decided to go to war. I, in turn, now shun the earth where my fallen men lie entombed."

"What kind of smith is your brother?" Morgan asked.

"Why, any kind thou needest, son. He makes the best clipping horseshoes in Lancaster County, free-swinging fireplace cranes, deep-thrusting plows, guns—oh, he maketh lovely guns for hunting, though none for warring. He made my ship house in less than a week and never drove a single nail nor spake one word to me as it was a-building. Then he and the other Brethren banned me to it. But what brings you young people to New Canaan?"

"I'm looking for my brother, Pilgrim Kinneson," Morgan said. "He went missing in the war at Gettysburg."

"Oh, child," the tree woman said. "I fear that multitudes of brothers and sons and fathers as well have gone missing in this war."

As Mother Bremmen, as the tree woman was called, fixed them a late supper of fish and vegetable stew, the wind came up from the west and the tree boat swayed in the limbs of the chestnut. Birdcall fell asleep with the rumbling cat in her lap and her head beside her plate. Morgan picked her up and placed her in the woman's hammock. Then he and Mother Bremmen sat by the light of the oil lamp while he recounted his story and traced out his route thus far on Jesse's stone. When he came to her sign, ᛈ, he asked what it was called and what it meant.

Mother Bremmen smiled. "No one knows the meaning of *Perth*. It's a mystery, like our own little lives."

When Morgan finished his tale, Mother Bremmen wrote something with a goose quill and elderberry ink on a dry chestnut leaf. She handed the leaf to Morgan. "This give to *mein* former brother, Joseph Findletter," she said. "In Trout Run, about forty miles southwest of Harrisburg, three miles northeast of the river. Here, I'll show you on your strange stone." She pointed to the symbol, ᛉ. "*Algiz*. It signifies, among other things, protection. My brother will protect you if necessary."

"You don't believe I'm going to find him, do you?" Morgan said.

"My brother?"

"No, mine."

"I never said that. Only that many a good man hath gone missing in the war and never yet been found."

Birdcall lay quietly in the hammock, her eyes shut. Asleep, she looked no more than nine or ten. It occurred to Morgan that he had no idea how old she actually was. The cat was curled up by her side, content as only a cat can be. Morgan knew he must be on his way before the killers realized their mistake and returned to the island.

"Mother," he said. "You need someone to help tend your garden, cut your wood. The child needs a home. You could care for each other."

Instantly Birdcall opened her eyes and sat up and swung her feet to the floor. Morgan could tell from her expression that she was torn between wanting to go on with him and wanting to stay with the motherly tree woman and her purring ship's cat.

"You need to go to school and learn to read and write," Morgan told her.

"There's a schoolhouse between here and New Canaan," Mother Bremmen said. "School keeps there five months a year."

"No school!" Birdcall cried. "You can't keep me in a cage like your littly owl, old woman."

"Then wilt teach thee myself from the Bible. Thou must know thy scripture," the tree woman said.

"I've never lived in a tree at all," Birdcall said.

"I want you to take good care of Mother Bremmen," Morgan said.

"Pass me that scattershot and I'll take good care of you," she wailed out. "Don't you see, Morgan Kinneson? I loves you, I do. And I hopes you'll die of the Black Death for abandoning me."

Morgan touched his hat to the woman, who clasped him in her strong arms the way his mother had when he had come into his teens and considered himself too big to be hugged but had not really minded.

"Here," Mother Bremmen told Birdcall as Morgan started down the rope ladder. "Wilt show thee a new thing. From this book, wilt teach thee thy letters."

"Make me learn them if you can, crone," Birdcall shrieked.

Morgan grinned.

"Look now," the woman said. "Dost see this gentleman with the two slanted legs and the crossbar like an apple-picking ladder? It's an *A*. The first letter in the alphabet. And here is a *B* that thy name, Birdcall, begins with."

"It does not at all," Birdcall shouted. "Never in all Christendom does me name begin with any such outlandish figure. And your *A* looks like a drunk man on stilts. What's next? In your so-called alphabet?"

"Why *C* is next, girl. See it here? 'Call,' as in Birdcall, beginneth with this goodly letter."

"Never, never, never!" cried the girl. "We'll have no vile, sneaking *C* in me name."

"I tell thee there is a *C* in thy name," insisted the woman, who, kindhearted though she was, had as strong a will as any woman or man Morgan had ever met.

"Then I'll barter me name away. I'll go before the highest magistrate in the land and change it to Nebuchadnezzar. What's next, now? Pray Jesus we'll have no more *C*'s."

This world, Morgan thought, this woeful, wondrous world. Dawn was breaking. Across the river on the east bank the trees, shrubs, grasses, and springing weeds were twenty different shades of green, all reflected in the river. He got into the hearse-boat and began to row south, his musket and scattershot primed and at the ready beside him.

FIVE

ALGIZ

ᛉ

And it was full spring as Morgan Kinneson worked his way down the river in his little floating hearse, past the blue-green of spruce and firs, the leafy, ever-changing green of maples and lighter green of oaks, the emerald of the sedges cloaking the banks, and the green of growing corn and wheat and clover in the fields, all reflected one shade darker in the crawling river. There was no sign of his pursuers. Toward evening he studied Jesse's stone yet again. So far it had done him little good. The more he pondered it, the more puzzling it seemed. Yet this much was clear. Whoever he might have been and wherever he had come from, Jesse Moses was no ordinary Underground passenger. Big Eva had said that *Nauthiz,* Morgan's rune, meant that everything was harder than it seemed and that everything was connected. His quest for Pilgrim was turning out to be far more difficult than he had ever imagined. And he could not help wondering, Were Jesse Moses and his stone some-how connected with Pilgrim's disappearance? Might the killers be hunting Pilgrim as well as him and the mysterious runaway slave girl? If so, why? A year ago, at home in Vermont, Morgan had come across Pilgrim's well-worn old solid geometry text. In it was many a recondite problem involving cones and cylinders and the devil alone knew what other configurations. Morgan had set himself the task of solving each problem in the book, and with persistence, he had done so, if only to prove that he could. If only he could unlock the mystery of Jesse's stone.

At dusk he entered a long bend where the river hooked east and then dived southeasterly. He tied up on an island just above Harris-burg, and in the summery twilight he located a crawfish under a flat rock in the shallows, the blue-shelled crustacean fast scuttling back-ward out from under the rock, Morgan's hand descending faster still. He baited the crawdad on a hook and with it caught a bass on the cane pole his uncle had given him. He cooked the fish on a rock shelf by the water. The bass was flavorful but no more filling than fish usually is. As night settled over the wooded bar, the river frogs began to croak. He and Pilgrim had used homemade tridents fashioned from hay forks to spear frogs for their tasty legs along the edge of the Great Northern Slang. On his fishhook he fixed a bit of red cloth cut from his shirt and cast it like a fly up into the bulrushes. Five casts yielded five lolloping bullfrogs. The cut-off legs jerked and twitched as if still alive in the fry pan his uncle John had given him. They tasted good but wanted salt. A generous sprinkling of salt and a good thick slice of his mother's bread, liberally buttered.

The lights of Harrisburg lay scattered over a ridge on the north side of the river. As Morgan contemplated venturing into town to buy bread, he hummed, rather tunelessly, for he was no musician, a catchy refrain to himself. *Satan's shoe, Satan's shoe.* With horror he realized that he'd been hearing the ghoulish ditty for some time from somewhere down the river.

Morgan kicked the coals of his campfire into the water and scrambled into the hearse-boat. He began to row hard toward the singing, which faded, then rose.

We'll hang Jeff Davis from a sour-apple tree.
Davis and Pilgrim and the gal all three.

How did these demons know about Pilgrim? Their raft, its plunder from the zealous millennialists covered with canvas, was moored to a wharf at the foot of the hill leading up to the lights of the town. The dreadful singing had ceased and the killers were nowhere to be seen. Morgan put in a hundred yards below the raft. Musket in hand, scattershot dangling by its cord from his neck, he headed up a dark and narrow street toward a dimly lighted tavern.

It was Saturday night, and the Sign of the Yellow Beaver Tooth was packed with roisterers. The Beaver Tooth was a wretched kennel scarcely bigger than a henhouse and fully as foul, with a rank buffalo robe for a door. Inside, a press of rivermen stood under a smoky low ceiling at a counter made from a rough plank supported at each end by a spigoted beer barrel. Suddenly a huge black man blocked his way.

"Where did you come by that double hog's leg round your neck on that string, boy?" the black man said in a very deep voice. "I'll take it off you for five dollars."

"It's not up for sale," Morgan said.

The giant grinned, showing teeth as large as piano ivories. "Step this way and I'll show you a sight you ain't seen before." He wore a blue vest with a silver watch fob; a Navy Colt revolver stuck out of his enormous waistband. "It will cost you only one dollar."

"I don't have a dollar."

"Well, you should view it anyway. I runs the show." The man put out his hand. "Swagbelly, some calls me. I have the questionable privilege of providing entertainment for this high-toned establishment tonight. Come along, boy. What I want you to see is out back. Consider this part of your free and accepted education."

Morgan could not figure a way to get past the giant without shooting him. The back room, a crib off the rear of the shed, was open to the sky and surrounded by a rude paling of pointed stakes. A knot of rivermen and townies was gathered around an enormous white bull raised a few feet above the dirt yard in a blacksmith's ox sling. The bull was bellowing and foaming. Morgan stepped onto an overturned apple box for a better look. Strapped to a board below the animal was a naked black woman, her legs spraddled wide. Cut into the leather ox sling was an opening through which extended the bull's engorged member, a full three feet long.

Morgan started through the crowd toward the white bull. "You weren't meant for this," he said to the bellowing animal.

He placed the muzzle of the scattershot against the animal's temple, thumbed back one hammer, and shot the white bull dead with the four-ounce ball. He whipped out the gypsy's dagger and cut the ropes fastening the woman to the plank and pulled her, dazed, to her feet. He threw his jacket around her.

"You've kilt old Zeus!" King George roared, going for his revolver. "Hand over the runaway, goddamn you. Where is she?"

As George drew his Colt, Morgan buffaloed him full in the face with the butt of the scattershot, clouting him down in his tracks.

"Why, boy, you've leveled old Swag," a man with half an ear cried out.

"Free suds tonight, boys, drink up!" Morgan shouted as he led the groggy woman through the stinking robe over the entrance and into the street.

"Who?" the woman in his jacket mumbled as he helped her down the hill. "Who you?"

"A friend," Morgan said. "Just a friend." But he felt more desperate, more untethered from his own friends and family and all that he thought of as his previous life than he had felt since he discovered Jesse Moses hanging dead from the rowanberry tree. He felt like a man at war, not with an enemy wearing a different-colored uniform, but with his former self.

BY DEGREES, as Morgan rowed down the night river in the hearse-boat, the black woman came to her senses. She told him that her name was Mercy Johnson and that she had run away from her plantation in Tennessee. So far from being safe and free in the North, she had been seized by the enormous slave killer and forced to couple with the bull in taverns and wherever men who were no better than beasts came together to get drunk and work evil. George had kept her in a state of semiconsciousness by lacing her drinking water with laudanum, but tonight she had poured it out and begged water from the spectators at the show. She'd planned to escape that very evening and run back to her plantation. "At home they was never nothing but harsh and cruel to Mercy," she said. "But they didn't make her lay with no bull. You

Northerners more wicked by far. You say you free the slave, then you use the slave so. Old Swagbelly, King George, want Mercy to peach on she gal cousin, run away just before me. He say tell him where that gal cousin headed or he gone let old Zeus rut on she till she dead."

"What is your cousin's name, Mercy? Did she have a little boy with her when she ran?"

"Never you mind no names," Mercy said. "Mercy headed back home."

"You listen to me, Mercy Johnson," Morgan said. "You don't need to go back south. I'll find you a safe place where no one will ever mistreat you again. Will you trust me?"

She looked at him, at the scattershot slung round his neck, the musket leaning over the thwart, the long dagger dangling from his belt.

"All right," Morgan said. "I won't ask you to trust me. I'll just ask you to trust yourself. Will you trust yourself?"

"Trust herself? Mercy done a good job so far trust herself. Run away from the Grace plantatia and land in a bull show because she won't peach on she cousin. What you grand idea?"

"Can you row, Mercy? Can you row a boat?"

"Row a boat? She reckon."

"Good enough. I'm looking for a little stream called Trout Run that empties into this river a few miles below here. We'll go up it a short piece and hide the boat back in the bushes. Come tomorrow night, you row back upriver. Go right on past Harrisburg. Past that bad place where I found you. Just upriver there's a big wide bend. You'll find an island at the foot of that curve in the river. Put up there during the day. Come dark again, row upriver. You'll come to another island about half a mile long. Go up the easy water on the east." He pointed. "This side. Put in at the cove in the island and you'll find a path through the briars. Walk uphill about one hundred steps. There's a big old chestnut tree there with a little house in it. Call up for Mother Bremmen. Tell her Morgan Kinneson sent you. That's me. She'll see that you get to safety."

"Trust herself," Mercy Johnson muttered. "Call up Mother Bremmen, live in they tree."

"That's it," Morgan said. But what sort of union drove fugitives back to slavery again? What sort of war laid waste to whole states, then allowed such evils as he had seen to reign unchecked? Why hadn't someone arrested King George and his gang of madmen? Was there no one left to rise up and denounce the savage coupling of a bull and a woman in the very capital of a state long renowned for its humane enlightenment?

Even Jesse's precious rune stone seemed a sham. Where on the stone was the pictograph of a runaway slave being forced to copulate with a bull? A madman killing fish because his sons had been taken from him? Women, children, and ancients being bid for on the block in York State, the heart of abolitionist country? *A beautiful chance for those wishing to see something of this life away from home, boys.* The bloodiest war in American history, which had already taken the lives of more than half a million men? A beautiful chance to travel? The absurdity of it all. The futility. And yet Morgan had not, when he'd had the opportunity, finished off King George. He was evidently not the killer he'd thought he was, though he might yet have to become one. That the gang would continue to pursue him until they killed him and obtained the stone or he killed them, he had no doubt. He resolved that the next time he saw his pursuers he would shoot them on sight, without compunction or remorse.

He thought about asking Mercy once more for the name of her

runaway cousin, but he feared doing so would only make her more suspicious of him. At first he had wondered whether she might be the runaway girl that the killers were hunting, but that did not seem to be the case. He wondered what the connection could be between Jesse, his rune stone, and the pretty fugitive, Mercy's cousin. Like the river he was following, the Susquehanna, the mysteries he needed to unravel seemed only to deepen as he drew nearer to Gettysburg and the Southland. He gave Mercy two of his three remaining dollars and left her and the hearse-boat in a copse of willows beside Trout Run just above its juncture with the Susquehanna.

M ORGAN WALKED UP into a deep ravine where, over more time than he could imagine, the stream had cut its way down to its present bed through alternating bands of red and yellow sandstone. In the gorge all was green—the mosses on the rocks in the streambed that had broken off from the cliffs, the ferns (it bothered him not to be able to tell their names, other than the common edible fiddlehead, as Pilgrim could have), the hemlock trees clinging to the ledges above. What little sunlight filtered into the heart of the ravine was tinted green, like the sky just after a thunderstorm. Yet Trout Run was well named. Dark little speckled trout like those he and Pilgrim had angled for on the mountain at home darted away from him. He longed to cut a wand for a pole and look under a rock for a wriggling worm to bait his hook so he could feel the sudden electric tug of a trout in the spring-green canyon and be a young boy again.

High overhead a natural rock bridge spanned the gorge. Morgan sat on a tilted slab of limestone in the brook and looked up at the stone arch and tried to imagine how it had been formed. Again, Pilgrim would know. Or at the least, from his geological studies with the professor, he would be able to cipher out what had likely happened. Was the stone bridge the roof of a former cave carved out by running water eons ago? It looked to be about sixty feet long and twenty feet wide and sixty or seventy feet thick. Ferns and blossoming laurel spilled over its sides, creating a wild and lovely park in the sky. He had seen a daguerreotype of the Natural Bridge of Virginia, once owned by Thomas Jefferson. Here was a miniature duplicate of that bridge in William Penn's Land, a splendid natural wonder he never would have seen had he not left Vermont, though he would have traded any number of such marvels to know that Pilgrim was alive and well and Jesse safe in Canada.

He hiked up out of the gorge into a sweet-smelling morning. Plowed fields, lush pastures, blossoming orchards, hedgerows abloom with white drifts of dogwood. The farmers tilling their fields wore black hats. Women and girls in black dresses and bonnets tended dooryard flower gardens more colorful and orderly than any Morgan had ever beheld. The little boys wore dark hats like their fathers, a comical and touching sight.

He stopped to ask directions at a crossroads store beside the brook, a dank and narrow emporium with a shaded gallery in front beautified by several tobacco-spitting, staring louts. The store reeked of harness oil and pickles. "Who are the black-clad farmers?" he asked the storekeeper, a lanky man in a full-length white apron.

"They call themselves Brethren. They're Quakers but not Quakers," the storekeep said. "Dutchers who won't go to war, though they were eager enough to help start it, concealing and abetting other people's runaway property. Now that they've touched off the powder keg, they'd rather lay up treasure on earth and leave the rest of us to put out the fire."

Morgan shrugged. "They seem like a decent enough community," he said.

As he headed up the road beside the brook, Morgan watched a boy in a man's black hat swing a well-fed trout out of the stream. The boy removed the hook and dropped the trout into his wicker creel. "Good fish!" Morgan called.

Under his hat, the young fisher had straw-colored hair and blue eyes. He was smiling shyly. *"Danke,"* he said, offering the pole to Morgan. "Wilt try thy luck?"

"I guess I'll save my luck," Morgan said, smiling back.

"Dost go to war?"

"In a manner of speaking."

"Mein vater says war is bad."

"Well, I can't argue with him there," Morgan said. "Good luck with your trouting."

"Gute luck at the war," the boy said gravely.

The brook flowed along the base of a round hill wooded on top. A railroad track snaked out around the hill, and Morgan could hear a train coming and loud singing. Ahead in the meadow a girl with the same straw hair as the boy, hers mostly hidden by a black bonnet, was driving a brindled cow and a red bull calf up toward the bars in a crooked rail fence, gently swishing a willow branch with the leaves still attached along their clean flanks. It was a pleasing sight, the girl and the animals. As the train steamed into sight, starting its looping circuit around the hill, the cow paused in the field for the red calf to suck. The milkmaid waited patiently. Morgan overtook her and touched his slouch hat. "Good morning, miss."

"My goodness," she said. "Didst fall off the train?"

"Fall off the train?"

"Yon war train." She pointed with her switch toward the locomotive. Now they could hear the words the men on the train were
singing.

When Johnny comes marching home again, hurrah, hurrah.
We'll give him a hearty welcome then, hurrah, hurrah.
Oh, the men will cheer and the boys will shout . . .

It was a troop train, twenty rolling carriages packed with blue
recruits headed south. Some of the soldiers had spilled over onto the
tops of the cars, singing and shouting and dodging cinders from the
locomotive. One fired his gun off into the sky. Morgan watched
them from the meadow. They seemed to be having a jolly time of it.
Some were drinking out of glass bottles that sparkled in the morning sunshine.

"I'm looking for the Findletter place," he said. "Joseph Findletter?"

"Just beyond the hill," the girl said. Morgan wondered if she
was the fishing boy's sister, if all of these Dutchers had light hair
like his own. The bull calf pulled hard on the cow, which swung
around and butted it with her head. The calf was almost too big to
suck.

Morgan touched his hat to the girl again. "I'll cut over that little
knoll, I reckon. Those boys on the train might ask me to come
along with them and not take no for an answer. I thank you for the
directions."

And the ladies they will all turn out . . .

Heading up into the little woods, Morgan could still hear snatches of the soldiers' song. Partway up the cow path he turned to wave to the girl and the boy, now trotting through the field to join her. The train was quite close to the cow and calf. A beanpole officer in colonel's epaulets, standing beside a small general with four silver stars on his hat, threw his empty bottle into the brook. Before Morgan had any idea what he was about, the stringbean raised his Yellow Boy carbine and shot the brindled cow through the heart. The animal collapsed onto its side as the calf continued to nuzzle its teat. The girl stood stunned. Then she grabbed the little boy's hand and made for the pasture bars, leaped over them, and cut for home through a field of young rye.

The blue-clad cow killer was now screaming in rapturous staccato phrases that made no sense at all. His miniature comrade the general fired in the direction of the retreating children. The straw-headed children were running across the field of sprouted rye, the girl's black cap was gone, her yellow hair flying. Morgan sprinted over the hilltop and down the other side to yet another rail fence. The tracks lay about a hundred yards off across a pasture spangled with daisies, buttercups, and the bright orange hawkweed his mother called Indian paintbrush.

He lay behind the fence, waiting. The Findletters' farm buildings sat across the pasture to his left, as peaceful as a painting. As the girl and her brother ran into the yard, a big yellow-bearded man emerged from the barn. The locomotive pulling the troop train huffed out of the curve circumventing the hill. The soldiers on the car roofs, led by the drunken colonel and general, were singing a slow, sad song. The two officers had linked arms and were swaying to the rhythm of the song and the rhythm of the wheels.

So green grows the laurel and so does the rue,
How sorry I am that I parted with you.
Against the next meeting our joys we'll renew
When we'll change the green laurel for the red, white, and blue.

The entire contingent on the train roof was standing with arms joined as they sang and swayed. Some of the men wept openly, and Prophet Floyd bawled for love of his country as he and Steptoe, disguised as Union officers, whinnied out the green laurel song. Then, "Morrr-gan," cried out Floyd. "Come out, come out, wherever you are."

Morgan sighted on Floyd and touched off his musket. The Prophet yelped as Morgan's ball grazed his hat. The two killers sent a hail of bullets toward the crooked fence and woods, but Morgan was already racing hard across the pasture toward the train, pulling the scattershot on the lanyard over his hat. The bullets came on, ripping splinters off the fence rails. Morgan ran low, angling to intercept the car directly in front of the Findletters' lane. The train was picking up speed on the downgrade toward the river. A searing pain in Morgan's left shoulder spun him around a half turn. Still he stumbled on. He could hear the bullets whining past his head. The train continued down the grade and out of sight beyond a windmill with a cobblestone base and white-and-blue wooden sails.

Morgan stopped running and put his hand to his shoulder. It came away wet and warm and red. He toppled over into the white-and-yellow daisies and lay weeping in the meadow, not from the pain of his wound but because if he died here, in a hay field in Pennsylvania, he would never find Pilgrim or learn his fate.

.   .   .

"WE MUST SEND THEE SOUTH, boy, to quell the rebellion. I truly believe thou couldst do so by thyself in a short week's work."

The man talking to him spoke in the deepest of baritone voices. He had a craggy face thatched over with a yellow, spade-shaped beard extending from just below his cheekbones to the middle of his chest. It was as if the yellow beard itself was speaking in a deep voice. His eyes were blue as cornflowers.

Morgan looked around. On the walls hung guns of every description. Squirrel rifles, six-shooters, carbines, rifle muskets. A workbench was cluttered with dressing rods, punches, bits, and bullet molds. Nearby sat a great swage-block gun anvil. Remembering the train of blue boys, Morgan thought he'd been taken prisoner and conveyed to some kind of arsenal. Then he recalled the man running to the girl and boy and realized that he was in Joseph Findletter's gun shop. Also that he was in considerable pain. His left shoulder ached as though someone had struck it full on with the smith's anvil hammer. He was naked to the waist, and the shoulder was heavily bandaged.

From behind the beard came a strange noise. The smith was chuckling. He reached into his apron pocket and removed a small chunk of metal and set it on Morgan's bare chest. "I tonged that out of thy shoulder, boy, while thou slept the sleep of the dead. It's a minié ball. We dared not call the doctor for fear word of thy whereabouts would travel. But the wound is clean. The tongs were red hot from the fire, and I scalded the flesh around the opening as well. The bullet chipped thy collar bone and penetrated the scapula, but thou art not the first two-legged creature I've cobbled back together. If thou intendeth to go to war against the entire Union army, however, thou must lie still. In the meantime I thank thee for defending *mein kinder*. Thou art a brave boy. I saw thee assault the train. It was a grand sight."

"I was angry."

"I must hope not to make thee angry then. Dost read the newspapers?"

"Not much lately."

Morgan fingered the bullet, cold on his chest. It could not have weighed an ounce. It was cylindrical and seemed grooved, though flattened on the end where it had smashed into his collarbone and shoulder.

"Canst endure a small laugh? Mirth, you know, is the sugar of life."

Morgan nodded. But he was puzzled. How could this jovial man have turned out his own sister?

"Listen," Joseph Findletter said. "From the *Lancaster Telegraph*, fresh off the press this morning:

On this Tuesday at approximately 9:15 o'clock in the morning a large party of REBEL RAIDERS attacked a troop train near the Trout Run general mercantile. The cravenly REBELS had laid an ambuscade for the train at the foot of Snapfinger Hill, from whence they rained down upon the unarmed recruits a murderous hail of small-arms fire from behind the cover of a rail fence. The COWARDLY TRAITORS then attempted to SWARM the train, which they rushed from both sides of the tracks. Their numbers were estimated at upward of one hundred strong. Their ghastly traitorous yell was heard as far away as West Lancaster. Under the direction of two officers, a colonel and a general who departed the troop train at York, a few brave boys on the roof of the rail carriages were able to hold them off until the train got across the river at the Billups Bend trestle. The survivors of the gang, most of which was SHOT TO FLINDERS, are now being hunted down.

Post Script. The treasonous leader of the Reb outlaws stopped at the Trout Run store just prior to the MILITARY ACTION against our troops. There, in an act of unparalleled AUDAC-ITY, he held the proprietor and several venerable patriarchs of the region at gunpoint and tried, unsuccessfully, to cow them into reciting the Confederate Oath. He is described as young, with thick unkempt light hair falling to his shoulders, heavily armed, above six foot tall and well set up, with mad gray eyes and an ALTOGETHER MURDEROUS ASPECT. Posters bearing a tolerable likeness have been distributed by the Lancaster County High Sheriff."

Morgan mustered a smile. Was there ever such a famous outlaw as the outlaw Morgan Kinneson, wanted for treason and murder in Will Penn's Land? Yet he was deeply concerned that the killers had left the train at York. Even now they might be combing the region for him and for the two Brethren children as well. But Joseph Findletter shook his head. "Thou art perfectly safe here," he said. "No one has ever discovered *Algiz*."

The smith nodded at the window over the workbench. Carved into the pane was the character Ɏ, which Morgan recognized from Jesse's stone. Outside the window he could see leafy green treetops. *Algiz* was located deep in the woods.

"This is my gun shop," Findletter said. "I no longer sell guns, but I come here from time to time to make them. Making guns is what I do. What dost thou? Art with the army?"

"I'm with no army. Didn't you look at the stone around my neck? Your sign is marked on it."

"Young sir. Never, unless you departed this life, would I or any of my family molest thy belongings. We do not fight. Nor do we steal. Nor do we pry into another's possessions or affairs."

Morgan lifted the stone on the thong over his head and silently handed it to Joseph Findletter. While the blue-eyed smith intently studied the etchings, Morgan closed his eyes. Talking had tired him. His shoulder throbbed. In the hidden gun shop he breathed in the scents of well-oiled metal, powder, wooden stocks, dead ashes in the coke forge. Also the deep green of the woods outside.

"Where didst acquire this?" the smith said finally.

"From a black man named Jesse Moses." Morgan thought he saw a flicker of recognition in Joseph's eyes. "Your sister sent me here," Morgan said. "Mrs. Bremmen."

"I no longer have a sister."

"Yes, you do, Joseph Findletter. And what you're doing to her is flat wrong. Shunning your own family? That's just killing someone a little slower. In my haversack there's a tree leaf with a message printed on it for you. From your sister. You still do have a sister."

"*Nein.*"

"Yes. Do you believe in Jesus?"

"Of course."

"Who did Jesus shun? No one. Shunning's about the most cruel punishment I've ever heard of. If a tall man and a short man, neither right in the head, come calling, notify me immediately. Also be on the lookout for a huge black man with a stove-in face. Whatever you do, don't let them near your children. I'm going to shut my eyes and rest now."

When he woke again it was night. He was weak and thirsty, but the fever was gone and he thought he might recover. Especially when he looked up and saw, gazing down at him solemnly, instead of the blacksmith and his talking beard, the girl from the meadow. A bull's-eye lantern glowed on the workbench behind her, and in its light she looked beautiful.

"Did they catch that big gang of audacious rebels that attacked the train?" Morgan said.

"Newspapers do not tell the truth. I am here to change your dressing. Also I have brought you some good soup. My father thinks he should not come for a time. He thinks the authorities looking for the 'gang' may be watching him. Or, worse yet, the men you warned him of."

As the girl removed the old bandage and cleaned his wound, then rewound strips of sheeting around his shoulder, he said, "I met your aunt. She lives in a tree."

"*Ja.*"

"Your father has put her aside."

"I know. Do not move, please. My name is Gretel."

"You're sparing of words, Gretel."

"Words bring trouble. Fighting words brought about the war. I tell this to my children."

"You don't look old enough to have children."

"I mean my scholars. I am a teacher."

"You don't look old enough to be a teacher."

"Next month I am sixteen. Then I will be marriageable and have children of my own. My father, the smith and horse doctor, did an excellent job removing the bullet from your shoulder. He does much of our doctoring for us—I mean us Brethren."

"He's a good man. Probably he saved my life. But he shouldn't put aside his sister."

"Perhaps not," she agreed, tightening the bandage. "And you should not shoot at people. Even bad people. I teach my children first to tell the truth, then to practice kindness. We must love our enemies."

"That's easier to do when they aren't shooting at us."

She pursed her lips. "Fighting is always wrong. So I was taught. So I teach my small scholars."

"If you knew my enemies, you might think differently. They were firing at you, Gretel. And at your brother. They killed your cow."

"Then we must pray for them that they will see the error of their ways."

"I'll leave that department to you. How long do you reckon before I can travel?"

"Three, perhaps four weeks."

"Four days is more like."

She shook her head over such stubbornness. Morgan wished she would take off her bonnet so he could see her hair again, but he supposed that the bonnet went with the rest of the costume. Her tanned, shapely hands on his shoulder and neck were warm and gentle, and a slight smile played at the corners of her mouth, as though she was secretly glad that he had fought for her and her brother. She was slender yet full-figured. Morgan wondered what she would be like if she were not a Brethren. He wondered if it might be possible for him to love this girl—or any girl. After all he had done and must yet do, how would he ever be worthy of anyone's love?

L YING FLAT ON HIS BACK in the smith's gun forge, Morgan found himself starved for reading matter and took that as a good sign. But what was he to read? The Brethren read little but the Bible. Morgan asked Gretel to bring him the gazette containing the story of his attack on the troop train, which he devoured from front to back like one of his beloved travel books. After being away from books for a month, even the advertisements made good reading. Poultices for aching teeth. Harnesses. A new seed-boring machine. Some of the notices offered rewards for runaway slaves:

> Run off from the subscriber, a likely yellow wench of 17 or 18 years of age, answering to the name Slidell. A girl of uncommon height, quick parts, and supreme insolence. A five hundred dollar reward, in United States currency, will be paid for the return of this fugitive to Arthur Dinwiddie, Grace River, Tennessee.

Reading this notice, which no newspaper in Vermont would ever have printed, rekindled Morgan's determination to enlist in the army as soon as he found Pilgrim.

Over the next several days he grew stronger. Joseph Findletter said he was a good healer, like certain mules he had doctored, too set in his ways to be laid low for long. "The pot and the kettle," Morgan said, and Findletter smiled. Gretel, who was on summer vacation from school, since the Brethren children were now needed in the fields at home, took him on slow walks over her father's farm. Things were done differently here in the land of the Brethren. The sandstone barns had brown tile roofs and double walls filled with stone rubble and were impregnable to weather, warm in winter, cool in summer, clean and sweet-smelling year-round. Gretel showed him how the thatched roofs of the stone outbuildings were fashioned from rye stalks tied off in bundles and woven through the rafters with hazel withes. She showed him how flax was soaked in water to soften the outer husk, then dragged through a scutching board with iron hackles and pounded into spinning thread. She said that because cotton had been raised by slaves, the Findletter family wore only wool or linen made from flax. She stitched elegant quilts for which she compounded her own dyes. In Gretel's personal garden grew calendula flowers for yellow, beets for madder-red, woad for blue. She too believed that mirth was the sugar of life, and she teased him gently as they picked tiny wild strawberries along the fishing brook, a full morning's picking barely enough to make a shortcake. "I wish thou wouldst stay and become one of us," she told him. "Hast read the Bible?"

"I have. I take from the Bible what I find useful and ignore the rest."

"That sounds much like freethinking to me."

"To me it sounds like thinking. I don't stop thinking when I open the Bible."

From the barnyard, where he was repairing a wagon wheel, Joseph shot the two young people a look. He was coming to like this outspoken boy from the mountains of Vermont. He decided to catechize Morgan further.

That evening at supper Joseph said, "We Brethren, friend Morgan, have a proverb for war. 'Better an unjust peace than a just war.'"

"My brother, Pilgrim, would probably agree with you. I wouldn't."

"Well," Joseph said, "we have another proverb. 'Truth is a medicine that must be given at the right time.' Let us discuss the matter another time. You are a good young man, Morgan, whether we agree or not. You protected my children."

"We must obey the father," Gretel said to him primly after supper. "Both the Father in heaven and His representative here on earth. My aunt was always quarreling with my father."

"Shunning's wrong, Gretel," Morgan said. "I know it and so do you. No doubt war is wrong too, but sometimes it may be necessary. I believe that this one the country's fighting is necessary. John Brown understood that. So does President Lincoln."

That night, lying on his narrow cot in the old gun forge, he pored over Jesse's carved stone by candlelight. He suspected that his father, and perhaps Pilgrim as well, knew more about the runic system than they had told him. Clearly the runes had been inspired by the ancient and mysterious symbols on the great Balancing Boulder atop Kingdom Mountain. Morgan wondered if the whole scheme could be a joke played by Pilgrim, with his great gift for satire and mimicry. What Morgan would not give to hear his clever brother take off the Brethren with their solemn old "thy" and "thou." And Pilgrim could have done the gypsy and Eva and little Birdcall, with her sharp tongue and good heart. Sometimes Pilgrim mimicked Morgan's purposeful mien and unswerving single-mindedness. Pilgrim could always make him laugh. Now in the candlelight Morgan studied Pilgrim's sign, ᛉ, which appeared in the Great Smokies. He looked at it so long that he could still see the ᛉ,

dancing on the plank wall above his cot when he reached to blow out the candle. He looked again more closely. This was no mirage. Someone had carved his brother's rune on the wall of the blacksmith's shop.

As Morgan stared at the rune, trembling with the excitement of his discovery, a plan began to take shape in his mind. It was worthy of the subtlety of Pilgrim's great hero, Odysseus, though Morgan couldn't imagine wily Odysseus, or Pilgrim either, getting himself wounded by the cowardly Steptoe and Prophet in the first place. That night he dreamed about being at home on Kingdom Mountain fishing for trout with his brother. "What are you waiting for, soldier?" Pilgrim said to him in the dream. "Are you going to get on with your campaign and find me or not?"

He woke at dawn with his plan complete. He would have to move fast, for his presence here placed Joseph and his family at great and terrible risk. He must leave as soon as possible. But not, he hoped, without further information about his brother. And not without a better means of defending himself. Where he was headed, his ancient, short-range musket would be of little use to him.

"Kindly check my bandage for me, Gretel," Morgan said the following morning. "See here where it rubs on my shoulder?"

She bent over, a strand of her golden hair falling out of her bonnet and catching the early morning sunshine pouring through the window inscribed with the sign of *Algiz*. Morgan slid his good arm around her and pulled her head close and kissed her.

"Nein," she cried, jumping back. "What ails thee, Morgan Kinneson?"

"Other than my wounded shoulder, nothing at all," he said.

Gretel shook her head but Morgan smiled. From the slight,

lingering pressure of her lips on his he knew that, Brethren girl or no, she too had felt some passion.

FOR MORGAN KINNESON FROM the northern mountains of Vermont, there now came a peaceful interlude in the heart of the land of the Brethren. How, he wondered, as he and Gretel walked hand in hand through her garden, could people who dressed so drably, who made a sovereign virtue of self-denial, and who lived so rigidly—much more rigidly than Christ himself, who after all was a seasoned old dog of the open road who loved to drink wine at weddings and tell stories to his fishing cronies—how could these people grow such beautiful flowers? His mother cultivated flowers, but not like Gretel's rows of deep red peonies, tall spice-scented irises, poppies orange as the belly of a spawning trout, lupines not just blue but every hue of the rainbow.

Morgan and Gretel and the boy, young Joseph, swam in the deep green pool beneath Jacob's Ladder, as the Brethren called the great stone arch above the Trout Run. The icy water of the spring-fed brook provided more relief to Morgan's healing shoulder than the hot compresses Gretel applied.

"Let me cut thine hair," Gretel said.

"I'll let you cut it when you cut yours."

"That will be when I am married. Then I must cut it."

"Not if you married me," Morgan said, and the girl laughed, her cheeks as pink as her own June roses. But that very afternoon the smith took Morgan aside and said to him, "If I make thee a rifle, wilt go away and not return?"

"Yes," Morgan said, detesting himself.

Joseph nodded. "Very well, then. Thou wilt help build thine own rifle. Working together, we can do it in one week. By then thou shouldst be well enough to travel again."

As he walked his ox into the treadmill that ran the great bellows above the forge, Joseph said, "We will make the new gun from thine old gun, like Our Lord turning old wine into new. See how beautiful the stock is? Curled maple, among the very strongest and most handsome of woods. And we'll use the long barrel, as well, for the barrel of the rifle."

"My grandfather cut the maple tree for this stock in the small of the moon in January when there was no sap in the tree," Morgan said. "So the family story goes, at least. Before the gun was passed on to me it belonged to my brother, Pilgrim. Then Pilgrim decided he was a pacifist like you folks."

The smith gave no indication that he recognized Pilgrim's name, though Morgan watched his face narrowly from the tail of his eye. The double bellows blew a powerful stream of air onto the glowing bed of coke and oak charcoal in the forge. Findletter's blue eyes gleamed with pleasure. He was happy to be making a gun again.

As he took apart the old musket, Joseph's hands seemed to work independently of his head. Over the years all of the craft and knowledge of gunsmithing had been incorporated into his strong sure hands, and he no longer had to think of what he did, any more than Morgan thought what he was about when he raised the weapon to fire. The burning coal and charcoal had a fierce, acrid smell. Joseph inhaled deeply, as though the scent of the forge were oxygen to him.

Ordinarily sparing of words, the smith talked steadily while he worked. "A gunsmith, Morgan, is a specialized blacksmith. The carbines I made by hand are now made piecemeal by machines in thy New England manufactories. But those machines only imitate what people did first. Machine-made guns never truly become a part of thee. When thou make and assemble a gun thyself, each part becomes a part of thee. Dost see? No winch 'em squinch 'em the trigger thou pinch 'em and then thou flinch 'em. *Nein.* Thy gun will be *made.*"

They spent most of the first day taking apart the old musket and pouring the molten homemade steel for the new lower barrel, which would fire heavy shot at close range in a way that would make Morgan's scattershot pistol seem like a child's popgun. The groove in the swage block anvil formed half of the circle of the lower barrel. The smith's concave hammer shaped the other half. The barrel was formed around a mandrel rod, which Joseph drove out when he finished the process. He let Morgan wield the swage hammer as he shoved the barrel along the groove in the anvil. The hammer rang loudly through the glen, *clang clang clang clang,* until it seemed to Morgan as though it and the gun barrel were extensions of his own two arms. Joseph's beautiful homemade swage anvil, sometimes known as a dumb anvil or buffalo head, had scrolled corners and a six-pointed star over the sign of *Algiz,* Y. On one end was a horn for forging horseshoes, on the other a gentle curve for welding wagon wheels. The anvil was pierced with several holes for truing the mandrel bars. Thus they forged the lower barrel, on the first day.

On the second day Joseph showed his apprentice how to bore and remill his old round musket barrel, which would sit atop the lower barrel, using a gun-boring machine invented and patented by the smith himself. The hand-cranked Findletter boring device drove a pulley attached to a reaming rod that screwed itself into the muzzle of Morgan's musket barrel. The tapered, squared-off working end of the rod enlarged the barrel to accommodate a .50 caliber bullet fired out of a self-contained cartridge. It took them most of that day to bore out the musket barrel properly. Like the shot barrel below, it was fifty-eight inches long.

On the third day Findletter showed Morgan how to rifle the top barrel of his new gun. The smith explained that the rifling guide etched spiral grooves inside the barrel to impart lateral spin to the bullet. "You must understand, lad, that a bullet from your old smooth-bore musket will begin to tumble over and over and go astray after sixty or seventy yards. The rifling grooves inside a barrel transfer a furious deadly spin to the bullet and keep it on course."

The rifling guide was a cylindrical pole made of the trunk of a young poplar, grooved to have what the smith called a slow twist, to which a metal rod was attached. To the end of this rod Joseph had brazed a cutting button with miniature teeth fashioned from the teeth of a saw blade. The rod and cutting button completed exactly one revolution in fifty-eight inches as the smith helped Morgan turn the poplar pole by means of a wooden handle at the end. This process they repeated five times. A bullet fired through the rifled barrel would fly fast and true.

The smith referred to Morgan's old cap-and-ball Hunter as a Kentucky musket or hog gun. The top barrel of the new gun fired cartridges with grooved bullets superior even to the minié balls that were causing such carnage in the war. On the fourth day Joseph inserted a breech-loading mechanism, first showing Morgan how to drill lock-plate screw holes with a bow drill, one of the oldest tools known to man. The handle for the lever-action loading mechanism had been fashioned from part of a plowshare heated red hot and then white hot in the coke forge. The irony of beating an agricultural implement into a weapon did not escape Morgan, who then made a request. He asked Joseph to affix ring seats to the bottom barrel so he could attach the gypsy's long-bladed dagger as a bayonet. Reluctantly, the smith did so.

On the fifth day they brazed on a peephole at the front of the top barrel and, at the opposite end, a pointed sight made from the tip of a rattail rasp, plunging the barrel once, twice, and yet a third time into icy water from the nearby trout stream to anneal the new welds. Then the smith showed him the art of strengthening the maple stock and the new walnut forearm grip with aqua fortis, just as a true soldier's heart must be fortified against anger or revenge or pity for his enemy or whatever other passions that might come between him and his duty.

One afternoon when Joseph had business in Lancaster town, Gretel took Morgan to visit her little schoolhouse on the Trout Run. To throw off any suspicious bypassers, he wore one of her father's dark hats and suits. It felt odd to be in a school again. Morgan sat beside Gretel on a bench built for a shaver not half his size, dressed all in black like a croaking raven. She was much amused by his embarrassment, but when he began to tell her the story of Pilgrim's disappearance she listened intently. He concluded his tale by asking her if, either before the great battle at Gettysburg or afterward, Pilgrim had stopped at the Findletters', possibly in the company of an elderly black runaway named Jesse Moses.

Gretel said that so far as she knew, no young doctor answering to Pilgrim's description had come to her father's place. About two months ago, however, an ancient black man, very frightened and carrying a tow sack, had appeared at *Algiz* one evening. She did not know the old passenger's name, but her father had hidden him for several days before sending him along upriver to her aunt Bremmen's on his way to Canada. Morgan felt his heart fall. It was very possible that Jesse himself, not Pilgrim, had carved the sign of *Othila* on the wall. He asked Gretel if anyone other than he and the fugitive Underground passengers ever stopped at *Algiz*. The past winter, she said, a beautiful young Creole woman from New Orleans, who had gone to visit relatives in Montreal, where she was trapped by the war, was trying to work her way back to Louisiana and had spent a night at the forge. The woman was fearful, Gretel said, of being mistaken for a Confederate spy. Gretel smiled. "She was as beautiful as a princess," she said. "I like to think that she was a spy."

"Well, maybe she was at that," Morgan said. "In these times just about anything is possible."

"It is," Gretel said. "I know it is not allowed to speak the name of a passenger or a conductor or stationmaster, but to prove thy point, Morgan, we even had an injured Confederate soldier seek sanctuary at *Algiz*. He was badly wounded in the leg. The father whipped it off for him just below the knee, clean as a whistle. He was from Alabama, and his way of speaking was an endless source of mirth for us. We could scarce decipher a word the poor fellow said. But he was very handsome, with fine black eyes and a ready smile."

"What became of him?" Morgan said. He was a little jealous of this Alabama soldier with the fine eyes, and he suspected that Gretel meant for him to be.

Gretel laughed. "He went off south with the Creole woman," she said. "He agreed to guide her back to New Orleans. But we all believed he'd fallen in love with her. For a long time we teased the father for running a courting station."

Gretel smiled again, a little ruefully this time. "I was beginning to think, Morgan, that it might be possible for thee to remain here as one of us and be happy. Until thou told me about thy great search for thy brother. Now I understand. Thou must find him."

"You're the first person I've met who thinks he's still alive," Morgan said. "No, the second. You and my cousin Dolton."

"I do think he is alive," Gretel said. She stood up and took Morgan's hand. Her hand in his felt warm and friendly but nothing more, and in fact that was how he felt toward her. She would make an ideal sister for a rough-and-tumble fellow like him. A few days ago he'd been tempted to give her his cedar drinking cup. Now, in accordance with Auguste Choteau's advice, he would save it for the one he loved, assuming that someday, when the war and all it had wrought in his life was far behind him, he might be worthy and capable of loving a woman.

"Pilgrim is alive," Gretel said again.

"You have a great abundance of faith, Gretel Findletter."

"And thou, too, Morgan Kinneson, have a great abundance of faith. Vermont freethinker or no, thou have an abundance of faith. But"—and here her full-throated laugh reminded Morgan of her father's quick laughter—"I still think thou look very well in a Brethren's black hat."

O N   D A Y   N U M B E R   S I X Morgan and Joseph Findletter blued the two barrels of the gun with a chemical solution of soft water from the farmhouse rain barrel, a handful of crushed bluestone from a quarry north of Lancaster, and a sloshing bedpan of "chamber lye"—Morgan's own urine. The finished barrels, which

Joseph polished with beeswax, had a blue-gray sheen, like the big lake at home under a gray November sky.

That afternoon they made lead bullets in a mold, and as the bullets began to cool they took them to the natural stone bridge and turned them out of the mold over the side of the bridge to fall into the green pool far below, the bullets assuming in flight the slightly cylindrical teardrop shape best adapted to the .50 caliber rifled bore of the upper barrel. They made one hundred bullets. It occurred to Morgan as he watched the bits of hot lead plunge down and down to the pool below, diminishing to tiny gray flecks, that the burly smith could easily snatch him up and hurl him off the stone bridge to his death, thereby ridding himself altogether of an alien suitor for his beautiful daughter. But Joseph Findletter was no killer. Morgan and young Joseph and Gretel waded barefoot in the lime-green water, groping with their toes for the oval-shaped bullets.

"I put a drop of silver on the tip of each one," Joseph Findletter said, smiling. "It is all that will kill the devil, thou knowest."

The seventh day was no day of rest for the gunsmith. He and Morgan walked to the top of Gilead Hill, across the glen from Snapfinger, where Gilead Brook fell down the sheer side of the glen in a white billowing curtain over the red and yellow sandstone. They carried a rank cabbage left over from the past winter, also a soft orange pumpkin and a twenty-ounce apple, a good keeping variety much prized by Morgan's mother at home in Vermont. They placed the cabbage on a jutting ledge. The pumpkin they set in the crotch of a hickory. They skewered the apple on the pointed end of a long stick, which they thrust into a crevice in the rock wall below the cabbage. Then they made their way back across Jacob's Ladder and up to the top of Snapfinger. Across the gorge, about five hundred yards away, the cabbage, pumpkin, and apple were all visible. The smith lay down on a carpet of shiny green partridgeberry leaves. He sighted with the gun, tinkered the peephole, levered a shell into the firing chamber with a smooth, oiled *snick,* took careful aim, and fired. The rock beside the cabbage flew into splinters. The smith tinkered the sight again with a little screwdriver and aimed once more. The rifle spoke with a booming *crack,* and last year's rotten cabbage cleaved neatly into two halves, one of which tumbled over the falls. Joseph stood and handed the gun to Morgan. "Now is the time to master your work. Practice makes perfection. It will take practice. The gun is accurate enough. Now everything depends on the man behind the gun. Do not be impatient."

In a single motion Morgan raised the rifle and fired. The pumpkin in the hickory crotch burst into a thousand fragments. The astonished smith could see bits of orange shell and fibrous yellow pumpkin guts on the trunk of the hickory and the nearby laurel bushes, and as he marveled at the gun he had wrought and at the deadly skill of Morgan Kinneson, the rifle spoke again and the apple on the sharpened stick vanished.

The reverberating echo in the glen died away. "It's a pretty good gun," Morgan said. "I wish I could pay you for it."

"No pay," the smith said. "I have never seen such shooting."

"My brother shoots better than I do. Or did before he gave it up. Pilgrim."

Again Joseph's open and expressive face showed no sign of recognition. "Morgan?" the smith said. "A confession. I do wish I were coming with thee. After the shooting of the brindled cow and the bullets fired at the children, I do wish. I have prayed for forgiveness. My sign, *Algiz,* means two things. Protection for others. Self-control for myself. So I am told, at any rate. I fear that my self-control is far from perfect. Do you still believe that I was hasty with mine sister?"

"I do."

"Well. I will pray for better understanding. In the meantime may I offer thee one word more of advice?"

Morgan nodded.

"From him who made thee thy gun. Now thou has a Joseph Findletter rifle worthy of thy talent. A gun years ahead of its time. Be worthy of it, young brother. The times thou dost not fire the gun, which I name Lady Justice, are more important than the times thou dost. Wilt remember?"

"I wish I could stay and get to know you people better," Morgan said. "I thank you for Lady Justice. You'll tell Gretel good-bye for me?"

"Aye," said the smith, with what Morgan believed was a mixture of regret and relief, which was just what he felt himself.

When Joseph Findletter held out his hand to Morgan, it was like putting his hand in the man's gun vise. Then the boy began to walk south and did not look back.

MORGAN'S BOOTS were wearing out. The soles were so thin that the dew soaked through. As for the uppers, they had long since pulled away from what was left of the heels. He'd had to ask Joseph Findletter for a couple of hanks of rope to tie them to his feet. A few more days and he'd be barefooted. Having come this far, he believed his shoes could get him the rest of the way to Gettysburg. He did not believe he could continue barefooted, though a year ago Pilgrim had written that many of the Rebels went to war unshod. Pilgrim's writer friend from Concord, Mr. H. D. Thoreau, had noted in his book, "Beware of enterprises that require new clothes." He'd said nothing about new boots.

Morgan had learned from the German Brethren of a shoe manufactory in Gettysburg. He had very little money left, but he believed he could barter services for boots. Footgear was the order of the day.

The morning after he left the Findletters' it began to rain. At first the rain fell gently, but quickly it gathered into a driving storm slanting directly into Morgan's face. He was glad that he and Joseph had taken the time to blue Lady Justice. The downpour continued all morning. The newly cut hay fields and the young grain fields and the leafy green woods were indistinct through the rain billowing in from the west.

The rain beat down. More troop trains passed on the railroad track beside the sloppy red clay road Morgan was following, but the recruits were packed inside the carriages out of the weather. No one took any shots at him or at the cattle grazing in the rain or at the chimney pots of the farmhouses or the drenched beehives in the meadows.

A year ago the Rebels had penetrated this country. In places they had laid waste to the land, burning some of the barns and houses and leaving only blackened foundations behind. Other farmsteads were untouched. Morgan felt strangely comforted knowing that Pilgrim had been in these parts doctoring northern and southern soldiers alike. Before the battle Pilgrim had written that there was a seminary college in the shoe manufacturing town. He had said that his greatest hope was that Morgan would someday attend college and study a profession. For now the open road was Morgan's college, hard soldiering his profession. He walked at double time. Gettysburg was not far away.

Passing a small field of tobacco, he pinched off a piece of broad green tobacco leaf and crushed it between his fingers. It had an intoxicating odor. He put the leaf fragment on his tongue but promptly spit it out like wormwood.

The seminary college and the village below it had been spared destruction during the battle, though some of the stone houses and shops had bullets embedded in their walls, the richly hued sandstone having absorbed the errant balls like caked mud. The shoe factory was now engaged in making boots for the northern army. When Morgan asked about exchanging a day's work for a pair of boots, the timekeeper at the gate laughed and turned him out of the mill yard, thinking him a craven straw-headed Dutcher dodging conscription. So much for his plan to acquire footgear at Gettysburg.

"KINNESON? PILGRIM KINNESON, YOU SAY? That's an odd name, you'd think I'd remember it." The quartermaster in charge of exhuming the battlefield graves and moving them up the hill to the new cemetery thumbed through his register. "No, no one here under—holt on. Holt on here, boy. I do recall a Kinneson."

Morgan's heart seemed to stop altogether while the quartermaster looked at a roll of names in a different part of his ledger. "Here he is, by God, big as life. 'Kinneson, John. Colonel of the New York Forty-fourth. Wounded July 3, 1863. Transferred to Elmira August 20, 1863.' That's our only Kinneson thus far, boy. Maybe your brother, what's left of him, will turn up, but I wouldn't stake much on it. Some of them stinking trenches we've uncovered? We can't tell blue from gray, they was tore up so bad."

Scarcely knowing where he was headed, Morgan walked down the hill toward the gravediggers. He paused near a group of gaily dressed young men and women, holidayers touring the battlefield. A strange little man in a blue uniform jacket and a dashing blue cavalry officer's hat with a long ostrich plume was addressing the group in a voice full of self-important confidence.

"Not since Troy had such forces been arrayed one against another," intoned the orator, who had an uncommonly small, nodding head set slightly off center on a neck not much bigger around than a celery stalk. "But do not suppose, good friends, that I report to you as a mere bystanding historian. My credentials? I, a Union spymaster, was battlefield advisor to the generals. It was I who recommended at the outset, when we received word that the Virginian was marching this way with seventy thousands of men, that we must occupy the high ground first. Grant says to me, says he, 'Colonel Garrick. A word with you, sir. Is the high round hill good ground to make our stand?' And I said, 'Aye, Odysseus'—I called him so, a little private joke between us in reference to the Greek version of his fine Roman name—'Aye, Odysseus. The big round hill is very good ground to make our stand.'"

At this a passerby with a wooden leg laughed out loud. "The general you're referring to wasn't within five hundred miles of this battlefield last summer," he said. "I doubt you were, either."

"Laugh away, sir," the elocutionist replied in an injured tone. "Were you here, then? Or were you among the good gentlefolk of Philadelphia who, when they heard our cannonading from afar, fled in their carriages to New York? Eh, sir? Eh?"

With a histrionic gesture the little man pointed out over the fields, over the remnants of the peach orchard shot to splinters less than a year before. "The long-legged insurrectionists from Texas pelted up through that orchard screeching defiance. Would you people care to hear their infamous cry?"

The party, grown to about thirty, assured their diminutive guide, now donning a gray tunic and a Confederate kepi, that they much wished to hear the Rebel cry.

"Very well," he said. Without preliminaries he whirled around with his eyes all fiery red, uttered a falsetto shriek, and rushed madly upon the holidayers, who fell away in startled disarray, all but the man with the wooden leg, who laughed in the orator's face.

"But we stood our ground, good people," the speaker went on, "while down below in the great rocks known as the Devil's Building Blocks the advancing Rebs were caught by our crossfire and killed like so many sheep led to the slaughter. Eeee! Eeee! Hear them shriek! Eeee!"

"What made the West Point–trained southerner suppose he could ever take these two hills, outnumbered and outgunned as he was?" asked a young man in a paisley waistcoat.

"Why, he had enjoyed some fine victories lately in which he was also outnumbered and outgunned. He had outgeneraled his opposite number before and thought to do the same again here at Gettysburg."

"Nonsense. He was out of choices. It was all an act of desperation," the wooden-leg muttered. The crowd, however, snake-fascinated by the little man, hissed his detractor into silence.

"Now, over there," the self-styled spymaster continued, shrugging out of his gray coat and into his blue again but neglecting to remove his Confederate cap, "where the little hill stands, presided the learned professor from the great state o' Maine, who held the hilltop like Leonidas at Thermopylae until he and his company had no more ammunition. Meanwhile the traitors were coming on hard and hard. Their objective? No less than to take the hillock and flank our forces here atop the bigger knob. I arrived just in time to advise the Maine men to charge down the slope with bayonets set, though their rifles were empty. Oh, good ladies. We paunched 'em and backstabbed 'em and drove 'em before us like the Lord drove the cattle from the temple. We harried them into the Devil's Pen, where once again we did general butchery. Aye, we did. Pick pick, stick stick. Eeee! Eeee!"

As he ranted on, the manikin seemed to be looking straight at Morgan.

"Now, see here, sir, really," said the undaunted one-legged man. "How could you be so many places on the battlefield doing so many things at once?"

"Sssss! Sssss!" hissed the merrymakers, but the little man grandly waved them silent. "I trow we have a naysayer among us," he said. "I ask you again, old Methusalah. Were *you* here?"

"I was," the man said. "And I tell you that you were not. You are a brazen liar. I say so to your face. Perhaps you would like to defend your honor against the charge?"

"I scorn to stoop so low. I am no hobbling cripple. I have nothing to prove."

To a serpents' chorus of hisses, the one-legged man turned on his wooden heel and stumped away, and the player called out that scoffers had walked up and down in the land before now mocking truth-tellers far greater than he. He said he would conduct the multitude down to the common graves, whose contents were being transferred to the new cemetery on the hilltop even as he spoke, and show them at first hand the horrors of the battle and its grisly trophies. All the time, the player never stopped talking. Paying no attention to the workmen transferring the bodies, calling the noisome fumes of the yawning graves more fragrant than all the attars of Araby, yea, the very frankincense of war, the lunatic clambered down into a mass charnel pit and held up skulls and faded blue and gray cloth and finger bones white as sticks of chalk.

"A tanner will last seven years," he cited. "Ha ha! This poor fellow was no tanner, I fear. Oh, dear people. Would that you could have been here to see it. On and on came the last great charge, rushing up the hill into the death-dealing maws of our cannons. We poured volley upon volley of shot into them, but they continued toward us. A few of my comrades at arms, I am sorry to report, took leg bail. Yes, they skedaddled, and for all I know they're skedaddling still. But I cried out, 'Double canister, boys. A dose of the double grape for the Johnnies.' On they came, now thirty paces off, now twenty. At ten yards we poured it onto them like Nelson at Trafalgar. Do we have here this afternoon any visitors from Vermont? Yes? The tall lad in the fringed jacket? That's very apt. Rallied by my exhortations, the boys from the Vermont Twenty-second held their ground and fought like panthers. We kept the charging Rebs from overrunning the cannons. It was glorious to see. Yet lookee. These sad bones and rags and bits of rotting flesh are all that's left."

To the horror of the tourists, the creature was now fondling the shreds of uniforms and fragments of bones, cooing to them as if to an infant. Pressing scented handkerchiefs over their mouths and noses, gagging and retching, the people began to stumble back up the hillside, just as the doomed southern charge had done.

"Wait, wait, dear playgoers," cried the necrophiliac, reaching into his carpetbag and withdrawing a black stovepipe hat and a false beard on a string. "Tarry one moment more. You haven't heard my presidential address. 'Fourscore and—' Oh, Vermont boy. Where's my audience? Where have they gone? Come, then. Let us go down to the Slaughter Pen without them."

On their way Morgan's guide, now accoutered in the beard and top hat, said, "Can you keep a secret, boy? I'm writing a book. A very great book about this great battle."

Morgan, who was appalled by this hideous farce at the site of the bloodiest encounter of the war between North and South, the place where his beloved brother had last been seen, knew not what to say. "I assume that you've written many books" was all he could manage.

To which the madman replied, "Why no, sir. But what bearing, pray, does that have? Any fool can write a book. All it requires is time, and not so very much of that. My book on the battle will be an original history, for I shall write from real life, not from conning over other men's books or second-handed reports."

"Did you know a medical corpsman from Vermont named Kinneson?"

"Only slightly. He was a fine gentleman by all reports. But let us return to my book-in-progress, for I love best to talk of it. I was here to see it all and, like noble Fortinbras in the play, I'll go forth, or my book will, to tell it all. Are you familiar with the immortal bard's old *Prince of Denmark*?"

"I am."

"What do you think of it?"

"It goes on a great while. I would have done for the wicked uncle in Act the First."

"Aye, but then there would have been no play. Or a very short one. Do you recollect the moment where old Polonius meets his quietus?"

Before Morgan could reply, Steptoe drew a long gleaming bodkin from his blue tunic and, uttering his crazed ululation, leaped toward his intended victim. Morgan, who had recognized the child killer the moment he'd laid eyes on him, caught him off guard by taking two short quick steps directly toward him. Before Steptoe could plunge the bodkin into Morgan's neck he found himself impaled on the gypsy's dagger attached to Lady Justice. Morgan lifted the screaming player off the ground and ran with the rifle straight toward a blasted peach tree. He drove the dagger point, on which the demon squirmed like a fly on a pin, into the dead trunk of a tree that not two years ago had borne sweet fruit. He stood back to regard Steptoe, still alive and glaring at him.

"Who sent you?" Morgan said.

Nothing.

"Who sent you?" Morgan said again.

"Oh, you needn't fret, lad. They'll find the gal and the stone long afore you find them," Steptoe said. "And when they do, every last one of your thieving, nigger-loving, so-called stationmasters will die a death worse than mine!" As if to illustrate his point, Steptoe gave one last anguished, defiant outcry and died.

Morgan yanked on the gun stock, but the bayonet was embedded in the fire-blackened tree like Excalibur in the stone. He put his foot on Steptoe's chest and heaved back. As gravediggers came running down the hill, Morgan took hold of the stock and twirled Lady Justice around and around until it came free of the bayonet socket, leaving the player, still in the incarnation of the president, skewered on the tree.

Backing away into the jumbled boulders, Morgan jacked a shell into the chamber of his rifle barrel and swept the gun from side to side as the horrified workmen took in the scene.

"Don't follow me," he said.

As he turned and began to run toward the woods, he heard someone screaming, a scream louder than any Rebel yell. Morgan realized that it was his own voice.

SIX

GEBO

X

As he'd promised his uncle John, Morgan had written to his folks, informing them that he had found no trace of Pilgrim at Gettysburg and now believed that his brother might have been captured or perhaps had even headed south alone in order to avoid being taken up for desertion. He said that he would soon be behind enemy lines himself and that it might be many weeks before he could find means to post another letter.

A week later, it was raining again, at first just a spattering of big drops on Morgan's slouch hat and the steep path he was following, then cold, drenching sheets of water. The fever he thought he had left behind in Big Eva's steam hut in the Mountains of the Bark Eaters had flared up again, and as he walked southward he was scarcely certain what he actually saw and what he imagined. A huge crop of ripe orange field pumpkins came bobbing down the swollen brown current of a river under a long covered bridge. It was a pumpkin freshet, yet the season for pumpkins was three or four months away. As he slogged along a forlorn ridgetop in the northern foothills of the Blue Ridge he found that he had no notion what time of day it was. It could be midmorning, it could be early evening. Nor did he have any clear memory of the countryside he'd passed through for the last several hours, whether open fields, wooded terrain, or village streets.

He came to a town at the foot of the mountains designated on a signpost as Mason Or Dixon. Mason Or Dixon was a stately little village with several fine stone, red-brick, and ornate wooden homes. Yet the place seemed to be deserted. Ahead on the village green was a pump, but when Morgan tried the handle, a stream of white sand poured out of the spout.

On the south edge of the village a land tortoise was unhurriedly working its way across the road. Rather boxy in appearance, the tortoise was about as large as a dinner plate with tan-and-orange-chequered markings on the sides of its shell. It would make a good soup for his fever, Morgan thought. The tortoise stopped, extended its leathery neck, looked at Morgan with its calm dark eyes, and spoke. "My name is Pilgrim," it said. "I can tell you how this town got its name and where to look for my namesake, your brother. But not if you eat me."

"Tell your story," Morgan said.

In the voice of a seasoned raconteur, the reptile began its tale. "You must know, Morgan, that this town was settled by two brothers. Their names were Mason and Dixon Alexander. Both were attorneys and learned men. Do you see those two great houses facing each other across the street? Those were the original homes of the Alexanders. Mason lived in the Italianate house of orange sandstone on our right. Brother Dixon resided in the big white Greek Revival opposite. Very well, then. Time ran along as time will, and their law firm, Mason and Dixon Alexander, thrived. Then they quarreled."

"Over what?" Morgan said.

"Nomenclature."

Morgan stared at the talking tortoise.

"That's correct," it said. "Specifically, what to name the town, Mason or Dixon. They argued over the matter for more than forty years. During that time no one knew what to call the place, so they referred to it as Mason Or Dixon. Finally old man Mason Alexander, who was upward of ninety, walked up to his tottering brother and shot him down in the street to settle the dispute once and for all. That very evening Dixon's oldest boy, Dixon Junior, who was seventy-three, gunned down his uncle Mason. From there it was off to the races. It was pure war, Morgan, with one Alexander shooting or stabbing another one every few years on down through four generations. All over nomenclature. I shan't trouble you with the grim particulars. In time the clans shot each other out, and by then it wasn't safe for anyone else to live in this town either. Mason Or Dixon has stood empty these last ten years."

"Why didn't they compromise back before their feud began? Call the town Alexandria?"

"Why not indeed?"

"Couldn't the war between them have somehow been avoided?"

"One would have thought."

The fever was coming over Morgan again. He needed to find a cold brook or at least a pump that pumped water instead of sand. He needed to stop this charade, talking to a reptile in an abandoned town with an outlandish name. He said to the tortoise, "Is there a moral to your fable?"

"I don't know."

"You don't know much, do you, for such a talkative fella?"

"I know you should inquire for your brother from the pretty girl at the sign of *Gebo*," the tortoise said. "And I know I'd like a ripe red strawberry."

With that the animal continued across the street, disappearing in the Johnson grass outside the old Mason Alexander place. Morgan walked on toward the soaring front of the mountains. That night his fever broke, and the next morning he wondered if he had imagined the pumpkin freshet, the town of Mason Or Dixon, and the talking tortoise named Pilgrim, with his tantalizing hints about pretty girls and runic signs.

Morgan ascended into the mountains through folds and creases bright with blossoming rhododenrons and azaleas. At close range the metallic colors of the azaleas made his head spin. What was the point of all this riot of color? Since leaving Vermont he had seen nothing but devastation and misery. The splendors of spring in the Blue Ridge seemed a bitter and ironic mockery of all human endeavor, including this monumental nonsense of walking the world looking for someone who might well no longer be part of it. God could mock him all he wished—that seemed the way of creation. Morgan did not have to add his own scorn and self-loathing to God's torments by continuing to prosecute a fool's errand beyond the endurance of mind and body. He was free to turn around and go home at any time. Surely he had fulfilled his duty to Pilgrim at Gettysburg, where he had discovered exactly nothing. As for *Gebo,* designated on Jesse's stone with the symbol X and the strange drawing of the entrance of a cave, Morgan had no reason to believe that he could find the place, much less learn anything of his brother there. He resolved to continue his search to the height of land atop the Blue Ridge, and then, if he had not learned anything more of Pilgrim, he'd go not one step farther.

At the summit of the peak he was climbing he happened upon a seep trickling out from under a boulder. A gnarled beech tree grew in the humus on top of the rock, its exposed roots reaching down the sides of the boulder to the water. He cleared away last year's pointed beech leaves, and the spring quickly filled the small cavity at the foot of the rock. He dipped up a cupful of icy water in the carved cedar drinking cup Auguste Choteau had given him. The tea-colored water tasted faintly of beechnuts and was so cold it made his forehead ache. While he waited for the scooped-out depression to fill again, he noticed where black bears had rooted in the leaves of the forest floor for last year's beech mast. Here in the mountains Morgan felt something like his old self for the first time since that twilit afternoon when he had followed the moose down the far side of his mountain at home and his troubles had begun.

The mountains stretching off to the south were as azure as their name. Vermont mountains, rarely blue, were never this shade. The closest they came was on hazy fall afternoons when they were tinted the slate blue of Morgan's eyes. Just down the slope the seep gathered itself into a tiny rill, which vanished in a bright palette of azaleas. Far below, ten miles and more, off at the western foot of the range, Morgan could see the glint of a winding river, which he judged to be the Shenandoah.

Then he heard the dogs. They were still some miles away, coming up from the south, the way he was headed. He checked his rifle to make sure it was in good order and started along the spine of the mountains. He walked in the seep toward the barking dogs, well aware that he was still heading south, not north, and no more able to resist whatever pull in his heart made him do so than he could have resisted gravity itself. So much for reason and resolve, he thought. Let the gods laugh at him. His feet had a will of their own.

He had not proceeded far when he heard a jingling like sleigh bells coming his way. He stepped behind a large tree of a kind that didn't grow in Kingdom County and waited to see what would happen.

A figure was coming toward him up the mountain. It was a girl, a willowy slip of a girl with long slim legs the rich color of the inside of a split cherry log. She was running in quick, lithe strides, the bells on a collar around her neck jingling as she loped along. Twice Morgan saw her look over her shoulder in the direction of the baying hounds. She wore a shortish dress as yellow as a buttercup, and her shoulder-length hair glinted chestnut in the sun. She looked to be about his age. She entered the azalea thicket, and yes, she was pretty—more than pretty, lovely against the pink, deep gold, molten orange, and rich salmon of the blossoms. Then, like the rill Morgan was following, she vanished.

The thicket was as dense as a wild rose brake. At close range the colors not only made Morgan slightly dizzy, they seemed to produce a harsh coppery taste in his mouth. He had to get down on his hands and knees and crawl to follow the rill through the flowering bushes, which ripped at him like claws. He hoped he wouldn't meet a bear with cubs to protect; in such close quarters she would tear a man limb from limb. In the midst of the thicket of color he felt a powerful draft of dank air. It was like a *glace du bois* at home, a cold pocket in the woods, usually under a stand of gloomy hemlocks beside a brook, often where something bad had once happened, a massacre or a blood killing. Just ahead, the little stream passed out of sight under an overhanging ledge of limestone. A steady breath of frigid air was issuing from the fissure where the brook had disappeared. Morgan realized that he had found a sinkhole, a natural chimney in the ground.

Vermont had few caves. The granite bedrock was too hard for the water to hollow out—stubborn and resistant like Vermonters themselves, Professor Agassiz had joshed Pilgrim. As Morgan followed the rill down into the chimney on his hands and backside, the cave smelled cold, like his father's icehouse at home. "Hello," he called out. "My name is Morgan Kinneson from Kingdom County, Vermont. I mean you no harm. Will you answer?"

"Hello, hello, hello," his voice echoed. "Will you answer, answer, answer?" As he leaned forward to listen for a response, he lost his purchase on the rubble. The stones rolled out from under him, and Morgan bounced down into the darkness below.

"Hoo, boy! What kind of soldier are you, Morgan Kinneson from King County? Can't even stay upright down a little hill?"

In the flickering torchlight the girl with chestnut hair was grinning down at him. She seemed highly amused by his mishap. The bell collar around her neck jingled softly when she bent over to check his eyes.

"My guns!"

"Don't worry, your guns are fine. You fetched yourself a knock on the head, child."

The girl gave him a drink of water out of a tin cup, holding his throbbing head while he drank. He was going to have a good knot on the back of his head.

"You aren't supposed to be down here, Morgan Kinneson from

King County. Only black folks are supposed to know about the Mind of God."

Morgan drank a little more water. "What's your name?"

"Old John Brown, ask me again I'll knock you down. Except you're down to start off with. Slidell is my name. Slidell Collateral Dinwiddie, on account of my grandmammy was from Slidell, Louisiana."

"I know who you are, Slidell. I read about you in a newspaper."

"Go long!"

"It's true, I did. In a notice offering five hundred dollars for your return to Tennessee. Is your name really Slidell? I never knew anyone named Slidell. That's a good name."

"It's a foolish name. Naming a fine young gal after a town, of all things. How would you like be named King County? Have to say, 'My name is King County, from King County, Vermont.' My second name is worse yet. Collateral. Collateral brought up the rear of the line when names got parceled out."

"What did you call this cave? The Mind of God?"

"You ask a heap of questions, Morgan Kinneson. Didn't your mama teach you it was rude to ask so many questions?"

The girl looked at him goodnaturedly. "Here," she said, "sit up. Taste Slidell's fish. Catsfish, only down in this cave they're as white as cotton and blind as bats. This flying squirrel? I have a sling made from a boot cord, see? See this little pouch? I put a stone in here, smooth and round from the brook, twirl it round my head like little David and look out, Mr. Flying Squirrel. Fly plumb into Slidell's fry pan. Now. This is the hind leg off a she-possum, boy. She-possom is the best eating there is. Fried up in her own nice grease, she-possom is a right smart of eating."

"What's this?" Morgan said. "Chicken?"

"Chicken? Wherever would Slidell find a chicken down this forlorn hole in the ground? That's rattling snake, child. Makes you crafty and cunning like the old serpent."

He took a bite of the snake meat. It was all right. Slidell smelled like the evergreens on the mountain at home after a fresh spring rain. Like the sweet ferns he put in his fish basket to keep his trout fresh.

Morgan examined Lady Justice. The butt of the stock was scratched a little, but otherwise it seemed undamaged. He stood up too fast and his head felt as though it might explode like Joseph Findletter's orange pumpkin. Standing, he was surprised to see how tall the girl was, only two or three inches shorter than him, and he believed that he had grown a good inch and maybe more since leaving home.

"I need to get on, Slidell."

Slidell shook her head. "Didn't you hear those dogs, boy? We need to get deeper into the cavern before they get here."

They made their way along a ledge above the stream, Slidell's pine-knot torch illuminating many a fantastical pattern on the damp walls of the passageway. They emerged into a vast chamber, where she lit other torches affixed to the walls. He was amazed by the dimensions of the underground gallery. Ten of his father's hay barns would have fit inside it with room to spare.

"Behold, child," Slidell said in a hushed voice. "The Mind of God. *Gebo*. Some six thousand years ago, when old God was fixing to make the stars and the sea and all things that creep on the earth and fly above it, He came here first and tried out His hand. See? He made an *image* of everything. This big chamber is His synagogue.

That block of stone there? Shaped like a chest? That's the Ark of the Covenant. No! Don't you touch it. Fry you right up like a catsfish."

In the torchlight the Ark of the Covenant was tinted all the rich colors of the earth—tan, ferrous red, ocher, amber. On its side was inscribed the symbol X. *Gebo.* Slidell lifted her torch over her head. "Speaking of fish," she said, "look here."

On the cave wall above them was an orange-colored stain shaped like a primitive fish. "First fish," Slidell said. "All the other fish were patterned after him."

"What kind of fish is it?" Morgan asked.

"God's Fish," Slidell said solemnly.

"What's that?" Morgan pointed at a tall stalagmite, white as snow and resembling a woman looking back over her shoulder at them.

"Lot's Wife," Slidell said. "My granddaddy found this old cave, him, fifty years ago. Named it *Gebo,* the Mind of God. Named the Ark, God's Fish, Lot's Wife too, my granddaddy did."

Beyond Lot's Wife the stream emptied into a small lake. A shelf of rock hung out over the water forming a low ceiling. Below the surface of the lake lay a wondrous city of soaring stone towers and parapets, battlements, fortifications, bejeweled avenues, cathedral spires hundreds of feet tall and colored ruby red, cobalt blue, gold, and emerald. Slidell laughed and pointed at the stone ceiling. In the torchlight Morgan saw that the stately underwater city was the reflection of the myriad multicolored stalactites hanging from the ceiling.

"Liberty Bell there ahead. See him?"

Beside the lake sat a rock as large as the Kingdom Mountain church belfry, shaped like a flanged bell with one side collapsed. "That's the crack in the bell. I imagine this bell rang so hard the day old Father Abraham freed us it split right down the side. Only bells

Slidell Collateral Dinwiddie heard at the time, the bells on this slave collar."

"What's a slave collar, Slidell?"

"Why, boy, a slave collar jingles so if the slave runs away the slave catchers can hear her and fetch her back. I ran away three times before, and after the third time master collared me. I swore a great oath never to take off this collar for the rest of my life. Never forget for one minute what being free means."

Morgan was examining the Liberty Bell. Scratched into its side, near the long crack, was what looked like a rune, but not one that he recalled from Jesse's stone or from the great Balancing Boulder: ᛑ.

He traced the symbol with his forefinger. "What does this mean, Slidell?"

"Means you ask too many questions, boy."

He looked at her.

"Means they're coming, is what it means. Now you come along. Hurry."

They coming. Jesse, too, had said *They coming.* Who was coming? Morgan wanted to ask, but Slidell was suspicious enough of him already.

They ventured deeper into the cavern. If Slidell's torch went out, Morgan figured they could retrace their steps by following the stream, now tumbling over a natural stone stairway. They climbed down the graduated falls. Slidell watched closely to see if he needed help, but he seemed recovered from his fall. "Look there, boy. Where the water drops over those columns. Hear the music? Like wind in a cypress tree at night? I call that God's Pipe Organ. Pretty, too."

Slidell pointed. "Look over yonder. Where the stream narrows down and the walls close in tight. See old Golia?"

They were wading knee-deep through a narrow defile behind God's Pipe Organ, the walls of the cave touching Morgan's shoulders so that he had to edge forward sideways. Depending from the lofty ceiling just ahead was a column in the form of a gigantic warrior. "Look, Morgan Kinneson. There's Golia's breastplate. See? There's his great throwing spear."

The stream flowed through Goliath's legs, spread wide like those of the Colossus at Rhodes in Morgan's illustrated *Wonders of the Ancient World* at home. Goliath hung over them from the spiked top of his helmet. Ever so cautiously they proceeded under him and came out on yet another underground lake. They sat on a bar of gravel washed down over the ages and looked back up at the looming giant. While they rested, Morgan told Slidell some of his story. He told her about his long walk south in search of his brother. He described his encounter with Sabbati Zebi and the Caliph of Baghdad, recounted his adventures on the Great Western Canal, how he'd met Big Eva and the president and Birdcall.

"How old was this vile young wretch?" Slidell demanded. "This Birdcall?"

Morgan suspected that she was jealous of the girl. "Oh, about three and twenty and very beautiful."

"I misdoubt she was either. About fourteen and skinny as a post and randy as a bearded billy goat. Probably got some terrible pox from her." She pretended to shudder.

"She was a little girl," Morgan said. "I left her with a woman who lived in a tree."

"You never! Now Slidell's heard it all."

The cave fugitives bent their dark and light heads together in the torchlight as Slidell told him about the remote and mysterious

River of Grace, flowing into the Tennessee, where she and her little brother, Solomon Dinwiddie, had been raised on Grace Plantation, and about her escape route up through the mountains to Virginia and *Gebo,* the Mind of God. Morgan related how he had skirmished with Steptoe and Prophet and received his first battle wound. He set Lady Justice on his lap pointed away from Slidell and told her how, under the tutelage of Joseph Findletter, he had fashioned the rifle from his grandfather's old musket and a few simple farm tools. How he and Joseph had made the minié bullets and formed them by dropping hot lead slaked with silver off the soaring stone bridge called Jacob's Ladder and then felt for them with his toes in the green pool far below with Gretel. He told her about Jesse Moses without mentioning the old slave's name, and how he had laid an ambuscade for Ludi and later, at Gettysburg, had impaled Steptoe on the blasted peach tree. Finally he told her how, with the Caliph's help, he had destroyed the evil Doctor Surgeon.

"A very pretty story," Slidell said angrily when Morgan finished his tale. "Breaking all ten commandments, killing people right and left, poking all the helpless young gals. You'll have a powerful lot of explaining to do to Saint Peter, Yankee boy. Setting elephants on folks. Walking the land ravishing babies on the canal and school-teaching gals in black bonnets. King David all over again, off to the races with long-legged Bathshe."

"Slidell, I didn't ravish anyone. Listen. I want to tell you some-thing. Something important. When you get to Canada, go straight to Montreal and look up Auguste Choteau. Tell him Morgan Kin-neson sent you. He'll help you. You should leave immediately."

Slidell frowned as if torn between two opposing thoughts. She got out a mouth harp and played "St. Anne's Reel," "The Church at

Bayou Teche," "Evangeline's Waltz." She played "The Battle Hymn of the Republic," which she'd heard as she came north on the Path of the Water Gourd. God's Pipe Organ gave back the melodies like ten thousand lyres and tabors and clavichords, echoing and reechoing through the massive galleries of the cavern long after Slidell had stopped playing. The lovely notes rising and falling mesmerized the two explorers. Suddenly Slidell seized Morgan's arm. As the echoing music subsided, he heard again the baying of dogs.

Howling with bloodlust, a brace of tracking hounds was swimming through the narrow passageway under the spread legs of Goliath. Slidell leaped up, produced her sling, cradled a stone in the rawhide pocket, twirled it around her head, and sent it rocketing straight to the temple of the lead hound. Morgan jacked a shell into the chamber of his rifle and fired, shattering the skull of the second dog, the roaring shot filling the chamber just as the two slave catchers in frock coats and tall hats and carrying torches appeared directly under Goliath. Morgan fired again, this time at the point where the stone giant's helmet was attached to the ceiling. The gigantic stalactite collapsed. Where the passageway had been, a wall of stone now rose forty feet from the floor of the cave to the roof.

JUDGING BY HIS HUNGER, Morgan thought they had been wandering downstream, deeper into the cavern, for several hours. Slidell's pine knots were gone, her supply of candles dwindling fast. In places the passageway was almost too narrow to admit them. Elsewhere the cave opened into atriums whose soaring height could only be guessed at. Often several corridors led out of these vast chambers. Morgan and Slidell cleaved to the course of the stream.

Might it emerge at the foot of the mountains? Or did some cavern streams merely empty into subterranean aquifers? All Morgan was sure of was that they must keep going to find out, since they could no longer return to the surface the way they had come.

The stream seemed to stay about the same size, six or eight feet wide, two or three feet deep. Somehow the current was still seeping through under the rubble from the cave-in. If they came to a tributary stream, perhaps they could trace it back to the surface. But they found no tributary.

When he studied a mountain he wished to climb, Morgan could almost always find the quickest way to the top. Hearing a bird in the woods, even the call of a great horned owl or the drumming of a cock partridge on a log, which seemed to come from all four points of the compass at once, he could walk directly to that bird. He could tell at a glance where the largest trout in a brook lay. He knew north by instinct on the darkest night of the year. Now, lost in the heart of a limestone cavern deep beneath the Dominion of Virginia, he felt helpless.

"What you studying on, boy?"

"You. You surely are pretty, Slidell. You're as pretty as a speckled pup."

"How flattering. Slidell puts him in mind of a smelly old dog."

Morgan smiled. She was acting nonchalant about their situation. She was being brave, but he knew that she was as terrified as he was.

"Listen, Slidell. We're going to get out of here. I promise you. Let's rest a little now. Then we'll make a big push. I know that this stream comes out at the foot of the mountain. It probably runs right into the river."

"What if I drift off to sleep? You promise not to leave Slidell?"

"I'd never leave you, Slidell."

Thinking of Jesse Moses, deserted in the sugar camp with Ludi Too and Doctor Surgeon nearby.

"Morgan? Will you hold me?"

"I will," he said, and for a time, Morgan could not tell how long, they slept in each other's arms. When they woke Slidell lighted her last candle.

"One hour," she said.

They moved along a shelf beside the stream, which split in two around a rock shaped like a lion. "God's House Cat," Slidell said. The stream was moving faster, the floor of the cavern declining sharply. They could hear the murmur of falling water ahead. Again the passageway narrowed. Now they were wading in icy running water up to their waists. Slidell led the way, bent over, her candle flame brushing the ceiling. "Company halt!" she cried.

Morgan ducked through the spume and started down the pitted wall behind the falls with the hot lighted candle in his teeth. It threw hideous shapes and every mad configuration on the perpendicular wall, illuminating paintings of cave bears, big-toothed tigers, men in animal skins. At the bottom his feet touched slick clay. He stood marveling at the images on the walls. Men hunting an elk, others spearing buffalo, still others sitting by a fire. He understood that he had come to a place that had been sacred to some long-ago people close in kinship to those who had carved the whale and ice bear and runes on the Balancing Rock on the mountaintop at home. He shouted up for Slidell to join him. As she descended, he caught her in one arm and was overcome again by her fragrance of wood smoke and woods on the first warm spring day, pine scent and wild mint and apple blossoms after a long Vermont winter.

Hand in hand, they walked around the chamber behind the falls as if viewing an exhibition of pictures in a gallery. The men and women in the paintings had long hair. In one tableau a young couple sat facing each other joined hand to hand like Slidell and Morgan, as if in matrimonial union, he wearing a set of antlers, she a wreath of laurel. But the largest tableau showed men at war, some hurling spears at one another. One man was about to crush the head of an enemy with a raised boulder. Another was pulling out the guts of a fallen victim and devouring them warm from the body cavity. One of the painted men was swinging an infant by the foot and dashing out its brains against a rock. One was in the act of raping a girl. And looming over the battle scene, many times the size of the contending figures, was a deity with the body of a man, the tail of a serpent, and the head of an eagle.

"Judas Iscaria!" Slidell shouted. But Morgan merely shook his head. The prophet of yore had been right. Be it 1864 or ten thousand years ago, there was nothing, nothing at all, new under the sun.

They made their way out of the cave within the cave and past the waterfall to the edge of another lake. The water was several feet deep and a transparent green in the low candlelight. On the white sand bottom Morgan saw the outline of a sunken canoe. It was a dugout, perfectly preserved, and reclining on its floor was the petrified skeleton of a man. Somehow Morgan was certain that this was the painter who had created the tableau on the walls of the chamber behind the falls. The artist had been left here as a sacrifice or perhaps had even taken his own life because he could not bear to leave the scene of his great creation.

· · ·

"I READ THIS BOOK back home at Grace Plantatia," Slidell said as they drifted on the lake in the dugout, waiting for some slight current to deliver them from the cave, if any deliverance there might be from such a place. At first Slidell had refused to get into the dugout because she feared the skeleton. Morgan had taken the boatman's remains, with the stub of their last candle for light, into the hidden gallery of pictures.

"You mean the Bible?"

"No, this book was called *Uncle Tom's Cabin*. Old Master A.D. would flay us alive if he ever caught us reading it. I hated it."

"I've read it. My whole family has read it. Is it not then an accurate protrayal?"

"No. It should show old Simon Legree sloping into the quarters at Grace, what A.D. called the breeding barn, poking his vile old hog into Miss Lisa Harris, breeding more slaves. You told me your story, boy, a little while ago. Now I'll tell you mine. Down Grace, down the great state of Tennessee, master didn't just study raising cotton. No. He raised slaves. Slidell was lucky. A.D. made me his housegirl. Teach his white children to say please, sir, and thank you, ma'am. Recite their abc's and wipe their lily-white asses. Where you think Slidell got her middle name? Collateral?"

"I don't know. Where?"

"Up until I was five year old I didn't have a middle name. That year A.D. had himself a bad season. First came the old weevil, creeping and creeping into the cotton. Next you know, along down the river rolled a big flood. In case we didn't have tribulation enough already, in waltzed sickness. Typhus got into the quarters and swept off half the people. So old master took out a loan with a slave buyer up north and put little Slidell up for collateral. 'Slidell,' he said, 'fetch me the family Bible where I recorded your name.' In between my two names, on the page marked 'Bondsmen and Bondswomen,' he wrote the word *Collateral*."

"You don't have to use that name ever again, Slidell."

"Don't have to, but I intend to. Same as I intend to leave on the slave collar. Also, I'm insured."

"Insured?"

"That's right. For two thousand dollars. Old Dinwiddie that we called A.D. insured me for two thousand spondaloons. He insured my granddaddy and my brother Little Prince Solomon too. Granddaddy kept Dinwiddie's accounts and did all the bookwork for Grace Plantatia. He was insured for three thousand dollars. Little Prince Sol was insured for a thousand dollars. Granddaddy was already training him to keep the books on account of Sol being a great prodigy. Reading the Bible at two, multiplying great sums in his head at three. Reciting 'Curious Little-Known Facts' from the *Memphis Gazette* word for word. The last time I ran off before this time, I brought Sol with me. Dinwiddie sent old driver Swag after us with the dogs, and we never got ten miles. That's when Dinwiddie fitted me out with my nice collar. Also branded Prince Solomon's buttocks."

"Slidell, wait. What do you mean? Your master branded your brother? Like a cow or a horse?"

"Yes, he did. This was right after our mama died of the black-blood cholera. He wouldn't have dared do any such thing if mama was still alive. A.D. said he branded Sol to identify him in case he ran again. I know better. He branded that little boy's backside from pure natural meanness. Worse yet, he made my granddaddy do the branding. He told granddaddy that if he didn't burn that little boy with the iron he'd hang up Sol and Slidell too in a bamboo cage and starve us to death just the way he had other runaways. That's how cruel he was."

Slidell paused. The dugout seemed to be turning a little, as if it had found some slight current. Morgan could sense the girl go tense. She too knew that they were moving, however slowly.

Still Slidell hesitated as, ever so slowly, the dugout drifted out of the chamber. At last she said, "My granddaddy didn't have any choice, Morgan. He knew Dinwiddie meant business. He'd starved many a captured runaway in that bamboo cage. Granddaddy had to put that sizzling iron on that little child. Then Dinwiddie hung Sol up in that cage anyway, said he was going to keep him there for a month on bread and water. My granddaddy told me to collect my possibles and hide them, because as soon as we could figure a way to get Sol out of the cage, we would all three run together. In the meantime granddaddy told me to go about my business as usual. So I set about to whitewash the inside of our little crib-cabin—that's what we always do after the black-blood cholera comes through. It was evening time. Sol was up in the cage in the cypress tree by the river. Granddaddy was working in his little kitchen garden the next cabin down. I was all alone—that's what I thought. I lighted the candle on the table and then in staggered Dinwiddie, drunk as old Lot. He gave the door a slam and said, 'Slidell, it's time you started earning your keep around here. Put down that bucket of whitewash and shuck off that smock and get over on that mattress, gal. I'm going to make a woman of you.'"

"Good God, Slidell. What did you do?"

"Gave out a scream like a swamp panther, is what I did. Dinwiddie grabbed me by the neck and commenced to drag me toward the cornshuck mattress. That's when my granddaddy came busting through the door. He knew right off what was happening. He picked up that big slopping bucket of lime whitewash and flung it in Dinwiddie's face. Then he took my hand and we ran. Past the kitchen garden, past the mock orange hedge all sweet in the dewy dusk, through Dinwiddie's prize rose beds and up along the River Grace. We ran deep into the Moccasin Swamp to the secret gathering place where the slaves go to worship on Sunday. Granddaddy told me to hide out there while he led Dinwiddie's slave catchers on a merry chase. Then in a few days I could break out Sol, and we'd all meet up here in *Gebo*."

Slidell looked at Morgan for a long moment. Then she appeared to make a decision. With her fingernail she drew a symbol on the clay floor of the cavern. "Granddaddy's sign," she said. "*Wunjo*. Means freedom. Granddaddy told me to look for it on the Liberty Bell. Meant Little Sol and I should wait here in the cave, he was nearby."

Morgan studied the sign Slidell had drawn, *Wunjo*. He frowned. The sign on the Liberty Bell had been different. Beside *Wunjo*, he scratched the symbol from the bell: ⌡.

Slidell took a deep breath. "*Wunjo* reversed." She hesitated, then said, "Means danger."

Morgan started to speak, but she cut him off and resumed her story. "Back in that swamp, granddaddy took off and I stayed on. Moccasin Swamp, boy. Where I learned to eat snake and be grateful for it. I lived in there off serpents and whatever other creatures I could kill with my sling and what little my cousin Mercy could bring out to me at night, and all the while I tried to think of a way to get Sol down out of that tree. But Mercy told me Dinwiddie had set a guard over him. He was using Sol as bait, you see. Bait to catch Slidell. So I figured I'd just have to come on ahead alone. I got here the day before yesterday and found that danger sign on the side of the bell. I knew they were chasing granddaddy. He left that warning so I'd keep on going clear through to Canada, not wait for him. Well, Morgan, I was plumb tuckered out after traveling all the way from Tennessee. So I decided to rest here for a couple of days, then press on this very night. Figured I was too smart to get caught—but this morning I very nearly did. I was out chasing a rabbit through the bushes and I came *this* close to running right onto those dogs."

The dugout was moving faster now, but Morgan was scarcely aware of their progress. "Slidell," he said, "tell me more about your granddaddy."

She thought for a moment. "Well, besides managing Dinwiddie's plantation, granddaddy is a carving man. Oh, yes. He is a great hand to carve about anything. Granddaddy can whittle out a baby dolly from a stick of yellow pine that looks more real than a real child. Something else, too. What old master didn't know, for years and years my granddaddy helped slaves run north. Not just Dinwiddie's slaves, either, but hundreds of others. That's why he didn't run sooner himself. He was helping the others. Every time Dinwiddie sent granddaddy north on plantatia business? Granddaddy was setting up more stations, finding more conductors."

Morgan drew in a sharp breath. "What was—what is your grandfather's name, Slidell?"

"His name? His name Jesse. Only the people called him—look out, boy! Sit still, you'll turn us right out in the drink. As I was saying, my granddaddy went by the name of Jesse Moses. Because he helped folks get to the Promised Land."

. . .

JESSE MOSES HANGING on the rowanberry tree. Ludi Too gut-shot in the wintery bog. Dinwiddie blinded in the slave cabin on his great estate. Images tumbled through Morgan's head. Big Eva telling him that *Nauthiz,* his rune, meant that everything was more difficult than he thought and everything was connected. Mercy Johnson, refusing to tell King George the name of her runaway girl cousin. Now Morgan knew who that cousin was.

Slidell's last candle flared and guttered out. The ancient boat drifted on through what seemed to be another narrow corridor. Morgan lifted his hand. The ceiling of the cave was just over his head. "Duck," he said. Then, "Slidell. He got in here somehow. The cave painter. He surely didn't come down over those falls up-stream in this boat. If he got in, we can get out."

Later they came to a lake where the current was imperceptible at first, but eventually it found them and nudged them forward. Morgan had not gathered the courage to inform Slidell about her grandfather's terrible fate in the wintery woods of Vermont. He told himself that she needed to concentrate on reaching Canada. He told himself that the news would be a distraction that would only further endanger her. He knew he was lying, that he simply did not have the courage to disclose to her what had happened to Jesse and his own part in it.

"What's that?" Slidell said.

"Wind," Morgan said. "No. Moving water."

Ahead was a dim light. The underground stream was rushing toward it. The noise of running water grew louder. Morgan was momentarily overcome by the sweet scent of fresh air and foliage, a thousand mingled green fragrances, as they approached another falls.

"Jump, Slidell," he shouted, grabbing her hand. The dugout capsized and shot over the lip of the falls. Morgan scrambled out of the water onto a rock shelf and pulled Slidell out after him. Not ten feet below them, running blue in the twilight, was the Shenandoah.

THAT NIGHT THEY SWAM TOGETHER in a deep pool in the river, and then Morgan built a fire on the sand and Slidell asked him to hold her again, and she was warm in his arms and as fragrant as pine and river water and autumn on Kingdom Mountain. For a time they slept. When they woke they kissed, and Slidell's bells tinkled gently. Morgan said her entire name and she his, and he built the fire back up from its faint coals because he wanted to see her as she was. She was beautiful. Morgan felt wholly alive again for the first time since discovering Jesse dead in the tree. Then, for an interval hard to measure except for the time it took the fire to die down again, they loved each other beside the river deep in the heart of the Blue Ridge, and the bells inside Slidell's slave collar rang out under and over and beside Morgan like a whole carillon, and he believed there could yet be something better to live for than he had heretofore imagined. Slidell was both gentle and wild, soft and firm, quiet and joyous, slow and fast, bold and shy, part of him and he of her yet fully herself, and her bells rang like steeple bells, on into the night.

At dawn they played in the river again. Slidell reached in under a cut bank and pulled out a thrashing catfish as long as her arm. To Morgan's amusement, she made him look away while she put her yellow dress back on. Over their fish breakfast she said, "Well, Mor-

gan Kinneson, I imagine God will smite us right down for breaking
His commandment."

"I doubt it," Morgan said, thinking that what he truly doubted
was God's existence. "I killed those two slave catchers, if in fact I
did kill them, in self-defense."

"That's not the commandment I'm talking about. I'm talking
about 'Thou shalt not commit adultery.'"

Morgan grinned. "What did you do it for, then?"

He was about to suggest that they might as well be smitten for
two such transgressions as one, when she said to him, "Morgan
Kinneson from King County, you listen to me now. Back in *Gebo*?
The Mind of God? I made myself two promises. Promise number
one was, I wasn't going to die without."

"Without what, Slidell?"

"Without what you just asked about."

"But we got out of the cave. You aren't going to die. You'll be
north of slave territory in two days. Three at most."

She shook her head. "No, sir."

"No, sir?"

"No, sir. Because there's something else. Something I didn't tell
you. When I was hiding out up in the Moccasin Swamp, my cousin,
Mercy Johnson, decided to run, too. Mercy and I talked about running together, but I was still hoping to free Little Sol from that cage
and bring him north with me. So I told her to go on ahead, and Sol
and I would catch up. Just before she fled, Mercy delivered me two
pieces of news. One good, one very bad. The good news, old driver
Swag, the slave killer hunting Jesse, had been taken up by bluebellies and sent north to be hanged. The bad news was that Dinwiddie
suspected Little Sol knew where Jesse and I were headed. So he had

Sol lowered down to the ground in that bamboo cage and told him to peach on Jess and me or he'd cut off Sol's left ring finger with the great tin shears. Little Sol, he refused, so old A.D. snipped off Sol's left ring finger. And still that good little boy refused to deliver Slidell and Jess over to that evil man. So Dinwiddie took up the tin shears again, and he snipped off Sol's right ring finger."

Slidell was weeping now, but when Morgan started to speak, to reach out to console her, she held up her hand and shook her head again and said, through her sobs, "That second promise I made to myself in the cave? I promised that if I ever got out alive, I'd go straight back to Grace, and one way or another I'd steal Sol and bring him north with me. I'm going south, Morgan. I'd be obliged if I could travel with you for a piece longer."

SEVEN

KANO

‹

Morgan had much to consider as he and Slidell headed south through the mountains. He had not yet shown her Jesse's rune stone because he did not know how to tell her that her grandfather was dead and he was responsible. As for Arthur Dinwiddie, the plantation owner who had tried to rape Slidell, Morgan had no doubt that this was Anno Domini, the blind man in the hideous green goggles who, after Slidell had escaped, had gone north and broken out the condemned killers from Elmira and sent them on their murderous rampage to acquire the stone and capture Slidell. But where were the two remaining escapees? They might be lying in wait for him around any bend, and if so, Morgan knew that they would kill Slidell as readily as they'd kill him.

Dilemma compounded dilemma. Morgan's duty was to find Pilgrim. Yet something made him wonder whether, by going first to

Grace Plantation and helping Slidell rescue Little Prince Solomon, he might learn more of his brother. Might there be a connection between Pilgrim and Jesse? Pilgrim had been a conductor. Could he have followed the same route south, from station to station, that Jesse had taken north?

On the pretext of stepping into the dense rhododendrons beside the path to relieve himself, Morgan took out the stone and studied it. Moving his forefinger down the drawings etched into the smooth surface from one rune to the next he noted that, not far to the southeast of the Mind of God, the rune ⟨ was accompanied by the likeness of a pillared manse. Perhaps the stationmaster there could tell him something about Pilgrim.

So it came to pass that he and Slidell walked on, trending southeast now, and as they proceeded Slidell confided to Morgan that at times her faith in God was all she had to rely on. Morgan, for his part, understood for the first time in his life something of the power of the religion of his forefathers. Like Slidell, they had believed in God. And he, operating on a kind of faith, believed in his brother and in his own ability to find him. In both instances that faith came less from outward revealed signs than from within. How many times had old Mahitabel told him that it was an evil generation of men who looked for a sign to bolster their belief? Perhaps she'd been right.

He wondered what his hero John Brown would do in his place. Brown had been a man of enormous faith. Probably he would keep right on walking clear to the end of the earth, that fanatical old man whose eyes could drill a hole straight through you to your soul. Brown would find Pilgrim and then track down Arthur Dinwiddie, and when he did, by God, mercy would be in short supply.

Morgan was now walking barefooted, as Slidell was. There was little difference in appearance between them and the mountain people they met, who went mainly barefooted and wore plain homespun. Morgan had read that most of the mountaineers of the Blue Ridge neither owned slaves nor sided with either faction in the war. The men and some of the women carried weapons and wore slouch hats to keep off the sun and rain. A pillared mansion? People looked at him blankly, and hurried onward. All but one poor fellow with a head as big as a blue squash. "They," he said, pointing eastward at half a dozen serried ridges. "Yonder."

"Where yonder?" Morgan said.

"They," the fellow said. He shook his big head and gave an exasperated sigh. Then he took Morgan by his sleeve and Slidell by hers and led them at a shambling lope over ridge and through hollow and dale until, in the early evening, they came to a hill on which was perched a very large, very dilapidated house with a pillared portico.

"*They,*" the squash head said yet again, pointing up at the big house. "They's Little Mountain." Then he whirled around and headed back to whatever bourn he had come from, leaving Morgan and Slidell alone on the hill.

At one time the columned house on Little Mountain had been a showplace. Now it was fast sinking into ruin, overrun with creeping vines, the roof slates falling off, the forlorn brick walkways grown up to weeds. The low stone stables behind the house had started to crumble. The pillars in front were cracked, and the door hung by a single hinge, revealing a high-ceiled entry hall open to the weather. Morgan and Slidell walked around the side of the house and stood behind a large oak to survey the place more closely.

In an overgrown garden sat a small cabin, a dispiriting single-room affair, not even as large as the sugar camp at home where Morgan had abandoned Jesse. Over the door a slanted board bore the faded words NAIL FACTORY and the symbol ❨. In the dooryard an old black man with a yellowish tinge to his skin sat in a home-made hickory rocker with hickory withes for its arms and back. The man looked to be tall and thin and had a tonsure of graying reddish hair. He wore a shabby suit of clothes that had once been elegant, a blue coat with shining buttons and a worn velvet collar over a high, faded stock. His ruffled shirt had long ago yellowed to the same jaundiced hue as his skin. His eyes, Morgan noted, were milky blue, and he guessed that the man was blind. In one hand he held a half-made shoe. Beside the rocker was a cobbler's bench and a last with the shoe's mate upside down on it.

An elderly black woman, darker than the blind man, was tending a fire under a kettle swinging from a tripod in an open-sided summer kitchen separated from the cabin by a dogtrot passageway. Off the summer kitchen a crooked chimney tilted away from the cabin. A homemade ladder leaned against the wall nearby.

"Ghosts," Slidell whispered. "From the old times. Run!"

Morgan whispered back, "They're not ghosts. Listen."

"I have been wondering lately, my love," the shoemaker was saying in the cultivated tones of an educated man. "I have been pondering over who will be remembered as the greater president. Father Abraham or my own father."

The woman looked up from her cooking fire. "Father Abra," she said, and returned to her fire.

"I think you are right in that, dearest," the cobbler said. "For Father Abraham freed us all, while my good father freed none of us. Not even my mother, whom he loved dearly."

"Why not, us gots to wonder?" the woman said. "He a enlighten man, weren't he?"

"Yes, very enlightened. But he was frail like the rest of mankind. He needed his fields tilled, his tobacco picked, his bed warmed by comely Sal, his nails made and sold by the keg to buy fine books. My father was a neat hand to fashion a nail, you know. And he built his own shoes at this very last. The one useful thing he taught me was how to make a serviceable pair of shoes. And a good tight-clinching nail."

"You, Tom," the woman said, stirring her comestibles. "Supper 'bout on." Morgan felt his mouth watering.

"Speaking of supper, you should have beheld some of my father's collations," the cobbler said. "Great banquets with monogrammed silverware and French china and leaded crystal. At his table dined ambassadors and plenipotentiaries. He sent a stuffed moose to the French court to impress them with our American fauna. He couldn't be expected to perform such acts of largesse and still free his people. Not even those related to him. He needed their labor, you see. Now it's all come to this."

The shoemaker gestured at the ruined mansion, the overrun orchards and gardens. When the woman poked the fire, sparks flew out of the crooked mud-and-straw chimney, flaring orange in the summer twilight settling over Little Mountain. In the outside fireplace a log collapsed, sending up an eruption of sparks. Instantly the entire chimney took fire. The wind blew sparks onto the roof of the cabin and back toward the tree where Morgan and Slidell were hiding. The sparks gusted and swirled toward the plantation house.

Morgan ran across the dooryard in the dusk, placed the homemade ladder against the summer kitchen, and scrambled up to where the chimney bent away from the wall. He braced his back against the wall and his bare feet against the burning mud-and-straw bricks, and by dint of a tremendous wrenching shove, he knocked the chimney down in a clatter of rubble and sparks into which he himself plunged.

Shielding his eyes with the inside of his bent arm, Morgan rolled out of the flames and jumped up to help the woman put out the small fires on the cabin roof with buckets of water from the mule trough. Slidell, her fear of ghosts notwithstanding, ran to the big house with a bucket of water and threw it on the smoking pile of broken boards that had once been the side gallery. At the risk of burning his hands as well as his feet, which were well scorched by the chimney fire, Morgan threw the boards out into the yard away from the plantation house.

After the flames had all been put out, Morgan sat on the cabin steps with his feet in a bucket of cold water. Slidell stood close beside him, still wary of the two elderly black people from the old times. When the woman brought an ointment of hog lard and waxberry wax, Morgan could smell his scorched soles.

"I think you feets be all right, boy. They just char a bit on they bottom," the woman said, rubbing the compound into his feet. "This chimbly cotching on fire business happen two, three times before. Someday the whole shooting match go up. Good riddance."

The old man rocked away in his rocker. "Once this was the grandest place in Albemarle County," he said. " 'Look on my works, ye mighty, and despair.' That's 'Ozymandias,' of course. P. Bysshe Shelley, whom my father knew personally and much admired. Father could quote the entire poem. So too can I, though I can't read a single letter. My father never taught me to read, you see. I can cite the first book of the *Iliad* in Greek, yet I can't write my own name. My father did not think the art of writing necessary for me to learn. Instead he taught me to make shoes. Our sign, *Kano,* you know, means opportunity. In my own instance, the opportunity to make shoes. Put your poor burnt foot here on my last, lad, so that I may measure it. Ah. You have a good broad understanding."

He chuckled, so delighted with his pun that he turned to Slidell and repeated it. "Your master has a good broad understanding."

"He isn't my master," Slidell said sharply.

The old man apparently saw better than Morgan had supposed. It occurred to him that ever since he had started out for Canada with Jesse Moses, months ago, very little had been as he had supposed.

"Be gentle with that foot, sir. It and the other must carry me another four or five hundred miles."

"They will heal. My good wife knows all the old country remedies. 'Twill heal very nicely. Other one now, if you please. Sometimes one foot is as much as an inch longer or shorter than its mate. For the heels of your boots I'll use olive wood. My father imported black olives and green olives from Portugal, but they never flourished. Our Virginia climate is not quite adapted for them. So we used the olive wood for boot heels and for the clogs worn about the house by the slave women. I make my own tacks. My father showed me how. Did I tell you he was a shrewd fellow to fashion a tack? He could turn his hand to most anything. He even tried presidenting. My mother wore fine dresses in the latest Parisian style. She visited Paris with my father after his first wife died—I call her his first wife. He truly had but one. My mother was her half-sister. Did I tell you that? The president ran mad when his wife died. He saw his dead wife's eyes in the eyes of my mother, so he took Sal into his bed and into his heart. Ah, well. All's one in the end. All three rest in Abraham's bosom. Shall we sing the 'Little Shoemaker's Song' now, my love? My father taught it to me when I was a lad."

The cobbler leading, his wife joining in, they sang:

I am a little shoemaker by my trade, I'll work in rainy weather.
Two finished pair I've made today of a side and a half of leather.
Whack de loo de dum. Whack de loo de doo.
Whack de loo de dum. Sal, will you wear my shoe?

Go hand me down my pegging awl, I stuck it right up yonder.
Go hand me down my sewing awl to peg and sew my leather.
Oh! I've lost my shoemaker's wax
And where do you think I'll find it?
Ain't that enough to break my heart.
Oh! Right here, Sal, I've found it.

Whack de loo de dum. Whack de loo de doo.
Whack de loo de dum. Sal, will you wear my shoe?

Slidell rolled her eyes as if they had stumbled upon a madhouse, but Morgan looked on in wonder. There was not a hint of viciousness in these good people, who in their day, Morgan supposed from the sign of *Kano*, ᚲ, over the door of their cabin, had helped many others to freedom. Yet what could they possibly tell him of his brother? And why would Pilgrim come here or head south instead of north in the first place? Still, he had to ask.

"No, sir," the cobbler said. "No man that I know of named Pilgrim traveled this way lately headed either north or south. Yet I have met many a pilgrim on many a long hard progress. Last summer I met a one-legged man riding south by night. I believe he was a Secesh deserter, for he had a very quaint way of speaking. What is vulgarly referred to as a peckerwood dialect from the Deep South. He was headed toward the Cumber, so I directed him to the sign of *Ansuz* and Two Snake. *Ansuz,* you know, means messenger. If you go there, Two Snake will give you a message. The one-legged deserter traveled with his sister, a nun sworn to silence. A dangerous business, escorting any woman through these parts in such times. They both rode the same mule and would not dismount."

Morgan privately consulted Jesse's stone while the shoemaker nattered on. The sign of *Ansuz,* ᚨ, to the southwest of Little Mountain in a region designated as Boone's Gap, was accompanied by two intertwined serpents. Could the shoemaker's one-legged deserter be the Rebel soldier whose leg Joseph Findletter had amputated, traveling south with the beautiful Creole woman in disguise? It wasn't much to go on. It was less than a little and had no apparent connection to Pilgrim. Yet it was all Morgan had. If the Rebel deserter had followed this route, perhaps his missing brother had too.

The shoemaker's wife cut her eyes at Slidell. "You ain't from up north," she said. "But wearing that sinful yalla dress? Tossing that long glossy hair, switching you tail like they mockingbird? You calling altogether too much attention to yourself, Jezbel. You gone get caught up and fotched right back to wherever you run off from. Come 'long with me."

The old woman led the protesting girl into the cabin. Meanwhile the shoemaker turned his learned discourse to the war. He shook his head. "Wouldn't my father the president have been saddened to see what's become of his great Republic, lad? And all because he failed to free his slaves."

"How do you arrive at that conclusion, sir?"

"Why, friend, had Thomas freed his people, other luminaries of the Dominion would have freed theirs. Old Virginia would have stayed with the Union like a good wife cleaving to her husband. Our noble general would have accepted the commission Father Abraham offered him and swept the Rebels from the face of the earth in a few short months. Will you take a delivery of shoes to the general in the capital? Though I don't approve his cause, I can't bear to think of his poor soldier boys going barefoot. My half sister who lives on Capitol Hill will return the wagon and mule."

Morgan could hardly endure the thought of going to Richmond with shoes for the general's men. It would delay him, not to mention the risk involved. And he did not wish to aid the enemy even in this small humane way. Yet he could not refuse the cobbler his request. And it was possible that the southern general, to whom Morgan's uncle John had written on his behalf, might have heard something of his brother. It was even possible that Pilgrim had been taken prisoner at Gettysburg, in which case the general might be able to help Morgan locate him. Richmond it must be, Morgan thought. Boone's Gap and *Ansuz* would have to wait, as would Arthur Dinwiddie. But Morgan was determined that he would not wait long.

Just then the cobbler's wife appeared from the cabin with a young field hand in tow. The hand wore a large straw hat, outsized overalls with hanks of twine for straps, a long gray duster coat, and mismatched brogans. Morgan began to laugh, upon which Slidell ripped off the hat and flung it angrily to the ground, revealing a hideously cropped head like a person with mange. And without further ado, she tackled Morgan and knocked him to the ground. Silently and fiercely Slidell pounded him with her fists until she could pound him no more. Then she began to cry.

"This the worst," she said through her sobs. "Dress Slidell up like a scarecrow and then make sport of her."

With that she pitched onto him again, clawing like a bobcat while he tried to fend her off, to justify, to apologize, until he feared for his eyes she was ripping at him so. Seizing her by one leg and the bib of her overalls, he none too gently tossed her into the mule watering trough.

The cobbler nodded gravely. "That's a woman worth hanging on to, son," he said.

"That a fine woman, love you a great lot," his wife agreed. "Yes, sir. You hang on to she, boy. You hear?"

As the cobbler worked on, he called out to his wife, "Dearest, where is the book Father left me? Would you please be so kind as to fetch it to me?"

The woman sighed and shook her head as if everything connected with their lives on Little Mountain was as futile and absurd as owning a book neither of them could read. But after a little time had passed she went inside the cabin and came back with a volume bound in red buckram. "Perhaps you could read to me whilst I cobble up your boots," the shoemaker told Morgan.

Morgan felt a surge of joy to be holding a book in his hands again. The book Cobbler Tom's wife handed him seemed to connect him with the many books Pilgrim had passed along to him over the years and therefore with Pilgrim himself. *The History of the Expedition under the Commands of Captains Lewis and Clark,* edited by Nicholas Biddle, had been published in 1814 in Philadelphia. After

Morgan had read aloud from it for three quarters of an hour, the cobbler bade him take it on his journey, that it was of no benefit to an illiterate maker of shoes but might inspire Morgan to go west himself like Captain Lewis and Captain Clark and see rare new sights and leave the war and all its evils behind him now and forever after. Morgan was so touched he could only nod.

By dawn his shoes were ready, and he and Slidell were on their way, in the cobbler's mule-drawn wagon, to the capital. The cobbler and his wife stood in front of the plantation house at the top of the Little Mountain linked arm in arm and swaying gently from side to side, singing the little shoemaker's song. "Whack de loo de dum. Whack de loo de doo."

B Y NOON they were passing a steady stream of gray-clad soldiers. Morgan had secreted his guns in the storage box under the wagon seat so as not to arouse suspicion. He appeared to be just another boy from the country, a lowlander taking supplies under canvas into town with a lanky young field hand in a straw hat along to help. Most of the soldiers they passed were barefoot, and Morgan felt for them, would have liked to turn over his cargo of shoes to these limping, tattered men. Tobacco fields stretched away from the road, a rich blue-green like mature corn and as aromatic as a Vermont balsam woods after a fresh rain. Morgan noticed that as the soldiers wrestled along the cannons and mortars that would defend the citadel of the Confederacy against the expected Union attack, they stopped frequently to pluck tobacco leaves and chew on them.

Slidell had not spoken a word to him since the day before. He wondered how much longer she would punish him. She'd allowed the cobbler's wife to stuff her slave bells with cotton, and she wore an odd red muffler over them. Morgan had never met anyone like her.

In time they came to a major pike on the north bank of a large river. They could see the steady files of blue troops on the far side. The wind was out of the south. Morgan smelled cured tobacco wafting up from the Reb capital's forty tobacco manufactories. Not far ahead loomed Richmond's big flour mills and the stacks of Tredegar's Iron Works, where the cannons now being deployed along the river had been founded. "Satan's own lair," Slidell muttered.

"Well," Morgan said, thinking of the tavern in Harrisburg and what he had witnessed there. Thinking of the women, children, and elderly folk being auctioned on the block at the Utica almshouse. Yet though he knew he had many a long mile yet to travel, Morgan Kinneson, approaching Richmond past brick kilns and textile factories and sawmills, past gin and beer distilleries, past a poorhouse and a prison and a powder magazine, watching the black foundry smoke pour out of the stacks over Tredegar's, and now nearly deafened by the roar of the rapids on the river, allowed himself a fleeting smile of amusement that he, a Yankee and an abolitionist from the far mountains of Vermont, had, in the guise of a bumpkin muleteer peddling shoes and in the company of a runaway slave, breached uncontested the defenses of the chief city of the Confederate States of America.

"HOY, YOU GODDAMNED YELLOW-HEADED 'GATOR bait from the stinking backside of nowhere, watch where you a-going."

Morgan had nodded off, and the cobbler's mule, in its mulish wisdom, had walked directly into a crossroads in front of a massive cannon being hauled along on a six-ox wheeled truck. A very irate soldier was screaming at him. Morgan drew hard on the reins, but the mule would no more back up than sprout wings like Pegasus and fly. The intersection was all braying mule and bellowing oxen and cursing soldier until Slidell snatched the reins away from Morgan. "Hear me well, sir mule," she shouted. "Now you're under the management of someone who knows all your wiles and guiles. Come up, now." She gave a furious jerk on the reins. "Come up, sir!" she shouted again, and somehow the animals were disentangled and the oxen drew the cannon onward. No one else on the street paid the slightest attention.

Slidell cracked the reins smartly. "I know mules," she said. "They are a miscreant outfit from start to finish. One good thing about them though."

"What's that?" Morgan said, terribly relieved that she was talking to him again.

"They can't make more mules," Slidell said. "God rendered them sterile for being so lazy. Go ahead and smile, boy. We'll see how you smile when He strikes you the same for laughing at Slidell and poking all the pretty gals on your way south."

"Slidell, I do believe you are jealous."

She gave him a sharp jab with her elbow. "And vain besides," she said. "Next time you forget that and laugh at Slidell, there isn't going to be a next time."

The general's home was situated between the capitol building and the river. At the gate stood a short, grinning sergeant and a behemoth of a fellow a good six and a half feet tall wearing on his head an incongruous little gray kepi.

"Message for the general, sir," Morgan said to the sergeant. "And a delivery of shoes." He tried to speak in the softly modulated tones of the southern soldiers he'd overheard, but besides his Yankee accent, which fell harshly enough upon the ears, he had a sharp carrying voice with, Pilgrim had once said, an edge like a well-whetted adze.

The sergeant drew his revolver and pointed it at Morgan. "Got us a Yank here, corporal," he said. "I do believe we have captured us a Yankee and his nigger. Just hand over your so-called message, boy. We'll see the general gets her."

"Easy, boy," Slidell said, drawing the reins tighter. Morgan did not know whether she was talking to the mule or to him.

"My instructions were to deliver it myself. It's from Colonel John Kinneson. He and the general soldiered together in old Mexico."

"Well, the general ain't to home to Yankee boys, Yankee boy. He's down in old Mex with Colonel John Kinnerson. Ain't that right, Corporal Mann?"

The giant with the corporal's chevrons, his uniform coat unbuttoned because he was too thick through the chest for any normal coat and some of the dark hair on his chest growing out through the holes in his ragged undershirt, stared at Morgan the way he might watch a snake sidewinding its way across the road. Trying to decide whether or not it was worth the trouble of killing.

"Corporal Mann here, that we call the Man Mountain, don't say much," the sergeant said. "Corporal Man Mountain Mann is a man of action, you mought say. Fight first and parlay arter if at all is Corporal Mann's motto. Corporal Mann"—the grinning sergeant lowered his voice as if to convey an important secret—"is about the fightingest man in Richmond town."

It fell out that at just that moment a gang of drunken soldiers was coming along the street dancing barefooted to a penny whistle. When they drew even with the general's house they stopped to observe the hoo-ha between Morgan and the two guards.

"I'll fight ye for it. Your letter," said Man Mountain Mann in a rumbling voice. "Catch as catch can, winner to carry the letter into the general."

The words were scarcely out of his mouth before Morgan had launched himself off the wagon seat, striking the fightingest man in Richmond town feet first in the chest. The new boots the cobbler had made him, into whose toes Cobbler Tom had inserted half-circle iron ox shoes, thudded against Man Mountain Mann. Unfazed, the giant laced his fingers together, lifted them high over his head, and brought them crashing down on Morgan's neck.

"It's a Texas two-step!" shouted a soldier. "I put a silver cartwheel on the Mountain."

Instantly the mob of celebrants formed a ring around the combatants. Morgan, on his feet again, circled clockwise. He feinted with his right hand and drove his left fist three times straight out from the shoulder into the Mountain's face. Blood flowed from the corporal's nose, but he doubled his hand and smashed it into Morgan's midriff, knocking him into the mule hitched to the wagon. The mule galloped off down the street with the wagonload of shoes, Slidell sawing on the reins and shouting at the animal to halt.

"Here," a faraway voice said. "What in the name of heaven is all this? My wife is sick, I've a meeting in twenty minutes to try to save what's left of the Confederacy, and you men have turned my yard into Blackfriar's Fair. What have you done, boys? Have you killed this young man?"

"I believe they may have, sir," Morgan said, staggering to his feet and saluting the general, for that was clearly who the graying man with the short white beard and the tired but commanding voice must be. "I believe they may have. But they have not quite defeated me yet."

At this the general smiled. "Well," he said. "I believe I know from my own recent experience exactly what you mean. State your business here, son. Kindly make it brief. Sergeant, fetch back this lad's wagon. A mule may bolt but it won't bolt far."

"Does the name John Kinneson mean anything to you, general?"

"It does."

"I have a letter to you. From Colonel Kinneson."

The general looked at Morgan with weary eyes. "Come inside, son," he said. "I'd be honored to receive a letter from my friend Colonel Kinneson. And young man? The next time you decide to go up against a fellow twice your own size, make as though to grapple at close quarters with him, and when he opens his fists, seize his thumbs and bend them right back until he cries uncle."

"What if he doesn't?"

"Well, keep bending until you hear them snap. Then he's yours. That's one truly useful thing I learned at the Point. Now you know it too."

The general's study occupied a small room overlooking the river. It was lined with books on wars and warfare, some in Latin and Greek. A large map of the Dominion of Virginia with the major campaigns laid out in black ink in a neat hand lay on his flat-top quartered-oak desk, which was otherwise bare except for a small New Testament, a volume of Caesar's *Gallic Wars,* and a framed daguerreotype of what Morgan judged to be the general's home plantation at Arlington. Before the desk was a single straight-backed chair. The general motioned for Morgan to sit down. As Morgan handed the letter from his uncle across the desk, he thought he saw the general's face light up to see his name written in his old friend's hand. The general read the letter quickly. Then he looked up at Morgan. "Colonel Kinneson has requested that I give you a safe-conduct pass through the Dominion to Tennessee and North Carolina." He smiled. "The colonel—John Bookworm to his friends—was and is a fighting officer and a fine and learned man. He and I were at the Point together. He received but one demerit." The general smiled again. "For reading after hours. I believe it was Catullus. He says you're his nephew and that you will have a story to tell me. Can you tell it fast?"

Economically, Morgan recounted the story of his long walk south and why he had undertaken it. The general listened without interrupting, though during parts of the narrative his face expressed quickened interest. When Morgan finished, he showed the general Jesse's rune stone.

"This is a most interesting artifact," the general said. "These strange signs—we had one carved on the woodshed at home where fugitives were welcome to stay. We pretended we didn't know about them, but of course we did. Here. The sign looked like this." On the stone, he pointed to the rune ↑. "My father didn't know what to call it, but he said he believed it meant the warrior."

The general smiled a wry smile and shook his head. "I fear that's not quite proven to be accurate in my case. The true warrior seems to be that dogged Illinois shopkeeper, my opposite number. As we speak he is poised to deliver the final blow to our noble experiment."

"You call slavery a noble experiment?"

"I do not. I mean our experiment in independence. Like the independence declared by our forefathers. But to return to your missing brother. Son, if I didn't have rather more pressing business at the moment I'd help you hunt down these demons myself, the way I hunted John Brown, and I'd hang them higher than ever we did that poor mad devil. But God bless you, boy, you can't live beyond the law for revenge."

"I don't want God's blessing or his help or least of all his interference. This has nothing to do with God. It's between me and Arthur Dinwiddie. Not to mention finding my brother. Will you give me safe-conduct to complete my work?"

The general looked at Morgan, looked at the strange old oval relic in his hand, then looked out the window over the river. He thought of the mistakes he had made, in comparison to which this Vermont boy's misguided quest for justice was a trifling nothing. Not listening to Longstreet a year ago when he said the round hill could not, *could not,* be taken . . . But he would not torment himself by enumerating his blunders again today.

"Son, I well remember hearing of your brother the surgeon and the great service he performed for my wounded as well as his own in the Slaughter Pen at Gettysburg. He subjected himself to murderous crossfire from both armies. But even if he survived, which I can scarcely suppose, why would he then come south?"

Morgan shrugged. "My brother was a pacifist. To get to a place where there was no war? He couldn't go north. He'd be shot for desertion."

"What evidence do you have that he didn't die at Gettysburg?"

"He just didn't, I reckon."

"How can you know that, son?"

"General, do you believe that Jesus Christ rose from the dead?"

"I do."

"Where is your evidence?"

"Why, it's all around us. In the universal spirit of love of our Lord and Savior."

"My question stands. What shred of evidence have you lately seen in your Confederate States of America or in our United States either of the universal spirit of love?"

"My brand of faith comes from my heart," the general said.

"Just so," Morgan said.

The general sighed. He got a sheet of paper and an inkwell and pen out of his desk. He wrote something and handed it to Morgan. It was a safe-conduct north for him and his Negro servant. This was not what Morgan had wanted, but it might serve him in a pinch, and the general knew well that what Morgan did with it would be up to Morgan.

Just then they heard a commotion in the street. It was the sergeant and Slidell, returned with the cobbler's mule and wagon. "In the wagon are boots for your men from a well-wisher," Morgan said. "Also some belongings of mine. The mules and wagon to go to this address on Capitol Hill." He borrowed the general's pen and wrote the address of the cobbler's sister on a slip of paper.

The general nodded. From another drawer of his desk he took a compass, which he placed in Morgan's hand. On the back were his three etched initials above the words "The good man's course is always true." Morgan privately thought that the inscription was an example of the kind of suspect reasoning that the little testament on the general's desk and all other testaments abounded with. But he nodded politely and held his tongue as he started to hand the compass back. The general closed Morgan's fingers over the instrument. "Put it in your pocket," he said.

"Let's walk a little," the general suggested. "Walk down to the river with me if you will. I'm stiff and"—smiling slightly—"you must be too. You took quite a drubbing from Corporal Mann. Next time, remember, go for the—"

"Thumbs," Morgan said, wriggling his.

Outside, the general lifted his graying eyebrows as Slidell removed from the wagon box Morgan's scattershot and Lady Justice and silently passed them to him. On the way to the river they passed a tobacco manufactory. "Don't ever use tobacco, son," the general said. "I don't and I'm proud of it. Tobacco is a bad business."

Then, "You fought Corporal Mann like a tiger. Well, that's how I'm fighting."

"You might better have fought to persuade the Dominion of Virginia to join the Union."

Slidell, slouching along behind, put her hand over her mouth.

"You Vermonters are plain-spoken enough," the general said.

They sat on a bench on a marge of grass on a low berm by the river. Slidell stood nearby. "Perhaps you're right," the general conceded. "None of us ever thought the war would turn into"—he waved his hand at the fortified city jammed with soldiers, the river filled with blockade runners and ironclad naval boats—"this. Sometimes, son, a man needs to know when to say 'enough.' Sherman already in Georgia and poised to cut the Confederacy in two. Sheridan raising Cain here in Virginia. My best fighting general, a man so devout he refused to give battle on Sunday, accidentally shot through the back by his own soldiers. The very first battle of the war and all battles thereafter no more nor less than bloody clashes between armed mobs. My opposing number has lost nigh two men to my one, Morgan. Yet he knows not the meaning of retreat. Whyever would we keep on?"

"Like he said, Virginia should have waltzed in on the side of the North," Slidell said.

"Good Lord," the general said, looking from Morgan to Slidell and then back to Morgan. "I see why Vermont still calls itself a Republic. Even your servants are outspoken up there."

"Again," Morgan said hurriedly, with a warning look at Slidell, "my point remains. Had you and your Commonwealth thrown in with the president, all this warring would be long over."

"Boy, you should go into the law. Here. Promise me that if you live through this madness you'll look into the law."

"I'll consider it."

"You've heard this one, of course," the general said, "apropos of why we've kept on. During a Sunday truce a boy from Massachusetts called across this very river and asked a boy clad in gray why he was fighting. 'Why, because you're down here,' the southern boy called back. Perhaps that's as good an answer as I can give."

"Well, I'm *down here,* General, in part because a devil named Arthur Dinwiddie sent another devil *up there*"—pointing north—"and killed a man I was responsible for."

"Son, I beg you, if you feel you must persist, to confine your imperatives to locating your brother."

Morgan said, "I thank you for the safe passage. And for the compass."

The general offered his hand. They shook solemnly, and Morgan touched his forefinger to the brim of his slouch hat. Then he and Slidell started up along the river toward the bridge to the south side.

"Son."

Morgan stopped, half turned.

"Son, I will say this much. I would not care to be a transgressor in your eyes and you to be pursuing me."

For the slightest moment Morgan hesitated. Then he said gravely, "No, sir. You would not."

EIGHT

ANSUZ

ᚨ

Up in the Cumberland it was high summer and raining a warm summer rain. Morgan and Slidell were overtaken by black night at a graveyard where, according to an old man they had met that afternoon, early on in the war two skirmishing patrols had been picked off by mountain people, stripped of all their possessions, and buried willy-nilly in shallow graves on the hillside where they fell. At the bottom of the slope was a pine marker with the message STAY A WAY scratched onto it. A little stream already coloring up in the torrential rain rushed along the bottom of the slope. Here, with Morgan's blanket over their heads and shoulders and their backs against the marker bearing the warning, the pair bivouacked for the night.

Slidell insisted that the place was haunted and seemed delighted

by the notion. With uncanny exactitude she mimicked the general—
"Boy, you should go into the law"—and Man Mountain Mann:
"I'll fight ye for it, catch as catch can." She told Morgan, whose face
was still badly swollen and bruised, that he cut a grand handsome
figure, and he wondered how, in her female scheme of things, it
was acceptable for her to hooraw his appearance when he was not
allowed to poke innocent fun at hers. He wanted to make love to
her again, but he was as wet as a soaked codfish and as sore from
the beating by the Man Mountain as if he'd been trampled by an
entire marching regiment and so tired that he slept like a dead man
straight through until dawn.

They woke in a mizzling fog that quickly turned back to driving curtains of rain. As they started up the hill, they could see
a blue-coated arm jutting through the red clay hillside and more
graves spilling out their contents. "What I tell you, boy?" Slidell
said. "The day of reckoning has arrived. Angel Gabriel wants a
word with you, Morgan Kinneson from Kingdom County."

Corpses clad in gray and corpses clad in blue, mortal enemies in
life, boon companions in death, tumbled down the slope in mori-
bund embrace only to be swept away by the freshet at the foot of the
hill. Morgan could not think what to do. Maybe drag some of the
disturbed dead to high ground, but fearing disease, he stood trans-
fixed as whole sections of hillside calved away, spewing out more
of the dead. The bones danced a macabre supine dance and clicked
together like hand-held spoons at a hoedown. Some of the deceased
seemed to be racing each other down the hillside. One poor soldier,
mere rags on bone, was hung up in a pawpaw tree whose roots
had pulled out of the bank. A skull came bowling down the slope,
greenish white in the liquescent light. It clacked off another skull
like a billiard ball, took a merry skip, and landed at their feet. Slidell

screamed. Without thinking, Morgan gave the thing a boot, and it arced high and came down in the stream.

Before long the rain stopped and the sun emerged. In the middle of the morning they smelled smoke. "Somebody has a whiskey still nearby," Slidell whispered. Shortly they caught sight of a boy of fourteen or fifteen, dressed in men's overalls worn backward. He seemed to be floating through the laurel, keeping pace with Slidell and Morgan.

Presently the boy emerged onto the narrow sled path they were following. He was riding a pig, a big, dark, razorbacked tusker with fiery little pig eyes that fixed themselves on Morgan as though the animal longed to devour him.

"Who you?" the boy said. "You the debil?"

Slidell grinned from under her straw hat. "You got that right," she said.

Morgan said, "I'm Morgan Kinneson from Kingdom County, Vermont. I'm looking for my brother, Pilgrim."

"Abide," the boy said. Abruptly, he steered his mount back into the laurel by its ears. Morgan and Slidell sat down on a bluish rock beside the path to wait. They could still smell smoke.

"That pig-riding boy a specter," Slidell said. "I tell you these mountains are haunted, Morgan."

She pronounced his name as if it were two words, Mor Gan, and again he wanted her so badly that he did not trust himself to speak. He was quite sure that she knew it and took delight in his anguish.

Some time passed, perhaps half an hour. Soundlessly, the boy reappeared out of the laurel. This time he was afoot. He beckoned to them. "Foller."

They pushed their way through the undergrowth to a step-across-in-one-step brook, which they traced up the mountainside. They came into a clearing where a man stood in a tin washtub wedged between two boulders. A pile of green juniper brush smoldered under the tub, on whose side the sign ᚨ, *Ansuz,* had been painted in bright ocher. The man, stark naked except for a slouch hat, was carving a walking stick into the shape of two intertwined serpents. His arms and legs were as scarlet as a fall maple leaf, and he looked unhappy.

"Two Snake got into the pisen trefoil plant with the shiny shiny leaves up Waycross," the boy explained. "Now he's obliged to smoke the pisen outen himself."

"'Tis true, 'tis true," Two Snake said. "Green juniper burned very slow will generally draw it out. See how it's ruddied me up already. By 'n by I'll come good as new with the pisen all gone. Juniper brush smoked green will kill pisen ivy dead as a hammer."

"How did you contract it?" Morgan said.

"Oh, a-fishing around in the laurel up Waycross looking for a rattlesnake den. Before I knowed it I was into the stuff in earnest."

"What do you want with rattlesnakes?"

"Why, I sell 'em. What else would you want with them? Just yesterday I sold a dozen walloping big snakes to a serpent preacher with a wagon pulled by a red mule. He said he wanted to set up a hollering church in Haint Holler and shoo out the haints. Good luck, says I. Haints are a sight harder to get shut of than that."

Slidell gave Morgan a look full of meaning.

"Well, how do you get shut of them?" Morgan said.

"Up Haint Holler? You don't. That's they stomping ground. What else besides me do ye think's in the tub? A-simmering in the hot water?

"Peanuts," Two Snake said before Morgan could reply. "Raintree Pettibone, my third cousin twice removed down in the lowlands, grows them. I boil them. I boil 'em sunup to sundown. Then they done. They good."

He nodded to the boy, who ladled out a handful of peanuts in the shell with a homemade wooden spoon and dumped them steaming hot into Morgan's hands. Then he gave Slidell a handful. Morgan popped one in his mouth and started to crunch it.

Slidell whooped.

"Jesus to Jesus and seven hands around, man," Two Snake said. "You must shuck them out first. The meat's inside. Sit ye, sit ye, strangers, and enjoy them."

Keeping an eye on the wild pig, which he did not at all trust, Morgan sat on a chestnut log in the swept clay clearing and munched peanuts. Slidell stood nearby eating peanuts. They tasted salty and a little like the corn his mother popped in a wire basket over a fire on winter evenings when the wind came howling down the mountain out of Canada. He nodded his appreciation at the red man smoking himself.

"Where hail ye from?" Two Snake said, turning himself slowly to get the full benefit of the steam.

"Vermont."

"Vermont," he said. "I never studied no Vermont."

Morgan pointed north. He was thinking of popcorn white as snow. Thinking of new snow on the mountain at home.

The boy said, "Two Snake says it's a bad day when he don't sell a walking stick."

"Two Snake has many a bad day," the smoking man acknowledged.

"Did you sell one to a tall doctor from up north?" Morgan said.

"Doctor man?" Two Snake said.

Morgan nodded. He could feel his heart beating fast.

"Tall. Taller than you by a widow's mite?"

Morgan nodded.

"Inquiring sort of fella? All full of questions about medicine?"

"Yes."

"Yankee, you say. Talked through his nose like you. Dark hair and dark eyes?"

Morgan nodded again.

Two Snake shook his head. "No such a body in these parts."

"No such," the boy agreed.

"Bide here with us for a few days, friends, and I'll show you what I know," Two Snake said.

"What do you know?" Slidell said.

"Why, I know how to bathe a pneumonia patient in mountain liquor to draw the infection from the lungs. I know all the old plant cures under the healing sign of *Ansuz*. I know snake doctoring. Powdered-up rattlesnake rattles to ease a hard birthing. Copperhead venom and gunpowder to drive out dropsy. Moccasin pisen's sovereign powerful for heart trouble. For strong diseases you generally need strong medicine. Why come is the snake the animal of Aesculapius? Because it's the cunningest critter there be, if we but know how to use its canny wisdom. Rattlesnake bite will cure the melancholic brown studies. Despair hath no show agin it. Nor does heartbreak."

Nor would the desperate or heartbroken patient, Morgan thought, judging from the size of some of the snakes he and Slidell had encountered earlier that morning basking on ledges beside the sled trail. He could only agree with Two Snake that the ministrations of one such gentleman would cure any human malady and permanently at that.

"Where then do you apply the bite?"

"On the outer ankle as a rule. That way they mought lose the foot but generally not the entire limb. All thought of the lost lover or despair dissipates during the crisis."

"I should think it might. What other cures do you know?"

"I know green juniper smoke will draw out pisen ivy. Slippery elm bark boiled in a tea cureth the dysentery. And fifteen pounds of coarse white salt will bile fifty pounds of peanuts. I know where to cotch serpents. You'd be surprised how many folks have a call for them. They's one crawling over your left boot this minute."

Morgan looked down. A yellowish brown snake of a variety unknown on Kingdom Mountain was slowly progressing over his boot. It stopped, raised its head, looked up at Morgan, and flicked out its split tongue.

"That's my big yalla breeding copperhead, Harley Thigpen," Two Snake said. "Old Harley's a corker. He has enough pisen stored up in him to fell a full-growed ox. Don't you move a muscle now, boy. Harley don't take much to Yankees. No, he do not."

With great deliberation, Harley Thigpen snaked on over Morgan's boot, watching him narrowly the while. Harley did, indeed, look as though he did not take to Yankees.

"Toss me that stick you're carving," Slidell said to Two Snake. "Mr. Harley about to meet his Waterloo."

"I'll whistle up the hog," the boy said. "Old Garadene'll eat him in a trice."

"No. Harley's my best breeder. Don't you twitch an eyelash, Yankee boy. The moment you stir, Brother Harlan will cut one of his capers."

"What should I do?"

"I'm studying onto it."

Brother Harlan laid his small, deadly head atop his brown-and-cream-colored coils to watch Morgan the steadier. Morgan looked at Slidell. "What should I do?" he mouthed.

"Can you roll?" she said.

"What?"

"Can you tumble backward ass over teakettle and come up onto your feet?"

"I reckon."

"Do it then. Quick as ever you moved in all your life."

Morgan tumbled backward, heels over head, and came up onto his feet. "Jubilo!" the pig-riding boy whooped. He reached out with a stick and swooped Harley Thigpen high into the air, caught him on the way down in his croker sack, and tied off the mouth. Altogether, it was a very hideous performance.

The boy grinned at Morgan. "You want to ride my pig? Go ahead. Try him out."

"Go on ahead," Two Snake said. "It ain't ever' man in this world can say he's rid a pig name of Garadene."

Morgan approached the razorback. Gingerly, he put a leg over its back and seated himself, and the pig set off around the clearing at a stately pace. Morgan held his long legs out away from its sides so as not to drag his feet. They went around the clearing twice. Morgan could not have imagined when he woke that morning that he would witness the resurrection of a company of skeletal soldiers and ride a wild boar. Then Slidell rode the animal.

"That's a good pig," she told the boy afterward. "I thank you for the ride."

"Yes, sir," the boy said. "He an easy mount and he'll draw a sled. I wouldn't butcher him for no amount of lucre."

"Cobbler Tom at the sign of *Kano* said you'd give me a message," Morgan said to the smoking Two Snake. "He said *Ansuz* means messenger."

"Brush Arbor Holiness," Two Snake said.

"Excuse me?"

"You'll find your serpent preacher at Brush Arbor Holiness Church. He knows you're a-coming. He said to tell you he knows what you want to know. You must go through Haint Holler to get there. Foller the brook. One thing more."

"What's that?" Morgan said.

"Up Haint Holler you'll come to *Dagaz,* the domain of the Melungeons. They's a grist mill with a windmill and a waterwheel in a place of high white cliffs. The miller and his woman and their green-eyed gal will be pale as flour. They will ask you to stop and bide the night. But you must not eat of their bread. Not so much as one crumb, no matter how keenly you hunger. And you must not accept the favors of the miller's daughter, entice you though she will."

Morgan touched his hat to Two Snake and the boy. Slidell scratched Garadene's bristly head. Then they walked on up the brook.

Never before had Morgan seen a stream increase in size as he traced it upward. As they walked higher, the stream grew deeper but did not appear to narrow. Near Two Snake's it was up to their ankles. Then it rose to their calves, then their knees. Also, it seemed to become much colder, as did the hollow it flowed through. High in the narrow glen beneath soaring white cliffs they came to a stone grist mill with a penstock and a waterwheel, not presently turning. Two millstones as large as the wheels of a giant's wagon could be seen inside the mill. Nearby was a house shingled with cedar shakes, and beside the grist mill stood a windmill with motionless wooden sails. On the stone base of the windmill someone had carved the sign ⋈.

"Hello, the mill," Morgan called.

The miller appeared in the doorway of the cedar-shake house, dusted white with powdered flour, and in a creaky voice he invited them inside.

Slidell pointed her finger at Morgan. "Don't you step across that threshold," she said.

Morgan studied the miller. Under the flour his skin seemed olive-colored. His dark curly hair powdered with flour looked like a wig. The miller beckoned to him again to come inside, and he did. The house, which was ice-cold despite the cherry-red blaze in the fireplace, was sparsely furnished with a deal table and two crude benches. A crooked ladder led up to a sleeping loft. The miller's wife and daughter were both olive-skinned and green-eyed, and their hands, arms, and countenances were well powdered with flour. A sprinkling of flour covered the table and benches and the puncheon floor. Bread was baking in an oven built into the side of the fireplace. It smelled delicious.

"Slidell's waiting out here, boy," Slidell called from the dooryard. "Don't you lay a lip over that bread. Stay away from that green-eyed gal."

Morgan backed up to the hearth. Though the flames danced madly up through the logs laid on the andirons, the fire gave scant heat. When the woman opened the oven and brought out the bread on a long wooden paddle, it gave off a heavenly scent. As he gazed longingly at the fragrant golden loaves, the girl gazed at him with eyes more longing still.

"Come," said the miller, beckoning again. It was an odd, slow stiff-armed motion as if he were drawing Morgan to him by some ancient trick of necromancy. Morgan sat at the table but put the yeasty-smelling loaf the miller's wife set in front of him in his haversack.

"I don't wish to pry, sir," he said, "but I couldn't help noticing that you have both a waterwheel and a windmill. I should have thought that one or the other would be sufficient to drive your grinding stones."

"Well, friend," said the miller in his rusty voice, "in drought-time when the water does not flow, the wind might blow. Or the doldrums might settle in and kill all breath of wind. Then the brook might run."

"I noticed that the stream seemed to grow fuller as I climbed up along it."

"Aye," said the miller.

A rain of blows fell on the door. "Morgan," Slidell shouted. "You come on out of there. Before they witch you. Keep your hands off that gal."

The miller's wife looked at him with beseeching eyes and inclined her head toward the door. The girl gazed upon him and licked her lips. "Take some bread, the staff of life," she said, cutting into a loaf. The honey-colored crust cleaving away released a fragrance so intoxicating it was all Morgan could do to resist. Suddenly overcome by weariness, he got quickly to his feet and allowed the girl to lead him to the mill, where she made him up a luxurious bed of sleeping robes. She held out her ice-cold hand like a princess. When he took it, she gripped his hand fiercely and looked deep into his eyes, then ghosted silently across the stone floor and out the door.

A moment later Slidell appeared. "Come on," she said in an urgent voice. "We have to leave this place."

Morgan could not rid himself of the sense that Pilgrim had been here, perhaps recently. From his haversack came the delicious scent of bread, but Two Snake had warned him to eat not of the bread nor accept the favors of the girl. Morgan began to pace around the room past the looming walking beams and axles that powered the grindstones. A sick weariness came upon him. He stepped outside to splash cold brook-water on his face and saw in the penstock the green-eyed girl bathing naked in the wan moonlight. Although this *Belle Dame Sans Merci* was immersed entirely in the water, her face and hands were as white as the chalk cliffs above the brook. She beckoned for Morgan to join her with the same slow circular motion of the hand and arm her father had made. He retreated back into the mill and resumed walking around and around the grindstones. Slidell, now overpowered by weariness herself, lay down on the robes and fell into a deep enchanted sleep.

Soon the wind rose. The wooden sails of the windmill high overhead began to spin and the waterwheel as well commenced turning, its paddles *clap-clap-clapping,* the gears of the wheel screeking, the mill vibrating as the stone wheels ground against each other. The unclothed girl appeared in the moonlight and again took his hand in her cold grip. When she saw that he feared her, she wet her lips and said, "Just hold me, Morgan. I need to be warm again." But he knew that he must not give in to his desire to lie with her or eat the bread or fall asleep.

"He was dark, but thou art fair," she murmured, and though

Morgan was not sure he understood what she meant, her words chilled him to the marrow. Something told him that he must not ask after his brother here, must not mention Pilgrim's name to these pale revenants of the Cumber.

After a time the girl went away, casting a sorrowful glance over her bare white shoulder, her billowing dark hair trailing behind her. The wind fell. The wooden sails of *Dagaz* ground to a halt. The waterwheel ceased clapping and the machinery inside the mill fell silent. Dawn broke, revealing a bilious smudge over range upon range of mountains. Only with difficulty was Morgan able to wake Slidell. They stepped outside, and Morgan slung his sack over his shoulder and checked and double-checked his scattershot and rifle. Without looking back at the mill or the house, he soldiered on up the brook under the white cliffs, Slidell following behind like a sleepwalker. Presently the rill turkey-tailed out into several seeps on a bald at the top of Haint Hollow. Spread out before them to the west was Boone's Gap, cutting through as many more mountains as they had already traversed. Far off to the southeast were the hazy peaks of the Great Smoke Mountains, the Shaconage.

This morning the loaf in Morgan's sack looked and smelled like any other loaf of bread. He wondered if he could now safely eat it but refrained from doing so. By degrees Slidell came to her senses. After walking a while longer they came out on another sled path. Ahead in a clearing, an elder with a waist-length white beard was frying bacon in a black iron spider over a meager fire. Nearby stood a lean-to made of chestnut bark.

"I hunger," the hermit said, turning the bacon with a forked twig. "Give me to eat."

Morgan reached into his tow sack and took out the loaf the miller's girl had given him and broke it in two. The hermit looked as frail as a man made of dry sticks, but he grabbed one of the halves and greased it liberally from the bacon skillet, then stuffed it into his mouth and gummed it down.

"Now the rest," the hermit demanded. "Be quick about it."

Morgan, who was so famished he felt weak, gave him the remaining half. The ancient wolfed it down, all but the heel, which he angrily threw into the fire.

"Where come you by e?" he said.

Morgan realized that he meant the bread. "A miller gave it to me."

"I'll wager he did," the hermit said. "All white-like? Beckoning to you like Gabriel a-calling muster? Gal with hands cold as the twentieth of January?"

"Yes."

"Put you up for the night at the mill?"

"Yes."

"Mill sails commenced to turn?"

"They did."

"Waterwheel go round?"

Morgan nodded.

"Didn't happen," the hermit said.

"Of course it happened."

"Nay. A year ago Yankee bummers kilt all three—man, wife, and green-eyed gal—and hanged them up on the mill sails and burnt down the whole shebang."

Slidell gave a gasp.

"Then how do you account for the bread?" Morgan said.

"What bread?" the hermit said and went inside his bark lean-to and didn't come out again.

They moved on into the wild Cumber up a series of ridges called

Satan's Staircase. Never had Morgan dreamed of such mountains as these. The mountains at home had one main spine running north to south one hundred and fifty miles. In places a few gentle foothills and ridges led up to them. The mountains of the Blue Ridge rose quickly in an orderly series of ramparts. But these peaks in the southern Dominion of Virginia were a devil's puzzle of tier upon tier separated by deep gulfs and troughs and roughs splaying out in every direction and bespangled with streams running all kittywampus through the laurel. The mountainsides were so steep that if they slipped and fell forward as they toiled up, they fell only a foot before hitting the sharp slope. In a hollow below a rock pinnacle, they came to a heap of broken caissons and battered cannons that appeared to have been run over the top of the stone spire high above.

They stopped to drink from a cold stream. "You're a good man, Morgan, whether you know it or not," Slidell said. "Feeding that old devil back there. Giving him the last of your bread. Trouble is, you're too serious. Don't know how to enjoy all the great pleasures of the world that God laid out before you." Playfully she smacked down the heel of her hand on the little pool from which they had drunk, spraying his bruised face with cool water.

Morgan grinned, but now that he had fed the rude hermit he wondered if he might have a stroke of luck. His mother had told him that any beggar who asked for food or a ride in a wagon or shelter from the night might be Our Lord in disguise. If you helped a stranger in need, she said, you'd have luck. His parents had helped every stranger in need who ever came to Kingdom Mountain, but they had not had much luck. One son had gone missing in the war. The other was simply gone.

Ahead was a glade in the laurel, then a great huckleberry barren, the berries still green, then a sweeping bald carpeted with red and yellow mosses, then a little tarn on a mountaintop with a stone house beside it. A woman, far from young and with a very grim countenance, sat on the roof of the house watching them through a copper-ringed spyglass.

"Mother, we have come a piece today," Morgan said. "And have a piece yet to travel. We are headed for Brush Arbor Ridge to make inquiry of a preacher there who may be able to help me find my missing brother. Could we trouble you for a bite to eat?"

"Does this look like a wayside stand? Get along with ye. You Yankee bummers have already stolen every morsel from this land."

Morgan looked off at the long views in every direction. This would be a fine place to live when a war wasn't going on. In the meantime the woman, who was dressed in widow's weeds, came down a ladder. "Come in, then. I might find ye a small bait, I might not. Leave your firelocks outside. I don't allow them."

Into the stone threshold of the house was carved the sign ℮. Morgan was not surprised. This remote mountain, far from the towns where slave catchers prowled, was a perfect locale for an Underground station.

He and Slidell had to duck their heads to enter the house, which consisted of a single room with a peat fire in the hearth. Hanging by their naked tails from smoky dark beams were all kinds of mice and voles. A kettle swung on a crane over the fire. Out of it the woman dipped some kind of stew, which she ladled into stoneware and handed to them. They did not ask what was in the stew, and she didn't say. She motioned for her visitors to sit at a stone bench at a low stone table and watched without comment as they ravened down the stew.

"Tell me a story," she said. "I'm starved for a story up here."

"They're preparing to cannonade Richmond."

"They can cannonade each other to atoms for all of me. Northern atoms, southern atoms. Tell me a *story*."

"A boy's brother went missing in the fighting. He walked a thousand miles searching for him."

The woman nodded. Morgan thought that she would surely ask whether the boy in the story found his brother. Then he would inquire if she had seen Pilgrim. Instead, she said, "Tell me another."

Morgan thought. "We met a miller and his wife and daughter, all three with dark skin powdered over with flour."

"Melungeons. Portagee they be, Christianized Moors from Lisbon fled to the American world ages ago to escape the Inquisition. Their ancestors were shipwrecked off Caroline. Over time they worked their way up into these forsaken mountains. Here they stayed. They too helped the runaways. My mother was one of them, and my former husband's grandfather. I never learned their lingo. You aren't telling me a story. I'm telling you one. Have another bait of stew."

"Did your husband die?" Slidell said. "I'm sorry."

"He died to me. Did you meet a satanic old creature with a long white beard down the sled trail a piece?"

"We met a hermit man," Morgan said.

"He is no hermit but my husband that was. He's dead to me now, though I watch him and his comings and goings through this copper-bound glass. I live to spite him. Come out onto my grounds. I'll show you an amusing thing."

They went outside, and the woman trained her ancient spyglass down the hollow, then handed it to Morgan. There in the glass was the hermit, on his knees, hands clasped as if praying, looking up toward the stone house on the hill. Morgan passed the telescope to Slidell.

"He's beseeching me to take him back," the woman said. "Which I most surely will, in seven times seventy years. Watching him grovel is my chief pastime since *Jera* fell into disuse and the dark ones stopped coming."

Morgan looked at the hermit again. "I thought he might be Jesus in disguise."

"Judas is more like. I caught him with the miller's wife two years ago and turned him out. Now I watch him with my Portagee ancestor's sailing glass. He's as dead to me as the miller and his family killed by Sheridan's bummers."

At this disclosure Slidell nodded with approval and gave Morgan a very significant look.

"The hermit, your former husband, told me that tale," Morgan said. "He said they hanged them from the windmill sails, then burned the place."

"For once in his life he told the truth. Point the glass further down the glen into what they call Haint Holler. No, further. What do you spy?"

"Woods. More woods. Flashes of the brook. A place that looks like a—"

He stopped. What he saw in the glass was the stone foundation of the grist mill, the ruined windmill beside it, the penstock, and the waterwheel. There had been a fire, but that was some time ago. Now vines encircled the blackened foundation. He handed the glass back to the woman, who laughed bitterly. "Next you'll tell me that you slept in the mill and the sails began to turn and the girl asked to warm herself in your bed. Oh, several like yourself have come by with the same tale. A Confederate boy with a staff carved into the shape of two snakes for a crutch, a shouting preacher with a wagon of slickery snakes. There's no accounting for what happens in Haint Holler, boy. Ye didn't lie with her, did ye? The gal? Or eat of their bread?"

Morgan shook his head.

"You'd say not anyway, like my deceased husband." The woman gave him a look as bleak as the windswept bald where she lived. "Here," she said. "Take this spyglass with you. It may save your life. But not if you venture to Brush Arbor Ridge. Cholera has claimed half the souls in that region and will claim half of the rest before it's spent. As for you," she said to Slidell, "your disguise is passable, but your gait is that of a proud, high-toned woman, swinging her hips along with her head held high. In dangerous company you must shuffle and scuffle and spit and draw in the dirt with your toe like a good-for-nothing young man. And you must not look strangers boldly in the face. Avert your eyes as if ashamed of your very being. Now then. Whoever you two may be, and I don't want to know, steer clear of Brush Arbor as you would of the plague, for they're one and the same. To travel there now is as good as a death warrant."

As they ventured on into the mountains Morgan began reading to Slidell, and she to him, by firelight, from the wonder-book Cobbler Tom had given him, chronicling the incredible journey of Captains Lewis and Clark to the Pacific. Morgan told Slidell that as Tom had recommended, he had a great longing to go West after he found Pilgrim and see for himself all of the splendid sights the captains had seen. Slidell laughed at this notion and said that the Teton Sioux and the Blackfeet would be glad to hear it, that his long, gold hair would adorn their scalp-poles handsomely. But on the off chance that he did make it through to the Pacific and back, she asked him to bring her a young buffalo-bison to pull her carriage in Canada, where she intended to marry a rich man and live the life of a fine lady. So they passed the time, two lovers and companions, spinning out their dreams one to the other as they trekked ever southward toward a future so uncertain that their fantasies seemed more real than the sober likelihood that Pilgrim was dead, so too Slidell's brother, Solomon, and at any moment they themselves might be shot by Dinwiddie's mad outriders.

After their encounter with the ghostly Melungeons, Morgan waited for Slidell to remind him that she had told him the Cumber was a place of specters. Instead she asked him why, when God had given so much to mankind and set all the splendors of the world before them, most of all the capacity to love and be loved, mankind was so determined to spurn these great gifts? She asked him if he thought Satan had so much sway on earth that he had corrupted all men and women and all of their works since time began.

"If I thought so," Morgan told her, "I'd walk Satan down like those killers I told you about."

"You the boy to do that, all right," Slidell allowed. "Better off to spend your time finding Pilgrim. Rescuing Little Solomon off Grace." She gave him a sly look. "Maybe even making an honest woman of Slidell."

Morgan smiled. "Slidell, you're the most honest person I've ever known. As for mankind, I want to tell you about a book I read."

"Not that foolish *Uncle Tom's Cabin* again. I've already told you what I think about that book. Good enough tale, I suppose."

"No, it's a book my brother sent me from college. It's called *Origin of Species,* by Mr. Charles Darwin."

As they walked along, Slidell from time to time practicing shuffling and scuffling like a good-for-nothing young man, Morgan outlined Darwin's ideas on survival and evolution. He wasn't sure that Slidell, now imitating the stiff-legged gait of a mule, now floating eerily along like the miller's green-eyed daughter—*Hold me, Morgan*—was paying the slightest attention.

That evening, however, as they sat beside their campfire feasting on a young tom turkey that Slidell had killed with her sling, she turned her direct look on him and said, "That's flat-out slap nonsense, boy."

"What is?"

"That book by Mr. Charles Darwin you told me about. I've been thinking about it, and it doesn't make one particle of sense. Now you listen to Slidell. Let's say mankind *was* made to survive. Why then would we spend the last three years killing each other off in this war, half a million or more? Why brand our own children? Run off with the miller's woman? That doesn't sound like survival of the fit. It sounds like the worst pack of rascals ever created, hell-bent to destroy the species. That's not all, either. This coming-down-from-the-apes notion? Why, that's more foolish yet. What did the great apes ever do that we have to blame them for us? Do the great apes kill half a million their kind? No, sir. Not that I ever heard of. Cut off their little ones' fingers? I guess they don't."

"I think Darwin believed that apes and men both originated from a common—"

"I don't care *what* he believed, boy. I'll tell you what I believe. Talk about *species,* I believe mankind is just about the worst ever created. Go to war, enslave one another, persecute our children, and then blame the gentle ape. No, Morgan. We're evil to start out with because we have chosen to be. Satan's just there to help us out a little. Which is why we must turn to Our Dear Redeemer, Jesus Christ, for salvation."

Slidell paused for a moment. In her passionate faith she seemed more beautiful than ever. Morgan wished that he could share her beliefs. He reached out and took her hand and looked at her in the firelight. If he could not believe in God, at least he could believe in this beautiful and noble young woman.

"I agree with the first part of your proposition," he said. "We're a pretty sorry outfit. But I've been wondering about something, Slidell. You haven't mentioned your father. Where was he when Dinwiddie was branding Little Sol and trying to force himself on you? Where was your father when Dinwiddie chopped off Sol's fingers with the tin shears?"

"He was right there," Slidell said.

"Your father was there? And didn't try to stop Dinwiddie?"

Again Slidell hesitated. Then, in a voice devoid of emotion, she said, "Dinwiddie is my father, Morgan. Sol's too."

MORGAN KINNESON WAS SPARING of words, but only very rarely was he at a loss for them. Now for a time he did not know what to say. It crossed his mind, thinking of Slidell's own father attempting to rape her and maim his son, the little prodigy, that the world held a depth of evil that he had not yet plumbed. After his encounters with Ludi, Doctor Surgeon, and mad Steptoe, he would not have believed it possible.

"I'm sorry, Slidell," he said at last. "I'm truly sorry. But you need to know this much. However wicked this world may be, you're still the best person I've ever known. After all this"—he gestured with the back of his hand to the north, the way they had come, somehow encompassing all of the evil that he had thus far witnessed—"after all this, I wouldn't have thought it possible. That I could ever love anyone. But I do. I love you."

"Oh, Morgan," Slidell said, weeping now. "No. No, no, no."

"Yes. You have to believe me."

"I do believe you," Slidell said. "But you musn't. You musn't love me. You don't know who I am."

"I reckon that's about the one thing I do know."

She continued to shake her head. "You don't," she said. "I'm not the best person you know, Morgan. I'm the worst. Slidell Collateral Dinwiddie? Slidell Judas Dinwiddie is more like."

Despite himself Morgan smiled. But Slidell said, "That night in the cabin with Dinwiddie? Before I screamed and my granddaddy came running?"

Morgan was sure he knew what she was going to tell him. He put his finger on her lips. "I don't care what happened that night, Slidell. You couldn't help any of that."

"It's not what you think. And I *could* help it. Before my grand-daddy busted in, Morgan, I pleaded and begged. I begged old Din-widdie not to ravish me. I called out to my dead mama to protect me. He laughed and told me my mama was rotting in the ground. I even told him I had the black-blood cholera, that if he touched me, he'd catch it certain sure."

"I'd have said the same thing, Slidell. That's no sin."

"Maybe not. But what I did next was. To save myself, Morgan, I told Dinwiddie that my granddaddy had a stone, passed down in our family for hundreds of years. That away back in Africa, some men with light hair like yours came in carved ships and gave that stone to our ancestors. On one side were strange letters, very faint. On the other, my granddaddy Jesse had scratched a map of the escape route north for runaway slaves. I told Dinwiddie Little Sol knew that map by heart. And I told Dinwiddie that if he'd leave me be, I'd get Sol to draw it for him. But old A.D. was crazy drunk. He said he'd tend to Sol and the stone soon enough, but first he intended to make a woman of me. That's when I screamed and my granddaddy rushed in. Oh, Morgan. Don't you see? I alone was to blame for Dinwiddie cutting off Sol's fingers, and still that good little boy would not peach and give up what he knew."

With that, the girl began to moan and sob and shake, but Morgan took her in his arms and said, "Slidell, I'd have done exactly the same thing. You and your granddaddy Jesse were planning to run off with Sol that very night. You just wanted to buy a few hours, not betray anybody. Now you listen to me. I'll tell you something a thousand times worse than what you told me. Something about myself. Can you stop crying and listen?"

Without waiting for her to reply, Morgan said, "Do you remember what I told you in the cave? About that poor black man I was supposed to be taking into Canada? The man Ludi shot and hanged?"

She nodded, biting her lower lip.

"His name was Jesse, Slidell. Jesse Moses. That man was your grandfather. He gave me that rune stone, slipped it into my pocket so the killers wouldn't get it. And when I think about the way I left him alone in that cabin, I agree with just about every word you said about mankind, with myself the worst of the outfit. I'm sorry, Slidell. I shouldn't have hidden this from you."

In the firelight, as he held out the rune stone, Morgan could see tears sliding down her face. He braced himself for her to spring at him, as she had at Cobbler Tom's when he laughed at her, but she simply wept silently as she took her grandfather's rune stone and turned it over and over in her hand. Then she handed it back and shook her head and after a little she said, "I know all that, Morgan. I suspected as much back in the cave." Then she smiled through her tears. "Can you stand to hear something good now? Stop blaming yourself for what you aren't to blame long enough to hear the other side?"

Morgan looked at the girl in the firelight. She reached out and took both of his rough hands in hers, which were soft and warm. "Morgan," she said, "there *is* a whole other side. To mankind. To us. There's the love of my grandfather for our people and their freedom. There's your love for your brother. And mine for Little Solomon. And God's for all of us, despite our fallen ways." She looked at him over their clasped hands and said, "And ours for each other. I love you, too, Morgan. And I do know you love me."

As the small fire died, high in the pine and oak woods of the un-frequented wilderness, they made love again. This time their passion was infused with all the bonds of respect and deep affection and understanding and the more ecstatic for these bonds, but at last, as they lay in each other's arms, and the embers of the fire faded into darkness, Slidell said, "Morgan, I must tell you one more thing. I know that you have it in mind to kill that evil preacher tomorrow at the Brush Arbor. The one who calls himself Prophet. I must ask you, not for my sake but for yours, not to harm him."

"Slidell, if I don't kill him, he'll kill me and deliver you and Jesse's stone to Dinwiddie. Other people, many others, will be murdered as well."

Slidell jumped up and blew on the dying coals, and a few embers flared. "Throw that stone in the fire," she said. "You have it by heart, Morgan. You no longer need it."

"I do need it."

A little wind sifted through the treetops. From off over some long-forgotten valley a night bird unknown on Kingdom Mountain cried.

"I need it to draw them to me," Morgan said. "Not counting Dinwiddie, there are still two left. The Prophet and the one you call Swagbelly—King George. I'm sorry, Slidell."

"I'm sorry, too," she said. And in that moment, he feared that he had lost her.

O N THE SORROWFUL DAY of the mass funeral for the people swept away by cholera at Brush Arbor Ridge, deep in the mountains of the Cumber, an itinerant divine who had but lately come to the region drew up his mule wagon in front of the house of worship just as the service for the dead began. He was dressed all in black, his face and hands as yellow as the six-foot rattler draped round his neck that he called Angel Jaundice and kept near his person at all times. He climbed down and, already shouting, wrestled out of the wagon bed a great walnut armoire. This was his serpent cabinet, which he manhandled into the church and up to the pulpit, where the elderly minister was saying the prayers for the departed.

"Avaunt thee, Ahab!" screamed the oracle, thrusting the frail old cleric down into the pews with the bereaved congregation. "I and my scaly apostles have come to bring you great comfort. We have come to resurrect your dead. Yea, say I again, to *raise your dead. Bo-bobalabah and Jabalabah.*"

Prophet Floyd stalked back down the aisle of the old country church, spouting in tongues, and thrusting Angel Jaundice into the stricken faces of the congregants. Holding out the Angel, Floyd invited the people, both living and dead, to come forward and take the host. As yellow poison oozed from the reptile's fangs, he likened the deadly fluid to the first sweet pressings of the grapes at the Canaanite's wedding and himself to a benevolent vintner come to trample out disease and death.

At that moment a tall figure in a slouch hat and a fringed jacket entered the church. As the stranger came forward, Floyd brandished a long horse pistol in his right hand. The snake was now wrapped lovingly around his left forearm, its flat head and a foot and a half of its body reared up level with the chalice into which its poison was dripping.

"Come forward, boy, and render up the nigger's stone and your black whore, and I'll tell you where you can find your lost brother," screamed the Prophet. "But first take off your hat in the house of the Lord. For you stand before Him risen."

"When I stand before the Lord I'll leave on my hat and ask him a question or two. Are you the one they call Floyd?"

"I am that I am," the Prophet replied and leveled his pistol at Morgan and drew back the hammer.

"Forgive me, snake," Morgan said and fired the lower barrel of Lady Justice point-blank at the lunatic and his serpent. Floyd dropped lifeless to the floor with a hole the size of Morgan's fist where his heart had been, knocking over the snake cabinet onto himself. A leather-red copperhead slithered out, followed by a pygmy rattler less than a foot long and as big around as a fat cigar. More and still more vipers spewed out of the cabinet, as if issuing forth from the Prophet himself. Angel Jaundice, though headless, went whipping off toward the coffins of the dead. Morgan backed down the aisle and out of the tabernacle.

From the sagging trestle table under the arbor, Morgan hooked a damp grape leaf wrapped around a piece of bread and ham. He folded two boiled eggs and a leg of roast chicken in another leaf and put them in his haversack. Slidell, who had witnessed the shooting of Prophet Floyd and the coming forth of the serpents, looked on with horror. Beside the empty snake wagon stood a small black boy in a big straw hat, patiently keeping the flies off the Prophet's mule with a catalpa-leaf fan. He continued to wave the leaf, seemingly oblivious to the uproar, the loosed snakes inside the church, the defiled dead, the screaming mourners.

Morgan unhitched the red mule from the wagon and climbed on its back. He motioned to Slidell to climb up behind him. The boy was looking at him. "Today's my birfday," the child informed him. "Twenty-two July. I'se seben." He grinned at Morgan. "Some fine birfday!"

"Happy birthday," Morgan said and flipped him his last round silver dollar. The child caught the coin in his mouth. He removed it and studied it for a moment. Then he put it back under his tongue.

Morgan and Slidell rode the mule down the ridge. At the bottom of the hill a branch ran under the road through a hollow log. He drew rein and swung down. When he held out his hand to Slidell, she shook her head as if she could not bear to touch him and dismounted without assistance. She continued to stare at him as though she had never seen him before.

"What is it, Slidell?" Morgan said. "Don't you think I can help you rescue Solomon?"

"Oh, child," she said. "How are you ever going rescue yourself? How are you going to stop all this terrible killing?"

"Go along now," Morgan said to the mule, swatting it across the rump.

Then he looked back at Slidell. "I don't know," he said. "I'm not sure I can. I'm not sure I want to."

The riderless mule walked on up the dusty track. Morgan and Slidell stepped into the water and started up the branch through the bright orange jewelweed that grew beside the brook. Morgan thought of the little boy chasing flies. "Today's my birfday. Twenty-two July." It occurred to him that his own birthday, July nineteenth, had come and gone. Without realizing it, he had turned eighteen. He was a man.

NINE

BERKANA

ᛒ

And so the soldier Morgan Kinneson keeps walking because walking is what he knows to do. He believes that if he can but walk far enough, now trending south by southwest by the general's compass, he will get where he needs to go even if he is not quite sure where that is. He will know when he arrives because his brother will be there.

In such a fashion Morgan had begun to narrate his journey in his mind, he had no idea why. There was a moment when he and Slidell stood at a fork in the trail at the very top of Boone's Gap near the cabin of an opium grower, surrounded by poppies in full blossom. One branch of the trail headed toward the southeast and the hazy outlines of the tall Shaconage, where he believed his brother might be. The other prong of the fork was a narrow sled path cutting off to the southwest, toward the Tennessee lowlands, the Grace

River, and Dinwiddie's plantation. Morgan reached into his haversack and took out the general's compass. Unhelpfully, the needle swung north, as compass needles are wont to do.

"Trouble?" the old opium grower at the little cabin overlooking the grand prospect said. "Trouble making up your mind which-a-way to go?"

Morgan looked up. "I fear there will be trouble enough whichever way I choose."

A few days back, before he killed Prophet Floyd, Slidell might have had something to say. Now she just looked off into the distance.

"You see here," said the grower, who had over his shoulder a haversack like Morgan's. "I am an old man and I have seen me a great pile of your so-called trouble. Much of it never happened."

"I imagine some of it did," Morgan said.

The old man spread out his arms, encompassing the mountains flowing away and away to the south. "Behold. These peaks and coves are called Satan's Puzzlement. They're a hundred miles wide and all horribly gashed by little hollows that lead to nowhere, sprigging off like this and this and this." With each "this," the opium grower closed and then snapped open his fingers to indicate the hopelessness of negotiating Satan's Puzzlement. "What's more, each leads to trouble. For they are populated with a race of people who would almost as soon murder you as their neighbor and near as lief murder their neighbor as a blood relation with whom they have fallen out. Murder is the order of the day in those hollows. My brother was murdered at eighteen by his wife of two hours. At their wedding party she saw him talking to her sister. They was only passing the time, was they. But in a jealous rage she gunned him down on the spot. She had just turned fourteen."

Beside the old man's cabin, the poppies nodded pleasantly in the breeze. "Opium is much in demand these days," Morgan said, to shift the subject. "You must get a pretty penny for it."

"I get nothing for it. I give half of what I refine to the North and half to the South and have never taken a cent in return. It is my small contribution not to the war but to the peace. The peace of mind of dying men. Here." The grower reached into his sack and brought out a pouch, like a soldier's tobacco sack. Embroidered neatly on the pouch in scarlet thread was the rune ∩. Inside were twelve brown pellets about the size of common clay marbles. One by one the old man dropped them back into the little sack. As he did so, he named each one. "Matthew, Mark . . . James, John . . . and last of all, Judas. Take these and use them well, son. Employed wisely, they will bring more peace and relief than all the religion in this sad world."

To hell and gone with it all, Morgan suddenly thought. If, as he suspected, his brother was a short three or four days away in the Great Smokies, he would compass off to the southeast, along the left-hand branch of the fork, and Slidell could come with him or not as she chose. But his feet, his damnable walking feet, took him instead off to the west toward Grace Plantation. He knew that whether he found Pilgrim or no, his work would not be done until he dealt with Dinwiddie and helped Slidell rescue her brother, if he was still alive to be rescued. He had given his word to do so, and his word was all the certainty he had left in the world. Slidell walked beside him, as silent as the surrounding forest.

So THE SUMMER WORE ON, and as Morgan and Slidell worked their way through Satan's Puzzlement they did not happen upon any feuding mountaineers, nor did they get caught in their crossfire. This, Morgan believed, would have greatly disappointed the old opium grower. One morning their path lay through the remains of a close-set stand of woods so recently burned over that the blackened trees were still smoking. With the fumaroles of smoke twisting above it, the scorched landscape looked like some stern Old World painter's vision of hell. Some of the trees were still on fire, and scattered through them lay the charred remains of soldiers shot in the flaming woods and burned to cindery outlines where they had fallen. Slidell refused to look at the soldiers' remains. For the most part she no longer spoke at all. Since the killing of Prophet Floyd at the Brush Arbor Tabernacle, she and Morgan had not made love. On the few occasions when it was necessary for her to speak, she would not look at him.

One evening at dusk they happened upon a double-crib cabin. From one of the two rooms came a horrible high shriek, like a woman in childbirth. Inside on a straw tick stuffed into a rough open coffin lay an old, old woman with long white hair. On the door of the cabin was the symbol ᛒ and the word *Berkana*.

"Who be there?" the woman called out between moans.

"Morgan Kinneson from Kingdom County, Vermont."

"Take my hand, then, Morgan Kinneson, for I'm about to travel over."

He knelt beside the old woman and took her hand in his, and she held it deathly tight and moaned.

"Where do you have pain, grandmother?" Slidell said. "Can I fetch you water?"

"No, no water. The pain is in my soul. Ye must forgive me, dear children. Oh, oh, oh! I've lived with my own ruined conscience for nigh sixty years, and I can live with it no longer nor die with it, neither. Please forgive me."

"Grandmother, I'm no preacher. I can't forgive you."

"Ye must."

"I don't know what to say."

"Say, 'I forgive you, Fair Susan.'"

Fair Susan gripped his hand the harder, as though she wished to cling to life a little longer or possibly take Morgan across to the other side with her. By now he had seen enough of dying to know that she had only a few minutes left in this world. She said, "Listen, child. Long before your time I was the beauty of these mountains. I was known far and known wide as Fair Susan. I loved my young lover, but he married another and oh, it like to split my heart in twain. One eve I slipped up the mountain to their little cabin and found my rival asleep. On the table in the room where she lay sleeping, as if placed there by the horned devil himself, was a cleaver. I seized it up and drove it into her heart. Oh, child. Can you forgive me?"

A thousand thoughts went through Morgan's head. How could he of all people, abroad on the land walking down other men, wicked though they were, forgive anyone? Only God had that power, and Morgan had seen scant evidence that God, if he existed at all, ever forgave anyone. But his heart went out to Susan and so, though he believed that such a blasphemous act would surely certify his own damnation, he said, "Susan, I forgive you."

"Oh," she moaned. "There's more."

More! Morgan did not think he could bear to hear more—he already had guilt enough of his own for any ten men to bear. Worse yet, Slidell was watching him intently. He was certain that he had no chance of reclaiming her esteem, but he could not bear the thought of continuing this blasphemous charade. And he doubted that he could have broken Fair Susan's grip save by chopping off her hand or his own with a cleaver like the one she had plunged into the poor innocent bride's heart.

"Can you forgive me, child, if I tell you the rest? For I'm more sorry than words can say. I thought that taking in the poor black runaways at the sign of *Berkana* would ease my conscience, but it never did. *Berkana* means rebirth. There was no rebirth for Fair Susan."

"How many fugitives did you take in, Susan?"

"Hundreds. Yet it never relieved my anguish for one moment. Can you forgive me again?"

"Yes," Morgan said despite himself. "I forgive you, Susan. But don't tell the rest. You don't need to."

She let out another moan. "I must. After I did my fell deed, the high sheriff came riding, and he took up my former lover for the murder. He maintained his innocence up and down and forward and backward, but they tried him at Parched Corn Courthouse and found him guilty, and they hanged him from a tall gallows for the world to see. I went to the hanging. Until the moment they pulled the trip, I intended to confess. In the end I had not the staunchness. And all these years since I've never told a soul. Can you forgive me?"

"I can," Morgan said. "And I do."

"Thankee," the woman said with a sigh. "Thankee. And now there's one more boon I must ask of you. I want you to sit nigh for another little while until I travel and then take Fair Susan's corse up the Sugar Fork and lay her to rest beside her poor lover that was wrongfully hanged. He lies buried outside the graveyard palings under a hackberry tree. There's a little stone there, carved like unto a devil's skull, that his murdered wife's people set as a marker. Promise me, child. Ye owe it to me, having forgive me."

The logic of this assertion escaped Morgan. He hesitated to bury the poor woman beside the man she had consigned to an unjust execution, and most of all he was loath to delay his journey by one single hour more. But she begged him so, and was so terrified to die alone and be buried apart from her beloved, that against all his better judgment he finally said, "All right, Susan. I promise."

"There's a spade in the dooryard and a sled to pull me on," Susan said, and she lay back in her narrow wooden coffin, which Morgan guessed she had made herself, and a little later she expired with some measure of peace. Slidell lighted the oil lamp on the trestle table, and in its glow he realized that the trestle was in fact the coffin lid. He wondered what Fair Susan's last name might be.

Unable to meet Slidell's eyes, he carried the lidded coffin with Susan inside out to the dooryard, where he found the shovel and the hand sled, upon which he pulled the coffin up the dry branch to the cemetery. Under the hackberry tree outside the palings he discovered a stone not much larger than his fist, carved into a hideous little devil's head. He picked the thing up and put it in his towsack, thinking it would be a fitting marker for the grave he intended to dig for Arthur Dinwiddie. Working by the thin light of a quarter moon he buried Susan. To his surprise, Slidell assisted him, taking her own turn with the shovel. From time to time she gave him a quick, considering look, but said nothing. When they were finished, Slidell knelt beside the new grave and somberly recited the Lord's Prayer, laying particular emphasis upon the forgiving of our trespasses.

The gulf between them still seemed as profound as that which now and forever separated Fair Susan from her own once beloved.

THEY CAME INTO A LAND of flat cane fields and rice fields flatter still, of stout riparian trees whose high-kneed trunks seemed rooted in black standing water. Their limbs were draped with moss, like the tattered gray beards of soldiers who had been young when the war began but were now grown old. These strange sights made Morgan uneasy. Like heartsick Ruth, he had come to an alien land. He wondered if the people who lived here would find Vermont alien.

One morning Slidell woke up weeping. She told Morgan she had dreamed that Dinwiddie was now starving Little Solomon in the bamboo cage in which he had murdered many a runaway slave. That night Morgan asked her what she planned to do if they were able to rescue Little Sol from Grace Plantation. She told him that she had hidden, on the edge of Moccasin Bayou, a small blue fishing boat. Originally, Slidell's plan was to row north with Sol on the Tennessee River, then up the Ohio to Illinois, and from there they would make their way on foot to Canada and freedom. Recently, though, she had begun to think that she and Sol might be safer going on with him if he would agree to take them north after he found Pilgrim. For the first time since he had killed Prophet Floyd, Morgan felt that there might yet be some hope for himself and Slidell, however slender.

They began to hear terrifying reports of Arthur Dinwiddie's Grace Plantation. Some said there had been a revolt and the plantation had been turned into a prison for former slave owners. Patrollers rode unchecked over the land, visiting atrocities on the population. Here in the Tennessee lowlands it seemed a war within the war was being fought, with armed factions preying upon the refugees pouring northward and upon each other. Anarchy obtained. It was perilous to travel by day, more perilous yet to move at night.

At a riverbank landing near a place called Shiloh, where some two years ago there had been a terrible battle, a horde of urchins, the oldest of whom could not have been twelve, came boiling out of the burned shell of a steamboat and set upon Morgan and Slidell with rocks and sticks, until Morgan was constrained to fire a warning shot over their heads. They seemed to be starving, and he had nothing to give them but that deadly warning to keep their distance. At the next town he heard that the steamboat children were from a Memphis orphanage. How they had gotten here and formed a guerrilla unit making sorties into the countryside for food and committing all the acts of rapine they were capable of, no one could say. Slidell shook her cropped head. "Weep for mankind," she said. "In such times as these, Morgan, weep for mankind."

It was the first time she had called him by name in weeks. As for her sentiments, he could only agree.

Grace Plantation? The graybeards on the square and leaning against the mossy posts on the river wharves pointed off to the south. Rumor had it that Union gunboats were even now assembling on the Tennessee to assault the plantation by water. If Morgan wished to see it, he had best see it quickly. Sherman had ordered that not one brick of the notorious Grace be left standing on another.

· · ·

Y ET WHEN THEY ARRIVED, the place was not what Morgan had expected. Not that any place was in these inverted times, when the one remaining shared objective of North and South seemed to be to dismantle, as violently and completely as possible, a civilization that had taken several hundred years to develop, with absolutely nothing to replace it save chaos. But the broad avenue between the mature white oaks and spreading copper beeches leading up from the levee road by the Grace River to the gleaming white mansion with soaring limestone pillars seemed placid and blessedly removed from the terror and anguish not ten miles away. The fields stretching off into the distance, rice along the bayous, then cane, then plain upon plain of cotton, bespoke bounty and content and perhaps an oasis of sanity in a land run amok. How Morgan loved the trees. Stately, tall, wondrously varied, they ranged over a spacious park stretching away and away from the great house. Some he knew by name, many he did not.

The plantation house, as big as the Kingdom County courthouse, was built in the shape of a steamboat, with three decks decorated with ornate gingerbread scrollwork and a cupola on top resembling a pilothouse. Under the porte cochere wound a drive of crushed pink shells, up which Morgan now walked alone, while Slidell waited near the river. It did not look like the scene of a rebellion. The beauty of the place made Morgan wish to read law there, or write up a narrative of his long trek, sitting high in the glassed-in pilothouse where Slidell had read Sir Walter Scott to her small white half brothers and sisters.

Then he thought of Arthur Dinwiddie, and he strode across the pink shells and lifted the brass door knocker in the shape of a liveried black child knocking, though even Morgan Kinneson from Vermont knew that no slave, child or adult, would ever have been allowed to come to the front door of the Grace mansion. He rapped sharply three times. He had entrusted his rifle, Lady Justice, to Slidell for safekeeping. Ludi's scattershot, both barrels primed and loaded, hung around his neck inside his deerskin jacket. With it he would kill Arthur Dinwiddie. And though he was certain that Slidell knew his intentions, this time she had voiced no objections. Not because she had changed her mind about the wickedness of all killing. She had not. Rather, Slidell knew that if they were to have any chance of rescuing Sol, she must let Morgan do his work as he saw fit. Morgan, for his part, was prepared to dispatch the plantation owner like a coiled snake in his path. That would end it, he believed. That would end it all, and he would be free to find Pilgrim.

A black child no more than seven or eight years old opened the big door, revealing a lofty manorial hall and majestic spiral staircase. He was dressed in a butler's suit and a tall red turban. "Why, sir," he said, "what a pleasure to make your acquaintance. Welcome. Welcome to the good ship *City of Grace*. May I have your name, sir?"

Morgan told the little boy his name. He noticed that the child's ring fingers were missing from each hand. The scarlet turban was a good foot high. "I am Little Prince Solomon," the child said with the greatest insouciance in all the world. "Come in now, Mr. Kinneson. The tour of the *City of Grace* begins here in the Great Hall. The Great Hall was conceived by Mr. Arthur Dinwiddie the First in 1763 when he drew up the original design for the house. Mr. Arthur Dinwiddie the First was the great-grandfather of the current Mr. Arthur Dinwiddie. Don't mind your boots, sir. Leave them on. Through this door have strode booted potentates stretching all the way back to General George Washington, of whom the current Mr. Dinwiddie is a great-great-nephew."

Little Prince Solomon made a gracious gesture, palm up, toward the circular staircase. "We will tour the second deck momentarily. But let us now view the first-deck staterooms. These portraits lining the Great Hall are of former Dinwiddies and their thoroughbred racing horses. Here's Bonnie Scotland. Here's Iroquois, here's Emperor Jack. The smoke color of the hall paint was selected by Mr. Arthur Dinwiddie the First to enhance and highlight the portraits. The ruby-colored fanlight over the door is the result of blending gold flake with molten glass. The woodwork is yellow poplar, sir. Yellow poplar was very abundant in the day of Mr. Arthur Dinwiddie the First. It was quartersawed to give the appearance of walnut or oak."

From somewhere downriver Morgan could hear cannon fire. With patrician disregard for the cannons, the child, his shiny butler's shoes clacking on the yellow poplar parquet floor, led the way into a double parlor. Here he resumed his well-polished narrative. "The twin parlors, Mr. Kinneson, with their walls of robin's-egg blue and their varnished sweet-gum ceilings, are furnished with Thomas Chippendale chairs and divans. The tall pier mirrors in gilded frames multiply the chandelier lights. The modern gasoliers were installed only recently for the sake of convenience. The painting of the current Mr. Arthur Dinwiddie, over the Georgia marble mantel, was done in 1848 by the renowned Savannah artist Mr. W. C. Llewelyn Chute."

In the full-length oil portrait Slidell's father was dressed in a riding outfit. He was still quite young and did not look like a cruel man.

"Where is the current Mr. Arthur Dinwiddie?" Morgan asked.

Little Prince Solomon placed a finger to his lips. "Won't you come this way now and see the ship's library, Mr. Kinneson? Like the parlors, it boasts a fourteen-foot ceiling. The oak bookcases help take up wall space. The bird's-eye maple breakfront and secretary were commissioned for the library by the first Mr. Dinwiddie. The maroon racing silks above the door are the oldest registered racing silks in what we once called the United States—united, I fear, no longer. We'll tour the stables and grounds presently." In an aside, like a player delivering a soliloquy, Solomon whispered behind his maimed hand, "Help poor papa, Mr. Kinneson."

"What?" Morgan said. "Help who?"

The boy made a rapid silencing gesture. Except for the distant cannons, it was still and very warm. Morgan had the sense that he and Solomon were being scrutinized by the Dinwiddie ancestors on the walls of the Great Hall. He no longer wished to write up his journey in this anomalous steamship of a house, which seemed to him more mausoleum than manor. A mausoleum of a way of life that, like Cousin Mahitabel's textile mill far to the north, had been sustained by trade in human flesh, and very soon, when the approaching gunboats arrived, would be dead.

The cannonading downriver seemed to be drawing closer. The glass in the many-paned windows shuddered with each blast. "Well, well," Solomon said. "We have just time to tour the grounds and outbuildings before the troops arrive." Then, "Old Swag rode in two weeks ago. He hung papa up in a cage."

From which he glided with perfect cadence back to his narrative. "Are you fond of roses, Mr. Kinneson? Come. We have one of the finest collections in the Confederacy. You must see our thornless Himalayan and the unique Grace Colony Black Beauty. A true black rose is unheard of, you know. Mr. Arthur's blossomed a fortnight ago. Just before the Reign began."

"The Reign?"

"Of King George the Terrible. Come now, sir. See our rare black rose. Mr. Arthur was working on hybridizing a blue one as well. It too may have produced a blossom."

As the early evening shadows crept over the manicured grounds, Little Prince Solomon led Morgan to the rose garden, showing him many a new cultivar developed by his botanically minded father. He conducted Morgan through an arboretum of exotic trees from Africa and South America, then down a path toward the crawling black river. Near several bee gums they came upon a thundering steam-powered cotton gin. In a nearby cypress tree hung a bamboo cage with an elderly white man inside it. He was wearing a filthy plantation owner's suit and green goggles. Twelve black men, whom Morgan judged to be former slaves, were holding a court below the tree, under the direction of a thirteenth, a black giant in a frock coat and top hat. The giant's nose seemed to have been recently broken. He was standing on the back of a tobacco wagon, and beside him, bolted to the wagon bed, was a gleaming silver gun with a crank handle and a ventilated barrel pointed straight at the man in the cage.

The huge man in the silk hat intoned in a grave voice, "And did you, Arthur Dinwiddie, after passage of the law prohibiting the importation of slaves into the United States from old Afric, did you continue to commission the theft and enslavement of Africans?" When the man in the cage refused to reply, his interrogator knelt beside the silver gun and began to turn the handle, sending a racketing volley of bullets into the branches of the cypress. The prisoner, grasping the bamboo poles of the cage, never flinched. "Fine, then," the judge rumbled. "Citizen Stoker, I bring you as witness. Did Ar-

thur Bedford Dinwiddie, also known as Anno Domini, breed and
sell into slavery some two thousand men, women, and children?"

"He did, Citizen George."

"And did he commission the murder of some thirty-five runaway
slaves?"

"He did."

"I put the question to you again, Mr. Arthur Dinwiddie. Did
you—"

"I don't have to answer your questions and I don't intend to," Arthur Dinwiddie said in a voice as dignified as is possible for a starving man in a bamboo cage. "Mr. Lee will be here shortly, and then,
gentlemen mine, we shall see what we shall see."

Citizen George fired another burst of bullets from the Gatling
gun. Then he gave a nod to Citizen Stoker, now building up a fearful blaze in the rumbling steam gin. Hiding among the bee gums,
Morgan heard shots from the river. The gunboats were arriving.
Citizen Stoker, stripped to the waist, his red galluses aglow in the
furnace fire of the clattering gin, smiled grimly.

"Jurymen, cast your stones, white for 'innocent,' black for black-
hearted villainous 'guilty,' as we know this man to be," King George
said.

"Help him!" Solomon whispered in Morgan's ear. "Help papa."

In the dusk a slender figure in a straw hat slipped out of the trees
along the river and passed stealthily through the bee gums. Slidell
slid in beside Morgan and thrust Lady Justice into his hands. "Sol,"
Slidell whispered. "Oh, Sol. It's your sister. It's Slidell, Sol. Come
for you."

The boy looked at her blankly. When she hugged him he stiff-
ened, still not recognizing her.

"Sol, I cut my hair," she whispered. "Otherwise, I'm just Slidell. Come, now. This man and I came back to rescue you."

"Rescue papa," the little boy said, pointing at Dinwiddie, huddled in the cage in the cypress tree.

Slidell shook her head. To Morgan she said, "I found my little blue boat. Right where I left it the night granddaddy and I ran."

Swagbelly stepped down off the wagon bed and removed his tall hat. As he walked from juryman to juryman, each one dropped a stone into the hat. Swagbelly took his hat to the steam gin, and in the light of the fire he dumped the stones rattling into his hand. Every one was black as obsidian. He strode back to the cage and stood beneath it with his hat over his heart.

"Arthur Bedford Dinwiddie, you have raped and pillaged and plundered. You have enslaved people on Grace Plantation for forty years. Into the land of Gath you sold your own children and nieces and nephews. You have ginned up the cotton and ginned up the lives of your people. Therefore I do sentence you to be ginned up in your own cotton gin."

"Do you think I care for your threats?" Dinwiddie snapped his fingers. "I don't care that much. General Lee is arriving as we speak. Can't you hear his boats? I'll whip you all again like the miserable curs you are. Even if I can't see you, I can still whip you."

"We gone gin up old Dinwiddie," Stoker said.

"No!" Little Sol screamed.

Morgan stepped out of the bee hives. "You men lower that cage and let him out. Be quick about it."

The jurymen fell back, letting go of the rope attached to the top of the cage. It dropped ten feet to the ground, split open, and spilled out the former plantation owner in a heap of rags.

King George laughed and came at Morgan with his massive hands opening and closing and made to seize his neck and throttle him. As Swagbelly lunged for him, Morgan grasped his huge thumbs, one in each hand, and bent them back onto the giant's wrist, breaking them at the second joint like matchsticks. Swag roared and rolled on the ground.

"Help Mr. Dinwiddie up," Morgan ordered the jurymen.

"Oh bee-gum man, hear us good," Citizen Stoker pleaded. "He they devil carnate. He send hundreds of chirren into bonda, kill all they runaway."

"I know what he's done. Assist him to his feet."

One of the men darted up to Dinwiddie and helped him stand.

"What's going on up there?" a nasal voice called out from the direction of the river. "What for's that cotton gin running at this time of night?" Citizen Stoker leaped onto the wagon bed, swiveled the Gatling gun in Dinwiddie's direction, and began to crank the handle, raking the area beneath the cypress tree with bullets. One struck the boiler of the gin, which blew up like an overheated steamboat engine, spraying some of the jurymen and Arthur Dinwiddie with boiling water. More shooting, as the scalded members of the court screamed and plunged into the river for relief. Morgan grabbed the wounded, badly burned, and screaming Dinwiddie by the back of his jacket and dragged him into the sugarcane, with Slidell and Little Sol close behind. Sol wailed as a torch flew out over the river. In its flaring incandescence, the oncoming blue-clad soldiers shot at the helpless men in the water. Someone discovered the Gatling gun and was finishing off the slaves in the river with burst after chattering burst. The soldiers were whooping, shooting at anything that moved now. The man on the wagon bed gave out a great hurrah and turned the deadly machine gun on the cane, sending a volley of flying lead in the general direction of Morgan, Slidell, and Sol.

A flung torch landed in the cane, which instantly took fire. Morgan wrestled Dinwiddie over his shoulders. Slidell grabbed Solomon's hand. They ran, fire licking at their heels. In its light Morgan saw, fleeing with them, rats and muskrats, rabbits, snakes, a lumbering turtle. "Shoot me, shoot me, I'm a dead man," screamed Dinwiddie. Shots, flames, snakes. A leaping buck deer. Wee hopping mice. Solomon wailing, Morgan plunging forward, on his back the screaming man whom he had vowed to kill, as light as dry sticks. Six months before, Morgan had been running his trapline and milking his father's cows in Vermont.

"I s PAPA going to die?"

"He's burned and shot up pretty badly," Morgan said, whereupon Slidell's brother burst into tears. Morgan was touched, and outraged as well, that the child could weep for the creature who had maimed him for life. They had reached Moccasin Swamp, where Slidell's rowboat lay hidden in a canebrake. A mile downriver, the attacking bluebellies were occupied in firing the plantation.

"For the sake of God, kill me," Dinwiddie begged. "You might better have let them gin me up."

"You had Jesse murdered," Morgan said. "Then you sent the others to kill me for his stone. Why?"

"They stole my property," Dinwiddie said. "Your so-called stationmasters and conductors. I meant to see justice served on them."

"Where is my brother?" Morgan said. "Where is Pilgrim?"

It was the very longest of long shots, but to Morgan's astonishment Dinwiddie said, "Ask Oconaluftee."

"Who?"

"Water," Dinwiddie pleaded.

Morgan gave the man a drink from his canteen. He dug in his haversack and found the pouch of opium balls the poppy man had given him. He put one in Dinwiddie's mouth like a priest giving unction.

Dinwiddie moaned.

"Papa," Solomon cried.

"Come to me, boy," Dinwiddie said, groping for the boy's hands. "Can you forgive your father for what he did to your poor little fingers? Oh, child. Can you forgive me?"

"Yes, yes, papa, I forgive you. Only just don't die."

"Listen, Sol. You must go with this Yankee man and do as he says. He'll see to it that you're well cared for. Won't you now, Yankee boy?"

"I will. In the meantime, where do I find this Oconaluftee?"

"Opium. Then I'll tell you."

One by one Morgan fed the dying man the balls of opium while Slidell tried to comfort her little brother with the good heart and the daguerreotype powers of recollection. Far off on the eastern horizon the moon was coming up, round and yellow as a wheel of Vermont cheese.

"You'll find him," Dinwiddie started to say. He was having trouble speaking. Frantically, Morgan pressed Jesse's stone into Dinwiddie's hand. "Show me," he said. "For God's sake. Show me on this stone where can I find Oconaluftee. "

In his frenzied hurry Morgan had forgotten that the blind Dinwiddie could not show him. Yet the dying man in the green goggles took in his hand the relic he had long coveted and, like some latter-day Teiresias, traced his forefinger from top to bottom. Then his jaw fell and his eyes stared up at the moon with blank intensity. The opium had done its work. For Solomon's sake, Morgan shut the lids and placed a long cartridge from Lady Justice on each one. He lifted Dinwiddie's finger from the stone. Beneath it in the pale moonlight was the name Gatlinburg.

"That's it," Slidell said. "That's where we'll find your brother, Morgan. Gatlinburg. You helped me rescue Sol. Now Slidell's going to help you find Pilgrim."

Morgan shook his head. All he knew of what lay ahead was that where he was going, no one could accompany him.

"I *will* come with you," Slidell said.

"You can't."

From his belt Morgan unclipped the carved cedar drinking cup. "This is for you, Slidell. Show it to Auguste Choteau of Montreal, Canada."

"You going to kill old Mr. Luftee?" Solomon said as Morgan handed Slidell into the little boat and lifted Sol onto the bow thwart facing her.

"I'm going to bury your father," Morgan said, and he patted the child's head and shoved the boat out into the bayou. He did not have much hope that they would make it to freedom. He would be surprised if they made it to the Tennessee River, much less Canada. Yet he knew that this was their best chance and that Slidell could get through if anyone could. As they disappeared into the trees, Morgan cried out her name. He thought she called back to him, but he could not be sure over the terrific detonations from the plantation house. In accordance with their orders, the Union soldiers were blowing up the *City of Grace*. The sky above the house was as red as a newly opened rose. With a cypress stick sharpened to a point at one end, Morgan dug a shallow grave beside the bayou and covered Dinwiddie's body with sticks and leaves. It was all he could do for the man. He thought of the stone devil's head in his towsack, but for Solomon's sake, and Slidell's, he left it in his sack. Then he began walking again, heading east toward Gatlinburg and the Great Smokies, unaware that he was weeping.

TEN

ISA

J

"A Yankee fella name of Pilgrim? Wall, now. We had Yanks enough here in Gat, I can tell you, when they druve Will Thomas and his wild red injuns out of town. I don't recall any Pilgrim. Did he come in the *Mayflower*?" The know-all pine-tar man chuckled at his own foolish joke. It was slack time for him, early fall, when the sap in the pine trees was not running much and he had ample leisure to hold court from his cane-bottom chair on the little gallery of his cabin. Grandly, he swept his hand up the single dirt track at the twenty or so log buildings that made up the town of Gatlinburg, Tennessee, toward the bloating carcass of a calf lying at the far end of the hamlet. "This ain't, you know, downtown Richmond or Atalanter. I never could cipher out what Little Will was fighting for here. A couple dozen shanty shacks, a few patches of undersized corn? It really weren't much of a battle. Not as battles in this man's war have went, it weren't."

Morgan was squatting on his heels in the tar man's dooryard, listening, which was about all you could do once the man got going.

"Where is Thomas believed to be quartered now?" Morgan said when the talker finally paused to draw breath.

"Oh, he's laying up yonder."

"Up yonder where?"

The pine-tar man waved the back of his hand vaguely toward the ridge upon ridge of mountains rising into the hazy blue air west of Gatlinburg. "Up there," he said. "In them Smoke Mountains. What they call the Shaconage. But you don't want to venture there, boy. Oh no, you do not. If the Cherokees don't take your scalp, the outliers waiting out the war up Sugarland will bushwhack you. If the outliers don't lay for you, why Oconaluftee himself will string you up. No sir, young boy, up in them Smokes they'll kill ye as quick as look at ye. Oconaluftee is the worst. He wears a stuffed rattlesnake for a necktie, does old Mr. Luftee."

"Where did he ever acquire such an outlandish name?"

"After the mountain he dwells on when he ain't out murdering people. It is a very tall mountain over in Caroliny."

"What is the tallest and wildest peak in these parts?"

"Why, that would be Great Grandmother. If you know exactly where to look from here, away off there, you can maybe just imagine that you see it."

Morgan did not imagine that he saw it—he did see it. Faint but definite, like a huge splitting wedge thrusting into the distant sky. *There,* he thought. *That is where Pilgrim would go.* He was walking again, headed down the street, past a boy poking at the dead calf's glazed eye with a stick, past a woman in gingham hanging out wash on a porch. Toward the far blue peak in the haze. The light over the hamlet receding behind him was golden. He had walked from Vermont clear to Gatlinburg, and the place was nothing. For all he knew he was not one step closer to finding his brother. Gatlinburg was just another little tumbledown war-torn settlement. The path he was following ran under some tall trees near a stream falling down from the foothills. In the two weeks since he had parted from Slidell, he had forged his way through Moccasin Swamp and on to Gatlinburg, yet at every waking moment he was intensely aware of her absence. What had she called out to him? Had she called out to him? He kept walking.

For all his determination, Morgan Kinneson was weary. He was weary in body and weary in mind, and Great Grandmother was still many miles away. For the first time since leaving home he felt a surge of panic to be alone and unable to see what was nearby in the darkling woods. He veered uphill off the path and traversed the slope slantwise under the trees until the stream tumbling down the mountainside was just a faraway hush. Using the general's compass, he sighted in on two soaring rock towers, dim in the twilight, like the chimneys of a giant's house. He walked toward them, passing an oak grove where a bear had rooted for mast. Soon he would have to stop for the night because unlike a bear he could not see in the dark.

The thought of stopping had no sooner crossed his mind than he smelled smoke. It seemed to be drifting out of a narrow side cove, where yet another rill spilled down the mountainside. He peered up the little crease. However dangerous the mountain dwellers of this region might be, they would know if a Yankee doctor had come through lately. Cautiously, Morgan started up the brook through the laurel. The tang of wood smoke grew stronger. He smelled meat cooking. He cut up the glen with the wind in his face, out around an open bowl, a cirque in the side of the mountain. Several hundred feet below, dark as the boulders along the little stream, were a few scattered cabins. He kept the breeze in his face so that any hunting dogs these people kept would be less apt to scent him. He eased his rifle over his head, then reshouldered it. It would not do to walk into a settlement in these mountains holding a gun at the ready. He started down toward the cabins, and as he approached, a woman sitting out on her log stoop in the dusk began to sing in a high, jerky voice:

All in the month, the month of May,
The green buds they were swelling.
They swelled till the pretty birds chose their mates
And Barbary her Sweet William.

By degrees, as the old tune that Morgan's mother had once sung to him proceeded toward its tragic conclusion, men, women, and children came to the doors of their cabins to listen. The men wore dark hats and carried their long-barreled mountain guns. Morgan wondered if they slept in their hats with their guns beside them like wives.

Will sent a letter through the town
To Barbary Allen's dwelling,

Saying here's a young man sick and he sent for you,
For you to come and see him.

A notion occurred to Morgan. He was no singer. He had never
been able to carry a tune, and Pilgrim made gentle fun of his un-
musicalness, as he did of Morgan's solemnity. Yet this was a song
that he knew well. If these people called such a nasal quivering wail
singing, surely he could do that much himself. The song went on as
hard-hearted Barbary slighted William and he took to his bed.

O mother, O mother, O fix my bed,
Go fix it long and narrow.

Whereupon Morgan began to sing counterpoint in the same
tremolo:

Sweet William he died for me today,
And I'll die for him tomorrow.

The singing woman gave a start. The men reached out their
long arms for their mountain guns, longer still. Morgan did not try
to conceal himself. That would bring a hail of bullets. He started
down the mountainside and sang on in some approximation of the
woman's minor key:

They buried Sweet William in the old churchyard
And Barbary close by the side of him.

He stopped, hoping, hoping. And yes, from below came the
woman's quavering voice, rich and low in the dew-laden twilight:

At the head of Sweet William's grave there sprung a red, red
   rose
And Barbary Allen's was a briar.

And Morgan, now walking in stately accompaniment to the ballad:

They grew, they grew to the top of the church
And they could not grow any higher.

The woman's answering voice was full of vibrato and deep sorrow:

They leaned and tied in a lover's knot
And the rose hanged onto the briar.

Morgan stopped in the woman's swept-earth dooryard. "Good evening, ma'am."

The singer stood, her copper-red hair falling down her back, her wide-set eyes as silver as new money. In her sack dress she was as spare as a girl, and Morgan could see that she had been and still was beautiful.

"Eventide to ye as well, son William."

There was a hint of irony and humor in her "son William," discernible more in her eyes than in her tone. Her voice was sharp with the ring of authority, and when the man at the nearest cabin shifted his gun Morgan's way, she made a short and queenly gesture with her palm straight out from her narrow waist and instantly he turned his gun barrel away. Whether she was the rifleman's mother or the matriarch of this clan Morgan couldn't tell. Only that he was now temporarily under her protection.

"Have ye tooken your nightly bait?"

"I have not."

"Be ye too dauncy high-born for porridge?"

"I like porridge."

"Then leave all your mickle weapons here by the house wall and venture in and be welcome to what I have. And afterwards ye'll tell us your story by firelight and we'll gather close to attend and then we'll determine what to do with ye. Come now, eat. No one in all the Sugarlands will dare molest your weaponry. Yet I do hope ye shoot better than ye sing, for meaning no offense, ye cain't croon a note."

As he stepped on to the gallery, leaving his guns leaning against the cabin wall, Morgan noticed, carved deeply into the woman's door, the sign ∫. Inside the cabin, the windows were covered with black crepe, as if there had been a recent death in the family. He devoured the porridge, which was no more than oats pounded into a watery gruel and slow-cooked for a few hours with raw molasses dribbled over for sweetening.

Outside, the men had built an open fire to sit around. Morgan sat on a log near the fire, the reflection of the red flames playing on his sun-darkened face and light mustache, his gray eyes trained inward on his own unswerving purpose. Some of the men and boys had been standing by the cabin admiring Lady Justice and Morgan's scattershot, but as the beautiful matriarch had promised, no one troubled Morgan's weapons. If he offended these people they might well shoot him. They would not steal from him.

"Why come ye armed amongst us? What draws you here to Hell

For Sartin?" the man who had shifted his gun said. At first Morgan was at some pains to understand him—the grace syllable in the word "here," *he-ear,* the name Hell For Sartin. Hell For Sartin must be the community of cabins.

"I am looking for my brother."

Maybe they had trouble understanding him as well, because after a few moments of silence the singing woman said, "He's questing for his kin," as though translating what Morgan had said into their tongue.

"Who be he, Barbary? What do they call his brother?" the rifleman said.

"My brother's name is Pilgrim Kinneson. My name is Morgan Kinneson. My brother was a doctor with the Union army."

"The kin he's questing for be a doctor man," the silver-eyed woman said. "Name of Pilgrim Kin."

"Kinneson."

"Kin-son. The son of kin. He is a-looking for kin."

"From whence?"

"Where hail ye from, boy?"

"Vermont."

"I ken it not."

"Far to the north."

"He comes from the Northlands."

"Up Pinch Gut? Kemper's Stand? Up Broke Leg? Where north?"

"Farther," the woman said. "Hundreds of leagues. Where the running ones go."

"T'other side of Old Mistress Grandmother? Caroliny?"

An old man back in the shadows spoke up. "I dropped down to Caroliny when I was a stripling. Tooken work in a mill. It was a shingle mill. Hied me home the next day."

"Why for was that, grandsire?" Barbary said fondly. "Why hied ye back so abrupt?"

"Why, Barbary, I didn't favor the drinking water. 'Twarn't sweet like ours. It tasted like unto metalwork. I hied me straight home."

"This boy is from far beyont Caroline. Tell us your story, Morgan Kinneson. Tell us all about your quest for your brother and leave out nothing. And if you met ary young women on your way and left them broke-heart, tell us that. For we love a sad tragic story of love above any other."

Morgan leaned in closer to the splits of dried hickory burning clear and bright on this fallish evening. He had told some of his story to Slidell. Told some of it to the southern general. Now he would tell it to these mountain people.

"Talk slow," the woman said. "For your fashion of speech is out-landish and difficult, and ye talk as much from your nose, the way we sing, as from your mouth, and the words fall rude on the ear to listen at. But above all leave out nothing, for we love a long story on a chill evening. No tales neither, story us no stories, but a spang-true chronicle. And if'n you left a sweetheart in your so-called Ver-mont, you must tell us about her. And when your story is finished, if we love it and love you, why we mought help ye find your kin. And if we do not love your story it will go the worse for you. Commence."

Morgan began his tale. He told of finding Jesse hanged and of the shoot-out with Ludi in the bog. That's when the copper-haired woman made him stop and directed the men to go to their cabins and return with their women and children. For she did not want any of the Allen clan of Hell For Sartin to miss hearing such a narrative. The women came forth with infants swaddled in quilts in their arms and with toddling children and school-age boys and girls who had never been to school a day in their lives, and Barbary made him start again from the beginning. Morgan recounted how he had acquired the gypsy man's elephant, an animal that none of the children and few of the grown-ups had heard of. He chronicled his adventures with Birdcall on the canal and his battle with Steptoe and Prophet on the troop train in the land of the German Brethren. He told of meeting the southern general in Richmond but doubted that they had ever heard of him either. They murmured approval when he described how he had bested Swagbelly at Grace Plantation by breaking his thumbs. When he finished, all was still. Then Barbary said to the other women, "Put the small ones to bed now." And carrying their sleeping infants and some of the toddlers as well, the women departed.

A boy of sixteen said to Morgan, "I am Barbary Allen's son, Noah Allen. A fortnight past I runned my blue hound Blue on a he-bear up Desolation Creek on Sharp Top Mountain. Along hobbled an old woman headed home to Broke Jug from Great Grandmother. She had been to a young doctor who flat cured her of the dropsy. He had brewed some kind of potion and told her how to concoct it herself. And he refused her metal coin. She said he was from the Northland. They call him Old Doctor Grandmother. But I misdoubt he was your kin, for the old woman said he was well wedded to a fair young wife."

"I would fain behold that young wife," Grandsire Allen cackled.

"I don't misdoubt but you would, grandfer," another man said.

"Grandsire worn out five wives with eight and thirty children," Barbary said proudly.

"And would willingly take another tomorrow," Grandsire said. "If one would have me."

"Ye are a regular old Abraham when it comes to getting children in your dotage, grandfer," a man said. "How many winters have ye?"

"Ninety and five. And eight sons shot by Sheltons and one shot last month by Oconaluftee. That would be my boy Quill. Barbary's man that was."

Morgan turned to Barbary. "Oconaluftee shot your husband?"

"Aye," she said. "Luftee and his devils cotched Quill up Fire Creek hunting ginseng. They tried to get him to peach on us'n and tell where we's laying out. Oh, they tormented him sore and sore, but Quill never said one word. So Luftee shot him."

Barbary stood up, her hair the color of the embers in the fire. "Get ye all and every one to your beds," she told the clan. "On the morrow some of ye must climb up Leather Breeches to Shelton Laurel and warn the Sheltons that Luftee is near."

"Why, Lady Barbary. The Sheltons be our sworn blood enemies."

"More the reason. If Oconaluftee kills their menfolks, there will be none left for us and our sons to kill. You will warn them. As for Luftee, I vouchsafe to you on the eternal soul of my beloved husbint Quill Allen that he shall be dealt with. Now to bed. You," she said to Morgan. "Bide here by the fire."

Some minutes later Barbary reappeared with two clean tow sacks and a rough bar of pearl-ash soap, a fresh white linen shirt, linen drawers, gray homespun trousers, also a pair of good wool stockings. She ordered him to strip off his tattered raiment and throw it on the wood coals. Morgan was mortified to disrobe before the beautiful Barbary, but she laughed and said in her throaty voice that as he very well knew she had a son his age and one older still and had had two more, as well as her man Quill, killed at the hands of Luftee, and he would shuck off his clothing instantly or she would lay ungentle hands on him and strip him herself. Aye, she would, and relish the task. So Morgan threw his old clothes on the fire and walked naked except for his boots to the cold stream in the mountain darkness. Barbary led him straight to a deep basin pool below a waterfall spilling over a trough of limestone, and without breaking her long-legged stride she tossed the clean clothing and tow sacks on the sand, and pulled her linsey-woolsey dress over her head, and walked into the pool up to her waist with her long hair floating out behind. She stood directly under the silvery shower of dropping water and beckoned to him with her eyes, silver as the falling water in the moonlight. Half mortified, half amused, more than half aroused by her womanly beauty, Morgan unlaced his boots for the first time since he had put them on at Little Mountain, though his old stockings were in rags and adhered to his feet like bits of sticking plaster. Barbary was soaping herself and laving water over her lovely shoulders and breasts and hair, then ducking under the falling curtain of water. As the icy jolt of the mountain water hit Morgan and he drew in his breath sharply, she grabbed his arm with a strength he'd never before felt in a woman and began to lather him well with the brick of soap, with no more regard for his modesty than as though she were scrubbing one of her own boys and they small again. Only the shock of the cold water from the falls drenching his head and back kept him from clasping her there in the pool, this tall, lovely songstress of the Blue Smoke Mountains. Soon she had soaped and cleaned him well, even washing away the remnants of cloth stuck to his feet and scouring his head and long hair, glinting like a cascade of dark gold in the mountain moonlight, then seizing his head and plunging it under the falls while, with her long musician's fingers, she routed away the dust and grease and sweat of weeks of walking. She led him to the dry sand beside the basin pool and flung at him first one of the tow sacks to use as a towel and then the embroidered cambric shirt and the drawers and stout linsey-woolsey trousers and strong stockings from her own roving sheep.

The clothes were a little roomy for him though comfortably so, but she made him leave his boots to air out on the chestnut log stoop before her cabin while she brought him inside and lighted a swinging Betty lamp with a taper from the coals in the fireplace. She seated him at the trestle table where he'd eaten his oatmeal with molasses and set on the table before him a glass jar of cloudy liquid. "Sup it slow," she commanded. "It's grandfer's best corn."

Morgan shook his head. "I take no spirits. Lest doing so deflect me from my task."

"Your task tonight for a certainty is a very different task," she said. "Have ye a sup."

Morgan took a sip of the drink, and for a moment he could not speak or breathe or feel any sensation but a flaring flame in his throat and chest followed by a spreading and delicious warmth. He raised the jar again, and the very fumes rising off the corn made his head swim. He took another sup and gasped as he had when the frigid shower of mountain water had poured down his bare back. He could feel the numbing heat of the whiskey usurping the will of his arms and legs, even his fingers. For this one night, he did not care so much about his mission. Seated across the pine trestle from him, her still-damp hair a dark, dark red in the lamplight, Barbary fetched up a gourd fiddle with groundhog-gut strings and the sign ∫

inscribed on its neck, and in the same unearthly treble in which she had wailed out "Barbary Allen," she sang.

Now red-haired Barbary had a good man named Quill.
Oconaluftee came for him to kill.
She'd borned two boys named Ab and Lot
Whom Luftee shot.
And when the leaden shot passed through
Her husband and her sons, it kilt poor Barbary too.

Barbary Allen set down her fiddle, wiped away her tears, and stood up. She went to a cupboard and returned with a long carving knife. "Which is your gun hand?" she said.

Morgan pointed to his right hand.

"Then hold out t'other."

He did, and so swiftly that the entire operation could not have taken five seconds, she made a cut in the palm of his left hand and another in her own and pressed her bleeding palm against his. "Now," she said. "Swear. Swear on the soul of your beloved brother that you will kill Luftee."

When he hesitated, she said fiercely, "Do it now or I'll slit your throat like a hog. Swear!"

So Morgan did, whereupon she bound his hand and prepared a place for him to lie by the fireside, and in the small hours of the night she sang a new ballad of her own composition called "The Ballad of the Outlaw, Childe Morgan."

From the far Northlands came the outlaw, Childe Morgan,
To hunt the demon-men.

For that they killed black Jesse, the man who was his friend.
Childe Morgan came to widowed Barbary Allen
Who, for all her many failings,
Had vowed revenge on him who slew her men.
She took her blade and boldly made young Morgan Allen kin.
Now, outlaw childe, go forth, go forth
And kill Oconaluftee and those men
Who killed your Allen kin.

BARBARY WAS SHAKING HIM ROUGHLY and repeating his name. He opened his eyes. It was coming on dawn, time for him to go forth as he had sworn to and kill this evil Luftee who had done Barbary Allen such a grievous hurt and to find Pilgrim, if Pilgrim was to be found. Then Morgan Kinneson's war would be over and he could return north, though whether to Slidell he could not foretell.

Barbary had been up and about for some time, preparing oatmeal with molasses treacle for him and for her son Noah, who had appeared with his long mountain gun. Barbary had softened his boots by rubbing them well with hog's lard and had cleaned Lady Justice with her dear dead Quill's wooden cleaning rods and a cloth soaked in oil made from camphor and, to assure its deadliness, the poisonous red berries of the nightshade plant. She had brushed Morgan's slouch hat, weathered as black as his boots, and sprinkled a little mountain rosewater inside the crown. The boy Noah was quiet and watchful as he cleaned his own long gun, and from time to time he gave Morgan a quick look that Morgan could not read.

Barbary's face looked haggard in the dawn light. "Noah."

"Yes, mother."

"Morgan is kin now. He has both the right and the beholdenness to destroy Oconaluftee. Killing is a business he knows about, just as you know the ways of the wild faunas and wee bright floras and the secret paths over which you have guided many a poor dark running one up through these mounts. You will guide him to the laurel where Luftee is encamped and leave him there to do his work."

Noah pursed his lips and frowned.

"Now go," Barbary said. "May Our Savior bless and keep you and make His light to shine down upon you in this sacred enterprise, Morgan Kinneson. Leave none alive and remember this. If you hear the mountain horns, one blast means gather. Two means sickness or accident. Three means grave danger."

"What of my brother?" Morgan said.

"Go up Great Grandmother," Barbary said. "And inquire there of the One-legged Man of the Mountain. Mayhap he can help you. But to reach him you must first venture through the land of Oconaluftee and slay the monster. May all-forgiving Jesus walk with you and steady your gun hand."

"One question more," Morgan said. "Where did you come by the sign on your door? And on your fiddle?"

"Grandfer carved e there so the avenging angel would pass over," Barbary teased him.

"My sign is *Nauthiz*," Morgan said. He drew it with his finger on the trestle table.

Barbary looked at him. "Our sign, *Isa,* means, so I was tolt, ice. The withdrawal of warm weather. It signifies withdrawal from the wicked world. A dark man give it to my Quill ages past. Now go."

As Morgan and Noah headed up the steep slope behind the cabin, they heard the strains of the gourd fiddle and Barbary singing the song that would soon gain such currency that it would be sung from one end of the Blue Shaconage to another.

From the far cold North came the outlaw, Childe Morgan,
To hunt down demon-men. . . .

"Tell again," Noah said as the song faded, "how it came to pass that you slew the wicked giant Ludi Too. I wish I had been there to help."

Morgan smiled at the boy's innocence. Noah reminded him of himself a few short months before. A boy-man, hunting a moose in the snowy Vermont bog. So young. So confident.

"Let's save our breath for climbing," Morgan suggested. "By nightfall there may well be more to tell."

"I'm for coming with you the whole of the way," Noah said. "I care not what Mother said. I intend to avenge my own people. I'd be honored for your help." Noah's eyes seemed to acquire a sly light as he added, "Now we're kin."

"Honor your father and mother," Morgan said.

"Aye," Noah said. "So I shall. I shall honor my father Quill Allen and my dead brothers by killing their murderer. In truth I need no more help than you do with your long walking."

"Well," Morgan laughed, "as for that, I *do* need help with my walking. These mountains of yours are a regular Chinese puzzle, Noah. Without a good man from this land to cipher the way for me, I'd likely turn myself around and be back in Gatlinburg by noon." Morgan got out the compass the general had given to him. "This instrument of mine is as useless here as a stopped watch."

Noah looked at the compass in Morgan's hand. "What o'clock be it?"

"It's a compass."

"What? A compass watch?"

Morgan showed him how the compass worked, and Noah jumped back when the needle swung north.

"What does this writing say?"

"It says the good man's course is always true. It was given to me by a good man."

"Your father?"

"No, though my father is a good man and more." Morgan told Noah who had given him the compass. He showed him the general's initials on the back under the motto. Noah nodded, but it was clear that he had never heard the name before.

Together they climbed skyward toward the encampment of Oconaluftee, though just who or what this man might be Morgan had no idea. He could not imagine what the murderous Luftee's connection was to Dinwiddie or to Pilgrim or to· him. It had occurred to him that Luftee, rather than Dinwiddie, might be the man who had set in motion the prison escape at Elmira, the murder of Jesse, and the search for the carved stone. It made no difference. If Morgan had his way, and he believed that he would, by sunset Oconaluftee's corpse would lie moldering on the forest floor and he would be climbing Great Grandmother Mountain to find Barbary's One-legged Man.

THOUGH HE HAD BEEN BORN with a compass inside his head, like a wild goose, Morgan would have been hard put to retrace a mile of his trek that day with Noah Allen. Every cove and brook split into a dozen more coves and brooks in half an hour's time. One especially steep knob called Acony Bell Mountain required a full two hours to go out around. They stopped at noon by a spring in a high cold pass, through which the wind rushed steadily with a terrible blasting roar, but before they had finished quenching their thirst Noah grabbed Morgan's arm.

"Sheltons!" the boy said. "You be all right but they'll kill me on sight." He pointed up the trail. "I'll meet you up yonder in the huckabuck roughs. You warn they about Luftee."

No sooner had Noah vanished into the woods than half a dozen heavily armed men in dark slouch hats like Morgan's own appeared on the path. They walked single file, and the tallest, who led the way, had a white linen cloth wrapped around the end of his rifle barrel. Morgan had not heard them coming. He had no idea how Noah had been alerted to their presence. The man in the lead nodded to him, and Morgan nodded back. The other men regarded him from the sides of their eyes, taking his measure as, one by one, they drank from the spring, some from carved wooden cups, some from their hands. Morgan could see them admiring his slung rifle without appearing to.

When they finished drinking, Morgan told them his name and that he was looking for his brother. He told them Pilgrim's name. The tallest man, who was three or four inches taller than Morgan, said, "Why come ye girded up with arms amongst us? To kill yer brother? Did he snatch away yer sweetheart? Do you ruction with him?"

Morgan shook his head and briefly told the men why he was carrying Lady Justice and the twin scattershot. When he recounted the killing of Ludi Too, one man removed his hat and raised his hand heavenward. Another squatted on his heels and with a little stick traced something in the sand by the spring.

After he finished his story the men were silent. Then the tall man said, "He ain't no red-headed Allen, that's certain." He put out his hand. "My name is Keith Vance Shelton. Have ye seed those demons that calls themselves Allens? We's under a flag of truce to parlay with them."

"A flag of truce?"

The tall man nodded at the white strip of cloth around his gun barrel. "We knows Oconaluftee kilt Barbary Allen's man Quill and two of her growed boys. Luftee kilt my brother Driscoll Shelton and Driscoll's son, and they bigged with child my niece Rosa Shelton who is but twelve year old. We propose to join forces with the Allens. To wipe out Luftee. We will settle up with that redheaded she-wolf Barbary and her wolfish clan later."

"Where are Luftee and his gang?"

"We ain't determined. Two day ago they up Baldy Dome. They come upon Wade Pearly's womenfolk and babies and mistreated them most atrociously. Tormented them fiercely to get them to give out Wade's hidey-hole up Clowers Mountain. Slow-hanged Wade's woman till they more than half stifled her to get her to talk, but she never did. Kilt one or two of Wade's babies even. Wade's people never talked."

"How many men does Luftee command?"

"Fifteen or twenty. The offcasts of mankind, tooken from prisons and madhouses, judged unfit even for the Home Guard. Some Union bummers as well. Satan's own crew and Luftee the worst of them. He stands six and a half foot tall and has dark whiskers and long dark side hair and is bald as a goose egg on top. He wears a stuffed rattler-snake necktie tied off in a bow. He carries a buffaler gun that shoots true as the gospels of Matthew, Mark, Luke, and John. When he turns his withering black eyes on you, it is as good as a death warrant."

"You must have suffered grievously at the hands of this Ocon-aluftee to be ready to join in league with the Allens."

"His crew murdered sixteen of our kin in Waynesville a fortnight ago. Old grandsires who had seen eighty winters and boys who had not seen fifteen. They digged a shallow trench and pitched them in, some still twitching. Them they finished off with a mattock hoe or buried still quick. One man danced on they graves to 'Juba' and clapped his hands, and Oconaluftee played on a lap harp whilst the slaughter did proceed. They all mad as crazed Saul that slang his spear at young David."

"What will you and the Allens do after you drive these killers out of your mountains?"

"Why, we'll take up battling each other again. If I ever cotch that Barbary out on the sled paths I shall big her myself. She is a high-toned woman and I would like to do a cornshuck mattress jig with her. Wouldn't she squirm like a wildcat though!"

From the laurel above a shot rang out. A rose-red bloom appeared in the middle of Keith Vance Shelton's forehead. The wound spread out like an opening blossom, and the tall mountaineer fell over backward.

"Hit's an ambuscade!" one of the Sheltons hollered. "To the laurel!"

They were off down the mountainside into the thick laurel. Blood gushed from Keith Vance Shelton's ruined head into the spring. Morgan ran up the slope. The boy Noah Allen, sheltering on his knees behind an orange boulder, was ramming powder and shot into his long squirrel gun. Morgan could smell powder in the air.

"He won't speak so of my mama," Noah screamed. "Never again he won't."

Morgan yanked him to his feet and dragged him bodily up the mountainside. "You bloody-minded little fool," Morgan spit out between gritted teeth.

"He was a-fixing to ravish my mama, the black villain."

"He intended to join forces with her against the man who killed your father and brothers."

"You leave me go. I aim to do for the rest."

"Listen to me, Noah. Those men will now go straight to Hell For Sartin and surprise your people and kill them if they can. Then they'll come back here for you. Can you cross directly over that steep knob, Acony Bell, and beat them to Hell For Sartin?"

"I aim to track they and pick they off one to a time."

"No. They'd lay for you. They'd pick you off. You cut over that saddle on Acony Bell, that path you told me of called Up to Heaven, Down to Hell. Get your mama and cousins and uncles out of the Sugarlands fast as ever you can. Take them down to Gatlinburg. If you try to dog the Sheltons, they'll kill you and yours."

Noah was shaking. Morgan reached into his pocket and produced the general's compass. "You're a good man, Noah. Like your father, Quill Allen. Your path will be true, just as the legend on the back of this compass promises. Keep it as a token to remind yourself who you are. Now run like your dear mama's life depends on it, for most surely it does. Go!"

Morgan placed the compass in Noah's palm and closed the boy's hand over it. He gave him a quarter turn in the direction of Acony

Bell, and off the boy bolted at a crouching gait, seeming to glide over the broken land more than to walk upon it. Morgan felt a deep fraternal affection for Noah despite his foolhardiness, and he wished him well, knowing that unless Barbary Allen could contrive some way to send him off to faraway kin he would not live out that week. He knew that he too was now a marked man, to be hunted by the Sheltons and shot on sight as an accomplice.

With the brass-bound spyglass he sighted in on the high peak of Great Grandmother, which he reckoned to be fifty miles away. He began to run, moving at the easy woodsman's lope he had learned from Pilgrim, the all-day pace that even in steep and tangly mountains would carry him thirty miles from sunrise to sunset. From time to time he reached out on either side of the path and turned up a laurel leaf to show its pale underside or kicked a rock a few inches aside to reveal a small fresh spot of earth or made a scuff mark with his boot. Despite what he had told young Noah, he was not at all certain that the remaining Sheltons would hit for Hell For Sartin. Instead they might trail him, particularly if he could leave just enough sign to convince them that two or more men, Keith Vance Shelton's shooter and Morgan and maybe a third bushwhacker, had come this way. If they began to overtake him, he'd have to get up on a knob and, with his superior range rifle, shoot them as they approached. He saw again in his mind the red rose spreading over Keith Vance Shelton's forehead. He ran at a smart pace.

As MORGAN SPRANG UP the mountainside he taxed himself for the bushwhacking of Keith Vance Shelton. Had he not approached the Allen settlement the evening before, Noah Allen would not have been with him today, would not have ambushed the Shelton chieftain. Yet he had not asked for Noah to guide him, nor had he exactly volunteered to avenge the deaths of Noah's father and brothers at the hands of Oconaluftee. *Everything is connected. Nauthiz means everything is harder than you think and everything is connected.* As Eva had prophesied, all that had happened since he'd left Vermont seemed connected in some way, and he was a cog in it all, but to what purpose?

At the top of a knob he paused to look back down the hollow and saw no sign of pursuit. Across the valley to the south, high on the bald of Acony Bell Mountain, he spotted, with the copper-bound spyglass given him by the woman who lived to spite her unfaithful husband, the tiny figure of Noah Allen bounding along like a roebuck. No one seemed to be dogging him, and it was likely that he would arrive at Hell For Sartin in time to warn the rest of the clan that the Sheltons were coming. Looking north, Morgan could make out quite plainly now the singular high, looming peak of Great Grandmother, slightly hazy but a deep shade of blue. It had rained here recently, and the shower had cleansed the air. It felt more like a spring morning than an afternoon in the early fall.

Five hundred feet down the north side of the rock knob, the faint path Morgan was following met another. One branch continued north toward Great Grandmother. The other, which appeared to have been much traveled lately, ran off at a westerly angle. Morgan studied the tracks. Six or seven men, all barefooted, had come through the mud on the path earlier that morning. Those could be Keith Vance Shelton's clan. But within the last hour a much larger band of men, many wearing hobnailed boots and two on horseback, had passed through heading toward Shelton Laurel. Morgan lifted

his head and tilted it to the west. From far away he heard the pro-
longed blast of a mountain horn. He heard it again and then again,
a kind of low-register bellow that seemed compounded of wind in
the pines on a stormy night, a freshet rushing down a mountain,
and the far-off sad whistle of a train. From the north came three
long answering blasts. And then the coves and glens and hollows for
miles in every direction echoed and re-echoed with the moaning
signals of three long notes repeated at about half-minute intervals.
As the mountain horns hummed out in concert, the hazy, blued
air over the unbroken forest seemed to quiver with their ominous
music. What had Barbary said? One blast meant gather. Two meant
sickness or injury, the call for a doctor or granny woman. Three
blasts, long and repeated, meant danger. There was no doubt at all
in Morgan's mind. Oconaluftee must be abroad with his killers. He
looked off at Great Grandmother, where the One-legged Man of
whom Barbary had spoken might be able to tell him news of Pilgrim. He was a day away at most, and with Luftee off in Shelton
Laurel he would likely have free passage. Yet he had given Barbary
Allen his word that he would kill Luftee. And how could he stand
by and let Luftee harm the Sheltons? Oh, the maddening impos-
sibility of all human choices! Morgan began to run again—away
from Great Grandmother Mountain and toward Shelton Laurel.

He believed that his only chance lay in reaching high ground
overlooking the Shelton settlement, but without Noah to guide
him he did not know exactly where that settlement was or whether
it lay exposed to any high ground. Plunging along in the prints of
the gang, he nearly bolted off the edge of a precipice where the
path bent sharply and descended to a stream he could have cleared
in a single leap. Here the trail ended altogether. But judging from

the water recently splashed on the rocks jutting out of the streambed, where the densely hanging trumpet vines had been hacked
away and laurel leaves broken off, he believed that Oconaluftee and
his killers had proceeded upstream. Morgan began to run up the
brook. He entered a cleft between the mountains where the tilted
rocks underfoot were slick and treacherous. Fifty yards ahead, a
sentinel of Luftee's raiding party wearing a skunk-skin cap with
the black-and-white-striped tail over one ear stepped out from behind a boulder, raised an Enfield rifle, and fired at him. The bullet
cut through the air an inch from Morgan's temple, smashing into
a pine tree clinging to the cliff on his right. Without slackening
his pace Morgan unslung his rifle and chambered a shell, lifted the
gun to his shoulder, and put a .50 caliber bullet through the sentinel's breast. The man toppled over into the brook and Morgan used
him as a stepping stone. A moment later he came to the edge of a
clearing.

Under the direction of a huge bearded man on a mule, the killers had rounded up the women and children and elderly people of
Shelton Laurel and were endeavoring to torment them into revealing the whereabouts of their menfolk. An old woman was being
slow-hanged over the limb of an oak, hoisted onto her toes by a
noose around her neck. A man with a feathered hat was busy dunk-
ing a squalling infant into the brook by its heels. A mountain lad
of twelve or thirteen, with an ancient fowling piece beside him, lay
dead of a head wound. Children were being chased down in the
high weeds and brush around the gardens. Partway up the bald,
a sharpshooter in a long duster coat plugged away at the fleeing
people. Each time he fired he doffed his hat and slapped it against
his thigh and whooped. Another raider was in the process of raping

a girl who could not have been ten years old. He was the second marauder Morgan shot, putting a bullet through the ravisher's neck. His next target was the whooping marksman on the bald. He estimated the distance at six hundred yards, with three hundred and fifty feet of elevation to account for. Aiming for the sharpshooter's head, he lodged a bullet in the man's gut and watched him roll over and over down the lichen-carpeted rock face like a tumblebug in a duster coat.

A stand-up fight against fifteen or twenty men was not what Morgan had wanted, though he had no fear for his own safety or for his life. He shot again and spun the bearded man, whom he judged to be Oconaluftee, right off his mule. He shot the man drowning the infant in the temple, the baby dropping unharmed, he hoped, in the sedges beside the brook. The hangmen ran for the woods but did not get far. From his bandolier Morgan fed Lady Justice one shell at a time, since he did not have leisure to reload all eight. He popped three of the four-inch-long projectiles out of their bandolier pockets and stuck them between his teeth like three short gleaming cigars. One by one he removed and inserted them in his gun and fired, hitting home each time with unerring deadliness.

The mule galloped round and round the meadow, dragging the wounded Oconaluftee by one foot caught in a stirrup. The woman who had been slow-hanged was crawling toward a cabin with her toddler child. As the mule thundered down upon them, Morgan shot it through the withers. It collapsed like an animal made of cloth. Luftee, detached from the stirrup, flew through the air, landing in a corn patch beside the cabin. The mattock man who had chopped the dying to pieces not a week ago lifted the hateful implement high over the crawling woman's head. Morgan shot him through the heart. There was a rustling in the corn patch where Luftee had gone sailing. Morgan lifted Lady Justice to his shoulder and pulled the trigger.

The meadow lay still in the early autumn sunlight. Morgan walked quickly to the stand of corn but saw no sign of Luftee. Instead, lying behind a shattered scarecrow were the lifeless remains of the toddler, still clinging to the straw leg of the pumpkin-headed figure as he would have to his mother. So far from dispatching the monster Oconaluftee, Morgan Kinneson had shot and killed a child.

HE JUDGED THAT Great Grandmother, where he hoped to find the mountain doctor Noah had told him of, was still twenty miles away. Perhaps farther, depending on how many ridges and hollows intervened between him and the mountain. He had staunched the gunshot wound in his side—he had not even realized he'd been shot until after the battle—by packing it with damp moss from a streamside boulder and webbing from the beautiful air trap of a yellow-and-black spider. He bound the wound with two strips of cloth cut from the bottom of Quill Allen's shirt. He felt a painful throbbing up and down his side and could not rid his mind of the picture of the poor dead toddler clinging to the leg of the straw figure. He knew he was eternally damned, not by Mahitabel's angry Jehovah but by his own conscience. And Oconaluftee was still abroad on the land. Perhaps the monster had headed east toward the mountain bearing his name. Morgan scooped up a dripping handful of brook water and laved it over his forehead. He kept walking. He knew that he must find the mountain doctor soon.

. . .

IT WAS EVENING. For some time he had been vaguely aware that he was ascending a steep mountainside. Ahead sat a small cabin in a meadow. As Morgan approached it, he saw, painted on the door, the symbol ☊. He stepped up onto the single log stoop, but before he could knock, the door opened and a tall man with a short dark beard, standing on one leg and leaning on a two-headed snake staff, said, "Yes?" Then, "My God, man, you're hurt. Come, let me—"

"Pilgrim," Morgan said, collapsing into his brother's arms and into oblivion.

ELEVEN

OTHILA

᛭

"I know you," Morgan said.

"Well, Morgan. I should hope that you do," the girl said, smiling. Dark hair framed her heart-shaped face, and her dark eyes were serene and amused, just as he remembered them from when he and she were both alive.

Reading his thoughts, she said in her mild accent, "No, Morgan. It is not what you suppose. I will explain when you are stronger, as you most *certainement* will be. We took the bullet from your side and sewed you back together again neat as a Christmas goose. Oh, Morgan. Silly *garçon* that you were to adventure into these mountains alone. But we are *trés heureux* to see you."

He was lying on a bed in an airy cabin with sunshine falling through an open doorway on the quilted bed cover. Bunches of herbs hung from the rafters overhead. Across the room stood a stone fireplace, and on a table between the bed and the door were more herbs and roots, as well as some small blue and green bottles. He could smell pennyroyal and some kind of wild mint and horehound and perhaps tansy. As the young woman spoke, she washed his forehead and face with a cool cloth, and though he felt weaker than he could ever remember feeling, his fever was gone and he believed he might live now that the bullet had been removed and he was stitched back up neat as a Christmas goose. What he couldn't get his mind around was that the lovely young woman was Manon Thibeau, Pilgrim's intended, who had wandered off to her death in the bog on Kingdom Mountain more than a year before. Moreover, she appeared to be with child.

"I thought we were both dead," he said.

"I believe not, Morgan." Manon's eyes were delighted by such a comic notion. "Can you turn your head? No, the other. I mean the other way, not the other head. You have but one head, I hope. A little more."

Through the window to his left he saw a one-legged man in a dark suit and hat limping up the lane, framed by the jumbled mountains in the background. The man was using a homemade crutch in the shape of two snakes, swinging along on the crutch and his single leg at a brisk clip, and as he approached the cabin he called out in a booming voice Morgan knew as well as any voice on earth, "Is he awake, the young layabout?"

"He is," Manon called back. The one-legged man shouted with joy, and then for a moment he was out of sight, and then he was swinging fast through the door in the sunlight, shouting Morgan's name.

"Morgan Kinneson!" he thundered, grabbing Morgan's hand. "You young devil. You walked all the way down here to get yourself shot when you could have done it as easily in Virginia. Look. Here's the ball I yanked out of your side, you rapscallion. Where have you been? I expected you months ago. You've grown six inches! Did you meet up with old Jess?"

Morgan tried to raise himself off the pillow but could only lift his arms to embrace his brother.

THIS TIME when he woke he knew that he was alive and so too was Manon and so of course was Pilgrim, though somewhere in his travels his brother had lost a leg.

Manon fed him some soup and tea. Afterward Pilgrim changed his bandages, working swiftly and expertly with Manon's assistance. She seemed, as she rewrapped the wound with cotton strips, as skillful as Pilgrim, who explained to Morgan that he was teaching his profession, including surgery, to his wife and that she already knew considerably more than most of his medical school colleagues and infinitely more than nearly any army doctor he'd met. He explained, in his confident, engaging fashion, that after walking away from the battlefield he had headed north, planning to return to Kingdom County, where Manon was waiting, and then possibly travel across the border with her to practice medicine in Canada. He had gotten only as far as Joseph Findletter's when he realized that the wound he'd sustained at Gettysburg had become infected. Posing as a wounded Confederate medical aide, Pilgrim had directed the smith in the removal of his leg. During his recuperation, he had carved his sign ᛟ, *Othila,* on the wall of the smith's shop. He had then secretly written to Manon, who, after feigning her disappearance in the bog, had made her way south by rail and stage to join Pilgrim in Pennsylvania. Together, in the guise of a southern soldier and his sister, the couple had stopped briefly at many of the Underground stations Morgan had visited, including Cobbler Tom's, Two Snake's, and the ghostly Melungeons', before venturing farther south to the primeval forest above Gatlinburg where Pilgrim had once spent a scientific holiday with his professor. Here, in an abandoned crofter's cabin on Great Grandmother, Pilgrim established his medical practice. The runaway Jesse Moses had been one of his first patients, brought to him by Barbary Allen. He had cured Jesse of malarial fever. Before continuing north, Jesse had painted the sign of *Othila*, ᛟ, on the cabin door, then etched it on his rune stone.

It was an astounding tale, but no more amazing than Slidell's and perhaps less so than Morgan's own, which he had not yet told Pilgrim and Manon, and part of which he dreaded to disclose. *Gots something important to tell you.* If only he had stopped to listen to Jesse, he might have avoided much of what had happened in the past several months. No matter. If, as Big Eva had told him, *Othila* meant separation, his long separation from Pilgrim had come to an end.

During the succeeding days Pilgrim and Manon did not press Morgan for his story but let him build up his strength by walking over the old sheep pasturage, to which Manon had some months ago introduced a small new flock purchased from Barbary. When Morgan first set out on his quest, he had believed that he must rely on himself alone and, moreover, that each man and woman in the world must do the same. Now he realized that without the help of others he never would have reached Gatlinburg and these southern mountains, much less survived here. Like his own ancestors, who, as the carved words on the door lintel at home stated, "lived in a house at the end of the road and were friends to mankind," he had befriended a fair number of people—Birdcall, Cobbler Tom, the runaway slave Mercy Johnson, Slidell, Little Solomon, the Findletters, and others. But the help he had given was negligible compared to that which he had received, and if there was great and unspeakable evil in the world, was there not also, as Slidell had told him, great kindness and love? Yet Morgan could not remember thanking a single person who had assisted him.

As the days blended into one another and the blue autumn weather maintained, with no word of Oconaluftee, Morgan began to relax his vigil. He loved to sit out in the sheep pasturage in the mild sunshine reading Pilgrim's books. Thoreau on Cape Cod, Emerson on self-reliance, Milton and Shakespeare on the good and evil in the hearts of mankind. On Great Grandmother he finished the wonderful account of the journey of Captains Lewis and Clark. And though he still longed to see the upper Missouri River, the Great Divide and the Pacific, he kept coming back to a thick old law book, Blackstone's *Commentaries,* which Pilgrim sometimes consulted in his secondary capacity as a kind of itinerant and impromptu justice of the peace. This tome was becoming Morgan's lodestone. So far from finding that periwigged old jurist Blackstone tedious in his strict recapitulation of torts and codicils and other legal terms he had never heard of, Morgan regarded him with fascination. With his absolutes, Blackstone suggested to him the comforting possibility of a realm where justice, such as it was, was meted out, however imperfectly, in high-ceiled chambers by men governed not by their immediate passions but by laws as ancient and fixed as the oldest pines rooted in these mountains. Morgan admired Blackstone's attack on the draconian Poor Law and on the savagery of the game laws, for which he had little use himself. He spent whole mornings and afternoons poring over the old volume, discussing what he had read in the evening with his brother.

During the daytime Pilgrim made his medical rounds on a gentle ancient nag that the Sheltons had given him for helping a woman of their clan with a hard birth. It was true, Pilgrim said, that the Shelton and Allen men not murdered by Oconaluftee had, in a fierce shoot-out on the very evening of the day Noah Allen bushwhacked Keith Vance Shelton, bid fair to annihilate each other almost to the last man. He did not know what had become of Barbary Allen, though her new song, "The Ballad of the Outlaw, Childe Morgan," had become popular among the remaining people of the Sugarlands. They had even added a verse:

He fit the Devil at Shelton,
Thirty kilt by one.
He felled Oconaluftee
With his fancy raffle gun.

Pilgrim did not interrogate Morgan about his great odyssey south, nor did Manon. Pilgrim had at last written to their parents to tell them that both sons were safe. Manon had written to her family to say she was well and with Pilgrim. When the baby came, which could be any day now, she would write again in the hope that a grandchild would reconcile them to her marriage to a freethinking Protestant. She and Pilgrim had recently decided to name their child, if a boy, Morgan. This disclosure caused Morgan to realize that he must not live with Pilgrim and Manon any longer under false pretenses. They must know who and what he was.

One warm September evening, as all three members of their small community sat on the log stoop of the cabin looking out over one hundred miles and more of mountains, Morgan told his story. It is a rare enough thing in this world to find anyone truly skilled at listening. To find two beloved friends capable of listening to a two-hour narrative without once interrupting, even when he told of abandoning Jesse Moses before Jesse had a chance to reveal that Pilgrim was alive and dwelling with Manon in the mountains near Gatlinburg, was remarkable. But when Morgan told of shooting the child in the corn patch, Manon took his hand and shook her head, and Pilgrim finally spoke out.

"No, Morgan."

"No?"

"Morgan Kinneson," Pilgrim said. "Hear me well. This monster, Oconaluftee? One of his most evil devices was using human shields. In my recent visit to Shelton Laurel, the dead child's own grandmother said that when she glimpsed the devil Luftee running in the corn, she fired her old hog musket loaded with buckshot at him, then saw that he was holding the child before himself. The little one was struck with buckshot. Your rifle bullet hit Luftee."

If in fact this was the case, Morgan felt strangely little relief. He was beyond the pale of normal human feelings, save the comfort of Manon's hand in his and the knowledge that there was still that much good in the world. For himself, there could be no hope or redemption. Slidell had known as much back in the Cumber.

T HE NEXT MORNING when Morgan came to the table for breakfast, Pilgrim put his arm around his brother's shoulder as he used to do when they were younger and walking the mountains, with Pilgrim telling him the names and secret ways of the birds and woods flowers, where the sleek and intelligent fishing otter dwelt along the river, and how their grandfather had once found a lost seal down from the St. Lawrence River and kept it for a companion like a dog. Some of the stories, like that of the seal and of the professor's gigantic betusked hairy elephants roaming the edge of the creeping walls of ice, were so fantastical that Morgan could never tell whether Pilgrim was recounting facts or spinning tales.

"Are you able to climb the mountain with me today?" Pilgrim asked.

Morgan looked inquiringly at Manon.

"I am perfectly fine to stay alone," she said. "This kicking man-child—I'm certain it is a Morgan, for he kicks far too hard and angrily for a girl—is a full week away from making his presence known. Go, Morgan and Pilgrim. Your luncheon for the mountain outing is ready. Cold baked beans. My own bread baked in the *petit* stone oven. Young Morgan"—she patted herself—"and I will be safe and content. Have the day with your brother, Pilgrim. He is nearly well, you know. Soon enough he will be off for the North-lands and his new life. I see a beautiful girl in it."

Manon's dark eyes danced with mischief, and Morgan's heart seemed about to break in two. But he said nothing.

On the way up the mountain the brothers talked freely about everything under the sun, as they had together at home. Morgan shared with Pilgrim his recent doubts about the violent actions of his hero John Brown, who it now seemed to him was no less a murderer than he himself. He spoke of the strange glyphs carved into the dwellings of the conductors and stationmasters he had met on his way south, how each conductor seemed to have a different reason for helping fugitives reach Canada and how, in some cases, those reasons had little to do with a hatred of slavery or a love of universal freedom. He asked Pilgrim if he thought that Jesse had set up the Mountain Branch of the Underground. Pilgrim said that he did think so, but he was much less certain about the provenance of the rune stone. It was possible, he supposed, that in accordance with the old myth Slidell had told Morgan, it had been passed down from one generation to another by Jesse's African ancestors. How they might have come by such a relic was unknowable. Like the similarly engraved Balancing Boulder at home, Jesse's rune stone would likely remain a mystery for all time to come.

"Now look here, brother," Pilgrim continued as he hopped up the mountain like a one-legged frog with a two-headed stick. "I'm in love with Manon—she is peerless. Peerless. And soon to present us with a son or daughter, also peerless. I'm about to be a peerless father. And you a peerless old uncle. Can you credit it?"

Morgan could not.

The game path they followed grew fainter as it climbed at a sharp pitch through twelve-foot-high laurel and dense, raking blackberry bushes, then waist-high huckleberries. Pilgrim continued to effervesce about his beloved mountains. "Manon is my cherished wife, but I have fallen in love with this land, brother. She teases me that these mountains are my mistress. The tall cardinal flower beside the brook, the flowering dogwood, the swift and amiable blacksnake."

"Why next you'll have me believing that you live in Eden, brother," Morgan said. "Though an old gaffer from the Sugarlands, an Allen, told me he once moved to North Carolina—you would think to hear him that it was as far off as Van Diemen's Land—and returned home the very next day because the drinking water was inferior." He looked off to the east. "Good God, Pilgrim. What is that massive soaring peak?"

"That is Oconaluftee, brother. There's a narrow lead threading up to the top. It's said that the blockaders, the first old mountain

whiskey makers who defied the tax laws, had impregnable strong-
holds in the caves hereabouts. One such rascal captured a cannon
from federal revenuers and mounted it atop Oconaluftee Mountain.
The only access to the peak now is by a long swinging rope bridge.
I've not been there, but I intend to go, now that the madman who
named himself for it is dead."

They sat on the rocky summit of Great Grandmother, eating
Manon's good lunch and looking far out over the flowing mountains, drained by many a well-concealed stream, cloaked in woods
and thickets made slightly indistinct by the blue mist that floated
over the highlands, so that it was difficult to say whether the more
distant peaks were true mountains or filmy clouds or mirages. It
was as lovely a scene as Morgan had ever beheld.

"I was especially taken by your story of our friend Joseph Findletter making you the rifle, the gun you call Lady Justice," Pilgrim
said. "Your account of shooting the big orange pumpkin across the
gorge is a grand tale. I can see it bursting apart in my mind's eye."

"Well, you could have hit it, Pilgrim. You always had a magic
touch with a gun. I expect you still do"

"Life plays us many a prank, Morgie. I was born with the gift of
shooting, but I haven't fired a gun in four or five years. Nor do I
intend to do so ever again."

"Brother," Morgan said. "You said you were wed to Manon, but
these mountains were your mistress. May I ask, has Manon been
your only sweetheart?"

Pilgrim roared with laughter. "Yes, Morgan. Manon has been
my sweetheart from our early childhood. There has never been another girl, and luckily she isn't jealous of my mountains so long as I
always come home to her."

Encouraged by his brother's good-natured candor, Morgan said, "Pilgrim, I must tell you that on my way south I met a girl who stole my heart."

Pilgrim seemed in no wise surprised. "Who was she, you young dog, you?" he said. "Some wealthy planter's daughter, no doubt, with a soft southern voice and a fetching black eye."

Morgan shook his head. "She was not. She was the runaway slave of whom I told you and Manon something last night. Slidell Dinwiddie. Jesse Moses's granddaughter. We became very close."

Pilgrim nodded but said nothing.

"Are you distressed with me, brother? For falling in love with a black woman?"

"Hardly, Morgan. You did what any young man might well have done. I'm only surprised that you didn't bring Slidell here to the Shaconage to wait out the war with Manon and me."

"She went north with her brother, the little savant. I gave her Auguste Choteau's name in Montreal. As for us, I mean Slidell and myself, she is a deeply and sincerely Christian woman. She found me, in my quest for the killers, unsuitable. I fear there can be no hope in that quarter now or in the future."

"Morgan, like many another soldier, both blue and gray, you have done only what you had to do. As for the future, it is more unfathomable than those far peaks that fade so subtly into the sky we can't tell them from the horizon. No one can know it. Not even Slidell's friend Jesus. Who, when it came to the future, mistakenly supposed that the Kingdom of God on earth was at hand and would surely arrive in his lifetime. Listen to me, Morgan. Let the future look out for itself, for I assure you that it will. I thank you for placing your confidence in me and telling me of your romance. The tale will travel no further. Now, brother, I will in turn tell you why I left my surgeon's post in Pennsylvania. And then we'll talk no more of war forever."

Quietly, with a measure of detachment suggesting that he had already put this part of his life behind him, Pilgrim began by speaking of the problematic, palliative nature of much of the field surgery he had performed during the war. Do what a doctor might, wounds to the brain, chest, and abdomen were nearly always fatal. One fourth of all amputations resulted in death. The higher on the limb the amputation, the greater the risk. Pilgrim counted himself fortunate that he'd been wounded just below the knee. Three inches to the north, he said, and he and Morgan would not be having this conversation.

Pilgrim paused for a moment, shaking his head. Then he continued his story. On July of the past year, the fighting at Gettysburg had been so fierce, particularly in the Wheat Field and the Devil's Den, that Meade had asked for surgeon volunteers to establish regimental medical outposts in those contested areas. With his head wrapped in a white flag and wearing white armbands, Pilgrim had crawled, under steady musket and artillery fire, into the Slaughter Pen. Using field tourniquets and emergency ligatures, he had provided first aid to more than forty badly wounded Union and Confederate soldiers. As the fighting inside the Pen continued at a greater intensity than anything Pilgrim had ever witnessed or imagined, six Union bandsmen impressed into medical service arrived with two cannon limbers cobbled together into a makeshift ambulance. Under Pilgrim's direction the wounded were piled onto the rough planks of the connected limbers, and the bandsmen set off at the double-quick toward the tent hospital on the ridgetop a mile away. The drifting smoke was so thick that all Pilgrim could see of the ambulance squad was their running legs. Before they were out of the Devil's Den, two of their number were shot dead. The remaining four were unable to pull their human cargo up the steep slope, and a moment later the limbers started to roll backward.

Pilgrim had just extracted, from the left shoulder of a southern captain, a Union minié ball that had entered on the right side of the man's jaw and had somehow traveled down and across the soldier's neck without severing the jugular. With the ball still gripped between his bloody thumb and forefinger, Pilgrim rushed to the assistance of the ambulance men. Seizing the long wooden tongue of the front limber and exhorting the four remaining bandsmen to follow his lead, he began hauling the jury-rigged cart of wounded blue and gray up the hill through the hail of bullets coming at them from all sides. The screams of the injured were inaudible over the steady racketing musket fire, the thundering artillery, and the deadly canister with its own horrible whining, like a million of quail or wild pigeons taking flight as one. Another ambulance man fell. And another. By some superhuman effort Pilgrim labored on. Then he was running quite freely again. His first thought was that more men had come to his assistance, perhaps pushing the rear limber from behind. But when he glanced back over his shoulder, he saw that the ambulance wagon was gone. Bits of the men he had but lately patched together were falling out of the smoke, which was now tinted rose red from the fine steady mist of blood raining about him like some latter-day plague. Pilgrim ran, screaming, unable to hear his own scream. He ran until he could run no more. Only then did he realize that he too had been hit, in the lower leg. His face, hands, hair, the once white flag around his head, all of his clothing and his boots, and the splinter of limber tongue he was still gripping were soaked in blood. He began to weep. Then he began to laugh.

Still clinging to the bloody tongue of wood—all that was left of his efforts—limping now and with his back to the battlefield, he began to walk. As he would tell Morgan a year and some months later, high on a mountain on the wild border of Tennessee and North Carolina, Dr. Pilgrim Kinneson was through with warring.

The two brothers sat side by side looking out over the wilderness. There was a little breeze. Pilgrim tapped the iron-shod tip of his two-headed snake staff against a rock.

"Well," Morgan said.

"Yes," Pilgrim replied. "We have each seen the war at first hand, Morgan. We each have sustained our own wounds, outer and inner. I suppose we will each be a long while recovering from them, and that is how it is. In the meantime let us enjoy this fall day together, two brothers and friends out on a frisk in the mountains. We can be grateful that the war and its wickedness has not reached, nor is it apt to reach, Great Grandmother Mountain. We are beyond its reach here. Now look. I brought fish lines and hooks. That crease in the mountainside below hides the brook that spills down to the base of our field. It teems with little trout as pretty as ours at home. Let's cut two poles and trout our way down to Manon and feast tonight on fresh-caught fish the way we used to at home. What do you say to an afternoon of sport? I'll wager I catch two to your one, the sorry loser to clean the fish."

"Done," Morgan said. "You never could outfish me, brother. You won't today. It's the one skill I surpass you at."

"That and girling it, evidently," Pilgrim said with a laugh. "Come now, you young Casanova, you. Let's see who the trouter is in the Kinneson family, you or your one-legged brother."

. . .

THE SLANT MIDAFTERNOON autumn sunlight illuminated the sheep meadow around the crofter's cabin and fell through the open door on Manon, sitting at the chestnut plank table crushing hickory nuts she'd picked the day before for a cake frosting to surprise Pilgrim and Morgan. She whacked each nut with a mallet on an oaken block, then picked out the meats with one of Pilgrim's steel surgical fleams. As she worked she hummed to the child within her, a tune called *"L'eglise à Ste. Anne,"* a reel she and Pilgrim had loved to quick-step to at schoolhouse junkets while Manon's father, old Thibeau, sat on the master's platform sawing out the tune on his homemade violin and clogging his feet in time.

Manon had a fine voice, low and mellow, with natural pitch, and she hummed the old tune loudly enough for its plangent resonance to float out the door and across the pasture, where her brown-and-white brindled cow grazed and her small flock of sheep was lying down under the watchful eye of the bellwether ram in the shadow of one of the sudden ledgy outcroppings where she had lately planted daffodil bulbs. She had an eye out, too, for the devilish wild pigs that roved the mountains and came in broad daylight, under the command of their captain pig, bold as newly polished brass, to root up her flower bulbs and potatoes. Morgan had left her his gun, Lady Justice, to deal with the marauding hogs.

From the far end of the pasture in the hickory grove, she heard an echo of the reel she was humming. Some mountain minstrel, perhaps Barbary Allen, was coming up the lead from the cove below playing softly in melodious counterpoint to her song. It was a zither, Manon thought. The instrument rang out joyfully, the small, bright grace notes and longer chords reverberating over the green field below and making her toe tap. The music was bewitching. Even the bellwether in the pasture stood up and looked down the lead. Manon could no more keep her toes still than keep her heart from beating. The zither sounded like the soughing wind in the tops of the forest trees—what neighboring mountaineers called the hickory wind—and the whisper of the brook falling down the mountainside on a still September night. The music had a silky texture and a rare gold color like the fall itself and seemed to perfume the air with the most delicate of scents, like the shy mountain flowers Pilgrim used to bring her at home, the spring beauties and woods anemones. Manon's feet were going faster, her nut hammer still poised over the block. She closed her eyes and passed her hand through her raven hair and sighed as she had when Pilgrim read her the "St. Agnes" poem.

When she opened her eyes she saw, coming up through the sheep pasture, what at first she mistook for the trained dancing bear in her old picture book at home with the brightly dyed cloth pages. The sheep fled up the slope bleating wildly as the bear came on. But it was not a bear. It was a man, monstrous, in a bearskin, beating on a zither of a kind Manon had no acquaintance with, a flat wooden stringed affair hung round his neck and jutting out from his midsection like a shelf. He beat it with mad vigor as he shambled along, bending his great head, over which the bear's own maw was draped, inclining his ear nearly to the zither and then straightening up and rearing far back as if about to flip over, yet always coming onward, now shuffling, now in the frenzied throes of a Cossack dance, now performing an intricate figure from a long-ago time when men had danced such dances in animal skins by moonlight. On he came, hammering loud and louder on his instrument until the clearing filled with music and Manon's small polished black shoes danced a little dance of their own, even as she reached for Morgan's rifle and sprang to her feet, upsetting the table and sending bowl and nuts and nutmeats and shells galley west on the puncheon floor. She feared that the noise would frighten the baby inside her. The child was her sole concern. Into the firing chamber of the great gun she levered a shell as Morgan had taught her, lifted the gun to her shoulder, and fired. The bullet ripped a splinter off the chestnut door jamb.

The bear man, filling the doorway, laughed as Manon jacked in another shell and fired again. The man's left arm fell to his side, one dulcimer hammer hitting the edge of the table and bouncing toward the hearth. He was wearing a rattlesnake necktie. Backlit by the peach-colored autumnal sunlight he stepped nimbly through the door, eliding with his one good hand into "Bonaparte's Retreat." An odor at once rancid and sulfurous filled the cabin. With his right hand the creature ripped off the bearskin and shook it, rippling black as a starless night, as a gladiator of old might shake a net to terrorize and distract a victim before sweeping him up in its meshes and driving a trident through his throat. Manon lifted the gun high and brought the barrel crashing down on his head. He staggered. She stumbled on a hickory nut and fell to the floor. Oconaluftee feinted left as his feet moved right. He hurled the bearskin over her head, and with a triumphant bellow he was upon her.

ORGAN LOST THE trout wager. He had caught a mere thirty-one fish to brother Pilgrim's seventy-eight. Pilgrim, he remembered, had the touch. He was connected to trout brooks the way he had once been connected to hunting and guns, through some deep affinity approaching magic that even Morgan did not possess. Watching his brother crutch down the boulder-strewn creek bed, his rod tip moving over the likely pools and pockets like a long compass needle attuned to trout, Morgan realized that while he himself understood how to read the woods and brooks and mountains for spoor of beast or man, Pilgrim loved them for what they were. That was the difference.

The bejeweled fish were so small, only three or four inches long, that they decided not to clean them until they reached the crofter's cabin. Morgan's penalty for losing the wager would be to carry the luncheon tow sack, now sopping wet and full of fish, while Pilgrim hopped beside on his snake staff, both brothers sogged to the waist from wading the stream, Pilgrim's arm looped affectionately round Morgan's shoulder. They were tired from the climb and the fishing, happy to be together, clopping along sweating like a span of weary mules, two joshing country lads out for a ramble, with the world and its bounty before them.

"No, brother," Pilgrim said, allowing Morgan to bear more of his weight, "were I you, which I realize I am not, I would not fret much about whom to marry just—"

The first shot cracked out from the direction of the farmstead, echoing and reechoing up the glen and across the valleys. Immediately Morgan knew the gun to be Justice. There was no other rifle like her in the Shaconage. He dropped the fish sack, the slippery little trout pouring out like so many precious fish-shaped gems in a sparkling heap on the green moss. He began to run, holding the scattergun away from his neck so it didn't bounce up in his face. Heedless of the ache in his side where he had been wounded, heedless of breaking a leg in a sinkhole or snapping an ankle between two fallen logs, he plunged down the mountainside like a leaping stag with the hounds at its flanks. Pilgrim vaulted behind him on his two-headed staff. The wound in Morgan's side was bleeding as he burst into the sheep meadow at full run, just as the westering sun

struck the opening on the mountainside before setting, illuminating the crofter's cabin in crimson light like a visitation. The door
was still open, and the splinter from the jamb lay like a dagger in
the dooryard. Morgan cleared the log step in a wild bound, skidded
on the dark, slick blood on the gallery. The floor of the cabin was
a-slather with curdling blood. The chestnut-plank table lay on its
side, one leg broken off, hickory nuts and shells strewn about like
the remains of a shelling bee. Pinned to the floor with the fireplace
poker was a sheet torn from one of Pilgrim's journals. Scrawled
across it in blood these words:

THE GAL FER THE NIGGERS STONE YR FAITHFULL SARVANT OCON-
ALUFTY ALSO KNON AS LUDI TOO.

N A U T H I Z

ᚾ

Morgan and Pilgrim followed the blood trail across the clearing in the fading light, to the path leading up the mountain. In the twilight, glistening on the scree like a slug's trail, was a broken thread of dark spots, some as small as pinheads, others the size of dollars. Morgan bent down, dipped his fingers into a larger puddle of the dark liquid, now coagulating into a viscous glue, touched his fingers to his tongue, and tasted the saltiness of blood. He could only hope that it was Ludi's.

"We'll make some pine links and follow," Pilgrim said.

Morgan shook his head. "That's what he's counting on. He'll bushwhack us. We'd stand no chance trailing him through the night forest. He'll lie up in the laurel beside the path and let us go by, then pick us off. We have to wait for daylight."

"Let him have the stone, then," Pilgrim said. "We'll give him the stone for Manon. Then we'll track him down and get it back."

Morgan had already turned and started down toward the cabin. Without breaking stride he called over his shoulder, "He means to keep her and the baby, too."

Pilgrim hurtled across the space between them, seized Morgan by the shoulders as if he would throw him down. "What do you mean, man?" he shouted. "Good Christ. *What do you mean?*"

It was the first time Morgan could recall hearing Pilgrim raise his voice in anger to him, but what he suspected was so horrifying he had no intention of explaining himself further.

"I mean that we will find them tomorrow. Giving him the stone won't matter. There's one way and one way only that we'll get Manon back. We have to kill Ludi Too. We have to kill Ludi Too, and this time we have to find a way to kill him so he stays dead." The two tall men stood face-to-face in the dusk, one standing upon a single leg and a staff.

"Brother," Morgan said. "You must be prepared to put aside your Quaker beliefs. Otherwise I'll go now alone and take my chances with an ambush."

"Brother, I *cannot* put my Quaker beliefs aside. They are who I am. But I promise to do all in my power to help you with what must be done and not stand in your way. I must and will come with you. And I still think we should start now."

"Pilgrim Kinneson," Morgan said. "You're the best and wisest man I know. But this requires a different kind of knowledge. My kind. We'll do this my way. Ludi may hear the cock crow tomorrow if he's near enough a barnyard to hear one. Let him listen well, for he'll never hear it crow again."

.   .   .

DAWN IN THE HIGH PEAKS of the Shaconage, with autumn ground fog and the mist from a hundred hidden streams layering over the valleys and the mountaintops jutting up pink in the rising sun. The monster had stopped at the fork in the game trail where one branch led to the top of Great Grandmother and the other slipped off the back side of the saddle on the east shoulder toward the Great American Dome and Oconaluftee Mountain. All night, while Manon lay bound hand and foot beneath his bearskin, the beast had sat under the stars and watched the switchback on the trail below. His pursuers had not come. They would find his trail today, but Ludi already had the jump he needed to reach his redoubt first. In the old blockaders' stronghold, approachable only by the swinging bridge, he would be safe from capture. And once the babe was born and they were on their way north with the stone, killing stationmasters and conductors as they progressed, none of the bungling thus far would matter. For Ludi Too, known in these parts now as Oconaluftee, was a man of character and conscience. He left no job unfinished once he had given his word, and he intended to keep his word to dead Dinwiddie and rid the mountains of the nigger-helpers once and for all, as Dinwiddie and Jesus had bade him.

It was time to wake up the young virgin. Gently, with his one good hand, Ludi played the waking song while he sweetly sang.

Good morning, good morning, my pretty little miss.
The virgin of my song. O Lor', says he,
Won't you marry me? She answers, I'm too young.

The younger you be the better for me,
More fitting to be my bride.
For I want to say on me wedding day
That I married before I died.

When she opened her eyes, the beast smiled kindly and sang the second verse again to comfort her and let her know she was safe, and he told her that she had naught to fear from him. Ludi's left arm hung useless at his side, yet he seemed not to notice. He untied her feet with his good hand and chafed the feeling back into them, working chastely with his huge beast-paw. She felt the baby move, thank God. It kicked her sharply. She gave a little moan, and he inclined his great head to her swollen belly and smiled and nodded as though to confirm what he already knew. Then he lifted his right hand into the air to give praise and cried out, "Hosanna! He cometh soon now, do the Child. The Son of Man do cometh. O, I will wed thee and blind thee and the babe, and all three on us will dwell like moles in a cavern beneath the ground. And you shall be called Mary and the boy Emmanuel the American Messiah. For his time be at hand, my virgin."

Although the monster seemed in earnest, there was also a terrible mockery in his voice as he continued in this mad vein while feeding her some broken dry pone and urging her to drink deeply from his canteen. "I shall let you see one more day, virgin queen," he said, "so look well on the wicked world you'll never behold no more nor need to."

As they started out for his stronghold on Oconaluftee, where the creature proclaimed that he would kill Morgan and Pilgrim, he helped her along, since her hands were again bound behind her. In her dress pocket, Manon felt the light weight of Pilgrim's surgical fleam, her last hope. The madman beat his dulcimer with one hand, and the notes chimed brightly through glens and dales as he sang.

> The first I see was a young banshee a-combing back her
>   locks.
> She says she see young Morgan amongst the high cliff rocks.
> With a ho ho ho and a rat tat tat and away with a bow wow
>   wow.

> The next I see was a partisan a-carrying his gun.
> He said he shot young Morgan as he come down the run.
> With a ho ho ho and a tiddy tiddy tat and away with a cat's
>   meow.

> The third I see was a terrapin
> A-crawling through the mud.
> He said he saw poor Pilgrim
> Washed away by flood.
> With a ho and a hi and a rat tat tat and a terrapin's loud bow
>   wow.
> With a tiddy tat tat and a brown barn rat and a terrapin turkle's
>   meow.

Manon worked her fingers behind her back. If she could twist her dress around to get at her pocket, she was as good as free, and the lunatic, with his horrible song of killing and terrapin turkles, was a dead man.

. . .

THEY WERE READY well before first light. Morgan checked his weapons by lantern light, and in his medical bag Pilgrim brought linen bandages and some herbal medicines to assist with childbirth. Morgan still had forty of the silver-tipped .50 caliber bullets for Lady Justice. As the first yellowish light leaked into the eastern sky over the Great American Dome and Oconaluftee, they started up the path that Morgan and Pilgrim had taken the day before. Yesterday's blood had dried to dark spots like shriveled black toadstools.

"Morgan?"

"Aye, brother?"

"You know this demon. Is he apt to harm her?"

"No," Morgan lied. "He wants the stone too badly."

As they pushed their way up the tilted mountainside, the laurel and hardwood leaves and evergreens now acquiring color in the dawn, Pilgrim said, "Luftee makes no effort to throw us off the trail. He must be badly hit. Gut-shot, I'd warrant."

"He wants us to follow him," Morgan said. "He has a place in mind to fight us."

On the shoulder of the mountain where the trail forked, one branch leading up to the summit of Great Grandmother, the other dipping into the huge valley between the Dome and Oconaluftee, they veered eastward, down into Lost River country. In the distance across the valley, resolving into form in the dissipating mist, Oconaluftee loomed, its massive brow overhanging the valley below. Just below the summit, in the side of the sheer rampart, a dark hole peered out like the sightless eye socket of a giant. This, Pilgrim said, was Polyphemus's Pupil, the cave where the moonshining blockaders had established their lair, hauling a small cannon to the rampart to guard their still in the valley against any who sought to prevent them from making whiskey.

Morgan glassed the defile leading up to a stone pinnacle about four hundred feet away from the cave and even with it. A hanging rope bridge with wooden foot slats connected the top of the pinnacle with the cave. Occupied by a single man with an accurate rifle, the stronghold looked as impregnable as Gibraltar. Still, there might yet be a way to finish Ludi for good and recover Manon. Once again a battle plan was forming in the mind of the soldier Morgan Kinneson.

As Morgan had perceived through the Portuguese spyglass, the blockaders' cave was not truly a cave but a natural dent in the face of the cliff under the beaked overhang of the mountain. Ever the gentleman, Ludi helped Manon up the defile to the pinnacle and then out over the thousand-foot-high rope bridge to the stronghold. There he lashed her to the ring bolt to which was chained the old rusted cannon, still facing out across the valley as if to repel revenue men. Earlier in the day Ludi had shot two fat gray squirrels and a grouse. It grew cooler as the sun lowered toward the western mountain, Manon's mountain, Great Grandmother. The considerate troubadour put his bearskin over her shoulders and drew its fearsome head over her dark hair. She looked down the sheer rock wall. Just below the parapet, a spring, framed with ferns and moss, came shooting out of the side of the mountain.

"We'll build a snug little fire and fry up these squirrels and the grouse in a savory mess," Ludi said. "For you, my dearest, must eat well to keep yourself and the babe in health."

The madman wore a tunic that was blue in front, gray on the back, and Manon saw that his vast trousers, previously concealed by the bearskin, had one gray leg and one blue, each with a gold stripe down the side. In his private lunacy, Ludi had made of himself a living mockery of the war.

Manon looked down past the gushing spring into the canopy of trees far below, beginning now to turn color for fall, recognizing the crimson and orange maple, purple ash, yellow birch. The spring fell down and down the red rock face into a deep blue pool. Ludi skipped to the lou to the gushing spring and pranced and danced as he exhibited his great member, as long as a stallion's, and peed off the edge of the parapet, squealing with glee as his urine arced out in the last rays of the sun and fell mingling with the spring water beside it. "Let us have a gloss on 'Sir Hugh,'" cried the mountain songcatcher, "pentameter mode as singed to me, with variations, by Mrs. Ale Sawyer at Black Cove Hollow afore I et her gizzard." He began to hammer on his dulcimer and to roar out over the valley below:

Bury Pilgrim's snake staff at his feet, his wood leg at his head.
When Childe Morgan calls for him, pray tell him Pilgrim's
    dead.

"You are safe now, virgin," Ludi crooned to Manon as he cut open the squirrels and grouse with his Arkansas toothpick dagger and washed them thoroughly under the icy spring and then washed his hands and scrubbed them well and said he would wash them again in water heated in his pannikin should he be called upon to deliver Emmanuel that night. He told Manon that she must not fret, that before blinding her and the babe he would sing them to sleep.

He set his pannikin on the fire to boil with the point of the dagger in the water to sterilize it for the blinding of Manon, bidding her to look well upon the world now, for soon it would all be but a bad memory and she would never have to view its cruelties again. He said he had popped out many an eye in a gouging brawl, and it would be quick and surprisingly painless.

Under the bearskin Manon worked her bound hands into her side pocket. Her fingertips brushed against the metal casing of Pilgrim's surgical fleam. She found the groove in the back of the blade and opened it and turned it ever so carefully in order not to slice herself, and while the beast cooked their evening repast, she began to cut through the cords fastening her wrists.

Oh, Ludi Too was in fine fettle. As he busied himself with supper he hummed bits and snatches of "The Ballad of the Outlaw, Childe Morgan Kinneson." He practiced with his Yellow Boy, shooting, with just one arm, and in quick succession, a raccoon feeling under rocks for crawfish in the plunge pool a thousand feet below, a peregrine falcon riding the updraft some hundreds of feet above the mountain's summit, and the top two feet off a rock chimney on a razorback ridge two miles away. In no instance did he seem to take aim but merely brought the carbine to his shoulder and fired in one swift motion. He cleaned under his thumbnails with the sterilized point of his dagger so that there would be no chance of infection when he gouged out Manon's eyes. Then he heaved on the rope handholds of the suspension bridge like a sailor, causing the rackety wooden crosspieces spanning the abyss to clatter and echo and the bridge to sway wildly. Ludi sang "Bye, Baby Bunting" and said the old bridge would make a fine cradle for a big baby like him. The setting sun, red and vast, rested on the top of Great Grandmother. Manon felt one cord give way, then another. She rubbed her wrists together to bring back circulation. *Soon it will be all right,* she silently told the child within her. *You're safe. You're safe.*

ATOP THE PINNACLE, which they had been the last hour climbing, Morgan and Pilgrim looked across the suspension bridge at Polyphemus's Pupil and the rock parapet. The cave in the cliff was more than five hundred feet away, and they could not see Ludi or Manon behind the rampart wall.

Morgan stood on a narrow ledge, steadying himself, with the lower barrel of Lady Justice across Pilgrim's shoulder and the rifle sights trained on the parapet. The suspension bridge, swaying beyond his sights, was distracting. Morgan made himself stand stock still, but the wound in his side had reopened. The gun barrel on Pilgrim's shoulder wavered.

"Give me the rifle," Pilgrim said.

"SING YOUR 'Sir Hugh' again," Manon said. "Before you blind me."

Ludi chuckled. He picked up his dulcimer hammer and began the old ballad, the notes falling on the valley below like the cascade of water now stained bloodred by the sunset.

She took Hugh by his hammer hand
And drug him to the wall.
She drug him to a great, deep well
Where none could hear his call.

She placed a penknife to his heart
The red blood it did fall.

On the last quavering note, Manon sprang at the monster and drove Pilgrim's veining fleam up to its handle in the side of his bull neck. He screamed, and she withdrew it and drove it home again. He rolled onto the cooking fire, lurched to his feet with the fleam jutting out of his left ear, blood from his neck and ear spurting onto the stone rampart. He started toward her with his Arkansas toothpick on high.

Manon, dressed in the bearskin, picked up a cannonball and clambered awkwardly onto the parapet. Ludi, in his blue-and-gray-pied garb, pulled himself onto the parapet.

"Shoot, for God's sake, shoot him," Morgan cried. He could feel Pilgrim's uncertainty, moving the rifle braced on Morgan's shoulder from the figure in the bearskin to the bloodied one.

"The bear-man, for the sake of Jesus," Morgan cried. "Shoot the bear."

The muzzle of the gun moved from one to the other. Ludi dropped the dagger and picked up the rifle and trained it on them. Morgan was no longer sure which figure was Ludi. Frantically, he sighted the old Melungeon telescope in on them. "It's the one with the gun!" he said. "Shoot the one with the gun."

In Morgan's ear, a shattering detonation. A new red patch bloomed on Ludi's bicolored smock, just to the right of his heart. From the parapet where Ludi, wounded, still stood firm, sighting over the rifle barrel, came another shot, a faint *pop* in Morgan's ringing ears. At the same time Manon, in the bearskin, lifted the sixteen-pound cannonball over her head and brought it smashing down on Ludi's bald pate, and he fell back onto the parapet.

. . .

MANON WAS MAKING her way toward them across the bridge, which was swinging wildly from side to side in the gusting wind. She grasped the hand rope with her right hand, her left hand over her stomach as if to protect the unborn baby. Morgan was running toward her. Twice he came close to pitching over the side of the bridge. Midway across he reached her and encircled her with one arm, holding fast to the hand rope with his other hand, and helped her back across the chasm. Then he was delivering Manon to Pilgrim, who sat atop the pinnacle with his hand pressed to his chest, blood seeping out from between his fingers and running down his side in a small unstoppable river. Manon screamed. She leaped the last foot from the rope bridge to the rock tower. She held Pilgrim in her arms as she said his name over and over and over.

"Pilgrim!" Morgan shouted.

Pilgrim shook his head. "No more, brother."

"Pilgrim!"

Pilgrim settled into Manon's arms. "No more," he repeated. Then he was gone.

"No!" Morgan shouted. "No no no!" Weeping, shrieking with grief and rage, Morgan turned and started back toward the far side of the swinging bridge. From the rampart, blood pouring out of his chest onto his blue and gray shirt and down his ruined skull onto his massive neck, came Ludi Too, Pilgrim's surgical fleam still jutting out of his ear.

"Where is your black bride-to-be?" Ludi said. "That caused all this fuss to begin with?"

"Where you'll never find her," Morgan said.

"Ah," Ludi said, "my hunting days are over, friend Morgan, that's true enough. This time you did me proper. You finally did do for me proper." He stretched out his bloody paw. "Here, lad. I offer you my hand in congratulations. At least we'll part friends."

The wind had dropped, and in the fast-falling dusk, clinging to the rope with his left hand in the middle of the bridge, high above the empty gulf, Morgan leveled the twin barrels of the scattershot at Ludi's head. "Why?" he said. "Why didn't you come for me? Why did you come here instead?"

"First you must pledge me a pledge, Morgan Kinneson. 'Oh, the swain pledged his troth to his Marion fair . . . ' I can't sing no more, Mr. Morgan. My music's all gone away. Swear that you'll pledge me a pledge and I'll tell you why I comed here to these mountains."

"I swear I'll blast your head from your shoulders if you don't tell me this moment."

"Morgan, you're like a son to me. I couldn't love you no more was you my seventh son. 'For it's very true that Ludi Too was son of a seventh son. And he and his son Morgan lived by the law of the smoking gun.' Pledge, lad."

"What is it you wish me to pledge?"

"Pledge that you'll kill me if I tell you whyfor I comed here." Ludi stood swaying on the bridge no more than four feet away from him.

No more, brother. No more.

"You're going to die anyway and soon," Morgan said.

"I wishes to die at your hand. Pledge that you'll kill me and I'll give you your why."

No more.

"My killing days are done," Morgan said.

"Don't you see, dear son," Ludi said. "You are the only one worthy to kill me. You alone can understand. You have give yourself over to the same quest for revenge and retribution I have pursued. Oh, Morgan," he cried in a high keening voice, though still with that hideous undertone of irony. "You must not forsake me in my hour of need *because you are me.*"

"No!"

"Tell me then wherein lies the difference? You can't. *You are me.*"

No more. Morgan turned away and started back across the bridge.

"I comed here because I knowed this was your destination, Morgan Kinneson. And had great faith that you would arrive."

Morgan spun back toward Ludi, who chuckled and said, "And I wanted to do for your brother before your eyes. In order to deprive you and the gal of him. There now's your why."

Profiled against the far peaks in the blue twilight, Morgan clicked back the hammers of the scattershot. Then he flung it as far out into the dusk as he could fling it, turned, and headed back toward Manon as Ludi, uttering one last cry, plunged over the side and, like some great, mortally wounded blue and gray bird, plummeted to the valley below.

THE WEATHER HAD TURNED sharply cooler, though Manon said there would still be some good Cherokee summer remaining, as the mountaineers called the stretch of warm clear autumn days that often followed the first deep frost. For the funeral she wore a blue dress she had taken out in the midriff. Morgan wore

Pilgrim's one dark suit, too big for him in the shoulders, the trouser legs too long by an inch.

The coffin sat on two wooden carpenter's horses by the open grave that Morgan had dug the day before. Manon stood beside it holding the baby. The air was fall-quiet. The singing black crickets and red-legged grasshoppers had been knocked down by the frost, and the birds were gone or silent. It was a windless afternoon. The dwindled brook at the bottom of the pasturage was too far away to hear. Even Manon's sheep were silent, standing atop one of the outcroppings around which the new daffodils would blossom in the spring. The bellwether ram watched the proceedings with his yellow eyes. Morgan doubted that the bellwether sensed Pilgrim's absence, though you never knew.

Morgan stood by the grave, in his hands the book he'd quarreled with for years. It was still closed, since mourners were continuing to arrive, some wearing their own burial clothing because they had no other suitable garb. Word of Pilgrim's death had traveled like wildfire, and scores of people had come, more than one would have guessed lived within thirty or forty miles of Great Grandmother. They were Pilgrim's patients, whom he had befriended and healed or whose children and old people he'd doctored. Men, women, children, stood grave and silent on the mountainside like that throng whose savior had long ago preached from on high.

"We will have no ranting at Pilgrim's funeral, Morgan," Manon had said the night before. She had begun saying "we" instead of "I" since the baby had come. Now she made it plain that she and her son, Morgan, would have decorum at the funeral. There would be no recriminations with a harsh and recondite god, no screeds on universal injustice, no references to the damnable war or to human iniquity. Morgan had looked at her for a moment and then nodded.

The sheep pasture was filling with mountaineers, the few surviving Allens and Sheltons standing opposite one another, Unionists and some Secesh, some families from as far away as the Sugarlands and Gatlinburg. By the edge of the woods, though no one had seen them emerge, stood half a dozen gray-clad Cherokees, men from Will Thomas's unit. For some reason, Morgan thought of Ludi's grave, thirty miles to the east. He had left it unmarked, burying the stone devil's head from the grave of Fair Susan's lover with the devilish creature himself.

Morgan began to speak. His voice was sharp, like a searching fall wind, carrying into every corner of the pasture. "Pilgrim Kinneson loved these mountains," he said. "He loved the seasons and the tall woods, the small brooks, the birds and all the animals of the Shaconage. He loved the people he doctored, and most of all he loved his family. His wife, Manon Kinneson, will stay on among you and carry on his work. You will cherish her and her child as you did him."

Morgan looked around at the listening people. "Pilgrim was not a believer in the ordinary sense. He was a Vermont freethinker and to the very end true to himself. But of all the words in all the books he had read, he loved these best." He opened Manon's Bible and read aloud from it. " 'Blessed are the poor in spirit, for theirs is the Kingdom of Heaven. Blessed are they that mourn, for they shall be comforted. Blessed are the meek . . . Blessed are the peacemakers, for they shall be called the children of God,' " Morgan concluded, and with his lips silently formed the word "Amen." Through her tears Manon nodded back to him. *No more.*

No one else spoke. No one pledged peace or offered to shake

hands with friend or foe. Such was not the way of these people. But one by one they filed past Pilgrim's closed wooden coffin. Some reached out and touched it. Some touched Manon or her newborn Morgan. Then they melted into their mountains. Manon and the baby had some time alone with Pilgrim, after which Morgan lowered the coffin and filled in the grave.

There was more food than any ten people could eat. Ham and bacon, berry pies, cornbread and more cornbread, a firkin of wild honey, even a few loaves of white bread, and jug upon jug of whiskey. After supper Morgan and Manon talked in the crofter's cabin. Morgan had built a fire in the hearth to take the chill off the air. As he had told the mourners, Manon would stay on in the Shaconage. She could already do much of what Pilgrim had been able to do for his patients, and she would learn, from his medical texts, most of the rest.

On they spoke, Manon cradling her newborn in her arms. She spoke of herself and Pilgrim, their early walks over Kingdom Mountain, their faithfulness to each other while Pilgrim was studying at Harvard and abroad in Scotland. She told of their shock over the families' opposition to their marriage and how, after Pilgrim had been wounded and walked away from the war, he had come up with the bold scheme to reunite and go south. The baby made a mewing sound in his sleep. "Hush, Morgan," Manon said, swaddling him closer.

Morgan chunked another split of hickory on the hearth irons. Manon told him that she had packed Blackstone's *Commentaries* in his haversack and that he should not neglect any opportunity to study it. Soon the baby roared to be fed, and Morgan carried his blanket up the hillside to sit beside his brother's last resting place.

. . .

DAWN ON GREAT GRANDMOTHER. The purple mountains rose from the fog as Morgan headed down the path toward the foot of the pasture. The yellow-eyed ram watched from a rock. Standing on the log stoop, Manon held up the baby. On the edge of the woods, Morgan turned and touched his finger to his hat. Then he walked into the trees, heading north.

EPILOGUE

In the Kingdom County courthouse, a curious relic sits under a glass case on a stand just inside the courtroom door. It is an ancient stone covered with drawings and odd symbols. Below it a brass plaque reads:

JESSE'S STONE

PRESENTED TO THE CITIZENS OF KINGDOM COUNTY

AND VERMONT

BY

CHIEF JUSTICE MORGAN KINNESON

UPON HIS RETIREMENT FROM

THE SUPREME COURT OF THE UNITED STATES OF AMERICA

IN MEMORY OF HIS BELOVED BROTHER PILGRIM,

MRS. SLIDELL COLLATERAL CHOTEAU OF MONTREAL, CANADA,

AND JESSE MOSES AND THE UNDERGROUND PASSENGERS

HE HELPED TO FREEDOM

ABOUT THE AUTHOR

HOWARD FRANK MOSHER is the author of
ten novels and a travel memoir.

About the Type

Bembo is an old-style serif font based on typeface cut by Francesco Griffo for Aldus Manutius's printing of *De Aetna* in 1495. Today's version of Bembo was designed by Stanley Morison for the Monotype Corporation in 1929. Bembo is noted for its classic, well-proportioned letterforms and is widely used because of its readability.